S0-BYK-652

INDENTURED LOVE

Emma raised her hand and slapped Will across the face so hard her fingers tingled.

"You *bastard*," she hissed. "Did you come here to debase me, to insult me? How much time did you spend making up such lies? Is that why you didn't come sooner?"

Will stood stock still. Emma could see the pink outline of her hand begin to appear on his cheek. His eyes shot fire as he glared at her. "We both know it would cost you nothing to sleep with a man—certainly not your *virtue!*" he spat out.

Emma gasped at the words. "You're...." she could not utter any words vile enough to encompass her rage. "How *dare* you speak of my virtue. If I have none it's because I was coldly seduced at a young age by a lying, faithless womanizer."

"I don't know if I'd bring up lying if I were you, not at this particular time, sweetheart." Will stepped toward her, unrepentant, and let his fingers caress her breast. "But I do wonder, Miss Emma...if you would compromise yourself for your country, what would you do for your freedom? Hmmm?" She slapped his hand away and he reached up to catch her chin again, this time in a grip from which she could not jerk away. "Would you lie with me again, Emma? Would you make love to me now, if I promised to set you free?"

Other *Leisure* and *Love Spell* books by Elaine Fox:
TRAVELER

ELAINE FOX

HAND & HEART OF A SOLDIER

LEISURE BOOKS **NEW YORK CITY**

This book is dedicated to Patricia Gaffney, in thanks for her unwavering encouragement and for making me laugh even in my lowest moments.

A LEISURE BOOK®

July 1996

Published by

Dorchester Publishing Co., Inc.
276 Fifth Avenue
New York, NY 10001

If you purchased this book without a cover you should be aware that this book is stolen property. It was reported as "unsold and destroyed" to the publisher and neither the author nor the publisher has received any payment for this "stripped book."

Copyright © 1996 by Elaine McShulskis

All rights reserved. No part of this book may be reproduced or transmitted in any form or by any electronic or mechanical means, including photocopying, recording or by any information storage and retrieval system, without the written permission of the Publisher, except where permitted by law.

The name "Leisure Books" and the stylized "L" with design are trademarks of Dorchester Publishing Co., Inc.

Printed in the United States of America.

HAND & HEART OF A SOLDIER

Chapter One

December, 1863
Richmond, Virginia

The tormented scream of a young man split the air, streaking through rooms and hallways in the makeshift hospital. Men whose fates were not as dire winced and turned away from the sound, while nurses and volunteers alike held their breath in agonized silence, waiting for its end.

Below stairs, Emma Davenport gripped the edge of the kitchen table as the anguished cry traveled up her spine to echo, perhaps forever, in the back of her mind. It was endless, excruciating, raw; but the silence that followed was suffocating. A sudden hush as thick, Emma thought, as if it had rendered her deaf.

She felt a gentle hand on her shoulder. "Are you all right, Emma?" It was Judith, her voice discreetly low and respectful of the ensuing silence.

Emma swallowed back the bile that had risen to her throat and nodded. She could not speak. As of this moment, and from this moment forward, her brother was a cripple. Her lively, devil-may-care younger brother was lame. In the upstairs parlor with the yellow-flowered wallpaper they'd sawed off his right leg below the knee, and they'd done it without anesthesia of any kind. A surge of anger and loathing for all Yankees shook her body. It was a familiar sensation to Emma, but Judith clutched her arm in alarm.

"Come sit down, Em," she instructed. "Sit down and put your head on your knees."

Defying the dizzy sensation that urged her to follow Judith's order, Emma instead raised her head. "If he can take it, I can," she said hoarsely. Tears choked her throat and burned her eyes.

"He's probably fainted," Judith stated. "And you look like you're about to do the same. Come now, you won't be letting anyone down if you just sit for a moment."

Emma let her friend lead her to the only kitchen chair left that had not been converted to firewood. She moved stiffly and landed hard in the chair as her knees let go of all pretense of strength.

A shiver racked her again. She clutched her elbows and drew her arms in to her body. The kitchen was warm but her trembling persisted. She stared down at her lap, at the threadbare material of her gown, and thought blankly that she was down to one petticoat now, and it had less life than a washrag.

A low moan rose from the room above them.

Judith's voice sounded reverent as she murmured, "God love him, he just won't stay down."

Emma's teeth clenched. "I hate them," she said lowly, voicing the thought that consumed her nearly every day from morning till night. "I hate them, I hate them, I hate them." She quaked, rocking back and forth with the words.

Judith bent over her. "Emma, honey—"

"You'd think they'd at least let the medicines through. It's not as if we can fight with them, for pity's sake." Hot, angry tears cascaded down her face and she did nothing to stop them. "My God, they're inhuman."

Against her will, an image of a handsome, laughing face rose up before her, his dark blue uniform a mockery of all the tortured, tender emotions the face called forth in her. "I *hate* them!" Emma cried, closing her eyes and turning her head from the vision. "I hate them all. I swear it."

Judith looked down on Emma's dark mahogany hair and shook her head. Her voice was quiet, wise. "It wasn't Will Darcy's bullet, Emma."

Emma made a sound that was halfway between a moan and a curse. "*Will Darcy,*" she spat with such venom that Judith winced. "How do you know it wasn't Will Darcy?" she growled, raising her head to stare resolutely before her. Her eyes took in nothing of the bare, battered kitchen; they saw not the meager, rotting stores of onions and potatoes, the shelves supporting dwindling stacks of chipped and dirty French china. They saw only death and blood, and betrayal.

She said flatly, "I hope he's dead." Then she buried her face in her hands, tears dripping freely from between her fingers.

She'd met Will Darcy at a ball in Richmond, through her father, who'd instructed him at West Point. "One of the finest military minds to come out of the place," her father, Gen. Custis Davenport, had said of him gruffly, "but a wilder, more irresponsible cur I couldn't imagine."

Because of this statement Emma had disapproved of him instantly, and had set her sights on his older brother, Brendan. Brendan was the handsomer of the two anyway. Refined, dark-haired, broader, and taller than his brother, he possessed an immediately arresting set of features on an aristocratically carved face. He simply *reeked* of sophistication, Emma had thought. And that brow—oh, that brow—what intelligence it spoke of. Directly upon setting her mind on him, Emma had blissful visions of their future together, replete with literary talks in his extensive library, philosophical discussions over dinner, and theological theory at bedtime.

Why everyone talked only of Will, she couldn't fathom. She'd seen them both enter the ballroom, and it was Brendan who had the superior look. He'd moved with a reservation and strength she'd admired, and he had a decisive, upward set to his chin that spoke of character. Will had merely flashed a grin at all the ladies within sight and moved from one conversation to another, with hardly a minute spent thoughtfully perusing the room as his brother did.

Emma's friend, Belle, who had met both the Darcys before, had chattered on about Will, but Emma already had herself mentally situated in a stately mansion with stately servants and a stately brougham with Brendan Darcy.

So it was with surprise that, when William Darcy gave her a jaunty bow and asked to be included on her dance card, she had fumbled for a reply and gone tongue-tied upon staring into his lively gray eyes. It was his reputation, she'd told herself. He was wild. Reckless. Brilliant, perhaps, as they said, but a rakehell. Why did all those women talk about him so wistfully? Everyone knew he treated women the way a drunk treats liquor.

But he'd charmed her. Charmed her completely. He'd teased her and laughed at her comebacks. The grin that had seemed so contrived was electrifying when directed at her. The merry, irreverent flame in his eyes was quick and intelligent, focused outward instead of in, inviting, not arrogant. He'd listened to her, really listened. He seemed to understand her. And he looked at her as if she were the only woman in the room.

Brendan Darcy faded to a pale shadow of his charismatic brother that night. For Emma, he might as well have ceased to exist, for over the next several months she fell so far in love with Will she'd even—

Well, that was a lifetime ago, Emma thought abruptly, slamming the door on the memories as she made her weary way up the stairs to her bedroom. She and Judith shared a bed these days, since the improvised hospital had swelled to such an unwieldy size. No matter that it was a large house—*palatial,* Will had once called it—she shared a room now. Everything was shared, what little they had anymore.

Nothing was as it used to be, Emma thought with a stab and

then a calculated hardening of her heart: not her room, not the house, not Will Darcy, and least of all not herself.

She pushed a fist to her lips to stop the sob that threatened to overwhelm her resolve. It was better not to remember those old days, the days when nothing and no one had been serious, not the way they were serious now. She was better off not feeling anything, as she'd trained herself these last two years. She was better off hating, and working, and hating, and coping, than she was when the memories of how it used to be overtook her and crippled her senses. Because nothing would ever be the same again. Nothing could ever be the same again. Not if the Yankees were chased into Canada. Not if the Confederacy took over the whole world. Because a Yankee had killed her father. Because a Yankee had shattered her brother's leg. Because Will Darcy was a Yankee. And Emma hated all Yankees.

* * *

Peter's face was as white as a corpse's against his brown hair. So Emma kept her gaze pinned to his clear dark eyes as a way of staving off the panic. He would not die; he simply would not die. He might look sicker and weaker than she'd ever seen him, but he could not die.

"So tell me more about this Private Perkins who so amused you all," she said brightly into those warm, living eyes. Her fingers briskly guided two knitting needles through sturdy gray wool.

"Oh, hell, Em, I've told you all the Perkins stories I've got." He waved his hand weakly. "You can't possibly tell me you're not bored to death with stories of camp life. I've heard every man in here tell you countless tales." His voice was weak but getting stronger. This was the longest statement he'd uttered since he'd been brought in a week ago.

Emma searched her mind for another topic to engage him, but could not set aside her worry enough to find one. She couldn't bear for there to be any silences, quiet moments in which she would look at his wasted body and remember the horrible moment they'd brought him home, not as a soldier on leave, but as another

11

emergency for the hospital set up in the family's city house. Not once more could she live through the memory of her formidable mother falling to her knees in a completely uncharacteristic display of weakness and fatigue at the sight of him.

"I never tire of amusing stories," Emma scolded, "no matter how many times I've heard them." The needles clicked a rousing tempo to this falsely chipper statement, but the yarn in her agitated hands more resembled a bird's nest at this point than the sock she'd intended.

Peter's lips curved into a vague semblance of his old ironic smile. "You've got that Miss Lipskin voice down perfectly," he teased, referring to their former governess. Then he sobered. "But I miss the old Emma."

Emma's lips parted in surprise and her hands stilled abruptly. "But I am the old Emma," she protested, not even convincing herself.

Peter shook his head. "You need to rest, Em. You've gotten so—brittle. I wish you'd take some time away from all of this." His eyes raked the room behind and around her. It was formerly the dining room, the ornate crown molding and sturdy chair rail attesting to its former opulence. But now it was crammed full of cots on which restless, mutilated men lay; and where there weren't cots there were blankets where more bandaged and fever-ridden soldiers writhed out their agony in as silent a manner as possible. For no one here felt as bad off as the next man, and no one wanted to impose his pain on any other. It was an odd, honorable code that broke the hearts of the women who tended them.

Just then Peter was seized with a violent, convulsive pain that caused his teeth to clamp shut and his face to clench like a fist. He tried to rise but Emma stood quickly and held his shoulders down.

"No, no, no, Peter," she chanted quietly, though she knew he did not hear her. "Don't. You'll only make it worse."

The stump of his leg lifted, as if he might prop it up with his foot; but his foot wasn't there and Emma knew that the pain Peter experienced was in a part of his body that was no longer attached.

Phantom pain in a phantom limb. A wicked joke.

A moment later the worst of it subsided and Peter lay back against the pillow, weak, sweating, and pale. "Sorry," he murmured. "Sorry . . . only making it . . . harder. Sorry."

"Oh, Peter . . ." She blinked away tears that threatened to spill over her lashes. "Don't be sorry. Please don't be sorry."

But he had fallen unconscious—or asleep. It was often hard to tell which. In any case, he struggled no longer, and after assuring herself that his breathing was regular, Emma straightened the covers over him and went in search of Judith.

That was it. She gritted her teeth silently. The last straw. There was no possibility that she could continue on here this way, knitting socks and boiling water, when she knew what could be done—what must be done. Despite the disapproval of her family.

She found Judith putting clean, if worn, sheets on a cot left vacant by a soldier who'd died of gangrene that morning. Emma had examined the poor man from head to foot daily to be sure she knew all the manifestations of the affliction in order to be able to detect if any one of them surfaced in Peter. As yet none of them had.

It was in an upstairs sitting room, adjacent to what used to be Emma's mother's bedroom, that Judith worked. Her blond hair shone jewel-like amid the chaos of blood and pain, and Emma thought she looked just like an angel of mercy.

"Judith," she called urgently, in a low voice. "I need to speak to you. Privately." She glanced around to be sure she'd disturbed none of the sleeping patients.

Judith raised her head quickly, panic in her eyes. "What is it? It's not Peter—"

Emma waved her hand. "No, no. Well, yes, in a way. But he's all right, right now anyway. I just left him sleeping. Can you meet me on the porch when you're finished here?"

Judith's eyebrows descended in an ominous line. "On the porch! It's got to be twenty degrees out there!" she hissed.

Emma gripped her hands together at her waist. "Please. It's important. I won't keep you long, I promise."

Judith consented with a short nod of her head, and Emma descended the stairs to the front door.

The slap of cold air on her face felt vital and reassuring as Emma stepped onto the front porch of the brick mansion on Franklin Street. It somehow reinforced her decision. Reality was cold, and war made people strangers to themselves. Her plan was dangerous but correct. It was the only solution.

She breathed deeply of the frosty air, felt it catch in her throat and pinch her cheeks, as she leaned against the railing, looking out onto the street. The smell of wood smoke carried on the dry, cold air, and she wondered if it would snow. How she used to long for snow, she remembered wistfully, when she was a child and snow meant sledding and snowballs and play. Now it meant more cases of frostbite, more hacking coughs and deadly battles with pneumonia, more work and more fear.

Judith emerged from the front door a moment later, frowning and shivering in the cold. A thin shawl was pulled across her bony shoulders, and her lips whitened to a line as she clamped them shut.

Before she could say anything, Emma stated, "I need you to write to the Darcys. In Washington. I need you to ask on my behalf if I can visit. Tell them I'm exhausted and on the verge of a breakdown. You've never seen me so badly off."

Judith's mouth gaped with Emma's opening line, and with the final one she snapped it shut. "Well, that's certainly the truth! What are you talking about?"

Emma took a deep breath. "Drugs. Medicines."

Judith sucked in a breath, eyes wide. "Are you crazy? Emma, think of the danger. You'd never make it through the lines. And you want me to help you get yourself thrown into prison? No, Emma. I won't."

Emma's chin raised resolutely. "I have no intention of ending up in prison. But if I do, at least I'll know I did all I could, instead of sitting here feeling helpless and . . . and angry all the time."

Judith wrapped her arms around herself and shook her head

decisively. "Your mother will never allow it," she said. "I don't know why you even want to discuss it; she'll never allow it."

Emma stood composedly in the biting cold. "She'll never know."

"What do you mean, 'she'll never know'?" Judith repeated. "Shall I just tell her you're napping or in the privy every time she asks where her daughter is?"

Emma scowled and narrowed her eyes. "She'll think I've gone to Charlottesville, to see Sue. I'll write Sue and tell her. Judith, you've got to help me with this. Don't you want to see Peter out of this misery?"

Judith's eyes rolled. "And seeing his sister in the Old Capitol prison for smuggling is going to set him right back on his feet again."

Emma winced at the choice of words and hugged her shawl tighter around her shoulders. "Sarcasm doesn't become you," she muttered. "And anyway I told you, I'm not going to get caught."

Both pairs of eyes strayed to the street as a lone Dearborn coach pulled by an old, wilted mare rounded the corner. Frosted air puffed from the horse's nostrils as it plodded by. Judith shook her head and looked back at Emma. "Why don't you write them yourself? Why must I be party to your demise?"

Emma turned back to Judith, sensing acquiescence. "I've thought about it—a lot—and coming from you it won't look so calculating, so self-pitying. If I were to write to them they might suspect something—they might think I'm trying to rekindle something . . . you can tell them I was worried about their reception of me . . . after, you know. . . ."

"Yes, I do know. And you *should* worry about it. They probably won't have you even if it is me who writes."

She waved off Judith's objection. "Of course they'll have me. They're good people, and for some reason they've always liked me. I hate to use them but they're the only choice I have."

"Have you forgotten that the last time they saw you you were throwing a glass of champagne in their son's face and telling him

15

you wouldn't marry him if the Lord Jesus Himself asked you to?"

Emma frowned. "Surely they understood. . . ."

"Emma." Judith moved to place an arm around her shoulders. "I know it's frustrating to watch the ones you love in pain. Believe me, I know how you're feeling. But putting yourself at such risk is not the way to help them."

"They wouldn't know it."

Judith threw up a hand and laughed shortly. "It doesn't matter if they know it or not. You're bound to get caught!"

"Sarah Stevens hasn't gotten caught. She said she's been through the lines a dozen times and never once been stopped."

"You'd be caught," Judith said certainly.

Emma pulled away. "Why would I be caught?"

"Because you can't lie, Emma. I've seen you try and you can't do it."

"I could if it meant this much." Emma chewed her lower lip. "Besides," she added slowly, uncertainly, "they'd never arrest someone traveling under the auspices of Colonel Darcy."

Judith snorted. "Don't you mean 'Captain'? And as I recall, you ended that affiliation most decisively."

Emma fixed her with a glazed, inward look. "No, I don't mean 'Captain.' " She thought briefly, then continued, "You're right, Will would see right through me. But Brendan wouldn't." She rubbed her hands together to warm them, but the gesture came off as slightly maniacal. "No, Colonel Brendan Darcy wouldn't see through me . . . he wouldn't suspect a thing."

"Br—" Judith couldn't force the word past her lips. She stared at Emma. "But that's insane!"

"No, it isn't."

"Brendan may be thick as a post, but he's not about to court his own brother's fiancée. Or ex-fiancée."

"Oh, yes, he will," Emma said, clenching her fists in determination. "He was interested in me once; he could be still—just a little. If I could seduce Colonel Brendan Darcy into a formal courtship, then I could smuggle more morphine back to the Confederacy than a dog has hairs. All under the protection of the United States Army.''

''You're insane,'' Judith repeated, flabbergasted.

Emma turned chillingly sober eyes upon her. ''No, I'm not. I'm right.''

Chapter Two

Will Darcy needed a whiskey. No, a brandy. French. Warmed, perhaps, as a toddy with a little lemon and sugar. Then a bath, hot and steaming, with a pretty maid to scrub his back and wash his hair. He imagined sturdy, feminine fingers massaging hot water and squeaky clean suds through his hair. Then afterward she would wrap him in a towel that had hung by the fire.

He sighed and for a moment nearly felt the steamy warmth suffuse him before the hard, stinging rain renewed its efforts and slapped him back to the present. He drew his slouch hat lower on his brow and tried to concentrate on something—anything—other than the mud seeping through the split soles of his shoes, and the thick, chafing itch of his wet wool trousers.

Home, he thought with a longing that was unfamiliar in its intensity. A few more miles, a couple more hours of slogging through mud, and he would be there. He pictured the Federal-style house on Massachusetts Avenue, yellow light glowing from the windows, and a hearty fire visible from the street in the oval room's hearth. The elaborate fan doorways would still have vestiges of Christmas clinging to them in the form of sweet pine garlands and that champion of devilish tricks, mistletoe. In his mind he could smell the pungent fragrance of pine, hot cider, and mulled wine. And he imagined himself settling down with his father in front of that fire to discuss the latest developments of the war from the comfortable distance of miles and long-dreamed-of warmth.

Then he would call on Josephine. Or Cristal. Or possibly even Annabelle, if her husband wasn't home on leave. Because God, he needed a woman. He needed that gentle touch, that warm soft flesh against flesh, as surely as he needed a good meal and a bath. Tenderness was an elusive concept, an all but extinct idea in the depraved world of soldiering. Women in general were nothing but a distant memory until one was back in civilization. It amazed him how easy it was to forget that civilization was the real part of life, and that the ever-present dangers of military life were the aberration. Somehow, in a remarkably short time, it seemed, Will had come to think of life in terms of twenty-four-hour periods. If he got through this mission, if he dodged this many bullets, if he suckered just one more rebel sentry, then there would be a to-morrow. Then he could think about the next mission, the next salvo, the next sentry.

His last mission had been one of the tougher ones of late. Of course, it hadn't needed to be. The assignment had been simple. He and four others had been left by the regiment to guard a bridge. They were to hold off the rebels—in this case a regiment of cavalry—until such time as the rest of their own regiment had regrouped down the road and made ready to slaughter the rascals.

Will and the four other men were chosen because they were considered to be the sharpest shooters in the regiment. And it had been easy to hold the Southern troops at bay from their safe, hidden distance because in order to cross the bridge, the rebs had to narrow to columns of two. But picking them off that way had seemed somehow cowardly to Will, and subsequently to the others, so they'd devised a plan.

As night drew deep and the rebels had slept, Will and a man

19

from Illinois called Shorty had waded through the waist-high waters of the river and emerged quietly on the opposite shore, scant yards from the enemy. After silencing three sentries, and only having to kill one, they had—with a most respectable imitation of a rebel yell—mounted two of the enemy's horses bareback and herded the rest across the river to their own troops. The boys had loved it. The enlisted men, that is. The colonel, however, had severely reprimanded them, concentrating his wrath on Will, whom he knew to be the real culprit. Then he'd sentenced them to fatigue duty for the rest of the march. This meant policing and cleaning the camp, building and unbuilding stables for the contraband horses Will had been ''so damned anxious to commandeer,'' as the colonel had said, and collecting food and water for the rest of the troops.

Will resented it, though he considered the feat worth the reprimand. And for a while he was considered a hero to the troops. That is, until he started winning all their money in the poker games he hosted in the temporary stables he'd so ably constructed. Then he got the reputation of a shark, and after a while was invited to sit out his own games or sit in his stables alone.

So he'd left. He hadn't deserted; he'd just made up his mind to join Allan Pinkerton in his Federal Secret Service and had politely excused himself from the regular army. Col. Nesbit had allowed it, but had, in a surprising conversation, apologized to Will for his perhaps overzealous enforcement of military code. He believed Will to be a good and valuable soldier, he'd said, though he conceded that Will's talent—or recklessness, as Will had heard him call it in previous conversations—would be more suited to a station under Mr. Pinkerton.

So here he was, finding his way back home on his own in the middle of a typically foul rainy Washington winter.

By the time he actually saw the glowing lights of his family's home, the rain had changed to sleet. His haversack was cemented to his back by a sheet of ice, and the scraggly beard he'd been obliged to grow over the last few days felt like the bottom branches of a pine tree in snow. Even his eyelashes were freezing together at the corners.

Wind lashed the rain and sleet around him, stinging his face and hands. Through eyes squinted against the horizontal sheets, he could just make out the large house with the rounded south turret. His body shook uncontrollably with the cold but by sheer strength of will—and the relentless vision of a hot brandy—he kept his feet moving steadily forward.

As he neared he could see that the house was ablaze with light. Will had no idea what time it was, but he felt it was late. It seemed as if it had been dark for hours, but there was no denying that everyone in the house must be up for all the lights to be lit.

Just as he'd imagined, he could see the fire in the oval room's hearth as he made his way up the walk. Though he could not make his feet move any faster than the slow plod he'd used these many miles, his heartbeat accelerated in anticipation. Forget the women, he thought with a sudden buoyancy. Forget the bath and the brandy, even. All he wanted was to sit before that fire and gaze on the calm, steady faces of his mother and father, and to let his young sister Stephanie mollycoddle him until he could take the fuss no more.

He reached the stoop and with painstaking slowness pried the haversack from his back to place it on the ground next to him. Bending his frozen fingers into half a fist, and hoping they would not shatter with the impact, he rapped on the door. Nothing happened. He could walk in, of course, but the idea of standing dripping and alone in the front hall depressed him. He wanted a welcome, an entrance. He wondered if he was losing his mind. He'd walked twenty-five miles in the dead of winter, he was starving, half-frozen, and beyond fatigue, but he wouldn't walk into his own house without knocking because he wanted a welcome.

He knocked again. His body rocked with the wind as he studied the fine lines of subtly cracking red paint on the front door. Finally, from the depths of the house he thought he could hear footsteps nearing the door. A voice spoke and was answered by a chorus of laughter from beyond, far enough away that Will thought he might have imagined it. He was just about to knock again when the door swung open.

Maggie's bright freckled face and curly red hair, barely sub-dued by the maid's cap, beamed out from the door as brightly as the lights behind her.

"Round back with ye, now. Cook'll set you up wi' a bowl of soup," she said, starting to close the door on him.

"Maggie," he rasped, his voice unfamiliar even to himself. How long had it been since he'd spoken? Two days? Three? He cleared his throat. "Maggie, it's me."

She squinted comically and bent forward at the waist toward him. "Who's it callin' me by me name, now? Do I—" She stopped and quickly clasped her hands under her chin. "Mr. Will?" She reached out a hand to his sleeve and pulled him into the light of the foyer. "It is! What in blazes're ye standin' outside knockin' for? Miss Stephanie! Mistress 'Livia! Lookit what blew onto the doorstep here! And this the most ugly of nights!"

Will bent and scooped up his haversack, smiling smugly to the side of himself that had thought he was crazy for wanting this. He wanted to sweep Maggie up into his arms and plant a cold kiss on that plump warm neck of hers, but he was drenched to the bone and not thinking clearly.

"Well, that's more like it," he murmured as she pulled at his wet greatcoat and divested him of his hat.

From down the hall he could hear the commotion Maggie's words had stirred. As his eyes grew used to the light, and the icicles on his lashes turned to water, he saw Steph running toward him from the parlor at the back of the house.

"Will!" she screamed in delight, launching herself at his chest.

He barely had time to protest that his rain-soaked clothing would ruin her silk when she landed with her arms around his neck, her slender body radiating warmth and welcome into his chilled body. His arms automatically encircled her, pulling her close.

"Oh, Will! We hadn't heard anything for so long! What are

you doing here? Why didn't you let us know? Where have you been?'' She pulled back and grinned up at him, her gray eyes smiling out of an impish face that would never be beautiful, but was never dull. ''You look like the very devil,'' she pronounced irreverently, but with such matter-of-factness that Will laughed.

''Stephanie!'' His mother's sharp reprimand was forgotten the moment she laid eyes on her son. ''William? William! How did you get here?'' She took his icy hands in her warm ones and leaned in for a kiss, more conscious of his wetness than her daughter had been, but her eyes shining with confusion and relief.

''I'm not quite sure.'' He laughed ruefully. ''But I know it involved a lot of walking.''

His father was there then, shaking his hand with violent enthusiasm, and clapping him on the back. And all the while Maggie was stripping him of his wet outer garments and then handing him a dry blanket, warm from the fire.

Will would remember later that it all took place in what seemed like seconds until the moment that time stood still. His mother was ordering a bath, his father was asking, half-fearfully, half-jokingly, if he'd deserted, and Stephanie was dancing around him like a trained monkey, chattering about some coincidence he just wouldn't believe—when he saw her.

His breath left him as if he'd been punched. And at the same time he felt as if God had brought him fully back to life by pouring molten lava through his veins. She was there. The woman he'd erased from his mind, but had engraved on his heart; she was there, in the flesh.

At the top of the stairs, in the quiet glow of a wall sconce, she stood with her hair and eyes shining like polished wood. She might have been a statue but for the warm-blooded flush on her creamy skin and the rapid rise and fall of her chest.

Emma Davenport.

Lady Em, he'd called her long, long ago—lifetimes ago. Back when she'd let him call her anything.

Quiet descended—suddenly?—Will was not sure. Perhaps he was hallucinating. He looked about at the faces of his family, to

23

be sure that they saw what he did, and he found them looking up at Emma as if surprised by her presence as well. But the surprise was belied by the furtive way they glanced back at him.

Will shook his head. Stephanie bounded up the stairs in her puppylike way with her hand outstretched, saying something Will could not hear. But he heard Emma.

"I'm sorry. I don't mean to interrupt." It was almost a whisper. She clutched a book, white-knuckled, and backed out of the candle's glow. She looked as shocked as he felt.

What was she doing here? The idea was too bizarre to comprehend. She couldn't have known he was coming; no one did. And even if she had, why would she come? She hated him. She'd said so herself.

He tried to stop it but the thought materialized with an energy all its own: Had she changed her mind?

Eyes riveted to her as she slowly took Stephanie's outstretched hand, he somehow managed to get words past his lips. "Hello, Emma."

She froze. Their eyes met and then hers skittered away. "Hello, Will." Her reply was soft and cool, giving nothing away.

He felt suddenly light-headed and had to brace his feet to balance himself. His father's strong hand took his upper arm and led him to a chair.

"Come, come now, Steph, Emma. Olivia, let's let this boy have a seat. He's nearly falling down with exhaustion." Will let himself be led to a deep wing-backed chair in the oval room, near the fire, just as he'd imagined. But in his mind he could see only one thing: Emma Davenport standing still as a work of art on the landing at the top of the stairs. Would she come down? Would she look at him? Would she disappear if he blinked again?

He turned back to the doorway and saw her enter, her arm looped through Stephanie's, tension making her face a beautiful, unreal mask. "I found the book," she was saying in that silky Southern voice, low and smoky. He loved her voice; he'd always loved it. He'd dreamed of it many a night but never realized it until this moment, hearing it again.

This was what he got, some part of him reasoned illogically. He'd so effectively blocked her out of his mind that she'd had no choice but to materialize here in his own house. He would never escape her. He was a fool to think he could.

Someone handed him a brandy, warmed by a flame to the glass, but even this dream realization could not break the spell that Emma's presence conjured. He lowered his eyes to the glass, closed them, and drank heartily, and still saw only her face, her still-cherished form.

"Your bath should be ready in a minute, darling," his mother crooned next to him. His eyes sought hers, anything to bring him back to reality. "Are you feeling all right?" she asked with concern.

"As well as can be expected," he said, and tried to grin. He failed. His eyes involuntarily strayed to the sofa across the fire. Emma sat still, a stillness only Emma could accomplish, and looked through the book she held.

"Tell us where you've been, what you've been doing! Oh, tell us everything!" Stephanie pleaded, giving away her fifteen years despite the grown-up clothes.

Will wanted to joke, to say something witty and deflective, something to break the tension. But all he could think of was, "I can't."

Emma's eyes whipped to his. She'd heard that. She'd responded. She was offended. She must be real.

Uneasiness in the room thickened at his remark while his eyes felt bound to Emma's by an invisible cord.

"I can't," he repeated. "I can't tell you anything." Because of her, he realized with a sudden jolt.

Emma would have given all she had at that moment to be able to chug a brandy down the way Will did. Every muscle, every nerve in her body was stretched taut and vibrating with a queer energy. So she sat motionless, feeling that if she moved too much or too quickly she would break something inside herself, and her fragile hold on control would be lost.

25

He looked awful. And he looked wonderful. His face was as dear and familiar as the faces of her own family; and her first instinct had been to run to him, much as she would have done if her deceased father had suddenly appeared before her.

But Will was sick, or exhausted. His jaunty posture was gone and the insubordinate brilliance of his eyes was missing, flattened, replaced by a scary hollowness. Of course he was shocked. She herself was shocked, though by being here in his home she knew the possibility of seeing him had existed. For his part, it was no wonder that he looked as if he saw a ghost.

It wasn't until after the initial moment of astonishment passed that she absorbed the presence of the hated blue uniform. Standing at the bottom of the stairs, with the new growth of beard, the unkempt hair, the tired eyes, and the muddy uniform, Will Darcy suddenly looked like every Union soldier she'd ever seen. That's when she'd felt the shudder of revulsion come over her and had to step back out of the light.

Since her arrival in Washington two days ago, the Darcys had treated her so like a member of the family that it was easy to forget their affiliation with the enemy. They were scrupulous in ensuring that the war never came up in conversation when Emma was in the room, and yet she believed they considered her to be impartial somehow, or maybe just ignorant of the politics involved. They treated her as they did Stephanie, as a young woman more concerned with dresses and balls than the events of the current strife.

Which was fine with Emma. In fact, the release from constant talk of battles and wounded, tactics and politics, had done more for Emma's peace of mind than she cared to admit. She felt guilty forgetting—for sometimes a whole hour at a time—that there was blood being shed.

But with Will's arrival the war returned. He was dirty and fatigued, hardened and wary. He was the enemy. How many of her people had he killed? How many of her neighbors, friends—kin? It galled her that he could then accuse her—by that subtly offensive disclaimer of silence—of being the enemy in their midst. She was here on a mission of humanity. How unforgivable that he could suspect her of the heinous sin of spying.

"Mr. Will, your bath is drawn," Maggie announced from the doorway. She was all smiles and coy looks for Mr. Will, Emma noted dryly. But then what woman exposed to Will's charm for any length of time was not the same? She herself had been won over in the space of a dance. Why should a servant be any different?

Will rose immediately at the announcement, and Emma noted again how tired he looked. His once-supple grace was replaced by a measured caution. In a small dark place in the back of her mind, she hoped that with rest his liveliness would return. Otherwise it would seem too much like one more death.

"Emma, I'm sorry. Were you dreadfully uncomfortable?" Stephanie stage-whispered after Will left with Maggie. Mr. and Mrs. Darcy remained, though Mrs. Darcy rose and moved toward the doorway. There she stopped and spoke quietly to her husband a moment.

Emma felt the blood rise to her cheeks and shot a furtive glance at Will's parents. They didn't appear to be listening and she was grateful for their lack of interest in her. "Don't be silly, Stephanie. It's wonderful for you. I'm so happy for all of you that he's returned."

Stephanie sat back and regarded her with outright cynicism. "Well, you don't look very happy. You look as if you're going to be ill."

Emma tried to laugh lightly—the sound just a hairbreadth short of hysteria, she thought. "Really, Stephanie, don't worry about me. What a shock *I* must have been to him. It's—it's him you should be thinking of." For some reason Emma could not bring herself to speak his name. In fact, she realized now, since she'd arrived here the only one even to speak his name in her presence had been Stephanie. And then only to say that they had no idea where he was and that they hadn't heard from him in weeks. Based on those words, Emma had felt relieved that the likelihood of seeing Will again was slim; but at the same time she'd had to battle an involuntary panic that perhaps something dreadful had happened to him.

"There's no question about that. It was obvious you were a shock." Stephanie giggled. "He looked as if someone'd stuffed a hot potato down his backside!"

Stephanie's laughter was swiftly quelled by a sharp look from her mother. Mrs. Darcy fixed her daughter with an imperious glare and suggested in an iron tone, "Stephanie Jean, why don't you have Martha bring some hot chocolate? I'm going upstairs to see to William."

"Oh, all right." Stephanie flounced up from the sofa and walked to the archway. There she turned to her mother. "But if becoming a lady means ignoring what's in front of your face as if it doesn't exist, then I hope I never grow up!" A quick nod of the head punctuated this statement, and she exited the room with a flap of her full skirts.

Mrs. Darcy excused herself and disappeared through the archway after her, leaving Emma alone with Mr. Darcy. He was a kindly man, with a gentle sense of humor, but he always struck Emma as shy. Alone with her now, he looked distinctly uncomfortable.

Acutely self-conscious, Emma debated whether the best way to handle the awkwardness was to acknowledge or ignore it, so she made the decision to ignore it. The only problem was that she could think of not one other topic to bring up with this man. She watched, caught in silence, as Mr. Darcy walked slowly back to the sofa. He wore maroon velvet and moved with the studiousness of age, a fragile, dignified man more comfortable with books than people.

"I hope Stephanie doesn't have to wake anyone for the chocolate," Emma said, painfully conscious of the inanity of the statement, considering the situation. "We really needn't have bothered anyone for it. I'm sure I'll be retiring soon."

Mr. Darcy shook his head. "Nonsense, it'll be no trouble." He lowered himself onto the brocaded sofa and stared at a spot on the table between them. After a moment he asked quietly, "He didn't look well, did he?"

Emma felt her stomach clench. It was obvious he wanted to talk about Will. Or rather, he needed to.

She took firm control of her breathing and tried to concentrate on this man's needs. Her own discomfort paled in comparison.

"No, he didn't," she agreed. She had to work to modulate her voice so that it would not tremble with the words. "But it's only fatigue, I'm sure. He'll be fine tomorrow or the next day."

Mr. Darcy nodded. "Yes. He's a strong boy. Strong and determined."

Emma nodded as well, then voiced her agreement as Mr. Darcy still had not looked up from his pensive study of the table. She felt her insides quiver with uncontrolled agitation and wondered how she would keep from making a fool of herself somehow. How could one man's mere appearance cause her such physical turbulence? She tried to take deep, steadying breaths.

After a moment more of silence, Emma became aware of Mr. Darcy's gaze upon her. As soon as her eyes met his, his flicked away, embarrassed.

"I'm so happy he's come home to you," she said quietly. "I really am. You must be so relieved."

She watched as he nodded his graying head again, studiously avoiding her eyes. Then he sighed. "But my dear," he said in the saddest voice she'd ever heard from him, "it's you he should be coming home to."

Emma's breath caught in her throat and she opened her mouth to speak. Nothing emerged.

Stephanie returned with the chocolate at that moment in a flurry of energy and stated that she'd sent Martha to bed because "she looked like a fox at the end of the hunt." She strode carelessly with the tray to the table, spilling chocolate from cups into saucers as she deposited it.

Mr. Darcy took the opportunity to engage Stephanie in conversation and break the tension that permeated the air between himself and Emma.

Emma tried to calm the relentless thrumming of her heart by handing out the cups. She was all right, she told herself. It was just the unexpectedness of Mr. Darcy's strange comment. Will's presence didn't have to change her plans. She would be fine. This would not affect her at all.

She reviewed again the simple steps she was to take. This first "run," Sarah Stevens told her, would be a trial, meaning she would only bring back one or two vials of morphine, or possibly chloroform—whatever they had a good supply of. Emma would be approached at an unknown time in an unknown location by a boy selling flowers. He was to offer her a yellow one and ask if she would care to buy from a war orphan. She would, and on the stem she would find a small slip of paper with an address on it.

In all likelihood, Sarah had said, it would be a shop she was to visit. She was to mention the flower—working it into conversation any way she could—and then buy whatever the proprietor prompted her to. Simple, Sarah told her. The drugs would be hidden somewhere within the product, and when Emma was alone she could simply tie the small vials to her hoop. Even if she was stopped at the line, not even a Yankee officer would presume to search under a lady's skirts, Sarah assured her.

It sounded simple enough, Emma thought. Virtually risk-free, though she knew the danger of thinking that way. But unless someone was specifically watching her she could not imagine how she would be caught. She was staying with one of the more prominent families in Washington. She would be seen at all the important socials. No one would ever presume that the Emerson Darcys were harboring a smuggler, of all things.

The only thing she figured she had to be nervous about was her ability to get Brendan Darcy to consider her for courtship. Because that was the only way she could think of to come back on a regular basis. Brendan was currently away on some secret reconnaissance for the secretary of war, Edwin Stanton, but he would be back by the end of the month. After that he should be in Washington much of the time. If he were to invite her back, she was sure no one would suspect her. Obviously her claim of fatigue would be good only once. But if her beau—or better yet her betrothed—was in Washington, *that* would be ironclad.

But Judith had predicted a snag, Emma recalled sourly. And what a colossal snag it was. Though Judith had not anticipated Will's appearance, she had been sure of his interference in some way—even if only in Emma's heart. Emma, Judith had asserted, would probably crack the moment she walked in the Darcys' door.

But Emma was determined to prove her wrong. She had been here two days already without a mishap, she reminded herself. Will would not be here forever, and once he left she'd be home free. All she needed to do was wait for Brendan to come home and all would be set. Surely Will would be gone by that time. Then all she had to do was get Brendan interested enough to invite her back.

It seemed simple compared to this evening's trial.

Chapter Three

Had it been a dream? It was so unreal. Even awakening in his bedroom in Washington seemed farfetched to Will, an insane manifestation of his loneliness and the constant fear. But then to have seen Emma Davenport, that was the oddest part of the dream. Emma, his Emma. Still beautiful, still remote. Emma of Richmond and honeysuckle, of the fine dark eyes and sultry laughter. Emma who calmed him and made him lose the desperate need to stir things up, make something happen, whether it be a good thing or bad. The Emma who made him feel sane and good, not wild and dangerous.

But even if it was a dream, it was not typical of those he had of her these days, the nightmare involving angry words, appalling accusations, and a wrenching pain he could not face while awake. No, last night had been closer to the old dream, reminding him of the night they'd met. She hadn't liked him then, either, but he'd overcome that.

He felt a surge of hope and immediately repressed it. They'd hardly spoken two words to each other last night, but he had her back in his blood as surely as if she were a spirit he'd ingested.

But still the question was unanswered: What was she doing here? Had she changed her mind? He nearly laughed at himself, at the pitiful fool he was to think anything might have changed. The look she'd shot him when he'd realized he could not speak freely in front of her had discounted any possibility that she'd forgiven his "disloyalty." No, she had not expected to see him here, that much was clear.

Will pushed another pillow under his head and allowed himself the luxury of waking up slowly. In the army the only thing between sleep and full, upright wakefulness was the piercing howl of the bugler. Most days you didn't even realize you were no longer sleeping until you found yourself standing in the middle of a crowd of other dazed men.

But here he could lounge. Here he could ring for coffee—hell, a four-course breakfast—and never even leave his bed. Here he had two feather quilts, four pillows, and a door with a lock on it. Here, probably not three doors away, was Emma.

He pushed back the covers and rose to a sitting position. A slight stiffness permeated his muscles, particularly the thighs, from his three days of walking, but otherwise he felt pretty good. He had slept like the dead after his bath, dreamlessly, thoughtlessly, without fear or hope. And because of that he felt a rejuvenation deep in his self. As if coming home had propped up that which had been knocked over inside of him—his soul.

The clock on the mantel said nine o'clock. He'd slept over twelve hours. He opened the huge oak wardrobe and stared at the abundance of clothes inside. Velvets and silks, wool, cashmere, cotton Marseilles and piqué. Coats of plum and bottle green, dove gray and dark blue. Breeches of fawn and slate, soft, supple, and fitted exactly to his frame. He knew he'd find this collection here, but he'd forgotten how lush it was. Luxury was a thing he'd known all his life, yet it was the thing he'd forgotten most quickly.

He dressed in the fawn breeches, a white shirt, and a brown wool jacket, with a waistcoat of cream silk. He was disgusted but

33

he had no trouble admitting that he dressed for Emma. Whether or not she'd come here to encounter him, he was going to make sure she wouldn't forget she had. Two years ago she'd discarded him absolutely; she hated what he was, what he believed. But she'd loved him once, too, he knew. And he could not believe that she was able to wipe that out completely, especially when he had so much trouble doing it himself.

The house was quiet. At first he thought he might be the only one home, or awake, until he heard soft voices from the dining room. They were hushed, as if afraid of being overheard, and they stopped completely when he reached the doorway.

Emma stood at the sideboard, near the chafing dishes full of eggs and sausage. She wore gray, somber and elegant. Stephanie sat with a plate full of muffins before her, generously slathering a large glob of butter on one. His parents lingered over coffee at either end of the long, casually dressed table.

"Willie!" Stephanie enthused, pointing at him with her muffin. "You're up! Now we can speak normally." She jumped from her seat and led him to his familiar place at the table. "There. Now the room looks right again. It's just awful having to sit here without any men at the table. Sorry, Daddy," she added over her shoulder. "But you know what I mean."

Will laughed and made an admirable effort not to look at Emma. "Where's Brendan? Or doesn't he count either?"

"He's off somewhere doing something for Stanton, Lord knows what. It's so boring that he can never talk about what he does. But he'll be back in a week or so. You'll still be here, won't you?" She'd reseated herself, but stopped in the middle of her buttering project to stare hopefully at him.

Will slipped a glance at Emma, who'd seated herself next to Stephanie, but she concentrated on cutting her sausage. "I doubt it," he said.

"Oh, Will," his mother said, disappointment evident in her voice. "We haven't seen you for months; surely you can stay a couple of weeks."

"I'll have to see. But I have the feeling I'll be required to report earlier than that."

Martha appeared as quietly as ever and filled a plate for Will, which she placed in front of him. "Good to have you back, sir," she said with a smile, her gnarled old hands clasping themselves shyly in front of her.

"Thank you, Martha. It's good to see you. How's your arthritis?"

"Oh, I'm doing fine, just fine. Only pains me every now and again. Thank you for asking." She backed quietly away from him, obviously both embarrassed and pleased by the attention.

Breakfast progressed as if two separate meals were going on, Will reflected. Portions of the conversation were spent with himself, some with Emma, but never did the twain meet, he mused. Emma neither looked at him nor spoke in his direction. She acted as if he weren't there, and for some reason he was reluctant to confront her. He considered asking her a direct question, just to see how she would avoid it, but he did not want to have their first words to each other be something meaningless. Something trite, such as, "We haven't seen each other in two years, but how do you find the sausage? A bit spicy, you say?" No, he intended to find her later and speak words that meant something. He intended to ferret out the reason for her presence whether she wanted him to know or not.

His opportunity arose later that morning. It was nearing noon when he passed the library on his way to the oval room and saw her perusing the shelves. Other than herself, the room appeared empty.

He stood for a moment in the doorway, watching her. She was absorbed in her study, head cocked to more easily read the titles, and did not immediately notice him where he leaned against the doorjamb. He studied everything about her, noting small changes and details he'd forgotten, from the way her hair shimmered like a smooth yard of silk wound into a demure style, to the carefully mended tear near the hem of her skirt. The dress would probably have been considered a rag a few years ago, he knew. He wondered what other deprivations his Emma had had to face in the last two years.

He did not move, but spoke quietly. "Are we going to speak to each other, do you think, or shall we just circle each other like wary dogs while I'm here?" He was gratified by the start she gave. Some women would have known he was there and let him look. Not Emma.

Her cheeks flamed but she quickly regained her composure. Her eyes, alert and excited, encountered his directly. "How are you, Will?" Soft, Southern honey, that voice. He felt a quiver along his nerve endings.

"I'm better today. More curious, less shocked. And you?"

He was sure he could see a faint curve to her lips. "Still shocked," she remarked.

He smiled at that and saw the flush deepen in her cheeks. "So I'm correct in surmising you're not here to see me."

She turned back to the shelves and pulled out a book, a thin volume. Poetry? "I'm glad you're well," she said carefully. "Your family was quite worried about you. You should write them more often."

"I don't write many letters," he admitted. "I'm not much good at them, I'm afraid." He watched her and knew they both thought of the letter he'd sent her after that fateful night she'd learned he was completely against the Cause. Her Cause. The night when she'd learned he would fight, to the death if need be, against all her family, all her friends, all her beliefs.

He decided to give up the polite parry and get straight to the point. "What are you doing here, Emma?"

She inhaled deeply and turned back to him. "Things are bad—down there. I-I needed to get away for a while."

His eyes narrowed. "Is that so? That doesn't sound like you."

She stiffened but her eyes did not leave his. "What are *you* doing here?"

That brought a short, reluctant laugh to his lips. He inclined his head forward. Touché. "Same reason."

She nodded, her eyes knowing, a little triumphant. Good dodge, he conceded. He straightened from his place in the doorway and moved further into the room, toward her. "You know, when I first saw you last night I thought I might be hallucinating. I was afraid I might have conjured you straight from my imagination. You looked too good to be true."

She turned and stepped back, her expression dark and forbidding. "Don't, Will," she commanded. "Nothing's changed."

He had not realized the extent of his hope until that moment. The words were barely out of her mouth when he felt the old anger well up inside him with surprising speed and strength. He clenched his teeth together and bit back an immediate, scathing reply. He froze where he stood, halfway between the door and her, smack in the center of the room.

"That's not true," he said, as calmly as he could. But his tone was like ice and he could tell she heard the bitterness. "You're here in my house. You're the recipient of my family's hospitality. You're consorting with the enemy, Emma. Forgive me for being curious about that."

Emma slapped the book facedown on the shelf in front of her and fixed him with a brutal glare, her flush from anger now. "I can't talk to you," she stated, raising her chin. She strode directly toward him and the door, her eyes on his, then shifted slightly to brush past.

He grabbed her arm. "Emma, wait." He closed his eyes and took a breath. God, what he would give to have her back in his arms, loving him. But he could not shake the feeling he had about her presence. No matter what she said, it was not like her to escape from a hardship. "We both know you're here for a reason. I'd just like to know what it is. Something tells me it's a strange one."

His grip was tight and he knew it hurt her, but she would not show it. He admired that even as he tried to beat it. "I've told you all I'm going to," she ground out.

"I don't think so." His eyes held hers. He almost felt he could plunge into her brain and see the reason if he just looked hard enough into those deep, marbled depths. But his hand began to take on the warmth of her flesh, and slowly, insidiously, he became aware of the softness of her skin over the firmness of feminine muscle. Cursing inwardly, he dropped his hand.

She ran her palm involuntarily over the place he'd gripped. Her eyes spat fire. "I'd appreciate it if you would make the effort to be civil from this point on. I've no wish to insult your kind family by telling them what an uncouth boor I consider their son to be."

He took a breath and said quietly, "At least I'm not a liar."

He was rewarded by a quick, blatant flash of guilt in her expressive eyes. The color in her cheeks drained away and she recoiled as if struck. One hand clenched in a fist at her waist while the other flashed out to steady herself against a chair back.

Her voice came out in a whisper. "I'm not—" she began, but stopped herself short. She looked near tears. "I don't know what you are anymore, Will. I don't know you at all."

For some reason that stung more than anything else she could have said. Will turned his face away, eyes closed, until he realized what he felt was shame. He opened his eyes to deny it, to glare back at her, but she disappeared through the door and all he caught was a glimpse of the mended hem of her gown as it whipped around the corner.

He stood frozen stiff by the encounter and tried to slow his breathing. But it, along with his heartbeat, continued to race as her image sprang resiliently before his eyes. She was blinding, he thought. He could see nothing but her. He walked woodenly to the chair on which she'd so briefly rested her hand and laid his where hers had been. She was lying. He knew it as surely as he knew the nuances of her face. She could not hide from him.

He circled the chair and sat in it, staring at the empty grate of the fire. It was chilly in the room, he noticed for the first time. Someone should have lit the fire.

From a distance, he heard the front door open and heavy steps start down the hall. He pivoted in the chair to face the door.

"Ho there!" Brendan's voice called into the dimness of the room. "What's this? The prodigal son?" He bent to deposit his traveling bag on the floor.

38

Will rose and extended his hand, walking toward him. "You're almost as unexpected as I was. They weren't planning to see you for another week or two."

"Things went better than expected." They clasped hands, each clapping the other on the shoulder with their free one. "Good to see you, good to see you." Brendan nodded with the words, studying Will's face. "You look unscathed. Father was worried you'd been wounded or killed, and that's why you never wrote. I told him it was laziness."

"You were right," Will said, squelching the age-old ire this innocent statement produced. It was a bone Brendan had always liked to pick. Brendan felt it his personal responsibility to point out to their parents at every opportunity what a wastrel Will was. And he seemed to think that if he joked about it Will would not notice the seriousness of his intent. "I've been lucky," he said casually. "Just grazed once or twice."

"Better grazed than razed, what?" Brendan chuckled.

Will grimaced. What the devil did Brendan know about it, sitting in his solid, oak-trimmed office, no doubt with his feet up on the polished surface of his desk? "I guess," Will said. He sat back in the chair before the cold hearth.

Surprisingly, Brendan seated himself in the one across from him. "So. How're things at the front?"

Will gazed at him. "Correct me if I'm wrong, but I thought you boys in the War Department kept up with that sort of thing."

"Now, now. No need to get testy. I know exactly what's going on, in all phases of the operation. I just wondered about the details, the little things. Morale and all that."

Will looked away and rolled his eyes. "Oh, the little things. Well, the little things are struggling but they may yet win the war for you big ones."

Brendan nodded. "Fine, fine. How's Mother doing?" he continued conversationally.

"Mother? She seems fine. Why?"

"She's been sick, you know." Brendan pulled a pipe from his pocket and opened the humidor on the table next to him.

Elaine Fox

"I didn't know." And Brendan knew it. It was his way of illustrating Will's neglect of the family.

Brendan nodded again and filled the bowl of the pipe in a leisurely way, tamping the tobacco down with a thick forefinger, then lighting it by moving the match in slow, methodical circles. Will wanted to hurl the thing into the grate.

"Mild catarrh, but enough so that we've been giving her quinine. And some laudanum to help her sleep."

"I haven't heard her cough since I arrived."

"Good, good."

"Who's treating her?"

"Dr. Wayson."

Will scoffed. "Surely you could have consulted someone with more to recommend him than that charlatan."

Brendan fixed him with a sarcastic eye. "We did the best we could without your venerable guidance."

Will stood suddenly and strode to the bellpull. "Need to get some goddamn heat in here," he muttered, yanking the cord. Why was it a conversation with Brendan always managed to get his goat? Why couldn't he just ignore the irritating taunts and not give him the satisfaction of anger? "How long have you been gone?"

Brendan exhaled a cloud of pungent smoke. "Three weeks, or thereabouts."

Will strolled back to the hearth, laying one arm along it and resting his head on the heel of his hand. "Then you don't know about Emma Davenport."

Brendan stiffened. "What about her?"

"She's here." Will watched him closely. "Visiting." He drew the word out pointedly. Emma had been a weak point for Brendan, as she had been for Will, but in a much more negative way. Brendan had been interested in her the moment he laid eyes on her, which was precisely the reason Will had approached her at that ball so long ago. Little did he know the grappling hook she'd lodge in his own heart. But Will's victory over Emma's heart had galled Brendan to no end, exacerbating the already nasty com-

40

petition they'd felt since childhood.

Will watched with gratification as the blood rose to Brendan's face and his previously casual posture turned anxious.

"Emma Davenport? Here? What the devil . . . ?" He placed his pipe in the tray next to him, where it clattered to its side, spilling glowing tobacco into the dish.

"You look a little pale, old man; you feeling all right?" Will's grin was evil. "Afraid she's come back to me?"

Brendan's eyes filled with dread, even as he made a visible effort to relax. "Surely she's smarter than that."

Will chuckled mirthlessly. "Apparently so. I don't know why she's here."

Brendan sank back in his chair. "When did she arrive?"

"Couple days ago."

"When did you get here?"

"Last night." Will smirked. "No head start for me, then. Gentlemen, take your marks. . . ."

"Very funny," Brendan snapped. "I thought she made it abundantly clear she wanted nothing more to do with you."

"Right you are. Maybe she's here for you this time." Will wanted to laugh at the flush of pleasure even the sarcastic suggestion produced in Brendan. "Or maybe she's turned coat and become a Yankee. I'd say they're about equal possibilities."

Brendan scowled and rose to his feet. "Where is she now?"

"That's right, brother, don't lose a second while she's in the house. You could be hovering over her right now, breathing down her neck, hoping she'll cast a kind word in your direction that you could lap up like a starving mongrel." Brendan strode past him. "Be sure to put in a word for me," Will called after him. "That's sure to put you in her good graces!"

The door slammed, leaving Will alone in the dim room, alone in the aftermath of another kind of skirmish. He was tiring of battles, he thought morosely. A second later the door opened and Maggie appeared.

"Sorry to disturb ye, sir; did ye ring?" She peered anxiously into his face. "Sorry it took so long; I was helpin' Cook wi' the bread. Had to wash me hands."

"It's all right, Maggie. I just wanted a fire. Ask Jonas to bring in some wood." He raked his hand through his hair and stared at the empty fireplace, feeling as if he could ignite something with his eyes.

"Yes, sir." She moved slowly toward the door, then stopped. "If ye don't mind me askin', are ye all right, sir?"

"I'm fine," he said in her direction. Then added, as an after-thought, "Brendan's home."

"Ach, well, then." Maggie nodded. "I'll just go and fetch Jonas fer your wood."

Just fetch me Brendan's head, Will thought sourly. A log like that could keep me warm for days.

"Say, Maggie?" Will called.

"Yes, sir?" She poked her head back into the room.

"Where is Miss Davenport?" He had a sudden hankering to skewer Brendan's entrance.

Maggie gazed at him with sage eyes. "Miss Davenport? She's in her room, sir, last I knew."

"Which is . . . ?"

"The blue room."

Will laughed in fatigue. "Thank you, Maggie." The blue room. Right next to his own. No wonder she invaded his dreams.

Emma composed herself and left her room, closing the door quietly behind her. This was going to be harder than she'd thought. Having Will in the house was like living with a mind-reader, an irresistible mystic. He frightened her, made her afraid of herself. He was different, she'd noticed, tougher, and at the same time so familiar it was hard to keep from touching him. She'd wanted to lay her hand on his arm today when she'd seen the anger blossom in his eyes, just as she'd done so many times in the past, circumventing an explosion with a touch and a look. He was smart and hot tempered, a dangerous combination. He knew when people were lying, as she was, and he had no tolerance for it. And he would get to the bottom of it if it killed him. Her only hope was that he'd leave soon. The sooner the better.

But at the thought a small, lonely piece of her heart cried out. It had been nearly two years since she'd seen him, and the sip she'd had of him was not enough to quench the thirst. How many times had she imagined that unstudied grace, that masculine tilt to his shoulders as he walked, the electric graze of his glance that sent tremors all along her limbs to her heart? When he'd smiled today it had seized her heart so violently that she'd feared she might pass out from loss of breath. That charisma, it just filled a room to bursting when he was there.

She started off down the hall when she heard a heavy tread on the stairs. *Please, please, please, Lord, don't let it be him.* If he caught her again in such a short space of time she was sure she'd throw herself into his arms, fighting and bloodshed be damned. Could they possibly avoid the subject of politics for the next forty or fifty years?

She was half-relieved, then, to find herself face-to-face with Col. Brendan Darcy, future target of her falsest charms.

"Miss Davenport," he said warmly, the expression in his gray eyes sincerely happy to see her. She'd forgotten how good-looking he was, and how much he resembled his brother. "Emma," he amended humbly. "How nice to have you here."

She was surprised at the warmth of his welcome and ducked her head with her swift curtsy to cover it. Had he forgotten that by rejecting Will she had also, by association, rejected himself? They were, after all, members of the same army.

"Why, Brendan!" She hated the coy sound of her exaggerated Southern accent. But if she was going to be an actress, she had to act. "Praise be, you've returned safely!"

Brendan stopped two steps shy of the top of the staircase, putting himself at several inches' disadvantage to Emma, who stood on the landing. She held her hand out to him. He took it in his. She had the momentary thought that it would have been nice to have been greeted like this by Will, though she knew it would

43

have been impossible. Instead she'd gotten a halfhearted approach and a full retreat.

Brendan raised her hand to his lips, letting them linger there a little too long. She pulled back, surprised, then remembered her objective. Perhaps this part would be easy. She clasped the hand in her other one. The back was wet from his lips.

She smiled brightly. "So you're back; I'm so glad. I wish I'd known you were coming; I'd have worn something prettier." Like the one other gown she'd brought—or owned, for that matter, aside from the worn calicos she wore daily at home. She'd had to buy contraband fabric at an exorbitant price in order to make the new dress. Sarah Stevens had made it most clear that it was imperative Emma not look destitute. She was a lady of stature and she had to look it, if only to get past the Yankees at the line. When Emma had protested that Sarah had told her previously that they'd never presume to question a lady of any type, Sarah had said there was no need to take any chances. Besides, Emma *was* a member of the social elite—she only needed to look it. And that required at least one new gown.

Brendan flushed at her compliment and inclined his head in thanks. "You couldn't look prettier to me, Emma," he said in a strikingly intimate tone.

Emma gazed at him, somewhat at a loss for words. Always before he'd been distant with her. What had brought about this change? Of course, before she'd been firmly attached to Will and therefore out-of-bounds, she supposed. But still, he was coming on a bit strong.

He continued, "I'm surprised, and of course delighted, to see you here. But I thought, that is to say, I would have thought, or imagined that here, well, that you might not want to be here. You know, as they say."

She smiled at his discomfiture, in control once again, and laid her hand on his sleeve. He looked almost childlike on his low step in all his discomfort. "I just had to get away. You don't know what it's like down there." She cast her eyes to the floor. Brendan's eyes followed. "I mean, in the South," she amended quietly. He looked back up, embarrassed. "I needed to get away from it for a while, you understand. There's only so much a mere woman can take." She fixed him with an innocently tortured gaze.

"I understand," Brendan said, covering her hand with his own. "You came to the right place. Here you can regain your gay heart. Perhaps I could help distract you, perhaps take you shopping one day this week. There must be many things you can't get in Richmond these days."

You can't even imagine, Emma thought. "Oh, Brendan!" she exclaimed daintily. "That would be heavenly. You know a woman's heart so well." She was about to be made sick by her own simpering, she thought with disgust. But Brendan was falling headfirst for the act. The heat of his hand seemed to increase the longer they made contact.

Brendan smiled at her benevolently. "It would please me to know your heart even better," he said. "But let me get cleaned up and then we'll chat. I don't want to offend your delicate sensibilities, having just gotten off my horse, you know."

Emma inclined her head and let him pass. She watched dispassionately as he proceeded down the hall in the opposite direction of her room and entered a door at the end of it. This could be too simple, she thought. She could find herself in a real spot if things went too quickly. She turned back to the stairs, and her eyes were caught by a slight movement on the first floor. Will watched her from the door to the library.

Her stomach plummeted as his eyes penetrated to the depths of her being.

He cocked his head thoughtfully to one side. "It would please me, as well, to know your heart a little better, Emma," he said darkly.

Chapter Four

Emma sat before the mirror and tried to make sense of the emotions warring within her. She studied the expression in her eyes, hopeful that she could see her own motives there as Will had tried to do. If she looked long enough surely she could see it, the force driving her to behave the way she did, to lie to Will, to deceive Brendan, to undertake subterfuge and secrecy in order to gain—what? She did this for a higher good, for the Cause, she thought righteously. The end justified the means, didn't it? It was right, wasn't it, this lying?

She sank her face into her hands, scattering brushes and bottles of scent, and planted her elbows on the dressing table. She fought back the urge to sob but the emotion welled within her. It was impossible to know what was right anymore. There was no way to separate the turbulence of her emotions from the turbulence of the world. How could anyone hope to get anything right while riding the dips and crests of the sea of war?

Though the plan had seemed so simple from her far-off vantage point in Richmond, it took on an unexpected complexity here in

Washington. It was easy to hate Yankees when they came in a huge, dark, evil column, like an alien, serpentine beast. But here they were people, individuals, friends she'd known for years, and the overall picture was hard to keep in mind.

She took a deep breath and raised her head. She would not allow herself to weaken. She'd formed a plan—a good one—and now she must adhere to it no matter what her fickle emotions told her. It would be easy to conquer Brendan, and impossible to ignore Will. She simply needed to plan accordingly.

She mentally chanted the commands she'd issued herself upon undertaking this desperate venture: Do whatever it takes to help the men of the Cause; Commit any crime to alleviate the suffering of men in pain; Do all within your power to relieve even one small corner of want in the Confederacy.

But the words did not charge her with determination the way they had all the way to Washington. She gritted her teeth. Surely she could ignore her own pain in order to provide relief to others. By feeling weak she was only indulging a spoiled longing for Will. She should have anticipated this problem and prepared herself to deal with it. She had been called to this duty in the same way that an evangelist was called, and she would not let the devil in the form of Will Darcy change any of that.

Her motives, she thought with a deep breath, were ultimately pure. So if her conscience pricked her about Brendan, and if her heart kicked her over Will, then this was her battle-suffering, these were her wounds. She would deal with them in the same stoic manner that Peter dealt with the loss of his leg. And she would count herself lucky in the bargain.

She straightened her spine and pulled the pins from her hair, dropping them into a cut-glass dish, created just for that purpose, which lay on the table. She relished the *plink* of each pin against the glass, firming her resolve with each one by recalling the tortured men for whom she toiled.

Stuart Mason, she thought grimly, a carpenter. His hands were blown off by an enemy mortar shell.

Plink.

47

Avery Cooper. He died of gangrene after refusing to let the doctor amputate his arm. He'd be no good to his family with only one arm, he'd said.

Plink.

Junior Bennett. His wife learned in two letters received on the same day that her husband had been ceremoniously promoted to captain, and then been killed by a marauding band of Yankees while he bathed.

Plink.

And so on until her hair lay in waves on her shoulders and in a river down her back. She had no tears for these innocent victims who suffered real pain and hardship; she was beyond that. What she had now was a hard-hearted resolve to change it, to fix what she could. She had to strike whatever blow was within her power for those men who'd risked all and lost. She had to share the burden of defending the convictions of her place and her people.

She thrust a brush through her hair, pulling roughly through tangles and causing her scalp to throb with each stroke.

She had a duty to perform here. And when she let her heart ache over Will she was simply acting like a spoiled child who'd had her candy taken from her. He followed his convictions, with very little of the turmoil she was experiencing, it seemed. That, if nothing else, should enable her to do the same. He'd gotten over her. She would get over him. And once she did, she would then and only then be a true asset to the South.

Emma was amazed at what could still be obtained in Washington to dress a dining room table. Food was abundant. There was no worry that the sugar would run out, or the coffee, or the fine, imported scotch whiskey. Flour was plentiful and used lavishly in the breads, cakes, muffins, and rolls that adorned the table, and the fine linen tablecloths were as white as the Northern snow.

From the unreal perspective of this graceful room, Emma shuddered as she recalled shredding yard after yard of fine combed cotton, complete with eyelet and lace, to use for bandages. She remembered one particularly low point in her morale when she'd had to stuff a wad of costly Brussels lace against a gash in a soldier's leg that would not stop bleeding. She'd hated herself then for even noticing the precious lace, let alone allowing some portion of her mind to be sorry about ruining it, because the man had a bayonet wound that would not heal. The importance of his life over a tablecloth had been obvious, ludicrous even to compare. But at that moment the lace had symbolized something, something huge . . . loss, destruction, an innocence forfeit to brutality . . . things she studiously kept from thinking about except when exceptionally tired. She'd cried over it, given in to the emotion without letting herself think the thoughts.

But here the table was perfect. Here the ladies would all have dozens of petticoats and fashionable dresses with shoes to match. Here the war was a long way off.

Emma turned from the dining room to the oval room across the hall. The Darcys expected guests for dinner, and were upstairs dressing. Emma wore the new dress that Sarah Stevens had insisted she make, but still she felt the inadequacy of it. She hadn't missed the fine things so much at home, where everyone was in rags because of the Yankee blockade, but here, where society seemed untouched by the war, she felt ashamed of the poor showing she made. A couple of years ago she would have been wearing a gown of merino wool or grenadine instead of serge, she thought ruefully, and it would have been an unusual shade of bottle green or peacock blue, instead of this dark, practical maroon. Before leaving home she'd been able to dress it up a little bit with some old black braiding that was useless for anything else, but the buttons were still steel and the petticoats limited to just one with a hoop. She had no earrings anymore and the place where one of her stunning diamond brooches might have gone years before was now occupied by a costume piece of fake gold and quartz. Even that had been an extravagance.

Well, there was nothing she could do about it now. Perhaps no one would notice. They might just think her taste in clothes more conservative than theirs. In any case, she was not going to be the lively addition to this party that she used to be at home, either in dress or in conversation. Since the start of the war her language had become so peppered with aspersions about Yankees and references to the cause that now she had to be very careful in conversation. She had to keep her thoughts to herself except when on the most benign of subjects.

The oval room was empty of people, and Emma took the opportunity to relax by the fire. The Darcys had wanted to have some sort of social while she was visiting, and though she protested, they decided that a dinner party would be best. Several of their neighbors were to come, including one very dull member of the clergy who happened to live nearby. Stephanie had warned her to stay clear of Rev. Bullock, but Emma thought that an involved ecclesiastical conversation might be just the thing to get her through this evening without a blunder. She'd had Martha put her place card next to his.

Unfortunately Martha—or someone else—had also seen fit to put Brendan on her other side. Emma grimaced as she gazed into the fire. She had to keep this flirtation from moving too quickly or before she knew it she'd find herself in a very sticky predicament.

"Alone again," a low voice said from behind her.

Emma knew by the trill of her nerves and the delicious sensation down her spine that it was Will. She consciously waited a beat before turning from the fire toward him.

She could almost have wept at the sight of him. Clean-cut and dressed to the nines, he was the essence of the man she had loved. How many times had she seen him thus and felt pride? In normal times he would have been her escort, her fiancé, indeed by now her husband. She felt a traitorous longing. If she could forget the arguments, the betrayal—the whole bloody war—she could easily throw herself into his arms.

He stood just inside the door, adjusting a snowy white sleeve. His coat was dark gray, his trousers perfectly tailored. The glance he gave her was wary, challenging, and just a tad uncertain. She

50

folded her hands behind her back and felt the warmth of the fire on them.

"Are you hungry?" he asked casually. He strolled further into the room. He made his way to the liquor cabinet and opened the solid wood doors.

As he moved she turned to follow him with her eyes. "A little," she answered in her most controlled voice, a studious mixture of indifference and reserve.

He poured himself a scotch whiskey and flashed her a look from the corner of his eye. "Can I get you a sherry?"

As she watched the amber liquid tumble into his glass, she recalled a night when the two of them had sneaked away from a party and she had gotten drunk with him on scotch. She wondered if he remembered it, then forced the memory from her mind.

"Thank you, no." She kept her back to the fire, feeling its warmth as soothing support for her clattering nerves.

Will's mouth quirked up on one side. He did not look at her. "Scotch, then?"

A sudden lump grew in Emma's throat. She'd wanted him to remember, but now she wished he hadn't. "No." The word emerged harshly, though she had not intended it to. A faint red stain appeared on Will's high cheekbones. He kept his face averted, carefully mixing water with his scotch.

"I'm sorry," she said then. He looked up, surprised, and she felt her own face flush. "I—I didn't mean to sound so severe."

He studied her a moment, his eyes shrewd, yet gentle. Emma had to clench her teeth together to keep from saying more—to prevent herself from moving toward him, into his arms, with the sure knowledge that he would take her, hold her, and keep her safe, forever.

"It's been hard for you, Emma?" he asked softly.

Emotion threatened to overwhelm her. Don't be kind, for God's sake don't be kind, she pleaded silently. Keeping her eyes averted, she swallowed stiffly.

She heard him place the glass down and knew that he came toward her, his footfalls soft on the thick rug. When she could see his shoes under her downcast eyes, he stopped.

"I wish I could help you." His voice was tender.

She closed her eyes. Her heart bled. She could feel it breaking open, running through her in molten waves, storming her veins and unshoring her defenses.

"Emma," he breathed. His hand rose to her cheek. "You have no idea how much I wish I could help you."

At his touch she raised her eyes, defying her own conviction, and let him see the naked longing revealed there.

It was a mistake. She knew it the second their eyes met. Years fell away like split trees and he stepped closer. Her lips parted, and her breath caught in her throat.

She tried to turn her head, but his gaze held her. "Don't pull away," he commanded softly.

She opened her mouth to speak, but no words came. His mouth descended to hers.

Their lips touched lightly, just the barest graze, but it was enough to ignite a firestorm of desire within her. She trembled with it as his face remained close and his hand moved into her hair, fingers threaded into the low chignon.

Though she stood motionless, her senses reached out to him. The warmth of his palm and the caress of his breath on her cheek melted her nerves. Her hands twitched by her side, her fingers aching to grab hold and never let go.

"Kiss me, Emma," he said.

A soft breath of air escaped her, a frustrated, anxious sound. Without her consent, her chin moved forward an inch and her lips skimmed his.

His hand abruptly tightened on the back of her head and his other rose to her waist. With irrefutable strength, he pulled her to him and his mouth consumed hers.

Her lips opened, drinking him in. Hands fisted in his coat, she pulled him close and dove into the kiss as ardently as he. Their roughened breaths met, their bodies strained and clung.

So beautiful, Emma thought, and so terribly, terribly familiar.

A tiny sob crept into her throat and she felt tears squeeze out the corners of her eyes.

Will pulled back immediately, parting the current of desire that joined them. Emma could feel the energy charge between them, could barely resist the inexorable draw toward him, but forced herself to lower her head.

"Emma—"

"Stop it," she breathed. "Oh, God, please stop it." Her voice was hoarse, her breathing ragged.

Will's chest heaved with exertion. His hands moved to her shoulders and gripped hard. "Emma, don't."

"Stop it," she said again, twisting in his hands. She spoke not to him, but to herself, to the demon desire that raged around and through her. "Stop it," she said again, unable to form any other words either in her head or on her lips. "Stop it," she growled once more, her voice harsh. Gritting her teeth against an overwhelming ache, she raised hard eyes to his.

He dropped his hands and took a step back. "Don't do this," he said. He watched her uncertainly, with something that almost resembled fear.

She shook her head, her eyes on him. "I cannot. I do not want this," she said deliberately, still shaking her head. She spoke to herself, to convince herself, but she saw the effect of her words on him.

Color rose to his cheeks and the muscles ticked in his jaw. "Tell me something else, Emma, but don't tell me you don't want this. We both know that's a lie."

"It's not a lie," she said, her voice shaking. "I don't want it. My mind, my heart—I do not want it." Another sob rose to her throat and she swallowed hard to rid herself of it.

He turned away and stood still a moment. She looked at his back, at the waves of his hair on his bent head, and felt her heart break within her. Her hand rose to her lips, still throbbing from his kiss.

After a moment he turned back to her, face hard, one eyebrow raised. "All right, then. If that's how you want it, we can talk

53

until we're joined by the others. Just like the old friends we are. Is that what you want, Emma? A little polite chit-chat?" he asked with arch joviality. "What shall we talk about?"

Emma could not respond. She dropped her hand and watched as he donned a brittle smile.

"Really, we ought to be able to entertain each other safely for ten minutes or so," he continued.

"I don't care what we talk about," she said quietly. Her knees felt weak. She wished she had accepted the sherry.

Will took a deep breath and said, "Well, good. That means we can talk about whatever I want to talk about." He strolled back to the liquor cabinet and picked up his glass. Downing half its contents, he turned back to her. "Is that right?"

Emma's gaze met his. She struggled to keep her voice neutral. "Yes. Whatever you want to talk about."

Will smiled, a forced smile that told her trouble was brewing. He was angry, and he had no self-control. If something was on his mind he spoke it. He had no guile, and no tolerance for it. Emma's palms began to sweat.

"I'm glad to hear you say that. Because there is something I'd like to talk about with you, Miss Emma. I'd like to talk about you. Can we do that?" His tone was patronizing, and Emma felt her cheeks burn as she raised her chin.

"I'd rather not."

Will shook his head. "That's a shame, because you've already said we can talk about whatever I want. Didn't you say that?" He refilled his drink, not bothering to cut the scotch with water this time. "Or didn't you mean it? Didn't you used to say what you meant, Miss Emma?"

"Don't call me that," she said in a low voice.

He raised his brows in exaggerated surprise. "What—Miss Emma? What shall I call you? In fact, while we're on it, who are you these days? It seems I no longer know."

"Stop it, Will," she demanded, her anger flaring with a welcome burst. "I don't know why you must make this so unpleasant by baiting me. I have no desire to humiliate you; why can't you leave me alone?"

The sarcastic expression on Will's face disappeared. He said nothing for a long moment in which Emma felt the fire engulf her in a suffocating warmth. Finally he leaned forward to within a foot of her and said in a low voice, "Because you're in my house, Emma. I can't leave you alone because you're in my house and I don't know why. It's no good reason, I know that. But it seems to me this would be the last place you'd come to, no matter how bad things got in Richmond."

She forced herself to maintain contact with those drilling gray eyes. "I was as sure as I could be that you would not be here. That's why I came."

"And just as sure that Brendan would be here."

"I have no quarrel with Brendan," she said quietly.

Will looked at her, astonishment clearly written on his face. "You have no quarrel with Brendan?" he repeated, dumbfounded.

She looked away, studied the pattern of the embroidered sofa.

He moved to block her sight of it, capturing her eyes with his again. "You have no quarrel with Brendan?" he repeated, until she could do nothing but nod, once.

"That's right."

He laughed, short and hard. "Forgive me for being so dense then, but what quarrel do you have with me that you do not have with Brendan?"

Emma shouldered her way around him, unable to confront those angry eyes longer, and moved to the liquor cabinet. Heedless of convention, she poured herself a sherry. "You betrayed me," she said flatly. "In case you've forgotten." She took an unladylike swig of the ruby liquid, then brought her fingers to her lips again.

"Emma," Will said, laughter—actual laughter—in his voice. "I don't know if it's just an oversight, or perhaps no one has told you, but Brendan's also a—a Yankee." He uttered the word in a

55

loud whisper, as if it were sinful and impolite. Then, in a harder voice, he said, "Just like me."

Emma whirled, breathless with anger. "No. Not just like you. Brendan was never engaged to marry a Southerner. Brendan was not about to embark on a life of shared morals and ideals with a woman of the South, nor did he represent himself as believing in and being a part of that world—as *you* did, Will. You belonged there, Brendan never did. And Brendan was already in the army when his commander called him up. It was his commander who erred by directing him to take up unconstitutional arms against his fellow citizens—"

"Oh, Lord," Will interrupted loudly, enunciating the words with great scorn. He raised a hand in exasperation. "In other words, I did it as a personal insult to you—"

Emma raised her voice. "I don't care to hear your justifications. I have no desire to discuss this with you now or at any other time—"

Will kept going, approaching her slowly across the room. "— but if it were my job to fight whatever battle came up you would have—"

"—and I'd appreciate it if you would stop tormenting me with—"

"—forgiven it as an occupational misfortune—"

"—ugly reminders of a heinous mistake—"

"—and taken me back—"

They were no more than two feet apart, voices raised as they spat the words at each other, when the butler amplified his voice above both of theirs to announce, "Mrs. Josephine Sinclair, Reverend and Mrs. Bullock, and Mr. Lawrence Price."

Shocked silence descended between them as their heads simultaneously swiveled toward the door. They were both out of breath, their cheeks flushed with emotion, and their shared mortification left them stunned into a kind of paralysis, staring at the newcomers.

Mrs. Darcy stood just before the guests, her face suffused with red, an outraged expression in her eyes. Emma felt herself shrivel at the condemning look and stepped back away from Will.

An extremely well-dressed woman with gorgeous red hair and piercing blue eyes recovered first. She swept into the room, her silk skirts rustling and her hand outstretched, beaming a smile upon the two of them. "William, I'm so happy to see you home." Her voice was breathy, seductive, and Emma felt her already frayed nerves stand on end like the hair on an angry cat's back.

Will took the woman's bare hand in his and placed a kiss on the back of it. His fingers did not immediately let go, Emma noted, unable to regain the breath she'd lost in her tirade.

"And who is your charming companion, William?" the woman asked, scorching Emma with a look.

Emma felt what small confidence she had begun the evening with contract into a ball of irrational, defensive hatred for this woman.

Will turned back to Emma and searched her face for a second; but Emma was too agitated to analyze the look. "Emma Davenport," he said in a flat voice. "This is Mrs. Josephine Sinclair. An old friend," he added enigmatically.

"How do you do?" Emma said coldly, with a minuscule curtsy.

Josephine inclined her head, her eyes not leaving Emma's. "I'm well, thank you."

At that moment Will's father entered with Brendan, the two of them ignorant of the argument the others had just witnessed. Their boisterous voices helped to relax the group, and Mrs. Darcy took the opportunity to deflect attention by explaining that Stephanie was indisposed and would not be down to dinner. Emma knew that in fact Stephanie was being punished for going out unescorted to buy a yellow-cover novel, the most cheap and vulgar of literature; but the others were in this way given the opportunity to act as if they'd noticed nothing between Will and Emma by expressing heartfelt concern and hope that Stephanie regained her good health soon. The Bullocks and the Darcys then seated themselves near the fire while Mr. Price and Mrs. Sinclair remained standing with Will, Brendan, and Emma.

Emma made a valiant effort to regain her composure. The instant dislike she'd taken to Mrs. Sinclair was unsettling, but she had no illusions about the jealousy from which it had sprung. How pitiful, she thought briefly, to have to be jealous of another woman's freedom to be nice to Will.

She gazed across the room as Mr. Price and Mrs. Sinclair talked beside her. The reverend was to be her dinner partner and he looked every bit as dull as Stephanie had promised. He was a short, portly man with beady eyes and a stony expression. His wife, older-looking than her husband, was thin and stoop-shouldered. Neither of them looked as if they knew the first thing about being happy. Indeed, they looked as if they'd never spent one moment smiling if they could help it. Emma wondered if that was how she looked now to Will.

She shifted her attention to the conversation nearest her. Mr. Price was an interesting-looking man, she thought, of indeterminate age, perhaps somewhere in his thirties. His white complexion and frail physique gave him away as probably having some chronic ailment that kept him from joining the army, Emma surmised. He had pale brown hair and light, possibly green eyes that were remarkably penetrating.

Will poured drinks for the men and was handing a sherry to Josephine when she mused to Emma, "Miss Davenport, I hope I don't embarrass you with this question, but aren't you from Richmond?"

Emma felt her face freeze at the woman's silky implication. At once, and without thinking, Emma replied haughtily, "And why should that embarrass me?"

Josephine had the grace to look flustered. She gave a breathy laugh and looked apologetically at Will. "Forgive me, I didn't mean that the way it sounded; but as an old friend of the family I have not been completely ignorant of the events in Will's private life. I'm afraid I just found myself overly curious if you were the same Miss Davenport about whom we used to hear so much."

Emma felt shame suffuse her from head to toe. Of course the woman would not be so vulgar as to imply that Emma should be embarrassed by her home. Where in the world had Emma's social graces deserted to? Assuming the worst and snapping back at a guest, even if that guest *had* meant offense, showed a lack of refinement that mortified Emma. Not to mention that all of these people were undoubtedly old friends of the Darcy family and now she'd disgraced them by acting ill-bred. She dropped her eyes to the drink in her hand and searched for an appropriate reply.

"Yes, Josey, that's her," Will drawled. "The Emma who jilted Will. No sense in beating around the bush, I suppose. Any other awkward questions we can get out of the way for you?"

"Oh, for goodness' sake, Will," Brendan blustered. "Show some tact for once in your life. You're both embarrassing Miss Davenport." He put a protective hand on Emma's elbow.

"It's all right," she murmured, and gently pulled her elbow from his grasp.

Will drained the last of the scotch from his glass and gestured toward Emma with it. "There, you see? She doesn't mind," he stated. "Don't worry, Josey, Emma doesn't get embarrassed. We couldn't embarrass Emma even if we tried our best, and believe me I've tried my best. She knows what she's about, Miss Emma does, and she never says what she doesn't mean." Will glanced at his companions, who gazed uneasily at the floor, the ceiling, anything but the two of them. "Come, come," he said heartily. "We can speak plainly around Miss Davenport. Can't we, Emma?"

Emma stared him down dispassionately. "I've never known you to restrain yourself, Will."

Will barked out a laugh. "There you are! She speaks plainly herself!"

Despite her discomfiture, Emma did not miss the familiar way Will had with Mrs. Sinclair, nor the featherlight touch of "Josey's" hand on his arm as she laughed stiffly at his mood.

"Leave it to you to make everything a joke, dear," Josephine said. "Of course, you're perfectly right, Brendan. We've been beastly to Miss Davenport." Josephine turned a contrite countenance to Emma. "Miss Davenport, I sincerely apologize. Please forgive me if I've made you uncomfortable. I hope we can start over on a better foot." She curtsied and held out a hand to Emma. "Good evening, Miss Davenport. It's a genuine pleasure to meet you."

Josephine's sky-blue eyes looked up at Emma with an almost pleading attempt at lightness. Emma reluctantly felt her dislike for the woman begin to fade.

She managed a small smile and curtsied back. "Nice to meet you, Mrs. Sinclair." They shook hands.

Lawrence Price, silent until now, looked between the two women as their hands clasped and murmured, "Well, would you look at that." He cast an unreadable look at Will and laughed, a sly, sinister sound. "I don't know how you do it, Darcy."

Will shrugged. "All I do is show up."

Mercifully, dinner was announced before conversation could progress more uncomfortably. Emma allowed Brendan to escort her to the table and even managed to keep her eyes from straying to Will and Josephine, who seated themselves next to each other across the table. Emma quickly realized that the danger of not sitting next to Will was having to look him in the eye, as he was seated directly across from her. She was sure if she extended her foot she would be able to touch his, so she kept her ankles neatly crossed beneath her chair.

The Reverend Bullock, on whom Emma had depended to keep her safely in mundane conversation, turned at once to Mr. Darcy on his right to continue a conversation they'd obviously started in the oval room.

Brendan turned immediately to her and said, "Emma, it's so wonderful to see you here, I must reiterate. I do hope you're finding the trip to be the relaxation you needed."

Emma took a last delicate sip from her soup spoon, then lowered it with a muted *clink* to the bowl before answering. No matter what, she needed to keep her ultimate purpose in mind with Brendan. "I can't express the good this trip has done me," she said quietly, hoping to keep her voice from carrying to Will. "I really don't know what I should have done if your family had refused to have me.''

Brendan's chest puffed up like a pigeon's. ''Refused to have you! What a ridiculous notion, my dear. You've always been a favorite in this family.''

Emma lowered her eyes demurely. ''Thank you for that. It's so easy to feel . . . awkward, at times.'' She cast a quick glance at Will that Brendan was sure to notice. ''But I am so enjoying myself,'' she added quickly. ''It's just that . . .''

Martha's gnarled hand emerged and reached for Emma's empty soup bowl, then Brendan's.

''Just what?'' Brendan prompted as soon as the maid had proceeded down the table.

Emma shook her head. ''Oh, nothing.'' She sipped her wine.

''Please, tell me,'' he persisted. ''You suddenly look so sad.''

Emma turned guileless eyes on him. ''Oh, I'm not sad, not at all. I'm just so happy to be here. I'm only afraid that my visit won't be long enough to truly help my jumbled nerves—in any sort of permanent way, you understand.'' The comment was so blatant in intent that she had to turn her flushing face away. She picked up a roll, broke off a piece, and chewed it nervously. The dry portion threatened to stick in her throat, the way the weakness she had to portray stuck in her craw.

Brendan turned partially in his seat toward her. ''Emma, you mustn't think you wouldn't be welcome again. You must come back, anytime. Of course.''

His movement and insistent tone of voice were enough to attract the attention of the others at the table, except for Mr. Darcy, who was completely ensnared by the Reverend Bullock.

Spearing her eldest son, who had rudely turned his back to her, with a disapproving look, Mrs. Darcy said to Emma, ''Are you well, dear?''

Emma could have kicked Brendan for drawing attention to them this way. ''I'm fine, really,'' she insisted almost desperately. ''Brendan, in his kindness, simply reacted more strongly than I intended to a silly comment of mine.''

Brendan recovered himself and sat straight in his chair. "A thousand apologies, Mother," he said with a stiff inclination of his head. His own cheeks flamed nearly as hotly as Emma's. He had always taken his stern mother's comments more seriously than Will ever did, and his extreme reactions to that woman never failed to shock Emma. Will placated and teased when she reprimanded him; Brendan looked as if he were ready to send himself to his room.

Mrs. Darcy nodded austerely, accepting the apology with obvious reluctance. "Now, you were saying, William?"

Will smirked in Brendan's direction and leaned back in his chair. "I was just telling Jo—Mrs. Sinclair a story that happened a couple of months ago." He glanced at Emma and his expression sobered. "But I was finished."

"Oh, do tell them the story—it's quite heartwarming," Josephine urged. She turned to the group. "Really, I almost cried."

Will eyed Emma a second, then turned his attention to his mother. "I don't know. . . ."

"Please go on," Emma said calmly. If he were trying to spare her something, she would have none of it. She would rather be treated as if she were not there, than to be tiptoed around.

Will cleared his throat. "Very well. I'd say it was no more than three months ago; we were set up in the fields of a farm near the Blue Ridge. At the edge of the field was a forest, beyond which was encamped the en—ah, the opposition."

Emma was grateful that the conversation continued between Mr. Darcy and Reverend Bullock. She felt acutely self-conscious when the war was brought up, and the adjoining conversation allowed her the option of insinuating herself into it if Will's tale became uncomfortable. But the issue of church funds for the needy was boring, even if safe, and Will's story was captivating.

"It was late at night and I happened to be up, enjoying the quiet. It was one of the first really cold nights of the season and, aside from the pickets, there were only about six of us awake and we were all huddled around the fire for warmth." Will toyed with his dessert spoon as he spoke, his eyes alternately focused on his mother and his own hand where it lay by his place setting. "Anyway, the sentry closest to me, Wilson, was on duty and just passing by my spot when we both heard a rustling in the trees. Wilson's just a kid and he became immediately agitated, fumbling with his musket, suddenly unsure if he'd even loaded the damn thing—excuse me, ladies," he added perfunctorily, in unison with his mother's admonishing "Will."

"So I got out my pistol and told the boy to relax," he continued, "and preceded him into the trees. Most likely it was just an animal. No soldier worth his salt would have created a racket like that coming through the brush—unless he'd lost his way in the darkness and thought he'd made it back to his own camp. Even then he'd have known to watch out for his own sentries."

At this point both Mr. Darcy and Reverend Bullock had stopped talking and listened to Will. Emma watched as Mr. Darcy spun his wineglass in circles on the soft smoothness of the tablecloth.

"Wilson was babbling something about his girl back home in Illinois and how if something happened he wanted me to write her a letter, care of her Aunt Phoebe, and tell her his true feelings, when we both spied a small white form coming through the trees." Will looked up and grinned at his audience. "At that moment, in the cold darkness, surrounded by great looming trees, I would have sworn it was a ghost. Were it not for the fact that Wilson was depending on me to be the calm voice in the wilderness, I'm sure I would have disgraced myself and run screaming from the woods. But the shape couldn't have been more than three feet tall, so we were feeling a bit braver than we might have, and as the thing grew closer we became aware that it was singing."

"Singing! Can you imagine?" Josephine was enraptured, hanging on his words though she'd just heard the story. "Go on, Will."

Will put down the spoon and folded his hands around one raised knee, pulling back slightly from the table to rest his ankle on his other leg. "Turns out it was a little girl in a white nightgown—couldn't have been more than five or six years old." He looked thoughtfully at the table, seeing, Emma was sure, the singing little girl and not the delicate cut-glass sugar bowl.

"I called out to her, real quietly. I said, 'Hey, princess, what are you doing out in the cold all alone?' Well, she looks up at me and says, 'That's what my pa used to call me.' She said it real matter-of-factly, but then she went on to say that her folks were both killed and that she stayed with 'the captain' now. The captain, she says, is going to let her ride her own horse someday. And she's got a drum, which is not a toy, and sometimes she marches with the drummer boy who has real feathers in his cap." Will paused, staring, remembering something. He looked up at his mother. "Turns out she heard this captain saying how he wished he had some tobacco 'like the Yanks over there.' So this little girl takes it into her head she'll just come and ask us for some—since the captain's a mite shy about asking for things."

Emma felt her eyes well with tears.

"What did you do?" Mrs. Darcy asked.

Will shrugged and gave a short laugh. "We loaded her up with more Lone Jack than her nightgown could hold. She held it up in front like a little apron, and went traipsing back through the woods happy as could be." He shook his head. "We didn't hear a warning shot so we figured she'd made it back through her own lines all right."

Josephine dabbed at her eyes. The table was silent.

Will stared at his plate. After a moment he took a deep breath and let it out slowly. "Couldn't sleep after that," he murmured.

Chapter Five

Walking down the windy street with an icy sun overhead, Will tried hard to keep his mind on the stunning woman beside him. Resplendent in emerald satin, red hair fiery in the bright sun, Josey Sinclair possessed all that any man could want and even employed every coy look in the book in an effort to monopolize his gaze. But Will could not stop his attention from straying time and again to the gracefully composed woman with the shimmering dark hair in front of him.

It didn't help matters any that Emma's hand was tucked cozily in his brother's arm, nor that she laughed at every inane thing the buffoon said. They'd be hard-pressed to shut Brendan up later after the whole day with an audience like that, Will mused sourly.

On Will's other arm, Stephanie bobbed like a kite on a short string, anxious to keep up with the group, but unwilling to tear her hungry eyes from the brimming shop windows. Will had to pull her out of the path of oncoming pedestrians on more than one occasion. When Emma stopped ahead of them to peer into a particular window, Stephanie excused herself hurriedly and ran to catch up to her.

"Oh, Will, look," Josey cooed beside him, pulling him and his preoccupied gaze to a shop window close by. In the window, on prominent display, was a silk hair net of gold thread, set with pearls, and a gold-and-pearl-studded fan for evening wear. "Isn't it just the most delicious set? Can you see them on me?" She turned her head prettily and smiled at him, pushing her hair into a brief semblance of a chignon so that he could get the idea. "What do you think? Shall I try them on for you?"

"I'm sure you would be ravishing in them," Will murmured. Yet all he could think of was the exquisite effect the combination would have on Emma. How he longed to be able to buy them for her, to surprise her, as he used to do.

Josey pouted. "Well, you don't seem very sincere."

Will forcibly turned his attention to her and pushed a smile onto his lips. It was time he stopped brooding after the damned woman who didn't want him and concentrate on the one who did. "But I am sincere, Jo. You look beautiful in everything you put on, and you know it." At her unconvinced expression he laughed. "Come on, then. Try them on. I promise you I'll be stunned by your beauty." He ushered her into the store, where they were met by a supercilious young man with a tendency to bow after everything Will said.

"The lady would like to try on the set in the window," Will said, crossing his arms and leaning back against a display counter.

The man bowed. "Yes, of course, sir." He scurried to the window. "I'm sure I haven't seen a woman more suited to this set since we put them out this morning," he called over his shoulder. "With your coloring, madam, they shall be the perfect accessory, to be sure."

As the man bent into the window well, Will saw that Brendan and Emma had doubled back with Stephanie to follow them into the store.

Beside him Josey clutched his forearm. "Oh, they're simply gorgeous," she gushed, eyes riveted to the set as it emerged from the window in the cherishing hands of the clerk. Her fingers reached out like a child's and impulsively plucked the fan from the display before the man could set it on the counter. He made a brief, worried sound, then pinched his mouth shut firmly.

Snapping the fan open with practiced ease, she spun to Will. Bright blue eyes skillfully lined with kohl batted at him furiously. "Am I devastating?" She laughed.

A corner of his mouth lifted. "Truly," he murmured as the rest of the party entered the shop and his eyes trailed away from her, "I am devastated."

Josey turned to pry the hair net from the clerk's protection, as Will's eyes drifted once again to Emma. She walked slowly to the opposite side of the room, studying the array of accessories around her and stopping to finger the black fringe on a maroon silk shawl. In the area between her and Will, Brendan protested vociferously as Stephanie plucked a red fur muff from a shelf near the door.

"It's not proper for a young girl, Stephanie. Perhaps an older, married lady, yes, but not someone of your tender years," Brendan pronounced.

Stephanie pouted and snatched the muff back out of Brendan's hands. "But no married lady would need it! It's too fancy, too carefree. It's for a young lady to catch a young man's eye, you dolt—ask the man, go on. Where is he?"

Will glanced past them to Emma, who wore a gentle smile at Stephanie's manner, and he felt his own lips curve in like fashion. How calming she was. Even after their argument, simply looking at her suffused him with a form of tranquillity. He could imagine her easily in ten or fifteen years just as serene, just as beautiful, overseeing her own daughter's wardrobe with just such tolerance.

"Well?" Josey's voice ripped his attention back to her.

Will barely glanced at the bedecked Josey as he shook himself from his reverie. It was pointless, and painful, to indulge in ruminations of that sort. What a weak-witted sot he was becoming. "We'll take them," he stated firmly to the clerk, reaching into his pocket for his money clip.

He felt, rather than saw, Emma's head turn in their direction at the words, and his eyes flicked briefly to her, catching a surprised expression before she could hide it. Then he turned his back to her. He glanced at the clerk. "Box them up, please, so she can carry them with her."

"Oh, yes, sir." The clerk bowed deeply. "The perfect accessory. I daresay you'll be pleased to see them on madam each and every time she dons them. A truly timeless gift—"

"Yes, yes, I know." Will sighed, turning to Josey.

Josey's eyes widened. "Will, really? They're awfully expensive—you didn't even look." Her tone was cajoling, but there was an underlying intensity to it.

He took her elbow in his hand and gave it a perfunctory squeeze. "I don't care. I want to see you in them."

Josey smiled brilliantly. "I'll wear them tomorrow—to the Atkinses'. You're going, aren't you? Oh, Will, you're so sweet." Before he knew what she was about, she perched herself on tiptoe and planted a solid kiss directly on his mouth. "Thank you, darling."

Will eyed her suspiciously, a wry smile on his lips. She was up to something. From the corner of his eye he could see Emma's startled face, and he suppressed a wave of irritation at Josey's impetuosity. "It's nothing, Jo."

Josey's lips curled into a slow smile. "Perhaps to you." Then, in a softer voice, she murmured, "Come by later. I'll pay you back." With that she gave him a wicked look, wetting her lips with a slow, deliberate tongue. Will closed his eyes and laughed briefly, disgusted with himself. He'd asked for this somehow. But still it pained him to think of Emma's conclusions.

The clerk bustled to the back of the store for a box as Stephanie gave up on the muff, bounded over, and enthused about the purchase with Josey. Will slipped out of the conversation and made his way toward Emma, who still stood near the maroon shawl. His eyes took in her flushed face, her stiff jaw.

"And have you found something you'd like, Miss Emma?" he asked softly. He hated the way he sounded, patronizing and contentious, when what he really wanted to do was say something, anything, to erase her hostility toward him, to erase the years of pain and alienation that had come between them. But he knew the conclusions she'd drawn about his relationship with Josey were correct and that something inside of himself had egged him on to reveal it. The whole stupid scene was of his own making and he could not now get out of it.

Brendan was engrossed in the study of a child's toy, a marble in a maze of some sort, and Will did not want to distract him, so he deliberately stood on the other side of Emma, near the corner, forcing her to turn toward him or be conspicuously rude.

She turned with hard eyes. "There are no *favors* you can buy from me," she said, unable to conceal the anger in her voice.

The barb stung but he maintained a bland expression. "Come now, Emma. Surely a simple souvenir of your trip would not upset your moral sensibilities," he baited, for reasons he could not define. Perhaps it was a need to crack that iron facade of indifference once more. Though she would never again allow him to see the desire revealed by her kiss, anger was preferable to indifference, for beneath anger was passion. "Come, let me buy you a trinket as well. For the sake of old times . . ."

Emma's chin rose stiffly and she tucked her hands underneath her cloak, pulling it close. "There is *nothing* I want from you, Will Darcy, least of all memories of past mistakes." She'd mastered her countenance and bestowed upon him a haughty look, one that cut him more deeply than he could admit. "It's a bit warm in here. I shall meet you all outside." She turned from him and strode to the door.

Will shifted to watch her go, assuming a blank expression as Brendan jerked himself from the toy to hasten after her.

"Clerk," Will said harshly, flagging the man down as he bustled toward Josey and Stephanie with the fancily wrapped package. Pitching his voice below their chatter, he said, "Wrap the maroon shawl as well and have it sent to my home." He handed over a card.

"Certainly, sir. Yes, sir, right away." The clerk bowed and

was about to rush off when Will stopped him, motioning him back with a forefinger. As the man stood expectantly before him, Will took the box for Josey from his hands and smiled. "Oh, yes." The man laughed nervously. "So sorry. Of course. I'll just see to the shawl now."

"Good man," Will murmured.

He turned his gaze to Josey, who stood alone at the front of the store as Stephanie left to find Emma. She wore a strange little smile and regarded him thoughtfully as he moved toward her.

"You're a generous man, Will."

He smiled and extended the package to her. "You know I'd do anything for you, Jo," he said casually. "You'll look beautiful in them."

Josey cradled the gift, making no move toward the door. "I know you'd do a lot for me." Her expression sobered as she looked up at him. "But it's for *her* that you'd do anything." She paused, her eyes narrowing. "Isn't it." It was not a question.

Will stopped. For the first time in a long time he saw Josey objectively, her eyes defensively hiding hurt or anger, her face lovely, but hard. It must be difficult for her, he thought for the first time, living with her decision to marry the desperately rich but querulous old Malcolm Sinclair. It was no wonder she craved the attentions of every young man she met; she was wasting her own youth on an old curmudgeon.

The price she paid for wealth, he told himself, and quirked a sad smile. "There's nothing I can do for her. But you . . ." He let the words trail off seductively. He didn't want to think about Josey's desperation; it looked too much like his own, though their sources were dissimilar.

Josey's brow raised. "Well, the shawl is a nice attempt."

Will laughed and looked up at the ceiling. "There's no hiding from you, is there? My God, woman, you've got the eyes of a hawk." He shook his head, chuckled quietly, and turned her to the door by her elbow. She moved stiffly under his hand, wanting, he knew, to be placated.

"Never fear, my pretty," he added. "I only feel sorry for her.

70

She doesn't have much anymore, you know. You can see how worn her gown is.'' Reflexively, he opened the shop door for her. ''And she's used to better,'' he murmured thoughtfully.

Josey eyed him cynically. ''So you're playing big brother? Come, Will, I know you better than that.'' Her eyes sparkled with frustrated anger as she spoke. Exiting the shop, they could just see the others down the block, waiting on the corner. ''You're still in love with her,'' she accused.

Will sighed without answering and shook his head, stopping in his tracks.

Josey stopped with him and faced him arrogantly. ''You're still in love with her and she won't give you the time of day, will she?''

He looked at her sternly. ''Josey, when you've spent a long time caring about someone it's hard to just turn it off when circumstances change.'' He sighed. She wouldn't understand; and he didn't know why he tried to explain it to her, perhaps to decipher it for himself. He watched a horse clop slowly by, its hooves sucking in and out of mud puddles as it went. ''I was in love with her . . . a long time ago. But love needs love in order to thrive. Ours suffocated years ago.'' As he said the words he felt their sad inevitability. Whether or not it was true now, it would be true enough in years to come. With every passing day he could feel the erosion, the weight of futility on the vestiges of the love they'd had. It seemed obvious now that they would either kill or be killed by those feelings.

Josey studied the sophisticated bow on the top of her package with a pout. ''Why, Will . . . how tragically poetic.'' She could not keep the slight sneer of sarcasm from her voice; but he understood it. It was the same way he felt himself—both angered and frustrated by the sentiment.

He forced a laugh. ''Tragedies are always poetic. That's what draws us to them.''

Up on the corner, Will could see Brendan and Emma talking. Stephanie gazed quietly into the street, when from the periphery of his vision he saw a small boy dart toward the group. The boy

71

skidded to a halt behind Emma and tugged none too gently at her skirt. Emma whirled. Then, seeing it was just a boy, she knelt to his height.

As Will and Josey neared, he could see Emma's pink cheeks and her quick glance up at Brendan, who appeared to be shooing the boy away.

"It's all right, Brendan," Will heard her say in exasperation as they got close. It was an odd voice, tense. The old bore must be getting to her, Will thought with no small amount of satisfaction. "What is it, boy?" she continued gently to the child.

From behind his back, the boy produced a sadly wilted flower. It had the look of something held too tightly for too long, but still he croaked, "Care to buy a flower from a war orphan?"

Emma reached immediately for her reticule, which swung from the belt at her waist. "Yes, I would. How much would you like for it?"

The boy went mute, staring at her.

"It's all right," she said quickly. "Here." She thrust a penny into the boy's hand and took the flower, rising quickly as the boy sped off.

"Good heavens," Brendan blustered, "he runs as if he stole the thing. As if anyone would miss a dead weed like that."

"Aren't you nice, Emma," Josey crooned with a dry glance at Will, "to buy from that boy."

Emma looked distinctly embarrassed and made great work of closing her reticule, then settling the flower in her hands, first one, then the other. "It's just so sad," she said quickly, "a war orphan. His parents dead, so sad. Now I suppose he lives on the street—selling flowers. . . ." She held the sorry bloom up in pitiful illustration.

"*Stealing* flowers is more like it," Brendan insisted. "I've half a mind to track him down and see how many others he cheats in similar fashion. You shouldn't have encouraged him."

Emma turned an appalled look on him. "But he's just a boy. An orphan! He must support himself somehow—"

"He's no more orphan than I am." Brendan took a step in the

direction the boy went, scanning the crowd.

"Would that that were true," Will muttered, sending Stephanie into uncontrolled giggles.

Brendan shot him a quelling glance. "I just think it's disgraceful the way the urchins in this town run rampant. Someday they'll take over from the decent folks, running free like that."

Emma laid a hand on Brendan's sleeve and Will felt a pang at the sight of it. He knew just how the touch felt, calming, tranquil.

"Please," she said, gentle force in the word, "it's only a flower. Let it be."

Brendan blustered to a halt, clearly disgruntled at having to cease his tirade in order to please the object of his desire.

"Now, there is one thing I'd like to buy," Emma said into the ensuing silence. "I have need of some yarn. Is there a general store nearby?"

"Oh, yes!" Stephanie replied, taking her arm. "Pope's. It's just down here on the right. And they have the most delicious gumdrops in a whole rainbow of colors."

They all started off in the direction the boy had taken.

Pope's General Store was large and very clean, with an extensive selection of yarns. Will watched Emma make her way to the stooped and graying proprietor to ask for yarn, though she had to pass right by an extensive collection of it to get to him.

"I'd like something perhaps in this shade," she said in a strangely brittle voice, pulling forth from her cape the tattered yellow flower.

The old man took the flower from her hand and studied it carefully. "No," he said in a voice that sounded like the creak of an old rocker. "I don't believe we have one just this shade . . . but if you'll step over here, I think we can find something you'll like as well."

Something about the exchange piqued Will's curiosity and he started toward them. Just as he neared, he heard the clang of bells jangle behind him with the opening of the door.

"Well, hello," a familiar voice said.

Will turned toward the sound. "Lawrence, what a surprise."

He altered his course to shake the other man's hand. Lawrence's pale eyes glittered from an uncharacteristically pink face. The cold, Will thought. Makes him look almost human in spite of those colorless eyes. Normally the man was whiter than a corpse.

Lawrence greeted Brendan, Stephanie, and Josey alike. Emma did not stir from her yarn mission.

"What brings you out into the cold today?" Will asked.

"Odds and ends. I'm a bit surprised to see you, though. Thought you'd have had enough walking for one lifetime." Lawrence gave him a thin, pointed smile.

Will laughed. "You would think. But the ladies needed something to do." He swept Josey with his eyes, then turned toward Emma. She handed the proprietor some coins.

"Good of Will and Brendan to take such good care of us, isn't it?" Josey said, always ready to add more men to her entourage.

Will was about to turn back when he saw the proprietor smile faintly, give a slight shake of his head, then pat Emma's hand. He was refusing payment. Will's brow furrowed. At that moment the proprietor's eyes caught his and, with a nervous laugh, he said something loudly about her being too generous. Then he went off about his business.

Emma took up the yarn and tucked it carefully under her cape before turning around. Will met her eyes. She blushed, then smiled at him.

He felt a chill descend his spine.

"All set," she said gaily, eyes glittering feverishly and a smile pasted on her face. She came rapidly toward him, gracing him with a benevolence of expression he thought he'd never again receive from her. "He didn't have the shade I wanted, but I think this will do. Are you all ready to leave? I've finished my— Oh, Mr. Price, how nice to see you again." She extended her hand to him, obviously grateful for the diversion.

"Miss Davenport, I can't tell you what a delight it is to see you here." Will's sense of unease increased as Lawrence's eyes took on the hooded look of a cat who'd just caught supper.

* * *

The following day bloomed bright and sunny as Emma planned her impending departure. She would have to wait a few more days, of course, just in case anyone did happen to be suspicious. If anyone were watching Pope's, her departure right after a visit to the general store might make her errand obvious. If this had been an ordinary visit she would have left just to spare the Darcys the burden of her company now that Will was home. But on this visit it was impossible. Even though they were probably as uncomfortable as she under the circumstances, she would have to wait.

She sighed into the mirror as she repinned a few renegade tendrils of hair. Though she was still flushed from the small triumph of obtaining the contraband drugs in full view of everyone, the memory of the occasion still had the power to make her hands shake. Will, as she would have predicted, had proven to be the one who unnerved her most. That moment when she'd turned from the kindly shop owner's face to the flinty gray eyes of the man who knew her far too well had been one of the hardest of her life. The smile she had forced to her lips was a veritable battle won, and she believed nothing she'd faced or had yet to face could be as difficult.

The fact that the drugs now resided in a dark corner of her traveling case in an upstairs closet made her nervous, however, and she was anxious to get on the road in order to avoid any accidental discovery by a maid or a servant. There was no adequate excuse she could make if she were to be discovered harboring several vials of morphine, and the Darcys would be justifiably horrified at her deception.

A knock on her bedroom door interrupted her reverie. Emma checked the tiny watch she wore on a chain and noted that it was still a bit early for luncheon.

She opened the door to find Maggie. "Beggin' your pardon, ma'am, but ye've a visitor in the front parlor." The housemaid curtsied quickly. Maggie did not like her, Emma could tell. And she knew precisely the reason.

"A visitor? For me?"

Elaine Fox

"Yes, ma'am. Mr. Price, ma'am. Shall I tell him you'll attend him now?" Sky-blue eyes drilled her in a challenging way.

"Yes. I'll be right down. Thank you, Maggie." Emma sighed as Maggie strode purposefully off. There was nothing to do about it. Though Maggie had liked her well enough when she was engaged to Will, now that she'd called it off there was no avoiding the woman's disapproval. It made her a little sad, for she liked Maggie and her easy sense of humor.

Pushing the irrelevant thoughts of Maggie aside, she reflected uneasily on the matter at hand. Lawrence Price to see me, she thought. What in the world could he want? She hadn't sensed any particular rapport with the man in either of their two short conversations, nor did she think him the type to offer a polite neighborly call. In an effort to appear less idle and distracted than she'd been, she picked up a book from the bedside table to bring with her. Peripherally, she was glad of having donned the gray dress this morning. In it she would feel a tad less like the poor relation.

Adjusting her skirts as she descended the staircase, Emma was surprised by the sight of Mr. Price standing in the archway to the front parlor, watching her approach. He gave her a thin smile— the only type he seemed to possess, she thought unkindly.

"Miss Davenport, how fortunate for me you are at home. I'm sorry to catch you before luncheon; I hope you don't mind." He gave a precise bow, short respite for Emma from those strangely pale eyes.

His hair, a colorless sort of brown, was cut shorter than the fashion, and his complexion was almost desperately white. But though one might think he'd fade into the background with such pallidness, instead he stood out with a remarkably poised composure. Stephanie had told her that he was asthmatic, and as such he was unable to participate in the war as a soldier. But he did *something,* Stephanie was sure, though she could not quite say what it was.

Emma placed a courteous smile on her face. "I'm happy to see you, Mr. Price. It is no inconvenience." She gestured to the beckoning warmth of the room beyond. "Shall we sit down?"

76

He inclined his head formally and followed her though the door.

"Miss Davenport," he began as soon as she'd seated herself on the sofa. "I hope you don't think me impolitic in coming here this way but I feel once you've heard what I have to say you will be glad of my visit."

Emma looked at him in genuine perplexity. "I'm sure I shall. Please sit down, Mr. Price; you're making me quite nervous standing over me like that." She smiled to soften the words, but could not ease the sudden trepidation she felt.

"Forgive me," he said absently, seating himself on the armchair across from her and leaning forward intently. "Permit me to be blunt," he said in a hushed tone that caused Emma to sit a little further back in the chair. He fixed her with his pale gaze, the line of his mouth firm. "I know what you were doing at Pope's store yesterday."

Emma felt her stomach drop perilously and blood heat her face.

"I know this," he continued, "because I am the contact; I sent the boy to you." His eyes were merciless, hot and cold at the same time, both determined and ruthless.

Emma swallowed hard. "What?" It was a breathless puff of air. "What boy?" Her hand involuntarily strayed to the base of her throat, clenching into a fist.

"You know what I'm talking about. Please don't be alarmed. I am not here to incriminate you."

Emma took a shaking breath through a throat nearly closed in horror.

He continued. "The boy, the flower, the shop, the medicines, I know about them all, Miss Davenport." He reached across the short space between them and took her other hand in his cool one. She looked down at their hands as if both belonged to strangers.

"I-I don't know what . . ." She couldn't complete the sentence. It was so obvious that he knew all.

He squeezed her hand gently, though for some reason it felt coldly impersonal, not reassuring as he must have intended, and then he let it go. "The reason I'm here now—I did not initially plan to make myself known to you—is to beg for further assistance on behalf of the Cause." He glanced quickly at the door, then back at her face. "I must be brief, for discovery here would compromise everyone. But we need for you to provide a very important service. More important, even, than your procurement of lifesaving medicines. What we need for you to do will save far more lives than any drug can. Will you consider what I have to say?"

Emma felt adrift in a churning sea of emotions. She was discovered. She'd been seen. She had failed.

She was necessary.

His words told her she could trust this strange man, but she didn't feel trust. "I—Mr. Price, I-I'm overwhelmed." She let her hand drop to her lap and her eyes followed. Beads of perspiration prickled along her hairline. She forced her eyes to his. "You're for the South?" she whispered.

He smiled again, with a touch more warmth. "As much as you are, my dear, perhaps more." He relaxed then, slightly, and leaned fractionally back in his chair. "There is a very important message that must be carried—"

Emma gasped. "But—but I've promised to carry no messages. The danger . . ."

Lawrence smiled, but Emma detected a sudden coldness. "Miss Davenport, what you are already endeavoring to do is rife with danger. Surely you are not afraid of any *real* help you can provide your country."

Real help, he said. Emma's face flamed, stung. "Mr. Price, I can think of no greater help I can provide than saving lives."

"But there is where you're wrong." His eyes held both urgency and calculation, and she was not sure which to trust. He continued with unerring reason. "Is not prevention better than cure? Would you not prefer that the men were not mutilated before you could save them?"

Emma's fingers twisted nervously in her lap. She had the fleeting thought that his voice must be what the devil's sounded like

78

in urging the weak to stray into sin. What he said made sense, but she felt in her heart, in some unexplainable way, that he was wrong. Wasn't he?

"Of course I would rather they weren't hurt, but . . ." She did not know how to continue. How could she say she did not want to prevent bloodshed?

He leaned forward again. "Don't you agree that to avoid confrontation is the best way of saving lives? If you could prevent even one battle, would it not be worth it?"

She shifted in her chair. "Of course."

"Miss Davenport, I am offering you the opportunity to enact just such a circumstance. Perhaps if I tell you all . . . Our troops are situated in a very precarious location. Union spies have betrayed us and their troops are prepared to attack. It is imperative that our army be warned as soon as possible." He clasped his hands so tightly together in front of him that Emma could see his knuckles whiten. "Other intermediaries are unavailable. In fact, our latest messenger was dispatched with the erroneous message that those very troops were well placed and undiscovered. Miss Davenport, you are our only hope."

Emma chewed her bottom lip. From the feverish plea in his eyes to the strained force of his words, it was obvious Mr. Price believed strongly in what he said. His hands clenched and unclenched reflexively as he awaited her answer. She could feel his eyes upon her.

"Please," he beseeched softly. "For the sake of hundreds of young lives, please say you'll help. If only this once."

Her shoulders sagged under the weight of his argument. She could not say no. To do so would be churlish, selfish—cowardly. Her eyelids fluttered downward to focus on her own clasped hands. She had promised Judith she would smuggle only medicines. They both knew that the penalty for spying was far more serious than for smuggling. But how could she turn away from such an immediate need? How could she decline to do anything that would help the Cause?

"I'll do it," she said lowly. Her voice shook but she felt the moment the words were out that it was the only choice she could have made. "I'll do it this one time only."

Lawrence Price leaned back with a deep intake of breath. "God bless you, Miss Davenport," he said, his own voice thick with relief.

Chapter Six

The vials were tied in three separate bags to the wide hoop beneath her skirt. As she walked she could feel the uppermost one hit bluntly against her leg, but moving it was out of the question. That operation would entail the laborious removal of her gown as well as several cumbersome petticoats. The touch of the coarse little bag caused her nervousness to swell, however, for it made the hiding place feel obvious. Would she have done better to have hidden them in her bodice somehow? One of them might have fit there. Or perhaps in her hat.

The maid had packed her belongings, and a manservant carried them downstairs to the carriage while Emma took a moment in her room to brace herself for the trial to come. She would be borne across the line in the Darcys' personal coach, after which she would be met by one from her own household. Emma was sure she would not breathe a single complete breath until she was past the Northern guards and safely ensconced in her own carriage.

The previous day Lawrence Price had brought her a tiny slip

of paper which she was to carry in one of the bags of morphine. It was a tissuey little thing that she immediately pushed up her sleeve, glancing fearfully around the room though not even a servant was nearby.

"Don't be nervous," Lawrence had said with an icy smile that did more to unnerve her than any of his other "reassuring" gestures. "They'll pick up on that quicker than anything else you do."

Fine, she thought now with anger, *fine*. She paced the room in agitation as she fumbled with the cheap quartz brooch at her breast. It does no good to tell one that to be nervous shall be their undoing. How could he possibly have believed saying something like that would dispel her unease? She was just on the verge of getting the clumsy pin clasped when a sharp rap on her door caused her to jump and prick the skin beneath.

She whipped the offending object from her chest and clasped it in her hand.

"Who is there?" she asked in a tone of such obviously forced pleasantry she again suffered premonitions of doom.

"Will."

Emma's stomach flip-flopped at the sound of his voice. They had not been alone together since the night they had kissed, and for a brief, nearly overpowering moment, she felt a longing to fling open the door, fall into his arms, and let him soothe away her fear and anguish. I wish I could help you, he'd said. And she had wanted him to. But even if she let him, could he really help her now—could he eliminate the reason for this subterfuge and danger? On the heels of that question rose anger—anger that he had thrown it all away, their past, their future, their love, all for participation in this barbarous war. For the moment it felt almost as if it were *his* war, this war that the North had precipitated.

She yanked open the door, clasping the brooch so hard in her other hand she could feel its inferior pronged setting pierce the skin of her palm.

"What is it?" she demanded into his startled face.

He recoiled slightly at the aggressive tone. Then one eyebrow

82

lifted in curiosity. "I've come to say good-bye. But I might well ask you the same question. . . . What is it, Emma?"

She frowned and glanced down at the brooch in her hands. She was doing a fine job so far of concealing her emotions, and this was a Yankee she knew. "I'm just irritated, that's all. I don't like traveling, you may recall, and I can't get this blasted brooch pinned properly."

Will laughed outright. "My dear, here . . ." He took her hands in his and, before she could form the words to protest, he took the brooch from them and unclasped it. "Let me help you."

Emma stepped back. "Don't be silly."

"I'm not the one being silly. Now come here."

She did not move forward, but neither did she move back as he calmly approached and took the fabric near her throat gently in his fingers. A swift heat suffused her face and she was conscious of holding her breath. Though she kept her eyes averted, she could smell the clean soap scent of him and could just barely control the shiver of pleasure that swept her as his fingers brushed the skin of her throat.

"There you go," he said softly when he'd finished. He stepped back just far enough to force her to raise her eyes to his. When she did, the expression of damage and yearning in his eyes nearly undid her. She slowly exhaled the breath she'd been holding as their gazes locked.

"Emma—" He broke off sharply as a maid clopped purposely down the hall and turned in at the open door.

"Oh, pardon me," Maggie said, with just a trace of exaggeration. "I was just checkin' to see that you had nothing else to go down, miss."

Emma shook her head. "Nothing, no."

Maggie's shrewd eyes assessed the situation. "And good mornin' to you, Mr. Will," she said archly.

Will's lips curved ironically. "Good morning, Maggie." Then, as she continued to stand there, he added, "I believe that will be all now."

"Well, then, all right." She nodded. She whipped a glance

from one to the other of them, then spun out the door, managing to achieve a subservient huff as well as the destruction of any possible tenderness between Will and Emma.

Emma stepped back away from him. "Thank you for coming to say good-bye, Will," she said formally. "There was no need to make the special effort. I'm sorry to have invaded your home, as you so clearly implied earlier, but now you may have it back again."

Disappointment showed on his face, and Emma felt ashamed of the childish manipulation of her words. Still, if she gave an inch she was sure she'd be back in his arms in a heartbeat—a weakness she would despise in herself for the rest of her days.

"You know I never said that. Though I must confess I am still curious about your visit." He eyed her speculatively.

"You needn't be," she said stiffly. She wished she could say it was her last, but in view of the headway she'd made with Brendan she suspected it might just be the first of many. But with any luck at all her visits and Will's would never again coincide. "What do you plan to do now that you've left your regiment?"

Will answered casually. "I'm entering a different branch of the service, one that requires a bit of training here in Washington. According to Lawrence I am to begin today, which is why I am here at this hour to see you off."

"Lawrence?" She bit off her astonishment.

"Yes. Lawrence Price. He's partially involved in the field to which I shall lend my negligible services." He shrugged deprecatingly.

"But I thought he was too sickly to soldier," she protested, genuinely perplexed. Though, thinking about it, if he were to be of any use as a spy he would have to be involved in the Union military in some way, if only to have access to pertinent information. The hypocrisy of such a role sickened her and brought to mind again the hideous turn her own project had taken.

"His health is fragile," Will confirmed, and leaned on the doorjamb with a noncommittal gesture. "He is merely—a consultant of sorts."

Emma nodded her head, comprehension dawning. "Ah, I see." And she did. Lawrence Price was involved in the War Department; that was what would keep him in Washington and keep him informed of important movements in the war. What danger he courted, she thought briefly.

Then the thought of her own danger intruded. She turned away from Will, and the movement brought the dull thumping of the vial against her leg. Her heart tripped an unnatural beat. She could feel his eyes on her back. Please leave, her mind wailed silently to him. Please leave me to gather my wits, rather than lose them all in your presence. Why did he choose to confront her now, while she was so deeply in the throes of her fear, and her unyielding guilt?

She turned halfway back toward him as she tried to modulate her voice to a conversational level, but it still emerged unrecognizably brittle. "So you begin today in Washington. How soon before you are back in battle?" In an attempt to appear casual she picked up a bottle of scent from her dressing table and turned her eyes toward him.

He smiled cynically. "Soon, Emma, never fear. Your compatriots will get another shot at me before long. Though I don't know what difference it will make to you unless you plan on coming back."

The flush that stained her face was telling, she knew. Oh, why wouldn't he end this charade and just leave? But there was nothing to do but to plow on through it. Her fingers toyed with the tassel on the bottle as she kept her face averted. "I have no firm plan to return, but the trip has been such a help to—to my strained . . . my strained nerves that—well, that I just don't know." She hated the tentative sound of her voice and clenched her teeth in annoyance. He was doing it on purpose, keeping her on the spot. Why must he push her all the time?

Will watched her dispassionately. "Yes, I can see that you're much more relaxed now."

Stung by the sarcasm in his voice, Emma whirled on him. "You wouldn't know anything about it," she growled with a ferocity that surprised both of them. "You—you sit up here in the lap of luxury with your—your *cream* and your fresh vegetables."

His mouth opened slightly. "My cream?"

"You wear thick wool—quality wool clothing without holes— and you have ample firewood and food and—and oil." She paced toward him and stopped. "Your family is *whole,* damn you, and you dare to criticize—" She cut herself off sharply and took a deep, quivering breath. In an effort to stop her threatening tears she pulled herself up straight and clenched her fist against the welling emotion. She clutched the forgotten perfume bottle in her other hand.

"Emma, don't. . . ." He shook his head gently; but the expression of pity on his face only infuriated her further.

"But don't you dare feel sorry for me, Will Darcy," she challenged in a voice strong with conviction. "I'll come through this a better person than you will. I'll show every last cheap, lying Yankee just what Southerners are made of, starting with you. You can't run roughshod over us, treating us like wayward children. We shall rule ourselves."

Will's sympathetic expression disappeared with the vehemence of her words. "And all those poor colored souls around you," he spat. "Don't talk to *me* about running roughshod, Miss Emma."

"You know we don't own any slaves," she shot back.

He threw up a hand. "What a happy coincidence!" he said facetiously. "You don't own any slaves. Well, good for you. Who do you think does, then? And if you're so opposed to slavery that you don't own any, how in God's name can you defend those who do?"

"I defend my country," Emma said stolidly. "I defend the South against a dictatorship by the North, by an economy independent of that which it condemns. How simple to say 'Abolish slavery!' without offering any viable means of doing so."

"As if that would make one whit of difference," Will muttered.

Emma glared at him and placed the perfume bottle on the table with a loud thump. "Oh, it's easy to be high and mighty, isn't it? You take to it quite naturally. But it becomes a bit more difficult when faced with practicality. Though practicality was never your strong suit, was it?'' She hit a nerve. His face flushed and his eyes glittered like winter sun on an icy sea. He was very angry; and in an awful, desperate way it gratified her to see it.

Will shook his head, staring at the floor as a muscle twitched in his jaw. ''I'm not going to argue politics with you, Emma.''

''Of course you're not!'' She laughed shrilly and pushed the dressing table chair in so abruptly it struck with a crack. ''You couldn't possibly. You haven't any answers.'' She felt a wave of fatigue sweep her with the words and leaned her hands on the back of the chair. ''No one has any answers. They just have guns.'' She shook her head in disgust, her shoulders drooping. ''Lord, I'm just so sick of guns.''

A silence stretched long between them while Emma tried to control her seesawing emotions. It was too easy to lose sight of the arguments when one was so tired. And the longer the conflict was waged, the harder it became to keep the ultimate purpose of it in mind. For Emma, the battle was becoming one against death more than the Yankees, though certainly the Yankees were the agents of that death. But it was times like these when she most felt the futility of the fight. In the same way that neither she nor Will would ever give an inch to the other, neither would either the North or the South give way to the other. They would just continue until all of them were dead, she concluded grimly. The prospect filled her with hopeless fatigue.

Will stirred and she turned tired eyes to him. ''I only wanted to wish you a safe journey,'' he said finally. ''And as disparate as our positions seem, I want you to know that you can count on me if you ever need help.'' His voice was tightly controlled.

''I suppose I should thank you for that,'' she said wearily. But the words sounded haughty, though she did not mean for them to come out that way. She regretted it immediately as she saw the expression on Will's face harden.

Without another word he turned and took the doorknob in his hand to close it behind him.

"Will—" Something she did not stop to comprehend forced the protest from her lips. He turned slowly, his expression unreadable. She stared, unsure what she meant to say next, but anxious to have their last words to each other be civil. Finally she pushed words from her throat, the only truly sincere ones she could utter: "Please stay well."

Her eyes pleaded for understanding, for forgiveness for her erratic behavior, maybe even forgiveness for the sin she was about to commit against his country. He had to see that she fought for her country as surely as he fought for his, didn't he? How could she make him understand the uniquely Southern devotion to tradition, to pride, as well as her own uncompromising loyalty to those who fought so strongly for the Confederacy?

His eyes, a study in gentleness and restraint, rested on her for a quiet moment. "And you, Emma," he returned finally.

She inclined her head and did not look up as she heard him leave the room. A moment later, she allowed her hand to touch the brooch that he had fastened; and she relived, in the private recesses of her heart, the moment his fingers had brushed her throat.

The light slanting through the curtained windows of the coach was dim. Pale gray clouds shrouded the sky outside, and the frigid air carried the sharp smell of snow. She shivered and slid closer to the coal grate. But the tired, dim coals seemed to spit only a thin stream of warmth into the relentlessly cold air.

Though how she could be cold she couldn't fathom. Since leaving the Darcys' she had not been able to slow the rapid beat of her heart, nor dry the dampness of her palms as her mind imagined the myriad possible failures as they passed over the line between North and South. She wished fervently that the crossing was over with and she, snug beneath her furs, was safely in the Davenport family coach heading for home. Instead she sat shivering and tense in the unfamiliar confines of the Darcys' brougham.

She did not even contemplate whether it was worth it. It was too late for ruminations of that sort, and anyway, heading back toward her life at the hospital, she could not imagine doing anything less to try to stem the tide of despair that afflicted those men. She had no further questions about whether what she did was right, either, for she at least knew that it was not intrinsically wrong. People were suffering, dying even, for want of the medicines she carried; how could it be wrong to risk so little to help so much?

It was only here that her mind circled again to the tiny, tissuey message she carried. Of course it made sense to prevent battles, if one were able, for that was the only way to prevent injury. Then why, if Mr. Price's logic was so valid, did she feel so corrupt, so duplicitous, for carrying the message? Was it only the increased danger? For she knew she would not be nearly as nervous if she only carried the medicines.

When Emma heard distant voices outside and felt the coach begin to slow, she felt her head swim with a sudden airless panic. Steady, she admonished herself, remember to breathe. You need only show them your travel voucher and you will pass through unimpeded. What right have these Yankees to bar your way? she asked herself in an attempt to muster some self-righteous indignation at the imposition. But it was impossible. She was completely awed by her apprehensions.

"Ho! Ho there!" the driver from his upper berth called to the team of matched grays. "Ho'd up!"

The carriage lurched over the frozen road as Emma wiped her damp palms on the skirt of her gown. She grabbed the papers from beside her on the seat and clutched them on her lap, hoping and praying that the door would not open. A second later it swung wide to reveal a short, stocky man in blue with a thick mustache.

"Good aft'noon, ma'am." He tipped his hat briefly and settled pebble-brown eyes on her. "Please step out of the coach, ma'am." He bent with the words and lowered the coach steps with an ungraceful clatter.

Emma thrust her handful of documents toward him, then, registering his words, pulled them back with a jerk. "You mean you want me to get out?"

"Yes, ma'am."

Behind the little man she saw the driver of the coach standing docilely next to another blue-clad Yankee whose meaty fist held the driver's arm in an officious grip. Two others flanked him on the right.

"I don't understand," she said, alarmed, unable to move.

The short man's flat face revealed nothing. "Just step down from the coach, ma'am." Perfunctorily, he held a yellow-gloved hand out toward her.

She half rose; spluttered, "But, but I—"; held her documents helplessly before her; then she grasped her skirt and awkwardly descended the steps. As she stepped onto the hard ground she could feel the dreadful little bottle bump against her thigh. It seemed to toll the word *guilty* like the clapper of a bell. She bit her lip.

"Thank you, ma'am. Please come this way." Short, hard sentences. The man was a soldier, not a person, she thought bleakly. The Yankees *were* different. She glanced at the other two soldiers beside him, and their faces were as closed and uncompromising as his. Had they been members of the Confederate army they would have treated her like the lady she was, she was sure; at the very least they would have smiled or offered their arm.

He started off around the back of the carriage and she followed. As she rounded the back of the coach followed by the other two sentries, the driver, and his guard, she could see the adjacent field filled with white canvas tents and more milling soldiers. In the woods to the left horses stood peacefully idle in clumps tied to the trees.

As they passed, a man headed toward the trees leading a lathered and muddy horse by its halter. The metal bit from the bridle in his hand clanged sharply in the cold air as he stopped to let Emma and the small party of men pass.

She could feel the eyes of soldiers on her face as she walked self-consciously through the camp. Though they followed a well-worn path through the tents and around camp fires, she had some trouble walking on the frozen earth. It had been mud at some recent point and deep grooves from horses' hooves had frozen into little potholes.

She tripped once and a man leapt out to catch her, chilling her blood with an open leer as he grabbed her hand. She yanked it back and continued walking, staring at the ground. So intent was she on meeting no one's eyes that she nearly walked into the stocky man's back when he stopped before a tent that was slightly larger than the others. When he passed through the flap she just caught a glimpse of three men leaning over a makeshift table.

She waited several minutes, then decided to brave the consequences and lift her eyes to her surroundings. Men stood in small groups around fires, their guns standing in tripods against each other. Canteens hung indolently from the deadly bayonets. Though the voices were muted, the banging of tin pots against cups sliced through the chilly air with an exaggerated clarity. As her gaze passed over the groups of soldiers she could see their eyes shift away, then feel them dart back to her curiously. It was an odd feeling, she thought, being the only woman in the midst of a hundred or more men.

The voices inside the tent were no more audible than those around her but she could tell when they stopped. A second later the tent flap was thrown open by the stocky guard and she was motioned inside.

Her only chance, she knew, was to be calm and self-assured, even haughty if she could manage it; so with a deep breath she raised her chin and strode into the tent.

The soldiers straightened politely as she entered and one in the corner she hadn't noticed before stood up and pulled his hat from his head to his chest. She nodded imperiously, her hands clenched in terror around her travel documents.

"Good afternoon, gentlemen," she said in a quiet but remarkably steady voice. "I trust we can make this brief. I'd like to be home by nightfall."

A lean, dark-haired man with major's stripes glanced quickly

91

at the colonel next to him, then gave her a condescending smile. "We'll do what we can." He directed a curt nod to the third man at the table, who immediately saluted. Swiftly he turned to leave, passing Emma with the self-conscious air of one trying not to appear interested in the goings-on.

The colonel was an older man with a wide face, a long mustache, and piercing blue eyes. He looked decent, Emma thought, and relaxed slightly. He stepped toward her and held out his hand.

Emma placed her hand in his and curtsied briefly. "Emma Davenport," she introduced herself formally.

The man shook her hand once and dropped it, his face stern. "Colonel Harding," he answered in a deep, gravelly voice. "Might I see your travel documents, please?" He again extended his hand.

With a flush of heat she realized he'd held out his hand for the papers, not her hand, and in acute embarrassment she thrust them at him. "I trust you'll find them all in order," she stated in a voice slightly too loud.

The man in the corner sat abruptly and began taking notes on a lapboard. The colonel glanced at her papers briefly, then carried them with him as he turned his back to walk around the makeshift desk. "Miss Davenport," he said finally, turning back to her, "we need to ask you a few questions. It seems there's been some—question about the purpose of your trip. Perhaps you can clear them up for us."

He pinned her where she stood with those pale blue eyes. Her stomach began to quiver. "Certainly," she murmured stiffly.

He pulled a stool from the table and sat, leaning his forearms on the table and shuffling through her papers. "It says here you were to visit friends in Washington, is that correct?"

She glanced fitfully from the colonel to the major beside him, who watched the proceedings with a bland eye. "Y-yes, that's correct. I visited friends. The Darcys. It—it's their coach"—she gestured vaguely behind her—"I'm traveling in their coach."

The colonel raised his eyebrows as if expecting more. When

none was forthcoming he looked again at the papers. "How long did you stay in Washington?"

"A week and a half."

He twirled the end of his mustache between thumb and forefinger. "Rather a short trip, wasn't it?"

Emma fidgeted with the fringe on her reticule. "I could afford no more time. I work in a hospital where I am needed." As soon as she voiced the words she could have kicked herself. *Idiot. How stupid to bring up the hospital. Of course the first thing they'll think of is smuggling.*

The colonel only nodded noncommittally. "What did you do while you were in Washington?"

"I visited friends, went to socials . . . oh, and one dinner party. Mostly I spent time with the Darcys. Do you know them? The Emerson Darcys?" She was floundering, sounding desperate, she knew. But didn't they realize under whose auspices she traveled? "Perhaps you know Brendan, Colonel Darcy. I believe he works in the War Department. A—a fine man. Our families have been friends for years."

The colonel watched her discomfiture dispassionately. "I'm sure it's possible we have several acquaintances in common, Miss Davenport."

"Yes, yes I'm sure we have. But the Darcys—"

The colonel turned to the major and began to speak over her words. "In fact, where *is* young Darcy, Major? Perhaps he could clarify a thing or two for us here." The two of them looked back at Emma simultaneously, as if to gauge her reaction.

"Young Darcy?" she echoed. Her stomach butterflied. "Are you talking about—"

Colonel Harding motioned to the major. "See if you can't find him, Major." He kept his eyes on Emma. "Now, Miss Davenport, you were saying? What else did you do while you were in Washington?"

Emma watched the major leave the tent. Young Darcy? No. They couldn't possibly mean . . .

93

"I-I did some shopping," she blustered, dragging her gaze back to the colonel. "I knitted."

The colonel cleared his throat. "Miss Davenport, it's not my intention to intimidate you, but you seem a bit nervous. Might I ask why?" He studied her while she contemplated a suitable answer. Should she admit to being nervous or was that a dead giveaway? Wouldn't anyone be nervous in a camp full of enemy soldiers whether or not they carried contraband medicines?

The silence stretched as her mind whirled. It was only when the colonel's expression changed from one of curiosity to one of resignation that she realized she had waited too long. No matter what she said now it would sound false.

The moment was relieved of some of its awkwardness when a loud, anonymous voice outside the tent yelled, "What the devil happened to you?"

The laugh that rejoined this comment stopped Emma's heart. *Will.*

"Breaking that damn horse you showed me." He was nearing the tent, laughing. "Showed a little more spirit than I anticipated from your comments. But they don't fight quite as hard when they're up to their hocks in mud." His voice was very close now, just outside the thin canvas wall.

The first voice—the major's, Emma realized now—continued, "Looks more like you been breaking a pig, Darcy." More laughter. "Hold up a second. Colonel wants to see you."

Emma looked at the colonel, who looked straight back at her. She knew trepidation was written all over her face. A second later Will burst unceremoniously through the tent flaps.

A reluctant smile split the old colonel's face as he took in Will's ghastly appearance. From knee to toe he was sloppy wet, covered with mud, and from thigh to face he was splattered with the stuff. Wet pants hugged his muscular legs, and his boots squished audibly as he walked. His shirtsleeves were rolled up to reveal mud-streaked, sinewy forearms.

"Colonel Harding." Will saluted with a smile, leaving a smudge of dirt on his forehead beneath the recklessly mussed hair.

94

Emma held her breath. He hadn't seen her. Instinctively she drew a step backward in the vain hope that he might never see her. "Bratcher said you wanted to see me, sir. Are you sure you wouldn't rather I clean up a bit first?"

Colonel Harding smiled faintly. "You break that stallion, Darcy?"

Will's smile was ironic but the glow in his eyes was sheer exhilaration. "I don't know if I'd say *break,* exactly, sir, but he's at least a little *bent.*"

The colonel shook his head. "You're a little bent yourself, son, even to try a stunt like that. You know that's the horse that broke both Sanderson's legs."

"What?" Will spun in mock fury to the major, who stood at the entrance to the tent. "You told me that horse was nothing more than rusty." He turned back to the colonel. "Said it hadn't been ridden for a while, since its owner had died of old age. Belonged to an old widow who rode it once a week to church on Sunday."

This brought a chuckle to the colonel's throat. "Couldn't you see the look of the devil in that animal's eyes, Captain?"

"I surely could, sir. But it was my understanding that it'd been a while since that horse had been to church." A white grin flashed from Will's dirty face as the colonel's laugh broadened.

As the three of them amused themselves, Emma had the thought that were it not for the major's unfortunate position near the tent flaps she could probably sneak out unnoticed. Almost more anxious to avoid Will than the interrogation, she glanced around the tent for another exit, even daring to take another step back into the shadows, when her eye caught that of the note-taking soldier in the corner. That pudgy-faced man pinned her with mean little eyes and cleared his throat loudly, drawing the colonel's attention back to her.

Col. Harding harrumphed the last of his laughter and straightened on his chair. "Darcy, we've got something of a situation here." Will's and the major's laughter trickled down to silence. "There's a lady here who claims to have been a visitor in your

95

home. Miss, come forward.'' The colonel gestured her from the shadows as Will turned in surprise.

"I apologize, sir—'' Will broke off abruptly as his mouth dropped open. "Emma."

Emma stepped stiffly forward, mortified to the core and feeling like an errant child. "Will," she said quietly, inclining her head. This was it, the final straw, she thought with a sinking heart. That Will should be here would surely be her undoing. Either he would help her to evade further interrogation, leaving her forever in his debt; or he would be here to witness her debasement, her humiliating arrest. Either way, she would be compromised forever.

Will's head swiveled from her to the colonel and back again. Clearly at a loss, he asked her softly, "Are you all right, Emma?"

He took one step toward her and stopped as the colonel spoke up officiously. "Then you do know this woman?"

Will turned back to him, his confusion evident. "Yes, I do. Emma Davenport. I've known her for years."

The older man sighed heavily. "Then this is a problem. I was hoping she was lying." He picked up her papers again, then tossed them back onto the desk hopelessly. "Has Miss Davenport recently stayed with your family?"

"Yes, she did. I bade her good-bye this morning, just before coming here. She was to leave after breakfast. Is something wrong?" He looked back at Emma, genuine concern in his eyes. She wished she could hold on to that look because she had the desperate feeling that it would soon be irretrievably lost.

"I'm afraid there is, Captain." The colonel's kind face looked genuinely regretful over what he was about to say. "You see, we have reason to believe that Miss Davenport is smuggling contraband medicines."

Astonishment lit Will's face before amusement took it over. "That's ridiculous." He laughed and glanced at Emma. "Emma's not a smuggler, for God's sake. I'd about stake my life on it."

Col. Harding's gaze raked him from head to foot. "From the look of it you'd risk your life for far less than that," he commented dryly. "But as it happens we have a very reliable source implicating Miss Davenport in the scheme. *Very* reliable.''

"A source—you mean a witness?" Will had unconsciously stepped closer to Emma, so close she could see the flecks of mud in his soft brown hair, make out the beginnings of stubble on the fine plane of his cheek. "What about proof? Have you found any drugs?"

"We were just getting to that. I'm afraid I'm going to have to ask you to drop your hoop, Miss Davenport. Most of the ladies who attempt this tie the bottles to their hoops," the colonel explained to Will. "Rather like hiding the money under the mattress."

Emma's face flamed hot at the sarcasm. "Colonel Harding," she spoke up at last, her voice quavering, "I'll have you know that I am not about to disrobe in a tent with four men, and I heartily resent your assertions about my activities." She took a quick breath, acutely conscious of Will's eyes on her, and continued, "How dare you presume to pull me arbitrarily off the road, detain me from my journey, then humiliate me by asking a slate of accusatory questions and requiring me to undress. I am a lady, not some common strumpet used to pulling up her skirts for whomsoever may ask it." Her chin came up as she felt some actual indignation surface. Ignoring Will, she lashed the other men with a scathing look. "I refuse to do it and I absolutely protest this base treatment. You are none of you gentlemen. I am positively shocked and humiliated to be in your presence for this travesty of a proceeding. I should think you would all be ashamed of yourselves. Now if you've no further indignities to request of me, I think it only decent of you to let me go on my way."

A thick silence hung over the room when she stopped. She could feel Will's scrutiny but could not gauge his reaction, and she was unwilling to look at him to judge. The colonel, looking suddenly fatigued, rubbed his hands over his face and slicked his thinning hair back on his head. Slowly he rose to his feet and came around the table toward her.

"Miss Davenport"—his voice was gentle—"if there were any way around this I would happily take it, but there is not."

97

"Colonel—" Will began.

The older man silenced him with an upraised hand. "Miss Davenport, I have only one question for you. Did you, while you were in Washington, buy a flower from a street boy with a message hidden on the stem, then subsequently visit an establishment known as Pope's General Store?"

Emma opened her mouth to speak but could utter no words. Her gaze flew to Will, who could damn her with a word. His face had taken on a kind of horrified fascination as he looked at her.

What could she say? To admit it would be to condemn herself to prison; to deny it would make her a liar before the world.

As she gazed into Will's face she saw comprehension bloom inside him. All of his suspicions, all of his conjecture about her presence in his family's house, now came to one stupefying and degradingly correct conclusion in his eyes.

She bit her bottom lip. I'm sorry, she wanted to say, I'm sorry for so many things. But the words were weak and inaccurate. Instead she closed her eyes and nodded.

Chapter Seven

"I'll have to ask you again." Col. Harding's voice penetrated her distress. "Please drop your hoop."

She glared at the colonel, whose expression now was hard as nails.

"Go on, honey," Will's soft voice urged. "Show them you're innocent."

She turned back to him. Faith and condemnation warred in his eyes. He wanted to believe in her, but only a fool could ignore all the evidence.

Emma clenched her fists on her skirts and turned furiously to the colonel. "Very well," she spat in a hard voice. "I'll do as you ask, since I've no other choice. I'll give you the damned medicines and you can throw me in one of your filthy prisons. But I'll not be ashamed of what I've done. I'll not be ashamed that because I had to watch my wounded father burn up and die of typhoid fever, because I had to hear my own brother's scream as they tied him down and amputated his leg without chloroform, because of the suffering and death I witness daily, I decided to do the one thing in my power to do—to procure a tiny amount of the lifesaving medicine our men need. Medicine that you shall now have the pleasure of taking away.'' Tears blurred her vision but she continued doggedly. ''But you won't be taking it from me. No, not me, a mere woman clumsy enough to be caught on the Richmond road. No, you'll be taking it from wounded, sick, and dying men, men too weak to fight. That's not warfare, gentlemen, no matter what you tell yourselves. That's murder. And I hope you rot in hell for it.''

She was breathless and just barely in control of a nearly overwhelming anger. She hated these men, hated them with more passion than she'd ever felt before. They were poised on the brink of defeating her, of taking the precious medicines for which she'd risked all. After everything she'd attempted and been through, the hospital would be no better off than before, the men would suffer no less and the women would suffer more by being shorthanded. For a moment she was filled with the vision of Peter writhing silently under the phantom pain of a missing limb. Failure. And it was all because of the intervention of these pompous, ignorant, self-righteous men.

Through her swimming eyes she could see their identically condemning expressions. ''Women cannot fight,'' she added in a more subdued, if no less angry, tone. Her eyes shifted to rest on Will, whose expression gave nothing away. But she could not hate him as he stood there before her, she realized sadly. As much as she wanted to despise him along with these other Yankees, she could not dismiss the feelings she had left for him. He was the one person in the room who could possibly understand. ''Nor can women challenge the enemy on any front but the final one, death. I just didn't want to lose one more battle for want of a weapon.''

She felt curiously flat all of a sudden, spent; all of her emotions were laid at the feet of these men and now it was up to them to decide her fate. In resignation she turned her back to them and pulled up the front of her skirt. It would be easy enough to drop the hoop, quite another matter to get it back on. But perhaps that would not be a concern. Perhaps they'd just throw her right into a cart and haul her directly off to prison. She was too drained to worry about it.

The hoop, weighted down by the little silk-lined bags, dropped with a quiet rustle to the dirt floor of the tent. She stepped out of it and bent to pick it up but Will swooped down before her. Their eyes met briefly as he rose with the crinoline in his hand.

He wasn't angry, she could see, but his expression was too complex to read. Hers, she knew, projected mute defiance. Her fear had disappeared.

The colonel took the garment and untied the three little bags. He motioned for the major to return Emma's hoop, which she then held limply in one hand.

Will's voice sounded warily into the silence. "Ah, Colonel, I don't know if you are aware of Miss Davenport's status as my former fiancée." Emma's shocked countenance swung to Will on an indrawn breath. The colonel also looked appropriately surprised. "I mention it only in the hope that it might give me some credibility in vouching for her character. In light of all of the facts, as well as Miss Davenport's bravery and obviously altruistic intentions, I would like to ask if it be possible—"

"Jensen," the colonel barked to the note-taking man in the corner. The man started violently and jumped to his feet, lapboard, paper, and pen clutched haphazardly in his hands. "See if you can't find me a cup of coffee somewhere. We'll hold the proceedings until you return."

The pudgy-faced man glanced from the colonel to Will; then he saluted. "Yes, sir."

"Major, perhaps you could help Miss Davenport step outside for a little air. I'd like to speak with the captain alone for a moment." The colonel stroked his ample mustache and gazed shrewdly at Will.

"Of course, sir," the major answered, approaching Emma.

As the man in the corner passed her and departed, Emma stepped awkwardly in her overlong skirts toward the colonel. "If what you have to say concerns me, I'd rather be present to hear it. In any case, I have no desire to be on further display to the

101

many men wandering about camp, particularly without being properly attired.''

The colonel eyed her assessingly, then shifted his gaze to Will, beside her. With a brief glance at Maj. Bratcher, he said, ''Very well. Major, you may take the air yourself.''

Maj. Bratcher clicked his heels together and bowed formally. ''As you wish.'' He slipped out between the tent flaps.

Col. Harding sighed heavily and fixed Will with a judicious look. ''Captain, I think I know the request you were about to make and I stopped you in order to save it from becoming a part of the record. As I mentioned earlier, we have evidence from a very reliable source of Miss Davenport's guilt. Damning evidence.''

Will smiled ruefully and gestured to the little bags on the table before them. ''I'd have little grounds to question her guilt myself.''

The colonel waved a casual hand over the bags. ''These are incidental. In this particular case it would be seriously detrimental for any suspicion of involvement to be associated with your family.''

''My family!'' Will protested. ''Surely you don't believe my family helped in any way.''

Emma stepped forward anxiously. ''Colonel Harding, I can assure you the Darcys knew nothing of my plans.''

The colonel jabbed an index finger angrily at Emma. ''I'll hear no more out of you, miss. You've done quite enough damage already.''

Emma stepped back in shock.

''Is it necessary to be so hard on her?'' Will objected, confusion evident in his tone.

''Captain Darcy,'' Col. Harding enunciated. ''If you will kindly stop playing knight to Miss Davenport's damsel in distress, I will demonstrate to you the gravity of the situation.'' With quick, deliberate movements Col. Harding proceeded to open the little gray bags and drop the vials onto the tabletop. Emma's heart thundered in her chest, knowing just what it was he looked for. It was the third vial he reached that thumped to the table to be followed by the slow fluttering of the jeweler's tissue.

Emma's eyes flew to Will, who turned a face frozen in incredulity on her. His breath left him as if he'd been struck, and he shook his head, pushing both hands back through his hair and closing his eyes.

"Will—" she began.

"What?" he barked savagely, eyes opening to drill her into silence. "What could you possibly have to say to defend yourself?"

For the first time in her life she thought it entirely possible that a man might strike her. She withered beneath his white-hot anger, the clenched rage in his jaw.

"You used my home," he growled, ominously low. "You jeopardized my entire family, deceived them into offering you help—"

"Captain," Col. Harding interrupted.

Will's voice stopped but his anger continued to seethe. He took a deep breath through flared nostrils and slowly turned his penetrating eyes to the colonel.

"I can handle this now," the older man said mildly.

Will took an angry, audible breath and let it out slowly. "You're right, sir. Perhaps it's best I leave now, before doing something I *might* regret," he ground out, turning a searing glance on Emma with the last words.

"I agree," the colonel said.

Will strode abruptly to the tent flaps and pushed them apart. Then he stopped and turned back once more. "Before I go, sir, can you tell me one thing?"

Col. Harding acquiesced with a shallow nod.

"What will you do with her?" His voice was flat, emotionless.

The colonel twirled the end of his mustache and replied almost casually, "She'll be taken to the Old Cap to wait out the war."

The Old Cap. Emma felt as if she'd been punched in the stomach. The Old Capitol prison in Washington. *To wait out the war.* She felt the blood drain from her face and had to place her fingertips on the desk beside her to keep from swaying. Her terrified gaze fixed on Will's face, but it was obvious there would be no help from that quarter.

Will's features were immobile as he appraised her coldly, the look in his eyes so remote it sent a paralyzing hollowness to the pit of her stomach.

"I suppose it's fitting," he said at last. "But it's not nearly what she deserves." Emma lowered her eyes and he departed, letting the tent's canvas flap close behind him with a soft, final slap.

She rode back to Washington in the Darcys' carriage with the Darcys' driver and a toothpick-chewing Yankee sergeant for company. On the box above, another Yankee drove and they were flanked on horseback by two armed guards.

Strangely, the foremost thought in Emma's mind was that Maggie would hate her now even more than she did before. Perhaps it was because Emma could not bear to think of the Darcys themselves, or perhaps it was a direct effort to avoid thinking of Will and his appalled realization of her betrayal, but Emma felt numb, unable to bring forth any tears or even any fear.

She tried to think about the hospital, about Judith and her mother, and what they would all think upon learning of her imprisonment, but she was not at all sure they would get word of it. Perhaps Lawrence, with his ties to the underground, could let her family know, but she wasn't sure they weren't better off knowing nothing, rather than knowing her to be locked up for a smuggler and a spy.

Her mother, in particular, would be horrified. She had always reprimanded Emma for being headstrong, and had warned her on more than one occasion that someday it would get her into trouble. But her mother could never have foreseen this amount of trouble, Emma thought. Her own daughter on the way to prison. The shame of it would stain her forever.

The Darcys' driver would not look at her. Though she gazed at him with bland eyes, he kept his face averted and stared out the window. She imagined he hated her and she couldn't blame him. She felt worse than bad, worse than guilty, worse than a failure; she felt useless. With her family already doing without her, with the knowledge that she tried to help and could not, with the knowledge that the one person in the world who had loved her above all else now hated her, she felt nonexistent.

No one spoke to her. It was only when the coach rolled to a stop that the Yankee guard got up and stayed her with an outstretched hand.

"Wait here. I gots to be sure they's 'nuf room here fer you. We done had a run a smugglers of late." The burly guard exited the coach, spitting the toothpick on the ground and slamming the door behind him.

Emma and the driver sat in silence in the chilly coach until the sergeant returned and motioned her down. He did not offer his hand nor wait for her to descend before he marched into the large brick mouth of the Old Capitol prison. Two other guards waited for her to alight.

A crowd of onlookers jeered as she exited the coach. She saw one man on a crutch because of a missing leg throw a chicken bone that landed a few feet in front of her.

"Git yerself another one, Sarge?" a different man called. "What'd this one do, trade skin for secrets?" A loud chorus of laughter rose up at this and Emma felt her face freeze in mortification. They were a motley bunch of people, but beyond them on the sidewalk strode ladies and gentlemen of her own class. She bent her head lest she be recognized. Imagine the Darcys hearing from some neighbor that their recent houseguest was seen entering the Old Cap under armed escort. Though she guessed they'd be hearing about it soon enough from Will.

The superintendent in charge was a stocky man with brown hair and gray eyes who seemed genuinely sorry to have to imprison "such a lovely young lady."

"Ah, wars do terrible things to otherwise good and charitable people," he lamented as he led Emma up a narrow staircase to the second floor. Here was a hallway onto which opened many doors that were guarded by sentries posted down the length of it. He led her a short way down the hall to a door labeled number four, which he opened to reveal a sparsely furnished but clean room.

"You let me know if there's anything you need, Miss Davenport, and we'll see if we can't procure it for you," he said with a kindly smile.

Emma smiled back uncertainly. This was certainly a civilized imprisonment. "Shall I be allowed my things?" she asked tentatively.

The superintendent nodded. "In good time. I'm afraid the boys have to inspect it first, but don't worry. They take pretty good care of the ladies' belongings."

Emma had a vision of large, meaty hands pawing through her undergarments and searching her pockets, but since she knew they would find nothing she did not worry. Besides, if she were here for the duration of the war, what else could they do to her?

It wasn't until after the superintendent left, closing and locking the door behind him, that she moved to the window to look out at the yard below. There, stark in the bare dirt of the fenced yard, sat a gallows, its trapdoor sprung and swinging in the winter wind.

Emma's stomach dropped, and her hands rose to her chin. Turning quickly from the view, she sat heavily on the bed. So this is what it came down to, she thought bleakly. After so much struggle she would now languish months, perhaps years, in this little room with the threat of death just outside her window. She would be no good to anyone and even a burden on some—those who chose to worry about her. She would, in fact, be better off dead.

She lay back on the hard mattress, her head on the flat pillow, and stared at the ceiling.

After an hour or more of this there was a commotion at her door; then the key sounded in the lock. She bolted upright and stood as the door swung inward. Two large men in blue hefted her trunk into the room.

"Yer things, ma'am," one of them said; then the two clomped

out of the room in heavy black boots. The door closed noisily behind them, the key scraped in the lock, and she was alone.

She moved to the trunk and opened the lid. There, in rumpled disarray, lay her things, tossed and twisted. She looked at them dispassionately, as if they tried to give some idea of her identity and failed. Worn cotton petticoats and thick stockings curled around the gray dress she'd made before leaving Richmond. Bending over, she pulled at the dress, operating mostly out habit to prevent what wrinkles she could. But as she pulled at the material something else caught her eye, a darker, richer fabric underneath the gray.

She tossed the dress aside and knelt beside the trunk to pull at the other, knowing even as she touched the soft, watery silk what would emerge. Up from the depths of the trunk, the heel of a shoe tangled in its fringe, came the maroon shawl she had admired that day in the shop with Will.

Tears burned her eyes as her face contorted with the effort to fight them. Damn him! she thought, pain tightening like a vise around her heart. Damn him, damn him, damn him. She dropped her face into the sweet softness of the material and took a breath, smelling the subtle fragrance of the refined little shop. It would just serve him right, she thought as a sob caught in her throat, if she were to cry all over it and ruin the silk with her tears.

After three weeks of doing absolutely nothing other than crying and fuming and fearing and hating, Emma thought she would lose her mind. She woke in the mornings before sunrise and paced the room until the tepid bowl of oatmeal and water was brought for her breakfast. Then, after spending the morning reading and re-reading an old issue of *Putnam's Monthly* left by the room's previous occupant, she was allowed to walk in the yard around the gallows for half an hour.

Afternoons she knitted with needles and yarn the superintendent had procured for her from his wife, after regretfully informing her that his wife did not much care for reading, so books were out of the question. She knitted a blanket, long and thick and brown, without any pattern, with the ugly, coarse wool that made her itch after fooling with it for too long.

But it was the boredom that threatened her more than anything. She was allowed no conversation other than those brief sentences exchanged with the guard when her food was brought, and she found herself sleeping upward of fourteen hours a day. Her lack of energy could well have been attributed to a lack of decent food, for other than the oatmeal at breakfast she was given only a dinner of water and potatoes or sometimes cabbage, with boiled chicken on Fridays.

She'd been offered two baths since she'd arrived, which she accepted with alacrity though it meant undressing in front of the escaped slave who was assigned to help her, a strange, surly woman who slapped her once when she asked a question about the previous occupants of the tub.

Her hair she wore in one braid down her back, and she switched dresses every two days in an attempt to feel fresh.

She allowed herself to wear the shawl that Will had bought, but only because the chill of the room was so pervasive that she did not want to add to her list of mistakes by becoming ill out of stubbornness. Still, even then she felt somehow unfaithful to the Cause when she used it. It wasn't because the shawl brought her any pleasure. On the contrary, it only served to remind her of Will, and that awful day in Col. Harding's tent when he had faced her with such contempt and accused her of deliberately jeopardizing his family. At the thought of that day she felt her face burn again in shame, even now, after weeks of nurturing her own outrage at his reaction. Surely he knew she would walk straight to the gallows before implicating his family. How could he possibly believe she wouldn't? And even if he did assume the worst about her, he couldn't honestly believe that the U.S. Army would take the word of a lone Southern woman against a family as prominent as his, could he?

Emma threw down the scratchy blanket she knitted, spun the pretty silk shawl around her shoulders, and stepped to the window. It was sleeting outside and all the trees were covered in a sheen of ice, crystalline against the iron-gray background of the sky. It might have been beautiful but for the slick, glistening surface of the gallows beneath the trees.

No one had been hanged since she'd arrived, but she wondered how many people had lost their lives there. She sometimes imagined herself walking up those wooden steps and feeling the rough hemp of the rope against her throat. She wondered what it would feel like to have the floor drop out from under her feet, and what she might think in that split second between realizing it was too late for rescue and the moment her neck snapped.

"It wouldn't really matter," she murmured to herself. "It doesn't even matter what I think now."

She'd taken to talking to herself, just to break up the silence of the days, and her voice sounded strange to her. It was odd how the prison was arranged, so that she never passed anyone other than guards in the halls and only saw the other prisoners from her window when they, too, were allowed to walk in the yard. But then they were so shrouded against the cold that they were nothing other than woolen blobs, without identities or even faces.

But this day she was startled from her reverie by the scraping of the key in the lock. It was far too early for dinner, she noted at once, and her heart took up a frenzied beating in anticipation of the change in routine, however slight it might turn out to be. Her fingers toyed nervously with the fringe on the shawl as the door opened. The day guard entered and pulled his hat from his head, a gesture so unexpected that Emma's mouth dropped open.

"Some'un to see you, ma'am," he muttered.

It took Emma a moment to realize that some reply was expected of her, so she snapped her mouth shut and inclined her head.

The guard stepped back out of the room. After a moment the door was pushed wider and Will entered, tall and broad, and acutely vibrant in the spare stillness of the room.

Though Emma had been without a mirror for three weeks, the look on Will's face told her all she needed to know about her appearance. Shock warred with pity and outrage in his countenance, and he turned quickly to hide it by dismissing the guard with a curt "That will be all."

When he turned back, Emma had mastered her own expression and gained fragile control of the thrumming of her heart and the butterfly lurching of her stomach. After all, though he was not responsible for her being here, he had at least been glad of it.

He took one anxious step forward and stopped. "Emma, I—" He spoke no more words but his eyes drank in her appearance, openly scrutinizing her face, her hands, her pitifully worn and bagging dress.

"Please sit down, Captain Darcy," she offered, her voice low and dusky after weeks of disuse. Her hand indicated the bed while she took the straight-backed chair near the window. It was when she remembered she wore his shawl that she felt humiliation swallow her. How shabby she herself must look compared to the beauty and elegance of the garment. And how pitiful to be caught wearing it, as if clinging to an impossible memory. She felt a slow, frustrated anger building at the sorry circumstance.

Will cleared his throat. "Are you all right, Emma?"

She raised her brows. "Don't I look all right?" she asked, daring him to tell her the truth.

She should have known what his response would be. "You look like hell, Emma; what do they feed you here?"

Emma laughed at that. Of course he would tell her the truth. She'd been too much apart from him to remember that he only prevaricated when it suited some purpose.

She waved a pale hand airily. "Oh, the usual, prison fare, you know." She sobered, calling forth her anger, willing it to the surface. "Though I must say . . . it's not nearly what I deserve." She watched in gratification as his own words sank in, dispelling the concern she had seen on his face and replacing it with wariness.

He shrugged. "You must admit I had cause to be angry," he said, maintaining his distance.

Emma smiled coolly. "I must admit nothing."

Will took a deep breath and studied her. "You know, I admire your gall, Emma. I wouldn't have thought you had it in you. What I'd like to know is how you got the information."

She sighed. "That's what they'd all like to know."

"Yes, I suppose it is." He stood then, and sauntered toward the window. Emma sat docilely, lacking the energy to move, needing her strength to nurture her anger, to quell the traitorous urge to run to him and let him hold her—though of course he would do no such thing now.

He stood just behind her, gazing out the window. "I'm wondering, Emma, how did you do it?"

She turned her head slightly at the words.

"Did you operate like most female spies?" he continued. "And when did you find the time?" His tone was conversational, admiring almost. He was close enough to touch her.

She decided not to answer him, and after a moment he rounded the chair in which she sat and stood close, facing her. He reached out to cup her chin. She followed his hand with her eyes, closing them when he touched her face. Even with all that had passed between them, he still had the power to melt her with his touch.

It took all the control she had not to take his hand in hers and hold it to her cheek. Her longing for contact, for companionship, for the love she knew she'd lost forever nearly overcame her, but she settled for merely turning her cheek fractionally into his palm.

He knelt before her and she felt his body near hers. She opened her eyes; he was very close, his lips near hers. She couldn't help herself; she raised her own to meet them, giving him the kiss. For a moment their lips met gently, chastely; then Will moved forward and clasped her head in his hands, crushing her lips with his own. She opened her mouth willingly beneath his, their tongues meeting and twining familiarly as her hands rose to his shoulders. He pressed his body closer, his chest hard against hers, the buttons crushed painfully against her.

With fast, fervent movements he slid his hands from her face, down her sides to capture her waist, pulling her up and off the chair so that their bodies touched all along the length of them. Emma thought she might drown in the delicious sensations as-

111

sailing her. His arms so tight around her body might have hurt if she had not been consumed by the same desperation, the same starvation, that he seemed to be experiencing. His lips on hers were punishing, but she reveled in it, letting the years roll back so she could allow herself to love him, just for the moment.

Finally the kiss broke and they held each other, panting breathlessly. Will's hands ran up the length of her back and he buried his face in her shoulder. They were suspended in time, aswirl in the tide of memory and emotion.

When they'd both regained their breath, he asked quietly, "How was it, Emma?" His voice was full of such pain she leaned back to look into his eyes. The expression she found there was so distant and anguished that she stared at him in confusion. "How did it feel," he asked slowly, "to make love for a cause?"

She stared at him, mouth agape, as a tingling numbness swept her body. "What?" she breathed.

He swallowed and penetrated her eyes with his. "I want to know," he said carefully, loosening his grip on her, "if it felt like that when you bestowed your favors to get the information."

She stiffened and felt a reckless nausea besiege her. "I did no such thing," she said through frozen lips.

He backed off, letting go of her, letting her body sink into the coldness of the room. His eyes were shuttered, unreadable. "Right." He nodded in artificial agreement. "Because you're such a *lady* they simply handed you the information for a kiss on the cheek, is that it?"

Emma jerked away from him, staring in horror. "You think I had—had *relations* for that message? You must know I wouldn't do that."

Will's expression gave way to anger. "Don't give me that," he said harshly. "It took our boys two weeks to decode that message and then to discover that it contained some of our most significant, closely guarded information. Pope's couldn't have given you that. You must have slept with somebody big to get information that good."

Emma raised her hand and slapped him across the face so hard

Will drew himself into a salute, willing himself to master his own enraged emotions and present an objective countenance to his superior. The general returned the salute.

"I'd like to finish this up quickly. I've a parade to attend in half an hour," he pronounced in a no-nonsense voice. "Has she confessed?"

"No, sir," Will stated. Nor would she ever, he knew. But he, as well as the general, had seen her victim's confession. He had seen the doomed, stupid man's own handwriting state that he had "erred in the extreme and quite foolishly, though not maliciously, revealed confidential military secrets, which had the potential to jeopardize the United States of America, to Miss Emma Davenport while under the influence of various sexual and physical pleasure arising from that woman's pursuit and seduction of my bodily person."

The man was a fool, an idiot, a horny, disgusting pig; but he had snapped like a twig under interrogation, and there was no doubt that the confession was genuine. The man had been Emma's lover. At first Will had refused to believe it. The idea was ludicrous, insane. He was ready to risk all to prove the absurdity of it. But then he'd seen it. It had to be true because he knew the man would hang for it. What possible reason would he have to lie?

It had been the final blow to his faith in Emma. Until that day in Col. Harding's tent, despite their estrangement, she had been a constant for him, his one assurance that goodness existed in the world, his proof of loyalty and truth. In an odd, perhaps warped, way even her rejection of him had been evidence of her integrity. She gave up love for duty. He'd understood it. He'd even admired it, though the devastation of it had nearly killed him.

But the danger she'd knowingly inflicted on his family and the prostituting of herself had repudiated it all. From the destruction of his beliefs an unquenchable anger arose. He'd forgiven her the repudiation of their engagement. He would even have been willing to forgive her the smuggling, which despite the duplicity had demonstrated an awesome courage. But the spying—no, the *dan-*

ger in which she had embroiled his family—and the fact that she had sold her own body for military intelligence just as any common harlot would, those things had proven too much for him to bear.

His anger sprang not just from the acts, the plain fact of spying or the physical performance of making love for information. It came from a betrayal of a much different sort. She'd been fundamentally untrue to her own character.

The general sighed and drilled Emma with a masterfully intimidating glare. "We have General Bondurant's confession, Miss Davenport. There is no sense in denying your involvement. What we need to know from you is who your other informants were and what information you are currently in possession of that was not conveyed in the cipher."

Emma swallowed hard and threw her head back. "I don't know what you're talking about."

The general's eyes did not waver. "Sit down," he ordered.

She did as she was bidden, sitting with a grace and dignity that spoke painfully of her refined and cultured upbringing. Will had an unbidden split-second memory of Emma's unparalleled grace as she dipped into a curtsy in a blue silk ball gown.

"As you seem like a reasonably intelligent female," the general proceeded, "I shall put it to you plainly. If you provide us with the information we seek, there is a possibility that we can effect an exchange with your compatriots and secure your freedom. If, however, you persist in this senseless parody of ignorance, we will be forced to hold you incarcerated until such information as you might possess becomes invalid with age. This could result in your imprisonment for quite some time, Miss Davenport. Do you understand me?"

Emma listened to his statements with obviously growing rage and barely concealed impatience. At his conclusion she came to her feet and faced him. "As you concede that I may have a reasonable amount of sense, I cannot say that I do not understand your words. You, however, seem to have missed the gist of mine. I absolutely do not know what you are talking about—"

"Miss Davenport—" The general's growl was surpassed by Emma's rising voice.

"I have no informants and do not possess any information that would be of use to anyone. I've never heard of nor met any General Bondurant, and I have no message other than that with which you caught me. And Colonel Harding made it quite clear that he knew exactly where I'd gotten that one—Pope's General Store. In light of these facts I suggest you set me free immediately—"

"Miss Davenport!" the general roared. "I haven't time for your arrogant prevarication, and your insolence tempts me to destroy the key to this door."

"General," Will broke in.

Gen. Ferguson swung an immutable hand up to Will. "Shut up, Darcy. A plea from you will only infuriate me further." He turned back to Emma. "You shall stay in this cell until you come to your senses, or until hell freezes over and your rebel countrymen come to set you free. Your superior attitude is doing you no favors with me, young lady. I can only believe you do not comprehend the seriousness of this situation. Do you realize that I can have you hung for your crime?"

Emma paled and opened her mouth to speak, but Will beat her to it. "General, I have no intention of pleading for Miss Davenport. I was going to say that I've just spent the last half-hour engaging in just such an argument with her." He felt Emma's eyes swing to his face and knew they both thought of the kiss. "I suggest you do not bother yourself further trying to convince her of her folly and merely let her suffer for it. It appears that will be the only way she will comprehend it."

Emma stared at Will in horror. The general turned to him with raised eyebrows. "Are you suggesting I hang her, then?" he offered, with just a trace of amusement.

Will forced a smile to his lips. "Only as a last resort, sir. She'll never see the error of her ways in that case. In the meantime, though, I suggest you keep her here, in this comfortable room"— he swept a disparaging glance around the sparsely furnished cubical—"to contemplate the error of her ways."

The general directed a considering look at Emma as he pulled a watch by the chain from his pocket. "And do you think contemplation shall lead her down the right path?" he asked, glancing at his watch. "Or might she only contemplate an untimely demise for the two of us?"

Will was able to muster a genuine, if wry, laugh at this statement. "She'll at least contemplate mine, sir. But I'm willing to risk it."

Gen. Ferguson looked at him narrowly and murmured, "Hmmmm." Then he snapped the watch closed and pushed it back into his pocket. "Well, in any case I haven't time to hang her now. Got to go march in this bloody parade. I'll leave her here, then, as you suggest, but I'll leave instructions for daily interrogations."

"Very good, sir," Will said, relief washing over him. Emma could hate him if she wished, Will thought, but siding against her was the only way to accomplish his plan. He knew it the moment she was apprehended, and he knew it today. The difference was his realization of the extent of her guilt and the enormity of the risks she'd taken on behalf of herself *and* his entire family. This time, his anger came to him far easier than it had in Col. Harding's tent.

The general turned to Emma, who stood like an angry child near the window. "Do you understand, Miss Davenport? You've been given a temporary reprieve. I suggest you capitulate during the interrogations or the temporary nature of your safety might expire."

Emma drew herself up and shot him a condescending glare. "If I weren't a lady I would spit upon you and your temporary reprieve."

Will saw the general's temper flare, and frowned a warning at Emma, which she ignored. But Ferguson controlled himself, no doubt thinking of the time, and settled for drilling her with a hateful eye. "Yes, I think we are all aware of just what sort of lady you are, Miss Davenport," he uttered disdainfully. Then, with a calculated arrogance, he turned to Will as if she no longer existed. "Let the colonel know I'll confer with him later on the Wetherington issue. Got to get this damn parade out of the way, before I can get anything done."

"Yes, sir."

"And have Wilson do something about that infernal trapdoor. Someone's going to trip and kill themselves on it one of these days." He stopped with his hand on the doorknob. "And thank you for your help, Captain. Good day."

"Same to you, sir."

The general casually returned Will's salute and left.

As the door closed behind him, Will turned to Emma. The frozen immobility of her face rendered her practically a stranger.

"How you must hate me," she said lowly, her hard face bathed in the cold winter light from the window. "You've even convinced him of my supposed profligacy."

"On the contrary," Will remarked, "he convinced me." He saw these words register with something akin to confusion and he mentally congratulated her for her consistency. He never thought her much for lying, but, he supposed, when life depended on it . . .

He sighed, suddenly overwhelmed with fatigue. "Give it up, please. They've caught him, Emma." It was obvious she would never admit it; why did he continue to prod her? "He's written his confession and they'll probably hang him. You'll be lucky if they don't do the same to you."

Her brows drew together. "Who?"

Will shook his head. Her obstinacy was not new. "Bondurant."

She gritted her teeth. "I've told you—"

He held up his hand and she quieted. Silence reigned for several minutes as he collected his thoughts. Finally, conceding to himself that there was no point to further argument, he moved toward the door. "Don't be stupid, Emma," he said when he'd reached it. "You're in real trouble."

She smiled coldly. "Thanks, in part, to you. Before you leave let me also thank you for pleading so eloquently on my behalf," she said, words dripping sarcasm. When he did not react she turned to look out the window and added morosely, "Besides, I've already been as stupid as I'll ever be. You of all people should know that." Her disdainful eyes shifted back to him.

Will laughed incredulously, without humor, and shook his head softly. "You amaze me, Emma. Still biting the only hand that can save you."

Emma's laugh of disbelief was shrill. "Save me? 'I suggest you leave her here in this comfortable room, General, to contemplate the error of her ways,' " she mimicked. "Thank you, Will, thank you for that heroic attempt to save me."

He cocked his head slightly. "You're not heading for the gallows, are you?"

She flashed a brittle smile. "Not today!"

He nodded once. "There, you see?"

She rolled her eyes theatrically, a flash of her old vitality.

He knew it was illogical to still feel the need to protect her, but he did. There, in the midst of all his pain and frustration, was the undeniable knowledge that he would perform one last act of fealty for her—foolish or no. He would—somehow, and in spite of the risk to himself—free her.

"I don't expect you to understand what I've done, Emma," he said, watching her. "Not today. But someday you will; I'll make sure of it. Someday you will know it all. As I do." His last words were spoken harshly, perhaps to defeat his sense of futility, perhaps to convey it to her. In any case, words were powerless, so he turned, grasped the knob, and opened the door. "Enjoy your stay," he murmured. "With any luck it won't be long."

Two nights later Emma awoke to a punishing grip on her shoulder and the growled, guttural words of the night guard in her ear. "Rouse yerseff and be quick about it."

Emma's fogged brain reacted by directing her to sit up so abruptly she swayed with dizziness. "What?"

"Git yer clothes on," he snarled, his dim form just visible in the ambient light from the window. She saw his head swivel

120

surreptitiously to the door and then back to her. "Git up, you stupid fool. We haven't much time!"

Belatedly, Emma realized she wore only her shift, and at the same time awareness swept her like a bucket of cold water. The man was taking her out of here; he wanted her dressed! Her heart thundered in her ears with sudden adrenaline. She wanted to believe it was good news, her freedom, and his movements certainly belied his fear of discovery. But at the same time she could not escape the demons that constantly foretold her doom. Could they be plotting some action against her? Something so heinous they could only perform it under cover of nightfall?

She rose quickly and, completely void of modesty, dressed rapidly before him in her maroon traveling gown. She did not have time to wrestle with her hoop so she donned the gown without it, with only enough time to grab the silk shawl before the burly guard grabbed her and pushed her toward the door.

She did not look back as they slipped from the room, stealing down the hall as quietly as they could. The man's beefy fingers pushed at the small of her back, directing her to a narrow stairway at the far end of the hall. The stone steps were slick with damp, and the smell of mildew was almost overpowering. Emma clutched at clammy walls with open, groping hands as she scurried down the steps, more than once losing her footing and having to grab at the sleeve of the man beside her.

"Dammit, ye'll bring us both down," he muttered the last time, pushing her hand from his arm.

Finally they were on the ground floor. "Hellfire and damnation!" the guard hissed as they approached the door. Emma heard the dull thud of metal on wood as the man grabbed at a lock on the door and let it fall. He fumbled for his ring of keys.

The lock was an old one, Emma could see now that her eyes had adjusted to the dark, and it was encrusted with rust. The guard continued to swear as one key after another failed to fit or to turn in the ancient fixture.

Emma glanced around the small landing and caught sight of a pile of rubbish in a corner. Ignoring the filth and the possibility of vermin, she pawed through it in search of something, she knew not what, that might help. The collection of old rags, mud, twigs, and what felt like a dead bird yielded nothing of value, so she scanned the rest of the enclosure. Spying the banister that hung from its broken perch, she clutched the wood and yanked. With a splintering of the few remaining balusters, the rail came loose in her hands.

The guard's head whipped up from his task and he spat, "Keep quiet, ye damn harlot. Do ye want us both t' hang?"

"Move aside," Emma hissed.

The guard looked at her in disbelief. "Have ye gone mad? That'll never work."

Emma braced her legs apart and hefted the rail to her shoulder. "Move aside," she repeated. Perhaps it was the determination in her voice, or maybe the fact that, had she swung it, the rail would undoubtedly have met with his head, but the guard stepped warily aside.

"Shud've asked for more money," he muttered.

Emma twisted her shoulders back; then with everything she had she swung the rail around at the lock. A near-deafening thud echoed up the stairwell, followed by the sound of corroded metal hitting the stone floor. The lock had not opened, but the metal link it clung to on the door had pulled effortlessly free of the damp, rotting wood.

The two of them stood stupefied for a second before the sound of footsteps in the upstairs hall revived them. The guard grabbed for the handle and pulled and they simultaneously pushed their way through the door.

The cold air slapped her in the face with the freshness of diving into a pool. Emma stopped dead and sucked it in greedily.

"Git movin'!" the guard prompted, pulling her arm.

Emma dashed after him, following him under the low branches of the trees near the prison wall. They emerged at the front of the building, facing the gloriously free and open roadway. Gaslights lined the walk, and she could see a short block away the rising scaffolding of the unfinished capitol dome.

The guard pushed her out from the wall toward the street. "Go!"

Emma took two steps forward, then glanced back in panic. "Where? Where shall I go?"

"Martin's Tavern," he grumbled lowly, glancing behind himself.

Martin's Tavern! Her heart leapt to her throat. *Will.* The only time she'd been there was with him. This had to be his doing. The joy and relief that flooded through her went unanalyzed, then disappeared under the guard's next words.

"Go up through Swampoodle. But keep to yerself; they's danger there."

"Swampoodle?" she gasped, horrified. The area near Tiber Creek was notoriously dangerous, replete with drunks, whores, and criminals of every sort.

"Keep to yerself. Ye'll be a'right. Now go!"

The sound of voices reached their ears and before she knew what was happening, the guard slipped back toward the open doorway. "Here!" he boomed toward the stairwell, causing her to jump nearly out of her skin. "This a-way! I got her!"

Emma stared at him transfixed in terror until he angrily motioned her away with his arm. As if pushed from behind, she grabbed her skirts, jerked them to her knees, and fled. *Swampoodle.* It was only a few blocks away, but was she going the right direction? She scanned her surroundings for a street sign but saw nothing as she bolted up the street.

Her braid beat a frantic tattoo against her back as she ran, locks and tendrils loosening about her face. As she pushed them out of her eyes, her mind spun in an effort to orient herself. It had to be after midnight. There was no traffic, and in this area of unfinished buildings and boardinghouses there was no one on foot. She reached the corner and stopped, gulping down air and gripping her skirts with painful strength. She whirled in quarter-turns in search of a street sign, noting as she did so that there was no one behind her. Finally she spotted a sign. B Street. If she remembered correctly that street up ahead . . . she began again to run . . . yes, it was—Delaware Avenue! She sprinted toward it and disappeared around the corner.

Here she immediately slowed her pace. She could see no one yet but she did not wish to draw attention to herself. With a supreme effort she tried to calm the hysterical sound of her breathing and unfurled the shawl, which until then had been wadded up in one hand. Gingerly she pulled it over her head and held it at her throat, hoping its fine quality would be hidden in the dark. With her other hand she held her skirts, keeping their awkward length from underfoot.

After a block there was no more light, which was in a way comforting and in another way terrifying. The only thing that kept one foot moving in front of the other was that at the end of this hideous trek she knew she would find Will. At this moment, in the fearful dark of the February night, surrounded by black, gaping doorways and hidden perils, she felt she could forgive him everything.

In an effort to keep her courage up, she concentrated on what this frightening trip meant—freedom. She could go home; surely he would help her to get home. Instead of the looming dilapidated frame houses around her, she envisioned the warm glow of the fire in the companionable inn. Instead of the seedy skulking figures that flitted through the shadows, she pictured Will, waiting for her among the jolly men and blowsy women of the tavern.

Emma kept her eyes on the ground as she walked, stepping over debris and around mud puddles that could have swallowed an entire brougham. Occasionally she spotted the quick slink of a ratlike shape around a corner or under a front porch and she shuddered.

"Pssst, hey!" a sly voice hissed out of the darkness.

Emma dropped her skirts and skidded sideways. Her eyes searched the darkness for the source of the voice.

"Here," the sly tone coaxed. She turned to her left and squinted into the darkened doorway of a ramshackle shop. "Hey, now, there's a pretty 'un." He straightened from his leaning position and moved a step or two toward the street.

Emma whipped her head down and continued walking. But the third step she took landed on her skirt and as she brought her other leg forward she collapsed on her hands and knees in the muddy street. The shawl fell back from her head, its corner landing in the dirt.

She scrabbled to her feet as the man approached her rapidly. She felt his cold fingers grasp her arm and pull her up and toward him.

"I got money," he cooed. "Where can we go?"

Whiskey fumes fanned out in a cloud from his mouth as Emma wrenched her arm free. "Let me go!" she snapped.

"Well, now, a little highfalutin, ain't we?" The man continued to approach her.

She snatched up her skirts and turned to run, but the man grabbed for her, his fingers lacing into the fringe of the shawl. Emma pulled but the man would not let go. He dragged inexorably on the garment. She had no other choice; she let it go. Then, with both hands on her gown and her feet free, she raced up the street, leaving the wretch holding a garment worth more than he'd probably make in a year.

She ran blindly, afraid to be too near the buildings, but nervous about running so conspicuously in the street. When she was finally sure that the man had not followed, she slowed, clutching her arms to her middle and widening her eyes in an effort to see anyone approaching before they saw her. The cold air burned her lungs and she missed the shawl for more than just sentimental reasons. As she passed a deserted storefront whose shattered window looked like an evil, toothy grin, she saw figures up ahead in the distance and heard the tinny twinkle of bawdy music.

Swampoodle.

She neared cautiously and saw groups of men lounging against the garishly painted buildings. Scantily clad women sashayed through the crowd, but for the most part it was men, lasciviously perusing the offered flesh and laughing meanly amongst themselves. Every few seconds one of them would spit into the street, narrowly missing a passerby or hitting one of the dogs scavenging in the gutter, to the accompaniment of much laughter.

Many of the men wore the blue of the Northern uniform, but other than that they appeared no less seedy than their comrades. And, more often than not, they were considerably drunker.

Emma kept her head down and trudged through the gutters with the mongrels. It was far better to keep her distance from the men and ruin what was left of her shoes than to risk being mistaken for one of the ladies of the night again. When she did dare to glance up she saw far more than she wished. In an upper window she caught sight of a woman, bare to the waist, caressing herself and beckoning anyone and everyone inside with a graceful wave of her hand. On a corner she saw a begrimed woman sobbing and clinging to the pant leg of a man whose other booted foot relentlessly kicked at her as he tried to break free.

When she sought to avoid the worst of the area and move a block over, she came across two men in close conference against a dark wall. She stopped in order to remain unnoticed and watched as one of them stepped swiftly back from the other and whipped out a knife. She turned and fled back to the relative safety of the crowds.

When Emma finally made it past Swampoodle, into a section of town that got progressively cleaner, she desperately wished she had not lost the shawl. First and foremost in her mind was the fact that walking down this public street, bareheaded and bedraggled, she would be a much more noteworthy spectacle than she'd been in the anything-goes area of Swampoodle. And that, when being pursued by the authorities, was a most dangerous thing to be.

After what seemed an eternity she saw up ahead the lights of Martin's Tavern, in front of which were parked several coaches. Men in livery loitered about, smoking and chatting, in markedly civil contrast to the bands of men she had recently passed. Though the scene was so familiar, so commonplace in her real, if distant, life, she felt uncomfortably conspicuous and wondered how in the world she would make it past the doorman in her muddy dress and her wild hair. She knew she looked like an impoverished waif in her hoopless gown, and she could only imagine what her face looked like, but she proceeded on in the resolute confidence that Will, once she found him, would handle everything. How she longed to see him, to know that his anger had been an act and he'd really meant to save her all along. How delicious it would be to disown the hard words they'd said to each other.

She was about to cross the street to the block on which the tavern stood when a voice came out of the darkness behind her.

"Thank God you made it." The words were clear but the voice was not Will's. Emma spun to see a man leaning against the wall of the corner building.

He straightened and stepped forward, his pale, ghostlike face slowly illuminated as he emerged from the shadows.

"Thank God you're safe," he said, the voice strangely chilling now as she recognized it.

"You," she breathed, disappointment sweeping over her like a cold rain. "I thought . . ."

He stopped a few feet away and studied her dispassionately. "Yes, it's me. Whom did you expect?"

"I—didn't know," she said in a small voice. But in her naive, hope-filled imaginings, she knew that she did not expect to see Lawrence Price.

Chapter Nine

"Where are we going?" Emma asked as they slipped away down the darkened street and around a corner into an alley. Her foot cracked through a thin sheet of ice and she stumbled slightly, feeling the icy sting of the muddy water seep through her shoe. Lawrence caught her arm in a steadying grip but did not slow his pace.

"To a friend's. We'll be safe there." He spoke in hushed tones but she could hear him clearly. For some reason everything he did and said penetrated those around him with a deliberateness that was impossible to ignore. Some people were like that, she thought briefly. No matter how softly they spoke, people strained to hear them.

"In order to allay any immediate suspicion," he explained matter-of-factly, "I've told them we're eloping and need a place to stay before leaving on honeymoon."

"Eloping!" Emma gasped, but she was prevented from stopping by the firm grip on her arm.

"I needed to secure a safe place for tonight. We'll take the train south tomorrow to pick up the Orange and Alexandria Railroad. With any luck, Lee won't be plaguing the Bluecoats to the south and we'll easily make it to Orange.'' He stayed her with a hand as they reached the end of an alley. Peering around the corner and seeing nothing, he continued, ''From there it should be a simple matter to secure a coach to take us to Richmond. Eloping was the only believable excuse I could concoct for showing up at their house in the middle of the night with a strange female in tow. They think it's terribly romantic.''

She looked in disbelief at the side of his face as they emerged from the alley onto another lamplit street. It was hard for her to imagine Lawrence Price marrying anybody, let alone eloping; she wondered how his friends would consider it believable.

He steered her to the left, across the street, and down another alley. She was thoroughly confused by now, with no idea either where they were or where they were headed. But she followed him faithfully. After all, he'd saved her from interminable incarceration and the daily threat of interrogation, not to mention possible hanging. Her only choice now was to trust him. And she did. He might have gotten her into the worst part of this mess, but he'd also gotten her out. And what did it matter what these people thought of her anyway? The chances of her visiting Washington ever again were very slim indeed.

After what seemed an eternity of winding through backstreets and alleys they arrived at the rear door of a sedate little brick town house. Lawrence knocked on the door lightly in a strange but distinct rhythm and it was opened immediately by a small woman in a nightcap and robe.

''Oooh, you've made it!'' Her ruddy round face beamed at them. ''How was the ceremony? Is the knot all tied nice and tight, then?''

Lawrence bent and kissed the little woman's cheek. ''Nice and tight,'' he murmured. ''Let me introduce you to my wife, Emma Price. Emma, this is Mrs. Thomas. As I told you, she was a close friend of my mother's, before my mother died.''

Emma experienced a strange sensation in the pit of her stomach

Elaine Fox

at the sound of her name meshed with his, but mustered a smile for the cheery Mrs. Thomas. The woman cast a curious glance down the mud-stained front of Emma's gown, then made an obvious effort to conceal her confusion. "So nice to have you, Mrs. Price. I'm sure Lawrence's poor departed mother would have wanted me to welcome you to the family for her."

Emma took the woman's extended hand and thanked her, wishing only to be away from the two of them to regain her bearings. The many strange turns the night had taken were wearing on her, and the surges of adrenaline she'd experienced left her drained.

"Let me show you to your room, then," Mrs. Thomas said mercifully. "I'm sure you'll want to catch a wink or two," she said, winking herself, "before leaving so early tomorrow morning."

"I imagine Mrs. Price would like to clean up a bit, as well," Lawrence added smoothly. "As you've no doubt noticed, she suffered a little mishap on the way here. She stumbled into a puddle, ruining her gown."

Mrs. Thomas laughed in apparent relief upon discovering that Emma was no street hoyden but a only woman who'd suffered a misfortune. If she wondered what had become of her hoop or why she had unkempt hair, she didn't show it. Perhaps she was poor-sighted, Emma considered upon watching the woman take the stairs with slow caution.

"That'll be a simple matter to fix. My poor late husband Harry always used to say I could fix up anything and make it right. I'll just straighten up that gown so it'll be good as new come morning."

"Please don't put yourself out," Emma pleaded, thinking the woman would have to stay up all night in order to fix the shambles the gown had become. "Surely you need your sleep, too."

At the top of the stairs the woman turned a determined eye on her. "Nonsense. I'm an old woman," she said. "I have all day tomorrow to rest up. Where're you from, dear?"

Emma's heart flipped in her chest at the sudden direct question and she glanced quickly at Lawrence for help.

130

"Go on, dear, you can trust Mrs. Thomas," he said smoothly. But before she had a chance to open her mouth he continued for her. "What she's embarrassed to tell you is that she is from the South, Virginia. But don't worry, darling," he said to Emma, taking her elbow possessively, "no one will think you married me just to escape that peculiar fate."

Mrs. Thomas laughed again. "Oh, no. It's obvious as the day is long that you two are in love. So nice to see it, too. You've got a good man, sweetie, a good man." She led them to a room down the hall and opened the door, standing back proudly to usher them in.

It was an unassuming room with a handmade patchwork quilt on the bed and good, solid oak furniture. In one corner sat a rocker with a knitted afghan over its back, next to it a little table with an assortment of three books by a lamp.

"I hope you'll be comfortable here. But after all, you've only a scant few hours left before the train." She busied herself turning down the bedcovers while Emma stood stiffly in the center of the room. "Now, as soon as you're out of that wet dress you let me know. I'll fix it right up."

Emma nodded, though the woman did not wait for an answer before heading for the door. "Sleep well," she sang with a little trill of laughter. Then she shut the door, leaving Emma and Lawrence in an awkward silence.

At least it was awkward for Emma. Lawrence sat promptly on the bed and began to unlace his shoes.

Out of the myriad thoughts that raced through her head, Emma tried to formulate a tactful question to resolve her discomfort, but they all sounded inane. Queries such as "Where shall I sleep?" or statements such as "She'll be expecting my dress" would all come out awkwardly naive, when really what she needed to know was how he expected her to sleep here in this same room with him without her gown and most decidedly not married to him.

She fidgeted nervously, trying to find the correct words without having to state the obvious problem. It was embarrassing enough to be, apparently, the only one who noticed the dilemma without having to actually speak it out loud.

"Miss Davenport." His voice startled her from her anxious reverie. "This is no time for modesty. We're here to save your life, for I can assure you it was in profound jeopardy. We can marry tomorrow, once we're safely out of the city, but rest assured I will not touch you tonight."

"Marry!" The word burst from her. One hand rose to her throat. "I—but I—"

He looked at her quizzically. "You don't expect I should compromise your reputation without providing the means to repair it, do you? What sort of savior would I be?"

She had sudden difficulty catching her breath. Visions of her mother hearing—somehow—that she had spent the night with this man, alone and unchaperoned, assailed her with graphic intensity. "I—I—but marriage!" She wished she could think; her thoughts circled stupidly with fatigue. Perhaps he was saying what he thought she wanted to hear . . . "Mr. Price, I can't imagine taking such advantage of—of your kindness. . . ."

"Miss Davenport." He smiled thinly. "Emma. I have suffered such guilt these last few weeks, knowing that it was I who led you to such a desperate pass. Because of what you attempted and then suffered for the Confederacy, I believed it necessary to risk everything to free you. I've even sacrificed my position in the War Department to return you to Richmond. If they were to find me now they would kill me for a traitor. And you, my dear, I can say with absolute certainty, had you not escaped with me you would have hung for a spy."

"Hung?" she breathed. "I would have hung? How do you know?"

"Because, my dear, I was in a position to know such things. General Ferguson gave the order yesterday after his interview with you. Apparently you angered him into thinking it would be useless to keep you." He smiled ruefully. "I don't know what you said, Emma, but he was the wrong man to tangle with. He's one of the most vindictive officers in the department. Young

Darcy made some comments that didn't help you either, I might add.''

Emma felt the blood drain from her entire being. Her body felt dead where she stood in the center of the room, paralyzed, as if she'd solidified into stone with his words. Will had wanted her to hang. It was true. Inside she'd known it, though she hadn't let herself think it. But now . . . yes, he'd practically said so in her very presence. To fight down sudden nausea, she held her breath until her eyes blurred dizzily.

If only she didn't feel so tired, she thought again. If only the world hadn't suddenly become such a thoroughly strange place. She had no one to trust now but this man, she realized slowly, her thoughts sluggish with despair, this odd, remote man who was all but a stranger to her. He knew the whole story the way no one else could. If her family were to find out all—about the smuggling, the spying, the *jail*—she cringed inwardly. And if people were to find out about this night, about her lone flight from prison through Swampoodle—her virtue would truly be destroyed forever. For herself, she would suffer the consequences. But for her family? Could she punish them so with her own sins?

She looked at Lawrence, the man who'd saved her life. How could she ever repay him for what he'd done for her? He'd risked his life, given up his future, and he'd had a position of power and usefulness to the Confederacy that her bumbling foray into spying had destroyed. Now he could never go back. And it was her fault.

She made an effort to block any thought of Will. But it didn't matter; her brain was too tired to muster much of an argument anyway. It seemed she'd made her choice long ago—by making too many bad decisions.

''What will you do?'' she asked, her voice barely above a whisper.

Lawrence removed his other shoe and did not answer immediately. After a moment he looked at her again, his eyes cool and detached. ''That's partially up to you. I have no desire to pressure you, but my plan was to accompany you to Richmond where I can take up the Cause from an administrative post. I can instruct others in the ways of penetrating U.S. organizations such as the War Department." His pale eyes pierced hers. "However, if we are to arrive there in scandal, unchaperoned and obviously alone—if I were to alienate your family in such an unforgivable way—I suppose it would be unwise of me to stay. You might be able to live with the stigma of speculation about our two nights together, unmarried, but only if I am not there to remind everyone of it at all times. I'm sure the Confederacy can find another, if less useful, place for my talents somewhere else."

Emma felt her cheeks burn with shame, for she wanted desperately to be able to cast him out in just such a way. For herself, she would much prefer to live down the scandal than to marry this peculiar, intimidating man. But after he gave up everything to save her, could she really discard him so callously?

"We could both weather the scandal. . . ." she suggested tentatively.

He looked at her disdainfully. "Come now, Emma. We both know it would be impossible, especially moving as we do in the most conservative circles of Richmond society. Don't embarrass us both by being deliberately obtuse, Emma."

She blushed to the roots of her hair. "I'm sorry. I'm . . . this is just all so sudden."

The knock on the door seemed to blast through the room. "Have you got the gown ready?" Mrs. Thomas called.

Emma's glance skittered away from Lawrence. "Uh, no, I . . . just a second."

"Ooh, sorry then. I'll just come back." Her voice trailed off down the hall.

Lawrence stood and stretched his hand out over the bed in a gesture of offering. "You sleep here tonight. I'll sleep on the floor. You can make your decision tomorrow. We'll leave at first light."

Emma swallowed hard, knowing she should tell him that, yes, his plan was the best and she wouldn't dream of standing in the way—again—of his usefulness to the Confederacy. They could marry tomorrow, then continue on their way. But everything inside of her recoiled at the thought. She turned her back to him and began to unbutton her dress. Her mind reeled with the information he'd given her, circling and rejecting, then circling again to the knowledge that Will had helped to convict her. . . .

A hot tear ran down her cheek but she made an effort not to sniff. No sense burdening Lawrence further by becoming a weepy female on him. She could see it all from his point of view, so logical, so sensible. How stupid to let these weak, maidenly emotions get in the way of such a viable plan. The only viable plan, really. Marriage would solve both of their problems. They could travel more easily—she, certainly, would be at less risk of being caught, as the authorities would be searching for a lone woman—and it would ease her way back into Richmond and counteract even the smallest suspicion that she might have been despoiled during such a dangerous mission and daring escape. The thought of her mother's reaction alone was almost enough to make her acquiesce. But primarily it would help smooth Lawrence's way into the bosom of the Confederacy, though she expected he was already well known there if he'd been their main connection in Washington all this time.

As she slipped the gown from her shoulders the lamp mercifully went out. Lawrence must have extinguished it to preserve her modesty. He was kind, in his way.

"Thank you," she whispered.

His voice emerged stiffly from the darkness. "I hope you have no fears that I have done any of this in an attempt to compromise you. I assure you I sought only your safety."

"Oh, I know," she cried softly. "Please, I don't mean to seem ungrateful. It's just—I'm just so tired. Please, forgive me."

Silence stretched taut for a second. Then, "Don't be silly," he said quietly. "There's nothing to forgive."

Will's fingers drummed incessantly on the table in Martin's Tavern. A half-empty mug of ale stood before him, and an unfinished plate of cheese and bread lay next to that. Something's wrong, he thought for the hundredth time. She should have been here by now.

He rose for what seemed the millionth time and looked out the window, cupping his hand on the glass in an effort to see outside. Nothing, nobody, even the carriages had left. He was one of only three people left in the bar. The English barkeep, who kept up a steady stream of stories about bawdy London wenches, a boisterous drunk, who laughed hilariously at everything the barkeep said, and himself, who was tied in a knot of anxiety in his corner by the window. Once again he moved to the doorway and stood on the stoop, studying first one side of the street, then the other. Perhaps she didn't remember the place, though he'd given instructions to that brick-headed guard to give her cab money and directions to the W&A Railroad, where she could conceivably find a cab.

He looked at his watch. One-thirty A.M. Something had happened. He felt his barely controlled dread expand with the thought and strode back to his table. He threw down some change and weaved through the tables to the bar.

"Barkeep," he called, throwing caution to the wind. "I've been expecting a woman—"

The boisterous drunk roared with laughter at the statement. "Haven't we all?" he crowed, slapping Will on the back. "Haven't we all!"

Will shot him an irritated look and raised his voice over the noise. "If she shows up while I'm gone would you ask her to wait for me?" He pushed a ten-dollar gold piece across the bar.

The man fixed wily brown eyes on him. "Why, sure, guv'ner. But we close at three, you know."

Will glanced at the clock on the wall. "I'll be back by three," he promised. "Just don't let her leave once she gets here. Have you got a piece of paper?"

The bartender bent and retrieved a scrap from beneath the bar. He placed the paper in front of Will and pushed over a pen and a bottle of ink which, judging from the dried ink encrusted on the outside of it, had apparently tipped a couple of dozen times.

Hastily Will scrawled a note, then folded it in half. He handed it back to the bartender.

"You'll know her when you see her. She's a beauty, though she'll be a little ragged. About so tall, dark auburn hair, brown eyes, flawless skin. Give her this, and tell her to wait."

"Aye, guv'ner," the man said, with no small amount of interest. "You can trust ole Wally, you can. I'll be lookin' for 'er."

Will left at a half-run through the front door.

It was cold, and that worried him. It was black as pitch with no moon, and that worried him. If she'd gone the wrong way she'd have ended up going through Swampoodle, and that drove his worry to near distraction. If that idiot of a guard hadn't given her proper instructions he'd kill him. That is, if he even saw him again. He couldn't go to the prison now. If they hadn't already discovered her escape they would in the morning, and his being caught in the vicinity would ensure his arrest. As it was, the fact that it was well known she'd been his fiancée would land him in some fairly hot water. He'd at least be put through the paces of an in-depth interrogation. It looked bad when they lost a prisoner, and they always looked for a scapegoat.

But all of that paled in comparison to what could have befallen her on her way to the tavern. He should have risked it and stayed near the prison as he'd originally planned. He could have come up with some excuse for being nearby. But, dammit, it was all supposed to be so simple. At least according to Lawrence it was. It was he who had obliquely suggested that if anyone were to be of a mind to help someone escape from the Old Cap that he knew of a guard who might be in need of some ready cash. It was all supposition and innuendo between them, of course. Lawrence, being in a position of much greater power than Will either aspired to or was likely to obtain, had much more to lose if he were to be directly involved with such a scheme; but he obviously anticipated what Will planned to do and he'd done what he could to help him. He'd also made it most clear that if Will were to be seen within half a mile of the prison that night it would bode badly for him. And in that case all of Lawrence's power couldn't

137

Elaine Fox

help him avoid the dire fate of a traitor.

So Will had succumbed to reason and hatched an alternative plan. She'd be perfectly safe in a cab, Lawrence had argued, and cabs were reasonably easy to catch near the train station even at that hour of the night. Besides, Lawrence insisted he have an alibi someplace far away, and the tavern was perfect. Emma knew where it was, and it was a significant distance from the jail. Of course the alibi was worthless now that he'd told the barkeep of his intention to meet a woman. But all he could think about was Emma, and the possible hazards if she hadn't caught a cab, or if she'd attempted the walk on foot, or if she was never told where to go. . . .

Will let himself into the house from the chilling grayness of the wet morning, and shook himself out of his drenched greatcoat. A steady rain had begun to fall shortly after he'd left Martin's, and he'd walked heedlessly through it for the rest of the night, searching vainly for some trace of Emma. Now, tired and beaten by his failure, Will rubbed his burning eyes and battled back another wave of guilt and fatigue. The sounds of breakfast emanated from the back dining room, low voices, Stephanie's quick laugh, the clatter of silver against china. But he did not feel up to facing them. Not now. From them there would be no sympathy, not for Emma's plight.

Though the sordid details had been mercifully withheld, when word had reached them that their recent houseguest had been arrested for spying, both Brendan and Will's mother had reacted with a haughty, outraged renunciation of Emma and everything they had once thought of the girl. Both made a point of demarcating to all who visited how callously ill used the family had been by the two-faced Confederate, when all they'd been trying to do was help the poor thing escape the tragedy of her unfortunate birthplace. And to think, Mrs. Darcy huffed on more than one occasion in Will's presence, she had once almost allowed a connection between the families. She shuddered to think of it now.

138

His father had reacted silently, as usual, but with sadness more than disgust. Will had the feeling that, like himself, his father was more disappointed in her than he was judgmental of her attempt to help the Confederate cause. But though there might have been some sympathy for Will's complex feelings from that quarter, he had never been close enough to his father to be able to speak to him about anything so close to his heart.

Stephanie, of course, had thought it wonderfully exciting and brave of her friend, but when the embarrassment of her entire family had penetrated her enthusiasm, she too had retreated to a kind of wary silence on the matter.

He should sleep, Will thought lifelessly as he pushed his wet hair from his forehead and moved toward the library, but it was out of the question, and probably impossible. Somewhere out there Emma wandered, unsafe and alone, and the horrid visions he had of what could have befallen her were relentless. She had escaped the prison. As the officer in charge of her interrogation he'd been able to confirm that much. But after that there were no clues. When he'd inquired about the guard who'd been on duty during the escape, he'd been informed that that man had apparently disappeared as well. So Will had combed the streets surrounding the prison for anyone who might have seen her.

Of course no one volunteered any information. Either no one had seen anything or they preferred not to get mixed up with the search for an escaped spy. In his uniform Will probably looked like just another incompetent jailer who'd lost his prisoner, and there were enough Southern sympathizers in Washington for some of them to revel in the escape. He hoped to God Emma had found one of them to help her.

He pushed open the door to the library and breathed a sigh of relief at its emptiness. Again and again his mind ran in the same tired circles about where she could have gone, who might have found her, how he could possibly track down a woman determined to hide in this sprawling, divided city. He should have told her of the plan when he'd seen her; but he'd been so angry, and he was not at all sure that she would have accepted his help, not after the things he'd said to her. At one time he might have called it her only flaw, that she could be stubborn even if it meant her own ultimate suffering, but with all that had happened recently he'd have to rethink that. The raw courage behind her actions took on greater nobility the more he considered it.

He strode toward the armchairs before the fireplace and landed in one with a grunt of fatigue. He rested his head on the back and closed his eyes. How would he ever sleep again, not knowing what happened to her? The pain and suppressed panic that gnawed at his belly were constant. What had he been thinking during that wretched interview with her in the prison? He should have pitied, not condemned, her.

He'd been thinking she could have landed his whole family in prison, some harder, still angry voice in his head reminded him. He'd been thinking about her hair tumbled all about her naked shoulders while Bondurant—

No, it wasn't right. Something wasn't right. She must have had a reason. A good reason. Perhaps one of her brothers was in danger. For her to give up all she had and risk her life the way she did, she had to have had a damn good reason. But he hadn't thought of that then. All he'd done was react in a self-righteous and jealous rage. How could he have shamed her without first trying to understand?

He groaned with the thought and brought his face forward into his hands. But how would he ever understand? The vision of her in bed with the corpulent Bondurant, seducing and enticing, brought bile to the back of his throat and a stiff pain to his chest.

The sound of the door opening pulled him from his desperate reverie. He turned his head enough to see Brendan enter the room and close the door behind him in a suspiciously circumspect way.

As Brendan neared, Will could see he wore a dark, assessing expression. "Out gallivanting?" he purred. He was up to something. Will's fatigue deepened.

Brendan strode slowly to the fireplace, then settled himself in the chair opposite Will, all the while watching his younger brother as if his very movements might betray where he'd been.

Will leaned his chin on his hand and fixed bloodshot eyes on his brother. "In a manner of speaking," he answered. Unkindly, he noted that Brendan's strong, square face was getting jowly with age and the once-trim body was thickening around the middle.

"Or out searching for your paramour?" Brendan added, his expression hard.

Though he still slumped with exhaustion, Will froze inside, his brain suddenly alert. "What do you mean?"

Brendan smiled cynically. "She's escaped, of course; I heard immediately. I wonder who might have helped her to do something like that?"

Will shrugged with forced casualness but did not take his eyes from his brother's.

Jowls aquiver, Brendan continued silkily, "Of course, it's already been established that she can be quite . . . persuasive when she wants to be." He laced his fingers and placed them complacently over the taut middle buttons of his waistcoat. "Perhaps the missing guard benefited from her favors and decided to sign on for more. After all, it's possible; who would have thought she'd stoop to screwing a blowhard like Bondurant?"

Teeth clenched, Will murmured ominously low, "When she could have screwed a blowhard like yourself?"

Brendan's eyes narrowed and he puffed up his chest in indignation. "Very funny. Certainly I was interested in her; she's a beautiful woman. But I would never have succumbed to that sort of treachery."

Will laughed ironically. " 'There is no virtue like necessity,' " he quoted.

Face suffused with red, Brendan poked a finger in the air at Will. "I wouldn't be so smug if I were you. You could be in a lot of trouble, Will. I haven't heard anything definite yet, but you're going to be the first one to whom they'll turn looking for her."

Will sat up straighter. "What do you know about it? Are they searching for her?" He half hoped they'd find her, sure that whatever she'd suffer on the streets would be worse than the Old Cap.

Brendan raised his palms sarcastically. "Of course. And they'll probably find her before long. How far could she get alone?"

Will nearly winced with the guilt those words inspired and sank his face into his hands again. Surely there was something he'd overlooked, someplace he hadn't searched that she could be hiding.

"Unless she employed the missing guard. Do you think she would be that clever?" Brendan mused.

Will raised his head, ignoring the last comment though it threatened to infuriate him. Damned hypocrite, he thought. The arrogant ass would have handed her Lincoln on a platter if he'd thought it would win him a place in her bed.

"Where's Lawrence?" he asked abruptly, possessed of an idea. "I need to speak to him and when I stopped at his house this morning no one answered."

Brendan waved a hand dismissively. "He's off and you're lucky for it. Imagine what he might have said about this."

Will shook his head. "Off where?"

He shrugged. "Stanton sent him somewhere—Tennessee, I think. Going to be gone a while, as I understand it."

"Tennessee!" Will's brow furrowed. "I just saw him yesterday. He mentioned nothing about a trip."

Brendan looked unimpressed with this information. "I've known about it a couple of weeks now. I don't imagine Lawrence feels accountable to you for what he does."

"No, I imagine he doesn't," Will murmured, thumbs tapping against each other as his tired brain traced an idea. "Can you get me in to see Bondurant?" he asked.

Brendan arched his brows in surprise. "Bondurant! Good heavens, no. Haven't you heard?"

A sinking dread hit his stomach. "Heard what?"

"The man slit his own throat. Just after signing his confession. Christ, the whole place was abuzz with the news. Apparently he had a knife hidden in his boot."

Will closed his eyes. Bondurant, dead. "Because of the confession, I suppose."

"I suppose. Though I'm sure I don't understand why. He might still have gotten off, or at least been released at the end of the war."

Will's mouth dropped open. "I thought they planned to hang him."

Brendan shrugged. "There was talk of it, but they had no real evidence that any information actually reached the enemy. Aside from Emma's role in the scandal there was very little else to convict him on. She had denied everything and with her gone, he might have claimed the confession was made under duress and walked free."

Will stared at his brother. "Lawrence told me it had been decided."

Brendan laughed indulgently. "Well, Lawrence. He is inclined toward bloodthirstiness at times, don't you think? I'm sure if it were left up to him, anyone with an ounce of sympathy for the rebs would be hung on the spot. Surprised he didn't have it in for you, with your, ahem, *weakness* for a certain female, even before she was exposed as an informer."

Will eyed him coldly. "Or you. Last I recall you were laying your obsequious lips all over her hand and fawning over every word she said, in public no less. And you, a servant in Stanton's own War Department. They may be investigating that before long."

Brendan pursed his lips and looked suddenly uncomfortable. "Look, you know exactly how I feel about that deceptive little bitch. She played us like a bunch of fools, setting us up as decoys for her little charade," he blustered. "I'll do everything within my power to find Emma Davenport and string her up myself, if I have to. And I've made sure my superiors know it." He rose with his anger and circled the chair, clutching the back in his square hands. "Imagine, her tramping around while a guest under our roof. We'll never live it down, never."

"And she could walk in here this very moment, strip to the

143

buff, and have you like an hors d'oeuvre in the palm of her hand,'' Will spat, his own anger mounting.

''Which is probably exactly what she did to old Bondurant,'' Brendan shot back. ''Oh, you thought you were going to be the first, didn't you? You and your virtuous Southern belle. There were probably dozens even before she snared you. Think of it, think of what you escaped by virtue of sheer, dumb luck. She would have cuckolded you a dozen times over before you were even married—''

Will surged from his chair, his fist connecting with Brendan's jaw. Brendan staggered back, tripped over the rug, and thundered onto the floor, arms flailing, curses spewing from his lips.

''Don't you ever speak of her in those terms again, you overbearing, pompous ass,'' Will growled, standing over the fallen form of his brother, chest heaving with the explosion of indignation. ''She's done more for her cause *this month* than you've done yet for yours, and she's got twice the courage in her left hand than you've got in your entire body.'' Will prodded his brother's fleshy stomach with the toe of his boot. ''You call yourself a soldier, sitting in your plush, guarded office growing fat and egotistical. But you know nothing of war and the compromises it asks of those who fight it.''

Brendan sniffed and ran his fingers beneath his bloodied nose. ''How pathetic,'' he sneered. ''Pleading for the dignity of the whore.''

Will glared at him, his breaths coming in ragged, rapid succession. ''If I thought I could escape hell for it I'd kill you for that right now.''

''Like you did the missing guard?'' Brendan queried, raising himself onto his elbows. ''Because there are only two possibilities I can conceive. It's obvious that you arranged it, and she escaped. So you either killed the guard to keep him quiet or she abandoned you and took him instead.'' He gave an ugly, triumphant smile. ''And from the look of you, I'd wager she took him instead.''

Chapter Ten

The train rumbled slowly forward out of the station, with black smoke belching ponderously from the smokestack. Link-and-pin couplings clanged successively down the line of cars as the heavy machinery groaned to life. Emma pressed her damp palms to her gown to dry them.

Lawrence folded the packet of worn papers that had effortlessly procured passage for them to Orange, and pushed them into an inside coat pocket. With a quarter turn, his stark, unchangeable visage fixed on her.

"You've made the right decision, Emma." His voice was cool but approving. "Marriage will facilitate everything for both of us. You may go about your business in the hospital with perfect impunity from what certainly would have been malicious gossip and moral censure. And I may find a position of some use to our cause without chancing reprisal for moral turpitude." His lips thinned into something she interpreted as smug certainty. "You might even be of greater use yourself as a matron. I assume you were prevented from helping the most needy in your hospital because of the likelihood of seeing what no maiden should see.''

Emma nodded. ''Y-yes, that's right. You're right, I shall be more useful.'' She tried to impress this point's significance on herself. After she was married, it would not be solely up to her mother, Aunt Caro, and Mrs. Jenkins to bathe the men and assist the surgeon. She could even help dress the wounds that were on men's torsos, not just those confined to limbs. In that way she could be much more help; there were plenty of others to help write letters and read to the men.

But try though she might, she couldn't distract herself from the conversation she knew she must have with her husband-to-be. As he turned his attention back to the newspaper he'd purchased, she dug her nails into the heels of her hands and steeled her fluttering stomach for the duty she must perform. It would be the most uncomfortable discussion she'd ever provoked, but now that she'd made her decision she could avoid it no longer. She did not allow herself to think of the relief with which she would greet any ''moral censure'' Lawrence might express after hearing what she had to say; she simply plunged into her dialogue and hoped for the best, whatever that might be.

She cleared her throat. ''Mr. Pr—ah, Lawrence . . .'' She did not look at him as he turned his pale eyes on her again. ''I feel compelled to—to confess something to you. I hope you'll understand, but if you don't I'll abide by your feelings completely. It's, well, you should know . . . something, about myself, before you commit to marrying me.''

He looked at her blandly. ''You needn't confess anything to me, Emma,'' he said. ''I have no desire to stand in judgment of you.''

She smiled wanly at him. ''No, I know that. But what I have to say—well, it's only right, and fair, that you should know it.'' Her eyes flicked briefly to the passengers around them, all of them out of earshot.

Lawrence sighed. ''Very well, if you feel that you must.'' He folded his paper in resignation and bestowed his undivided attention upon her.

146

"It's about Will, uh, Darcy," she began awkwardly. Though she'd been intent upon telling him her secret for some time, she'd completely overlooked the problem of figuring out which words to use.

His thin lips smiled. "Yes, I think I know him. What of Will Darcy?" When she floundered with wordlessness again he added, "Might this have something to do with the fact that he was your fiancé?"

Emma nodded, eyes on her fingers knotted in her lap. "Yes. Yes, in fact it does." She took a deep breath. "You see, for a time he was—somewhat more than my fiancé." She glanced up at him quickly—his expression remained neutral—then back at her hands. Words turned this way and that in her mind as she struggled to find the right ones. How did one confess a sin that one had absolutely no remorse for? Her mortification came solely from the fact of having to say the words aloud. And how did one confess a sin such as this to the man one was about to marry? "You see, he—I . . . Well, we . . ." She bit her bottom lip. She was painfully aware of his cold eyes on her, penetrating her face, and she thought the whole thing would go much easier if those hard shark eyes would just look directly into her brain and save her the trouble of words.

"Tell me, Emma. Say what you have to say." He was an angry schoolteacher, aware that she had not done her homework. She endured a breathless moment of silence wherein her mind went completely blank before he shifted impatiently.

"Are you trying to tell me, Miss Davenport, that Will was your lover?" he asked.

Her eyes squeezed shut as she felt her cheeks burn with mortification. The bald statement sounded so shameful.

"That's right," she whispered, nodding. "I'm sorry," she added more audibly. "It's just that we planned to be married. We were sure, we were so sure. . . ." Tears stung her eyelids but she did not let them emerge.

To her surprise, Lawrence placed an icy, white hand on both of hers where they lay twisted in her lap. "Don't be concerned.

I am not interested in your carnal experiences, past or future.''
She tried to turn toward him but managed only to stare at his
knees, unable to meet his eyes. ''Ours shall be a marriage of
convenience,'' he continued in a businesslike tone. ''I thought
you understood that. I shall no more seek bodily pleasures from
you than you, I feel sure, would wish to seek them from me.''

Emma then forced her eyes to his, awash in relief, disbelief,
and a vague sense of foreboding. ''You have no intention of—of
consummating?'' She forced the word out of her mouth. With
any luck and no misunderstanding, this would be the last awkward
conversation they would ever have. A guarded lightness infiltrated
the beating of her heart.

His lids lowered slightly. ''Absolutely none.''

His stark answer and ominous look crushed any relief she'd
been about to feel. He was like a hawk, she thought with a twinge
of inexplicable fear. He had expressionless, birdlike eyes that saw
all and gave nothing away, ever. She tried to remember seeing
any sort of lifelike expression on his face and could not.

She let out a long breath. ''All right. Then . . . then I'm sorry
to have burdened you with my confession. Please try to overlook
it.'' A little voice inside her head began to whisper worries she
could not quite hear. Though she knew she should feel nothing
but relief at his assertion, something inside her was suddenly,
deeply nervous. Was it the thought of a marriage without any sort
of future? Without children? What of the life she'd always envisioned for herself of a husband, a home, children, grandchildren,
love?

She tried to squelch the thoughts. She'd been given a gift, a
bit of mercy. She had dreaded marriage to this man because she
was patently unattracted and absolutely not in love with him. To
learn now that she would not have to sleep with him, would not
have to propagate children who might have that same moonlike
coldness and strange aloofness, should have filled her with comfort.

Ignoring her unfounded trepidation, she concentrated on what
might be good about their future together. She would still have

her life, her independence, her work. Once this horrid war ended, she could devote herself to something else, perhaps become a nurse full-time. There were plenty of people in the world who led rich, happy lives without children, or a husband they loved. And she at least felt she could respect Lawrence, if nothing else. That should be enough for any marriage. She would not have to worry about him becoming a gambler, or a drinker, or any of the other disreputable things that could destroy the life she might make for herself. Indeed, she was fortunate to find someone who would not expect from her the love she had given to Will—the love she was sure was dead without him.

She settled herself more firmly in her decision. "Then I think we shall do well together," she said firmly, though the words sounded odd to her, as if she hadn't spoken them.

Lawrence squeezed her hand and let it go. "I know we shall," he agreed. "Now try to get some rest. We'll meet with the preacher in Orange and all will be well."

The book closed with a clap, and the justice of the peace, a young man with blue eyes and a baby face, beamed at them. "You may"—he waved a hand encouragingly—"you know . . . kiss the bride."

Emma stiffened and shot an uncertain glance at Lawrence. Without hesitation he turned to her, leaned in, and deposited a cool, deft kiss on her cheek.

For some reason, Emma felt the impulse to murmur "thank you," as if he'd handed her a cup of tea, so polite and impersonal was the action. But she stopped the words in time.

It was certainly the strangest wedding service she'd ever attended, Emma reflected, little more than jumping over the broom as plantation slaves did. And it was so perfunctory that it was easy to cling to the feeling that it wasn't real. After all, she reasoned, keeping panic at bay, she felt no different and nothing would really change . . . except for the fact that this strange man would be present in her life. For the rest of her life . . .

She stopped the thought before it could go further. The baby-faced preacher ushered them over to a worn, brown desk and dipped a pen in the inkwell. He handed it to Lawrence and slid two sheets of paper forward.

"If you'll just sign these documents, here"—he indicated a spot with a pudgy finger—"and this one here." He clasped his hands before him and watched Lawrence sign, smiling benignly. He was altogether too satisfied for Emma's mood.

"And you, miss—ah, madam." He laughed jovially at his mistake. "Mrs. Price, please. Sign opposite your husband on each of these papers. These are identical copies, you understand. The new couple"—he smiled encouragingly at them—"that's you—keeps this one. In case you ever need proof, you know. Things are so uncertain these days, society in an uproar and all that. And it can be something to show the grandchildren someday." He pushed the one on the right toward her.

This was not even happening, Emma thought absurdly as she shifted her focus to the spidery writing on the page. It was too illusory; she felt too detached. Perhaps it was the dryness of the ceremony, the brevity, but it struck her as more of a transaction than a wedding, like buying a yard of cloth.

She leaned toward the table and the man's white finger where it pointed to a spot on the page. "Sign here, opposite your husband." She scraped the ill-trimmed pen-point across the page, noticing as if from a distance that she'd missed the indicated line with her last name. *Mrs. Price* . . . She turned to the other document. The letters became indistinct, swimming before her eyes. It wasn't until a tear struck the page, running Lawrence's signature, that she realized she was crying.

"I'm sorry," she said in a breathless voice. She brushed at the wet spot, streaking black ink across the page and onto the side of her hand. She bit her bottom lip as both Lawrence and the preacher moved to blot the paper. Neither of them handed her a handkerchief.

"It's all right," she said when they finished and she'd regained her voice. She took the pen from the inkwell and signed her name again, firmly, straight along the line.

There. It was done. She turned away from them and concentrated on straightening her gown, donning her gloves, and swallowing the lump that had grown in her throat. She heard Lawrence ask where they might find a coach, and listened with half an ear as the preacher embarked on a long explanation of the erratic stage schedule and the fact that there wasn't a horse to be found for love nor money because the soldiers—both sides—had commandeered them all.

Emma straightened her shoulders and moved toward the front door. Air. She needed some air. Never mind that the rain still pelted the windows; she needed to get out of the room.

As she stepped onto the front porch the wind sprayed her face with a fine mist from the downpour. The road in front of the preacher's home was deep with mud and, apart from the steady drumming of the rain and the splash of water off the roofs, nothing stirred. No horses tramped through the street, no coaches sloshed by. The town was completely quiet.

After several minutes Lawrence joined her. She felt stronger in the cold, raw air and was able to face him without any outward sign of emotion.

"We might be in luck," he said dryly. "There's a mail wagon due through here today on the route to Richmond. Reverend Fellows says there's a chance we might secure passage on his buckboard."

Emma turned dry eyes to her new husband. "His buckboard?" The thought of continuing their journey in the driving rain in an open wagon threatened to fill her with desolation. On the other hand, staying in the tiny town and waiting for more comfortable travel arrangements was equally distasteful. She wanted to be home. She wanted to get back to her life, get back to her self, get back to some kind of normality. This forced numbness, while momentarily accommodating, was alien to her and, she was somehow able to admit, it felt a little scary.

"Correct. His buckboard," he said, looking ominously out at the empty street like a crow searching for carrion. "And we'll be lucky to get that. There's not a horse to be found for miles." He sighed heavily, the first sign of fatigue Emma had seen from him. "Come. We'll get something to eat over there." He indicated a building toward the end of the street with an unreadable sign over the door.

Though she was not in the least hungry, Emma followed Lawrence into the rain. Mud immediately slogged the hem of her skirt, dragging at it heavily, and she bent her head against the driving wind. Her hair ran with rivulets of rain onto her cheeks, plastering itself to her skin. Would this journey never end? she found herself thinking. Would she ever arrive home, or would she just continue to exist in this strange world she'd created when she embarked on this failed mission? It seemed a lifetime ago that she'd left Richmond with the hope of returning so quickly with blessed, lifesaving medicines. But somewhere along the line things had taken a turn they shouldn't have, and it now seemed as if she were living the wrong life. It was a feeling she'd never had before, and she had no choice but to blame herself and her headstrong overconfidence for it.

They blew through the doors of the inn with a blast of cold air and rain, and clattered across the wooden floor to the restaurant. The dining room was empty but for one waitress and one patron sitting alone at a table with a generous portion of pot roast before him. As it happened, the patron was the mail carrier and when they joined him at the long plank table, he agreed to give them a seat in his buckboard.

"Good t' have comp'ny in God f'saken weather sich as we got," he said, giving them a toothless grin.

Emma smiled wanly in return, thinking she might just pass out from fatigue, when a whiff of roast chicken caught her and awoke her ravenous stomach.

Two hours later her kidneys felt as if they were being thrown against her backside and her stomach slammed into her rib cage as she wondered at the wisdom of consuming such a large meal before embarking on a journey in a buckboard wagon. She was wedged between two large canvas bags of mail, which were as drenched as she was, and sat upon a third. Though the road was rutted and thick with mud, the driver kept the horses going at a steady clip that bounced them out of holes they might have sunk into at a slower pace.

Lawrence sat beside the driver and clutched the seat with pale, frail hands. Emma had the fleeting thought that with his infirmity, he oughtn't to be out in this kind of weather, but she knew instinctively that he would object to any suggestion of circumspection on account of his health. And she had no desire to stop the wretched motion of the coach, even if she did feel most acutely like throwing up, for each bounce and clatter brought them closer to her home.

They arrived in Richmond in the dark of night. It was only about nine o'clock but the town was dark, the rain relentless. The buckboard creaked up to the large, looming house on Franklin Street and stopped, harnesses jingling as the steaming horses tried vainly to shake themselves free of the driving wetness.

Emma climbed stiffly down from the back of the wagon and waited uncertainly as Lawrence shook the driver's hand and disembarked. It appeared there were people in the house, other than just the patients, for the small front parlor lights were lit and she knew that it was the only room on the first floor not designated for the wounded. She could see shapes moving against the drawn drapes and wanted nothing more than to be inside in the warmth and dryness.

But she did not immediately run for the door, as part of her demanded she do, primarily because she was peculiarly unsure of her reception. By now they would have heard—something—about her plight, wouldn't they have? At the very least, Judith would have cracked and told all—the lie about Washington, her affiliation with the Darcys, her plan for smuggling. Judith herself was probably sick with .worry, Emma realized with great guilt. After all, didn't they have enough to worry about with all of their men off mired in danger? Did she really have to add to the troubles by doing something stupid because of some misguided notion of her own valor? Did they even know she'd been imprisoned?

She was supposed to have been back weeks ago, and while she

knew her mother would be worried, she also knew she would be intensely angry at Emma for lying about her destination in the first place. But still, inside, Emma wanted nothing more than to run to her mother and have everything be forgiven, as if all she'd done was miss dinner. But she knew it would not be so simple. Even when things were their bleakest and Emma had had the childish fantasy of burying her face in her mother's skirts to have her hurts soothed away, she'd been impeded in the dream by the sure knowledge that her mother would be livid over her deception.

So now, in the muddy, rain-soaked street, she waited patiently for Lawrence to descend from the wagon and escort her like a stranger to her own door.

And what would her mother say about this odd man she brought home as her husband? Emma intended to put the best possible face on her hasty marriage, portraying it as a positive choice and not one made in desperation. But would her mother see right through the pretense to the colossal mess she had made of her life? Of all things, Emma thought painfully, she hated most being a disappointment to her mother.

Emma drew the line at turning the bell. Steeling herself for she knew not what, she gripped the cold brass knob and let them both into the high white foyer.

Strains of violin music could be heard from the parlor as Emma rounded the opening door warily. The room was lit with more candles than normal, though not nearly as many as they used to use before the war, and fifteen or twenty people milled about, oblivious to the opened door and the bedraggled couple who stood dripping in the marble hallway.

Emma felt odd, a outsider in her own house, and Lawrence suddenly looked more alien than ever against the adverse backdrop of homey familiarity. His face looked haggard with exhaustion, his eyes more dead than usual.

"Perhaps we should . . ." She paused and gazed about the hallway. The cherry bench was missing. "Perhaps we should leave our wet coats on the floor here somewhere."

Lawrence began to comply when he looked behind her and

straightened, donning an imperiously detached countenance over the worn lassitude he'd revealed to her.

Emma heard a swish of petticoats and started to turn.

"Can I help you?" a soft, familiar, feminine voice, rich with a Virginia cadence, asked.

Emma turned fully to gaze into Aunt Caro's bright brown eyes. She stood still as Caro's eyes widened in disbelief, letting the shock of her appearance sink in fully before speaking.

"Hello, Aunt Caro," she said then with a tight smile. How much did they know? What could she expect their reactions to possibly be?

Aunt Caro shrieked. Moving forward with a speed Emma rarely saw in her, she threw her arms around her niece's shoulders and clutched Emma's sopping body against hers. She smelled of homemade soap, Emma noted nostalgically, and her hair against her cheek was the softest thing she'd felt in months.

"Emma Louise! Saints preserve us! The Lord's seen fit to answer our prayers!" She pulled back and beamed into Emma's face. "Child, we thought we'd never see you again." Tears filled her eyes and she swept at them impatiently.

"Eva!" Caro turned to the crowd of people who had begun to gather at the door to the parlor. "Somebody get Eva! The prodigal daughter's returned!" She laughed merrily.

And then Emma was surrounded. Judith ran from the parlor and engulfed her in a painfully tight hug. Peter emerged on crutches, and Mrs. Jenkins, Doc Waters, and Uncle Smith were all there. And then came her mother, who'd been in the kitchen.

Tears welled over Emma's eyes at her mother's expression. No anger, no condemnation, just pure, unadulterated love and relief radiated from her mother's face.

"Oh, Emma," she cried softly, running to her. "Emma, my foolish, foolish child. You're safe." She took her in her arms and pressed Emma's head against her shoulder as she did when Emma was a child. "My darling girl," she breathed, her tears mingling with the wetness of Emma's hair, "what in the world made you think to try such a thing?" But the words were a coo of relief, and her arms could not have been more welcoming. Truly, the prodigal daughter.

She was cocooned in a cloud of warmth and family, drinking it in as one too long in a desert of loneliness. At last, the endless need for stamina was at an end. She thought she could stay in that protected circle forever, until slowly, one person after another began to notice Lawrence.

Though he stood stiffly to one side, he was not one to shrink into the shadows. And when Emma's mother turned her attention to him, he stepped unequivocally forward and held out his hand to her.

"Madam, I am Lawrence Price," he said distinctly, in a manner that seemed to Emma even more haughty than usual. "I apologize for the abruptness of our arrival, and the awkward circumstances under which I am obliged to introduce myself, but it could not be helped."

Her mother offered her hand with a smooth, unconscious grace. "If you helped to bring my daughter home, then I am most grateful to make your acquaintance, Mr. Price."

Emma, seeking somehow to distract everyone from the inevitable, said, "Yes, he did, Mother. He was such a help to me. Have you heard anything about—about my plight?" She stumbled over the words.

Her mother turned sad, kind eyes back to her. "Yes. We received a letter from Will, several weeks ago. It was short, but most compassionate. He told us about your attempt to procure medicines, and said that you'd been caught. But he assured us you were safe and that he'd see you were brought back to us as soon as possible."

Emma felt a sudden inability to catch her breath and was afraid to speak for the emotion welling in her chest.

Her mother turned to Lawrence. "If you are his means of returning Emma to us, then I am most deeply in your debt."

Lawrence fixed his pale eyes on her and bowed coldly. "I thank you for your appreciation, but I am not an agent of William Darcy's." He flicked an unreadable look at Emma, then at her apparent inability to speak, proceeded. ''Perhaps we should have mentioned this immediately, but I, Mrs. Davenport, am your daughter's husband.''

Emma's stomach dropped and the suppressed tears broke free to fill her eyes. Then the whole house took on that awful, alien familiarity again as everyone in the room turned their shocked eyes on her.

Chapter Eleven

September, 1864
Richmond, Virginia

God, how he longed to see her.

Will pulled his slouch hat lower on his brow and leaned back against the warm brick archway of the building. In front of him was the market square—scant blocks from Emma's house—which at this time had little more than greens to offer, at exorbitant prices.

From beneath the shadowed brim of the hat he peered about at the milling crowds of ladies gingerly picking through the meager fare. Surely she would come, one of these days. Just a glimpse of her, that was all he asked. He certainly had no intention of speaking to her, nor even allowing her the opportunity to see him, for that would be far too dangerous. He just needed to know that she was safe. That she'd made it back.

Vaguely, in the back of his mind, the question intruded again: What would he do if she never came, if he never saw her? Would

158

he dare go to her house? Try to see her through the windows late at night, even though Confederate guards roamed the city at all hours in search of able-bodied men to conscribe into their weakening army?

They were desperate, the rebels were. The Federals were firmly entrenched around Richmond and Petersburg, holding the city under siege, only awaiting the right moment to attack and take over. Periodically scouts were sent into the city to gauge the number, readiness, and morale of both the troops and the residents, and now that Will was one of them he planned to use the opportunity for his own ends as well . . . to search for evidence of Emma.

When they'd first arrived near Richmond back in May, Will had been desperate to discover if Emma had made it back, but penetrating the city at that time would not only have been stupendously unwise, it would have been directly against Pinkerton's orders.

Then he'd thought of asking some of the local children who approached the Union troops with their shy questions and blatant curiosity if they either knew the Davenports or had parents who knew them. None of them had, but he did meet one fearless urchin who regularly made trips into Richmond to loot abandoned buildings. He knew the Davenport house—just down the street from Lee's own—and the next time he went, he was under strict instructions to look for Emma Davenport.

The boy came back triumphantly sporting a kepi squashed onto his rumpled hair and showing off a booty of two stale loaves of bread, three buttons from a Confederate officer's uniform, a bum Ketchum grenade, and—oh, yes, he remembered passing the Davenport hospital and seeing "a purty lady with dark hair goin' in with a market basket all fulla bottles and bandages and such like." But that was all.

Enough information to tease, enough ambiguity to make Will crazy.

But now he was here himself, inside the city, dressed as a farmhand in battered clothes and an old slouch hat. He leaned heavily on a crutch and wore stained bandages on his right leg to ward off any questions about his ability to serve in the army, as well as to give the impression of a loyal Confederate.

As the hot September sun beat steadily on the cobblestone square, Will reclined negligently against a wall of the market, hopefully looking as if he'd just unloaded one of the wagons and awaited the end of the day to load it back up. But all the while his quick eyes scanned the crowds for Emma.

Occasionally he'd study a passing officer or well-dressed matron to ascertain if it was someone he knew from his days in Richmond's tight-knit society—the one real fear he had of the assignment—but mostly he searched for Emma. In vain, it seemed.

Will had come a long way from the jealous anger he'd indulged before Emma's disappearance. For it was after he'd discovered that her escape from the city had taken place without him that he regained his senses. As he searched all of Washington for even just a sign of her, imagining every sort of hardship and struggle she might encounter, he felt the obvious truth creep back like a shamed puppy too long gone from its master.

She was innocent. Innocent of the heinous charge of trading sex for secrets, anyway. And the other crimes were, at least to him, justifiable. It was true, she had endangered his family, but he knew now she had not realized it. Her courage had been matched only by her naivety. And the spying, well, it was no worse than what he was doing at this very moment. But he'd been blinded by a jealousy that began with his suspicions of her and Brendan and exploded with the seeming proof of her profligacy with Edmund Bondurant. It was a twisted, possessive, aching rage that had sent him mad with fury at the thought of Emma, his own impeccable, exquisite Emma, with another man's hands upon her. And now he hated himself for the coarse way he'd treated her.

Gen. Bondurant had not taken his own life. A doctor examined the body after the rumors of suicide had coursed through the city, and he had declared that there was no way Bondurant could have had the strength and the exactitude to do what had been done

A Special Offer For
Leisure Romance Readers Only!

Get
FOUR
FREE
Romance
Novels
A $21.96 Value!

Travel to exotic worlds filled with passion
and adventure —without leaving your home!
Plus, you'll save $5.00 every time you buy!

Thrill to the most sensual, adventure-filled Historical Romances on the market today...

FROM ▐▌ LEISURE BOOKS

As a home subscriber to Leisure Romance Book Club, you'll enjoy the best in today's BRAND-NEW Historical Romance fiction. For over twenty-five years, Leisure Books has brought you the award-winning, high-quality authors you know and love to read. Each Leisure Historical Romance will sweep you away to a world of high adventure...and intimate romance. Discover for yourself all the passion and excitement millions of readers thrill to each and every month.

Save $5.⁰⁰ Each Time You Buy!

Each month, the Leisure Romance Book Club brings you four brand-new titles from Leisure Books, America's foremost publisher of Historical Romances. EACH PACKAGE WILL SAVE YOU $5.00 FROM THE BOOKSTORE PRICE! And you'll never miss a new title with our convenient home delivery service.

Here's how we do it. Each package will carry a FREE 10-DAY EXAMINATION privilege. At the end of that time, if you decide to keep your books, simply pay the low invoice price of $16.96, no shipping or handling charges added. HOME DELIVERY IS ALWAYS FREE. With today's top Historical Romance novels selling for $5.99 and higher, our price SAVES YOU $5.00 with each shipment.

AND YOUR FIRST FOUR-BOOK SHIPMENT IS TOTALLY FREE!
IT'S A BARGAIN YOU CAN'T BEAT! A Super $21.96 Value!
▐▌ LEISURE BOOKS   A Division of Dorchester Publishing Co., Inc.

GET YOUR 4 FREE BOOKS NOW—A $21.96 Value!

Mail the Free Book Certificate Today!

4 FREE BOOKS

A $21.96 VALUE

Free Books Certificate

YES! I want to subscribe to the Leisure Romance Book Club. Please send me my 4 FREE BOOKS. Then, each month I'll receive the four newest Leisure Historical Romance selections to Preview FREE for 10 days. If I decide to keep them, I will pay the Special Member's Only discounted price of just $4.24 each, a total of $16.96. This is a SAVINGS OF $5.00 off the bookstore price. There are no shipping, handling, or other charges. There is no minimum number of books I must buy and I may cancel the program at any time. In any case, the 4 FREE BOOKS are mine to keep—A BIG $21.96 Value!

Offer valid only in the U.S.A.

Name _____

Address _____

City _____

State _____ *Zip* _____

Telephone _____

Signature _____

If under 18, Parent or Guardian must sign. Terms, prices and conditions subject to change. Subscription subject to acceptance. Leisure Books reserves the right to reject any order or cancel any subscription.

A $21.96 VALUE

4 FREE BOOKS

Get Four Books Totally FREE – A $21.96 Value!

▼ Tear Here and Mail Your FREE Book Card Today! ▼

PLEASE RUSH
MY FOUR FREE
BOOKS TO ME
RIGHT AWAY!

Leisure Romance Book Club
65 Commerce Road
Stamford CT 06902-4563

AFFIX
STAMP
HERE

with his own hand. Someone had killed him. And that someone, Gen. Ferguson and his cronies all believed, was Emma Davenport. The fact that she could never have gotten into the cell that Bondurant had occupied without having to pass four guards and two outdoor sentries seemed not to matter to those wanting to throw the blame quickly.

But Will knew without a doubt that Emma could never slit a man's throat. And at the moment that indisputable fact hit him, he also knew that she could never sell her body for military information. It was so obvious he wondered how he could ever have believed otherwise.

And now, sweating in the hot Richmond sun, scouring empty faces, hoping she'd made it, praying she was all right, he knew he would never forgive himself for not believing her immediately.

Sweat trickled down his temple. He pulled off his hat, held it so that it blocked any straight-on view of himself, and wiped the side of his face with his sleeve. Damn, it's hot, he thought, pushing the wet brim back onto sweat-dampened hair. Surely hell could not be worse than this combination of anxiety and affliction.

His shirt stuck to his back, and his skin prickled beneath the weight of the sun. He tried to envision, for a second, falling into a cool pool of water, clothes and all, and he closed his eyes with the imagined sensation. The blast of bracing water would instantly cleanse away the dirt and grime that covered him, camouflaging him. Soothing cool fingers of water would lift his hair and bathe his head, unclouding his senses. He would drink of the cold, clear stuff, gallons, then float atop the invigorating, undulating surface.

The picture was so vivid it brought him another vision, one of a dark-haired nymphet in chemise and pantaloons, diving into just such a pool one summer in the mountains of the Shenandoah Valley. They'd gone there, he and Emma, along with all of Emma's family and servants, of course, on a holiday some years ago. It was just two weeks after they'd announced their engagement and they felt as if the world cradled them in feather-soft hands. He'd never been happier in his life. And never would be again, he knew now.

Elaine Fox

They'd stayed at the summer cottage of some friends of Gen. Davenport's. Yankees, Will recalled with a wry smile. And they'd celebrated their engagement with bottles of champagne and apple brandy, and food such as he now believed he would never see again. Pheasant and turkey, beef and smoked ham, summer squash, green beans, sweet corn, and ripe apples. Raspberries, clotted cream, mint juleps.

He and Emma exerted no small amount of cleverness in escaping the watchful eyes of Emma's sharp mother, her domineering father, and her two genial but overbearingly protective brothers, Buck and Peter. Of course, it helped that there was such a vast supply of apple brandy and that Will was so deft at creating cool, soothing beverages with it. All day long, he plied the group with sumptuous drinks, gently but effectively reducing their fears of overindulgence, convincing them it was little more than residual tension from their everyday life that made them decline just one more small one—all the more reason to relax while on holiday.

So eventually, Emma and Will, high on their own drug of exuberance and hope for the future, wandered successfully off together to the relief of privacy at the swimming hole.

Once there, Will stripped immediately and unself-consciously on the rocky overhang above the oxbow lake, while Emma crept behind a boulder to slip out of her summer frock.

He dove in, and relished the shock of exhilaration the coldness induced. From underwater he could see the sun glinting off the ripples above him and he glided upward effortlessly with a smile on his face. He broke from the water to see Emma, feet bare, hair loose, arms crossed over her chest, laughing with embarrassment and delight.

"Is it cold?" she called.

He laughed and flipped wet hair back out of his eyes. She was incredible. Through the sheer material of her shift he could clearly see the perfection of her tiny waist, and the pantaloons proved no barrier to the delicately rounded hips and her strong, slender thighs. He wished she would uncross her arms so he could see

162

the pink, firm peaks he knew were beneath them.

"It's warm. It's a bathtub. Dive in, Emma." He grinned as she laughed again.

"Liar." Her cheeks were delicately flushed and her eyes glittered with unsuppressed delight. "It's cold as a dog's nose and you know it."

He laughed, the sound bouncing joyously off the water and rocks. "A dog's nose? How bad could that be?"

He watched as she uncrossed her arms and pulled her heavy hair behind her in both hands. The unimpeded view this motion gave him caused his breath to catch and his nerves to tingle.

"Come on, Emma," he said gently, his eyes burning into hers. "We're finally alone. Come to me." He stretched a hand out of the water toward her.

She eyed him seriously for a moment. "Right away, darling," she said, her voice a husky purr that sent a shiver of anticipation up his spine. Then her lips curved into a wicked smile.

Before he knew what she was up to, she jumped from the rock, tucked her knees into clasped arms, and landed with a tidal splash that submerged him under rollicking water. He sputtered through the careening waves that plowed into his nose and mouth, and rubbed his eyes to clear them.

She came up laughing, water dripping from her thick black lashes. One hand pushed away the mass of wet hair as she treaded water before his coughing, wheezing form.

"I'm here, dear," she said sweetly, but the wicked smile was back.

He eyed her sourly, extending the cough a bit longer than necessary, then suddenly dove beneath the water, caught her by surprise, and grabbed her feet. He intended simply to pull her under, but while he was there another idea struck him. And before he gave it too much thought, he grasped the waist of her pantaloons and pulled.

Even beneath the water he could hear her shriek, and though he might have paused at that, he also heard her peal of laughter as he pushed away, garment in hand. He came up several yards

163

away in time to see her spinning herself in jerky circles, looking for him.

The moment she laid eyes on him she pointed an imperious finger and commanded, ''William Darcy, you get back here this instant with my underclothes.''

He cocked his head at her and wrapped the legs of the garment around his neck like a scarf. ''Is that the way you'll speak to our children, Emma? Because it sounds a bit unfriendly.''

She raised a haughty eyebrow. ''You and I shall never have children if you do not bring back my drawers this instant.''

He backed up to a rock over which the water lapped and rippled shallowly, and sat, watching her tread water in the depth of the pool.

''Now, Emma, I know it's fashionable for young ladies to appear completely ignorant of all things physical, but if you think that we shall conceive children only when you're wearing your drawers you're in for a considerable shock.''

With a sound of aggravation she dipped under the water for a second. Then, head back and hair sleek behind her, she reemerged a yard or two closer.

''Will,'' she ground out, ''my arms are getting tired.''

''Come sit here,'' he offered, magnanimously sliding over on the rock to make room.

She rolled her eyes, making him smile.

''I'll be the best gentleman I know how to be,'' he swore, raising one hand. His fingers caught in the lace of her pantaloons and he swatted it away impatiently, holding the hand up again primly.

''Well, that's a hollow oath if I've ever heard one,'' she grumbled. ''Really, now, Will. I'm getting tired.''

He smiled sweetly. ''Come here. I'll give them to you for a kiss.''

Her dark eyes held his. She was trying to look angry but he could see the laughter in those dark brown depths. She was the most perfect creature he'd ever seen. She was creamy pale and deepest dark. Fine brows etched against white skin. High cheekbones framed by midnight wet hair . . . hair that swept down over ivory shoulders to float ethereally in the water.

"I love you, Emma," he said with complete sincerity. "Don't you trust me?"

She swam a yard closer, then reached for the rock and pulled herself up. Will unwrapped the drawers from around his neck and handed them to her with a smile, letting his eyes linger on the perfect outline of her breasts molded by the wet chemise. "You're beautiful, you know."

"And you're a cad," she said. But she wasn't angry. In fact she looked as if she were not quite sure what to do with the garment now that she'd gotten it back.

Will let his hand stray to her shoulder, where he traced a rivulet of water down her arm. "Do you love me?" he asked slyly.

Her eyes met his, calm, no-nonsense, knowing he was up to something. "You know that I do."

His finger moved back up her arm, slowing to brush the side of her wet breast. "And so you'll marry me?"

Her lips tilted slightly up as she took a deep, satisfied breath. "You know that I will."

Will was acutely conscious of the narrow current of water lapping between their bodies where they sat in about three inches of water. It was enough to keep the feeling of coolness, the sensuousness of bare skin uppermost in their minds.

His finger circled her taut nipple. He felt a current of excitement shake her body. "And when will you marry me?"

She pushed a wet tendril of hair from her shoulder to her back. "Anytime you want." Her voice was soft, breathy, and her eyes took on a hooded, unconsciously seductive expression.

He felt himself grow hard despite the cool water, felt the fire in his loins. "Now, Emma? Would you marry me now, this moment—this perfect, private moment that belongs only to you and me?"

Her lips parted and her eyes dropped fractionally. He could see the pulse at her throat beat rapidly. She knew just what he meant.

She raised her eyes back to his and they seemed to glow with some undefinable emotion. It was as if she floated in a cloud. "Yes, I would."

The air electrified around them. He reached his other hand out to cup her neck, his thumb at her cheek, and pulled her forward. Their lips met tentatively. They'd kissed many times, done even more than that many times; driving themselves to the brink of complete frustration whenever they were alone together. But now, with the tacit agreement between them, their actions took on an awesome significance.

He traced her lips with his tongue in the same motion his fingers traced her nipple and he felt her shudder. "I love you," he murmured, so softly he wasn't even sure she could hear, but it felt good to say.

He turned more fully toward her and let his hand slide from her neck down her arm to her waist. He pulled her closer, his tongue delving into her mouth as his hand traced the silky wetness of her chemise along firm skin to her hip.

She sighed against his lips, a soft, feminine sound that caused the blood to pound ravenously through the shaft of his manhood. With barest restraint, he pushed her back against the smooth, water-worn surface of the rock. Her arms tightened around his neck, but she leaned back pliantly. One knee came up as she reclined and he let his hand trail from her hip to the juncture of her legs. Beneath the wet material of her shift he could feel the soft hair that covered her most private place. He pulled the wet chemise up with his fingers, an inch at a time.

She stiffened slightly as he reached the end of the material and his hand grazed the bare skin of her inner thighs. He paused, letting his fingers entwine in the hair there. "You're so beautiful," he murmured against her lips. Then his fingers found the spot.

She tried to suppress a gasp of surprise but her eyes flew to his as his fingers parted the folds to probe the silky softness of her. He drew his head back and met her eyes.

"I'll stop anytime you want, Emma," he said quietly, letting his fingers convince her otherwise.

But she drew in a deep, shaking breath and let her head fall back as he moved his fingers back and forth over the sensitive area. "God, no," she breathed. "Don't ever stop."

Her hands clutched his shoulders as her hips raised to meet his rhythmic movements. Blood thundered through his veins at the sight of her straining breasts, her flushed cheeks and parted lips, and he didn't think he could wait much longer.

She moaned when he took his hand away but grabbed his arms as he raised himself over her. She turned on the rock to give them both room to stretch out, and he lowered himself onto her, keeping most of his weight on his elbows.

His hips descended so that his organ touched the sleek wetness his fingers had just stroked. Gently he pushed against her, gritting his teeth against the desire to plunge into her quickly, savagely. Her thighs widened instinctively at the touch. He pushed the tip of his manhood only slightly inside, gauging her readiness, nearly drunk with the nearness, the wetness, the tightness.

"Are you sure, Emma?" he asked, his voice a harsh whisper.

Her eyes opened to his, glazed with an all-seeing intensity. "Yes, Will. I'm sure. I want it." Her face was glowing, determined, sure. A smile, the likes of which he'd never before seen on her face, and which threatened to take what was left of his breath away, curved the lush fullness of her just-kissed lips. "Do it, Will. Make love to me," she whispered.

He groaned and closed his eyes, pushing slowly into the silken cavity. He was clutched by the velvet smoothness inside her, and for a second he thought he'd have to let himself go. But he held his breath and dove further into the heavenly feel of it.

"My God," he breathed.

She answered with an unintelligible murmur.

Then, unable to maintain the lingering pace, he thrust himself forward—hoping the quickness would make it better for her—then he lost all cognizant thought as primal need overtook him.

She gasped once and clung to him, causing him to slow. But after only a second her stiffened muscles relaxed and her legs wrapped around his waist. He twined his fingers in her hair and

167

cupped her head in his hands as he pushed into her with renewed vigor, a torrent of pleasure bursting behind his eyes. Her gasp became panting and her throat issued soft, kittenish sounds of pleasure. Each one sent him further into the abyss. He was consumed by a driving, uncontrollable desire, and she met his movements with a need equaling his, a force equaling his.

Great waves of pleasure engulfed him, sweeping up his body to the ends of his fingers, the crown of his head. He was awash in the feel of her, her skin beneath his hands, her breath on his cheek. The thundering rhythm of the blood through his veins was matched by that of his hips as he plunged into her again and again.

As soon as he heard her shattering gasp of fulfillment and felt her body pulse around him, he let himself go. An explosion of pure passion rocked him from head to toe. Muscles in his arms and shoulders jumped and tensed with the sweet assault to every nerve in his body. Reflections of the sun on the water burst behind his closed eyelids as every ounce of life force emptied from his body into hers.

They lay spent on the sun-soaked rocks for what seemed an eternity before Emma, with a sleepy smile, turned to him and said, "Promise you'll never leave me."

He chuckled at the irony. "Emma, at this moment, I don't think I'll ever even leave this rock."

She'd laughed softly and stroked his hair. After a moment, she'd repeated, more seriously, "Really, Will. Don't ever leave me. I don't think I could bear it. I just love you so much."

He'd caressed her cheek then, and felt such love and devotion well up inside him that he thought he would burst with it. "Emma, you'd have to kill me to get rid of me now."

Which was almost exactly what happened, Will thought with a stabbing pain and the surprising sting of tears behind his closed eyes. She'd sent him away, she'd thrown him out of her life, and it had nearly killed him.

Until the day last winter that she'd shown up again and breathed new life into the dormant love that lay inside him, he'd thought it was dead. He thought he'd mastered it. But all it took was one more look at her, one more chance exposure to her spirit and beauty, and he was captured again, newly alive, newly imprisoned.

He opened his eyes to the bustling marketplace around him. What a long way they were now from that blissful time in the Shenandoahs. He stood in a Richmond market, sweltering in a spy's skin, just blocks from that familiar mansion on Franklin Street, and yet he could not seek her, could not speak to her, could not even acknowledge her if she happened by. She should have been his wife by now. They would have had children most likely, one probably two or three years old. The thought made him almost queasy with longing. How had things gotten so warped? Was this war to go on forever? War between North and South, war between ethics and ideology, war between love and honor . . .

The market tables before him swam with the heat. He closed his eyes and rubbed the sweat from them with his fingers. Good God, he was getting light-headed from the sun. He pulled a bandanna from his pocket and mopped his face.

It was the pressure, he thought, swallowing hard. He took off his hat, momentarily forgetting his disguise, and peered up into the relentless summer sky. It was only perspiration that caused his eyes to sting so, heat and airlessness that put that tightness in his throat. . . . He ran the bandanna along his damp hairline. He needed some water. He looked around the square for someone with a dipper and bucket. Surely there was at least some water. . . .

He straightened abruptly from his leaning posture to venture forth in search of water. But he lost hold of his crutch with the motion and was only able to graze it with his fingers before it clattered to the ground. Heads swiveled to the noise so he bent swiftly, hiding his face and trying to favor his right leg as he reached out for the thing. But before he could get to it he saw it lifted by a slim, feminine hand.

He tried to rise without putting weight on the supposedly bad leg, but had to hop several times on the other foot to avoid tumbling forward into the skirts of she who held the crutch. But when he gathered his balance and looked into her face he nearly capsized again.

She gasped, eyes wide and mouth open, and nearly dropped the crutch.

Will squashed his hat back down on his head and grabbed the crutch as it left her fingers. ''Thank y', ma'am,'' he said into her frozen face.

She stood motionless, the woman he'd just made love to again, if only in memory.

He nodded curtly and tipped his hat, pushing it even lower on his brow this time. ''Thank y', ma'am,'' he said again, in an identically numbed tone.

She snapped her mouth shut and nodded jerkily back once. Then she spun and moved swiftly through the crowd, heedlessly pushing people aside, to disappear onto the street.

Emma. He let out a long, slow breath, his heart still threatening to erupt out of his chest. She was alive. She'd made it. She'd slipped out of Washington and gotten safely through two lines of war to make it home. She was thin and she was pale, but she was more beautiful than ever, his brave, brilliant Emma.

His eyes still watched the gap in the crowd through which she'd disappeared. *Emma.* She was safe. Thank God, she was safe.

And now, with just a word, she could have him killed for real.

Chapter Twelve

Emma strode rapidly down the street, barely breathing. In front of her she saw nothing but the suntanned face and clear gray eyes of Will Darcy—in homespun farmer's garb at a Richmond market.

She felt her breath shorten with the long, fleeing strides but dared not slow for a second lest her panic overtake her. Will Darcy, in Richmond, spying. She needed to flee, to escape the deception, because in one way or another she would surely have given him away.

Her heart thundered in her chest and her cheeks burned from more than just the sun's rays. How could he have come here, of all places? For God's sake, Emma wasn't the only one who could recognize him. There were dozens of people, perhaps hundreds, who would know him on sight. He'd be arrested—or worse. Spies were always treated more harshly than other prisoners of war because of a general feeling that they were not playing by the rules—they were cheaters. Therefore they were worthy of a fate no better than that which a pack of marauding wolves might receive.

At last, unable to maintain the pace, Emma slowed her stride, then stopped and leaned against a lamppost, panting. She ran a shaking hand across the perspiration on her forehead and swallowed hard. What was she to do? How could she keep such a heinous secret? And how could she continue to live her life normally, knowing he was so close? She closed her eyes and reveled momentarily in the memory of the sight of him. How had it come about that she could not go to him, smile at him, tell him how happy she was to see that he was alive and, for the most part, well?

She opened her eyes and looked about herself. There was no one around. She straightened, shifted her empty basket to her left hand, and ran the other primly down the skirt of her dress. One thing was certain. She had to forget about seeing him. She could not give away his presence to anyone or something awful would happen to him. Even the people she trusted could let something slip in an unguarded moment. No, she had to go back to her home and her husband—and live normally, as if nothing unusual had happened at all.

Not that her life could be said to be normal, she thought with a small, wry burst of cynicism. She lived in a house full of wounded and dying men, she worked with friends and relatives with whom she barely spoke, and she shared a bed with a stranger she could not even like.

She pictured again Will's face as he saw it was she who held his crutch. He'd been stunned, that much was obvious. But how could he have thought he would not see her? He was so close to her house. Had he taken the risk intentionally, or was he reluctant to be there? Could he possibly have forgotten how close she lived to that market? Or did he for some reason think that she was still imprisoned in Washington?

The questions were too numerous and unanswerable for her to ponder. All she knew was that Will Darcy was in Richmond, even now not two blocks from her house, and there was nothing she could do about it. She certainly couldn't go back and talk to him, ask him what he was doing here, ask him how she was supposed to keep this secret—just speaking with him might give him away. And besides, after their last parting, she was not sure he would participate in a conversation of any sort with her.

And she absolutely wouldn't go to Lawrence, regardless of the fact that he'd once been a friend of Will's. He was the most devoted Confederate she'd ever seen, constantly warning her of the evils that Yankees were capable of and telling her just what to do when they finally did break through Richmond's defenses and swarmed the city. She was to disappear as quickly as she could—out of the city completely, if possible—in order to avoid the dire, unspeakable fate she would suffer at the hands of such an ungodly enemy. And then he would go on to recount horrible, bloody stories of the retribution practiced on the Union prisoners by the Confederate guards where he worked at Libby Prison. Surely, he would add at the end of the particularly gruesome ones, the Yankees will be looking for revenge on behalf of those prisoners.

Then he would fix her with those pale moon eyes and say, "They'll have no compunction about making even the most mindless Southern belles pay for the atrocities of this war, Emma."

The mere thought of it made her shiver. In fact, the mere thought of Lawrence made her shiver. He still had not touched her, to her profound relief, and she was fairly sure he never would. Indeed, he seemed almost repulsed by her on the rare nights when he was home in time to see her undress for bed.

It was fortunate, but still somewhat odd to her, that most every night Lawrence stayed late into the evening either at work or at one of his *secret spy* meetings, as Emma mentally called them. Though he had a job at Libby, Lawrence had indeed become an asset to the clandestine efforts of the Confederacy. When it was discovered that Lawrence's original contact had been killed, Emma had introduced him to Gen. Carruthers, a longtime friend of her father's, who was very high up in the Confederate secret

173

service. Gen. Carruthers had taken Lawrence under his wing and, as he mentioned later to Emma, had found him to be a very valuable participant in the chancy game they played.

Though she was happy he was a benefit to the Cause, Emma was particularly glad that the activity kept Lawrence away from the house for such large blocks of time. His presence had become so oppressive to her, indeed to everyone in the house, that she was beginning to feel suffocated by her own life. Everything she did Lawrence suggested how she might do better. Everything she said in his presence was in some way naive, or erroneous, or sometimes just plain stupid. And even though he had no designs on Emma as his wife in a physical way, he had some very strict ideas about the sort of wife she should be in other ways.

The most irritating was that when he was in the house she was expected to wait on him hand and foot, to the exclusion of all else, including her duties in the hospital. Another tiresome requirement was the endless circuit of parties and socials he required she attend with him. Now that the Confederate Army was so close at hand, defending the city now besieged by Union forces, there were far more soldiers in town than ever before. Gen. Lee had even given his approval for socials of all sorts to be held in order to improve the morale of the men. So the townsfolk went out of their way to accommodate him. This meant that Emma had to accompany Lawrence to every social and introduce him to everyone she knew, even people she knew only by sight.

The barrage of social activity might have done a lot to relieve her depression from working with the wounded all day, but Lawrence's presence and demands made it an uncomfortable activity. If she did not pay sufficient attention to him in public he would chastise her later. If she did not show him what he considered to be enough respect or if she did not keep quiet when he spoke, she was reprimanded, frequently in front of others. If she dared argue or even disagree with him, which she had done once or twice in the beginning, she was cut to the quick by a scathing insult, a haughty condescension, or the swift reminder, if they were alone, of her moral turpitude to keep her quiet and put her in her place.

But even worse than the public embarrassment was the humiliation she suffered during their private quarrels. He never failed to remind her of her "promiscuous sexual history," as he referred to her relationship with Will, and pointed it out as the most disgusting moral failure that could afflict a young lady. It was also no doubt the cause of her other lapses into sinfulness, such as her tendency toward impertinence, her selfishness, her flightiness, and, most wickedly, her "openly inviting and flirtatious ways with the patients."

Emma could barely stand to think about his accusations, for though she knew that he was being deliberately cruel, he always had concrete reasons for the accusations he made. She did tend toward the impertinent, speaking her mind the way she did, though she had learned to control it of late. And she knew she must seem flighty to him, for whenever she saw him coming she got flustered and tried hard to avoid any situations that might awaken his ire—such as talking too long to one person, or volunteering any substantial thoughts or opinions in a conversation. As to being flirtatious, she did try to be nice to the men in the hospital, for it seemed to cheer them up, though lately she confined herself to tending the unconscious men and managing the removal of the corpses, something no one else wanted to do anyway.

Several times Judith or Peter, even her mother once or twice, had tried to talk to her about her marriage. But Emma was so ashamed of her reasons for marrying—namely fear for her precious reputation and her pathetic gratitude to Lawrence—that she was reluctant to confide in anyone that she'd married for any reason other than a desire for the match. Though she could not bring herself to feign love.

And then there was the inadvertent way she'd compromised the Darcys that fueled her guilt and kept her half-believing the things Lawrence said of her. She still could not recall what possessed her to use them in such a way, what prompted her to think that it was all right to employ their house to, essentially, spy from. She could only chalk it up to that selfishness that Lawrence saw in her.

In any case, it all amounted to her estrangement from her friends and family. It was easier to exist in her own world, to separate herself mentally from not only her husband, but from all those things that would make him angry. For when he was angry he intruded upon her self-made cocoon and made life an ugly hell, as opposed to the quiet solitude she was able to make for herself by ignoring that which was around her.

She took the long route home, calming herself after the disturbance of seeing Will and telling herself that there was nothing she could do about his presence. Though she knew Lawrence would consider it another moral failure not to turn Will in, she simply could not do it. Besides, she thought dismally, how much damage could one more spy do? The enemy was so close to invading the city anyway, it seemed only a matter of time before it happened. And she was so tired of war, so bone-wearily exhausted and depleted, that sometimes she almost believed she didn't care who won anymore, as long as the bloody thing ended.

But that was blasphemy, she knew. And she would certainly never dare to utter such a thought in the presence of her husband. Instead she just plugged along in her routine, putting all thoughts, interesting or upsetting, into a mental room she never visited. It was to this room that she sentenced Will Darcy now. Before, if she thought of him at all, it was memories of the days before the war when they were so happy. No match could have been more perfect, she'd thought then. They were alike in so many ways, and yet different enough to always be stimulating to each other. But most important, they'd been in love. Desperately, completely, deliriously in love.

In her stronger moments she was thankful to have the memories, to at least have experienced such a love. But in her weak moments, of which there were many, many more, she found the memories far more painful than she could bear, and the experience seemed a cruel jest compared to the life she now led.

She let herself into the house quietly, hoping to attract no notice. But Judith was just descending the stairs as she closed the door.

"There you are," Judith said. "We've been waiting on those turnips for the stew—" She arrived at the base of the stairs and peered into Emma's empty basket. "Where are they? Did you already give them to Cass?"

Emma untied her bonnet slowly, folded the ribbons around it, and set it on the makeshift hall table. "No, I, ah, arrived at the market and experienced such a wave of dizziness. . . ." She pressed her own forehead with the back of her hand. "It must have been the heat."

Judith's eyes became dark with concern. "You do look pale, Emma." She approached and pressed her forearm where Emma's hand had just been. "You feel a little warm. Why don't you go upstairs and I'll bring you some cool water?"

Emma shook her head. "You've got enough to do without waiting on me, too. I'll just go up and lie down a little while."

"Nonsense," Judith stated. "You go ahead; I'll be up in a minute. You've been working yourself to the bone lately. You deserve a little waiting on."

Emma would have protested further but Judith held up a hand and walked purposefully off toward the back, saying, "I'll only be a minute." And anyway, some cool water in a darkened room sounded heavenly to Emma. She ascended the stairs.

As she approached her bedroom she anticipated the bliss she would feel spending even just an hour alone. Lawrence was almost never home during the day, and at night Emma worked so late she frequently passed out quickly, so that before she knew it Lawrence had come and gone and it was morning again.

But this day it was different. As soon as she entered the room she saw him, sitting on the bed, for the desk had long since been sold for food or scrapped for firewood, with papers spread about him. His thin hair was mussed and his shirt was loosened at the neck.

He looked up from his work and pinned her with hard, impersonal eyes. "What are you doing up here at this hour?" he asked.

Emma's hand flew nervously to her forehead again; then she moved it to pat some loose strands of hair into place. "I-I felt dizzy. I thought I'd lie down a moment."

His eyelids drooped fractionally and he raised a palm over his papers. "As you can see, that would be impossible. I'm busy here."

Emma backed one step toward the door. "I see. All right." She started to turn, doorknob in hand, when Judith appeared behind her carrying a dripping glass of water.

"Now you just come right in here—" She took Emma by the arm and started to bustle her through the door when she too caught sight of Lawrence. She froze momentarily. Then, taking a deep breath, she dropped Emma's arm and moved further into the room. "Mr. Price, might I ask that you move your business elsewhere, perhaps to the parlor? You see, your wife had a dizzy spell this afternoon and I think it best that she lie down."

Lawrence looked at her coldly. "I'm afraid that's not possible. As you can see, I'm hardly presentable to the public in my current state of disarray, and the work I am endeavoring to complete is most important. I'm sure my wife will be fine if she sits for a moment." He indicated a wooden stool by the window that had recently been used by someone patching a leak.

Judith's cheeks reddened and a look of angered determination blossomed in her eyes.

Emma stepped forward quickly. "He's right, Judith. I'll be fine if I sit for a moment or two." And she really would be, if she could just get out of this room.

"He's not right," Judith asserted, turning an indignant glare back to Lawrence. "Mr. Price, if you could even make just a bit of room to one side . . . Surely you can see that Emma needs the rest, if only for a short while."

"Miss Spencer," Lawrence intoned, "you obviously have no idea of the importance of my work. If my wife is tired, it is not sufficient reason to impede the progress of the Confederate Cause—"

178

"The Confederate Cause can surely wait out the course of an exhausted woman's nap!" Judith snapped.

Lawrence drew himself up slowly. It was only a slight straightening of the shoulders but to Emma it seemed a far larger motion. "The Cause waits for no one," he said icily.

There was something about his mood that caused even more weariness than usual in Emma. It was clear to her that she would suffer for this confrontation later. "Really, Jude," she said with a hard look at her friend. "I'm fine now. Don't worry. Just being inside the house has helped."

Judith spun on her and swung a hand out in exasperation. "You're not fine, Emma. Look at yourself. You're white as a sheet and thin as a reed, and you've been tiptoeing around this brute of a husband of yours ever since you got back!"

"Judith, please!" Emma shot a quick glance at Lawrence. His eyes narrowed dangerously.

Judith continued. "And you, sir, have given no thought to the well-being of your own wife. Has it occurred to you that paleness and fainting spells are symptoms of a woman in a family way? She could well be with child."

Astounded, Emma's mouth dropped open and she felt an immediate urge to throw up.

Lawrence stood abruptly and glared at Emma. "She'd better not be," he said in a deadly quiet tone.

Judith stared at him. "I beg your pardon?"

Lawrence strode across the bare floor to Emma and gripped her arms in his long, bony fingers. "Well?" His eyes froze her where she stood. "Is what she said true? Are you with child?"

Emma swallowed and looked at him incredulously. "Of course not!" She stepped back, shrugging off his grip. He released her immediately. "Of course I'm not with child. Judith, whatever made you say such a thing?" Astonishment at Judith's words and alarm over Lawrence's response caused the question to emerge much harsher than she intended.

Judith looked mortified. Whether she was shocked at Lawrence's reaction, the escalation of the scene, or Emma's sharp words, was hard to tell. "I'm sorry," she said in a forced, dignified tone. Her eyes reflected confusion as she looked at Emma, her voice defensive. "I only meant to help."

Emma felt panic edging around her, tweaking her nerves. She knew *she* would pay for Judith's words, but would Lawrence's wrath extend to her friend? She looked into her husband's white face, at the vein that throbbed in his temple. Her gaze locked on her husband's pale glare. "Please go, Judith," she said simply.

Judith started to leave, then turned to Lawrence. "I'm sorry for what I called you, Mr. Price," she said stiffly. "But I do think she needs to lie down."

When Lawrence didn't answer, she turned and left the room, closing the door with exaggerated care behind her.

The click of the closing door had barely been heard when Lawrence's hand whipped out and slapped Emma hard across the face. Emma's head jerked with the force of it and she gasped, stunned, unable to stop involuntary tears.

"You stupid, stupid woman," he hissed at her. "How dare you bring such disgrace upon me?"

Emma clutched her cheek in her hand. "Disgrace?"

"Have you lain with someone? Are you with child?" he demanded, voice rising.

She took a step back, heart thundering in her ears with fear and outrage. "No!"

"Don't look so appalled, my *dear*. It's not so unbelievable. We both know you'll throw that whore's body of yours around wherever you please." He stood close without touching her, one pale hand fisted between them. "But if I find out you've had carnal knowledge of someone I'll make sure you go directly to your place in hell." His face was suffused with red, and his already mussed hair shook with his rage.

Emma had difficulty finding her voice. This fury was beyond anything she'd ever seen. "I haven't—"

Lawrence ignored her. "It's disgusting," he continued, his lips curling with the words, "those people thinking you might be with child. How dare you let them believe that?"

Confusion swept her. Was he jealous? Or was the mere thought of pregnancy repugnant to him? He acted as if people could possibly surmise a baby from her would not be his. "But even in their groundless suppositions people would think it was your child," she protested.

"My child!" he scoffed and gave her a disgusted look. "As if I would touch that soiled body of yours. God knows how many others have had their hands on you, mauling your breasts, putting themselves inside your little box of feminine sin. I'd as soon wallow in a trough with a pig," he spat.

The words were more of a blow than his hand had been. Though he'd been malevolent for some time, he had never been so vehemently malicious. "I've told you," she insisted, her voice low and quaking with indignation. "There was only Will. No one else has touched me. Not *you*, not anyone."

"I don't even like them thinking that I touch you," he spat, then shook as a small tremor overtook him. "It's disgusting."

Emma held her breath as she was struck by a sudden clarity. "Shall I tell them you don't, then?" she asked quietly. "Shall I tell them you shudder with revulsion at the sight of me? How would that play with this charade you insist on perpetuating?"

His already cool eyes frosted completely. "You'll say nothing," he growled.

But she couldn't stop. Her anger pushed her beyond fear, beyond sense. "Perhaps I shall tell them how warped you really are, Lawrence. Do you think anyone would be surprised about what a perverse, unnatural marriage this really is?" Her voice rose with the words until he whirled on her again.

The *crack* of skin against skin split the room. Emma's cheek stung as if burnt and her head snapped sideways, but she did not move.

Silence reigned as she turned her face back to him and they glared at one another. Finally Lawrence's voice rose like molten lava from the chasm between them. "You slut." Her breath left her as if he'd actually struck her in the gut. "Have you forgotten what I've done for you?" he snarled. "I saved your useless, ornamental life. I plucked you from the threshold of death after your stupid, disastrously inept failure to do even one simple thing

181

right for your *cause*," he sneered. "And you, what have you done in return? You've burdened me with worries and rumors and then watched as I worked to make a significant contribution to the world." He bent to her face, close enough that she could smell his breath and see a wild, unhinged look in his eyes. "Cream rises to the top, Emma," he breathed ominously. "And everything else sinks. That's how I know that if I wait long enough one day you'll come to me carrying some bastard child, expecting me to take care of it. Well, I'm telling you right now, I'll kill you if I find you've copulated. I will. I'll slit your throat."

Emma stood paralyzed, one hand clinging to her cheek. He was crazy, she suddenly knew. The look on his face was rabid. Her anger evaporated and a bone-deep terror took its place. She tried to move but could not. She was transfixed by his shimmering eyes and the sudden silence of the room.

Finally, he straightened and stepped back. His expression was glazed by a sort of other-worldliness, as if he'd just been in the grip of a spirit more powerful, more deadly than his own.

"Now go," he muttered.

She tried to bend her locked knees and dipped suddenly when she succeeded, catching herself awkwardly against the bedpost. He turned coldly detached eyes on her stumble.

"I won't come back," she said low, half-thinking he would be glad to know it but in the back of her mind knowing there was no place else to go.

One thin eyebrow raised calmly. "You'll come back," he said. "You'll come back because I need you."

A chill racked her body as she backed toward the door.

He didn't move, but his eyes held hers with an eerie fascination. "You can't escape from me, Emma, so don't even try it. I can find you. I *will* find you."

Her fingers found the knob behind her. It was warm beneath her cold fingers.

Lawrence's voice was strangely calm. "It's only when I don't need you that you'll exit this masquerade of ours, Emma. When I don't need you, and not before."

Chapter Thirteen

The heavy rumble of guns, cannon, and mortar shells racked the very air. Though the fighting was nearly eight miles away, Emma felt the cloud of dread as if it hovered directly over her head.

She straightened from her position over one of the many new occupied pallets in the foyer and brushed the hair out of her face with a sweat-dampened forearm. Pressing a hand to the small of her back, she arched her spine against fatigue and looked around at the fifteen or twenty new wounded, fresh from the fighting at Fort Harrison. Would they even have enough water? she wondered. For at this point there was so little they could do for the men that cool, clean water seemed precious enough.

"Miz Price!" The door slammed back against the inner wall, and the thundering roll of less-distant gunfire filled the hall. It was Dee, one of Aunt Caro's houseboys who had been recruited to help tear clothes into bandages and boil those used ones that were salvageable.

He clattered across the marble in oversize boots he'd taken from one of the dead.

"They're bringin' more!" he announced breathlessly, glancing back behind himself as if he'd been chased by a corpse. "There're so many more! Miz Polivah say she ain't taking more and this is the only place lef'!"

Emma sighed and handed him the canteen she'd been using to distribute water. "Here, keep going down this line. I'll try to find Mrs. Jenkins. We can't possibly take another man."

Dee nodded vehemently. "That's what I told 'em. I told them that already."

Emma pressed her fingers to her eyes. She'd been awake for twenty-four hours and her eyes burned with fatigue and the ambient sulfur that hung in the air. "Well, I'll just have to tell them again."

She stepped over a limp set of legs and moved to shut the door. But she paused midway as she looked out onto the street. Everywhere were wagons and mules loaded down with wounded. Old men carried stretchers filled with Richmond's youth toward homes that had been opened for shelters. The hospital was full, the doctors scarce. Even the Davenports' makeshift infirmary was beyond capacity.

Walking swiftly through the busy streets in a long, hoopless gown and carrying a fully laden basket over one arm was Judith. Just the sight of her sent a feeling of comfort and control coursing through Emma. Since the beginning of the war, when Judith had come to stay with them after losing her mother to cholera, she'd been a mainstay for Emma. She was strong, wise, witty when needed, and always sympathetic, and Emma didn't know what she would have done without Judith and her uncanny resourcefulness. Even now she carried a basket full of bandages when everyone in the city was clamoring for what linens could be found.

"Emma!" she called, and waved a hand imperatively to stay her. Breathlessly, she strode up the walk to the stoop. "Fort Harrison's falling," she announced, eyes sober with fear and concern. "Soldiers just off at the depot said we're going to lose it. One man said he'd lay money on the Yankees taking over Richmond by nightfall.''

Emma felt her breath go shallow, and her eyes bore into Judith's perspiring face. "They're invading?" she breathed.

Judith shook her head and untied the laces of her bonnet with one hand. "Not yet. Our only hope is that Lee can shore up our defenses west of the fort. The way I understand it, Harrison's as good as lost now."

"Lost," Emma repeated on a long expulsion of air. "My God, they're so close. What will they do if they invade?"

Judith shook her head and brushed at the sheen of moisture on her forehead with delicate fingers. "I don't know. I just can't believe they'd be able to get past Lee. He's got practically our whole army down there!"

Emma's lips pursed wryly. "The last couple hours I've started to believe we've got most of it in here."

Judith's mouth dropped open in despair. "Oh, no. Not more?"

Emma nodded. "Dee did what he could, but he's just a boy. Poliver said we're the only place left with even floor space."

Eyes closed, Judith sighed. Then she took a deep breath. "Well. This is the best I could do." She held up the basket of bandages. Perhaps enough for three, maybe four, men. Not the fifteen that had arrived in her absence.

"And that is a miracle," Emma said, putting her arm around Judith's shoulders and walking her into the hall. "Have you slept at all?"

Judith laughed shortly. "I think I dozed off for five minutes or so waiting at the depot for Dr. Wilcox." Emma laughed. "Anyway, I'm no more tired than you, or your mother, or Mrs. Jenkins, or any of the others." She stopped short inside the door and sighed at the sight of so many more men.

"It's not as bad as it looks," Emma soothed. "Most of them just need stitches."

Judith rolled her eyes at her. "You're lying to me."

Emma smiled. "That's right. And didn't it sound nice?"

All through the day the women in the house on Franklin Street worked at cleaning, feeding, watering, stitching, and doing whatever was within their power to make the torn and mutilated men more comfortable.

Emma's mother was a tower of strength, directing people and materials wherever they were most needed and keeping track of it all with masterful precision. They worked until they were dead on their feet, and until the ceaseless thunder of guns became one with the perpetual moans of suffering from the wounded.

Peter, his leg now healed enough to allow him some mobility, made himself useful scrubbing down tables after stitches or amputations, and helping to monitor men in need of watching after surgery. The Davenport house was lucky enough to have a doctor twice a week for a half day, so they made the best use of it by accepting some of the more seriously wounded men.

But all day long, no matter how busy the clinic became there was no escaping the constant dread of enemy invasion. Every blast of cannon that sounded closer than the others, whether by a shifting of the breeze or actual retreat, sent them all into a frenzy of activity to distract themselves and the men they tended. Though, Emma noticed, the soldiers fresh from battle were far less jumpy about the prospect of invasion than the civilians. She marveled at their ability to ignore the constant battle noise, but she guessed that after being in the thick of it they probably couldn't even hear it at this distance.

It was shortly after dark when the shelling stopped. Emma hadn't even noticed it was gone until her mother, as scrubbed and tireless-looking as ever, found her in the back parlor, kneeling by the unconscious form of a hollow-eyed, white-faced corporal who would probably not make it through the night.

The first she noticed of her mother was the cool, delicate hand on her forehead. "You're exhausted," her mother's calm voice stated. "Why don't you go on to bed for a while?"

Emma shook her head and looked up into her mother's dark, sympathetic eyes. "I don't think I could sleep now. I'm still running on nervous energy. Why don't you sleep, Mother?"

Her mother regarded her thoughtfully. "You saw him come in, didn't you?"

"Who?" Emma asked, but her gaze slid away from her mother's.

"You know who. You're going to have to straighten this out, Emma Louise," she said firmly. "This is no way to start a marriage, with avoidance and fear."

It was true. She *had* seen Lawrence enter and make his arrogant way past the carnage to their room. He'd been gone all day, either at the prison or somewhere else, but Emma didn't care which it was. She only wished whatever he'd been doing had kept him longer. She was grateful he had no desire to help in the hospital, for, as ironic as it seemed even to her, the time that he was away and she worked until she was weary to the bone, was time far more happily spent than the three or four dark hours they were alone together to sleep.

It wasn't as if he were violent to her, or even mean, after their last confrontation. He just made her feel anxious and unhappy in a way that was much more vivid than when she tended to other people's needs.

"You're right," she said quietly. "I know. We just need to get past"—she swung a limp hand over the sleeping bodies around her—"this."

Mrs. Davenport pulled up her skirt with one hand and knelt beside her daughter. Casually, but with care, she reached a slim white hand out to feel the pulse in the corporal's wrist. "You know," she said softly, "sometimes the moment we're waiting for, the perfect moment for everything to become right, sometimes that moment never comes. And then something else happens and it's too late."

Emma sighned inwardly, feeling acutely sad that this close motherly chat had to be wasted on a situation so hopeless.

"Emma," her mother said firmly.

Emma turned obedient eyes to her mother.

"You married this man, and in a lot of haste. There must have been something there to create such urgency in you. I know you very well, my girl." She put unyielding fingers beneath Emma's chin. "You do nothing without thought. Now I did not feel the need to remonstrate when you brought home a perfect stranger as husband—a man about whom we knew nothing and whose family are strangers to us. I trusted you to have made the wise decision you are capable of. And I trust you now to abide by that decision and make the best of it."

Desolation swamped Emma. It was only at moments like these that the permanence of her situation became obvious to her. Most of the time her marriage seemed just one more hardship of war to be endured. Not a lifelong commitment that would be with her long after the shooting stopped.

She blinked rapidly to hide her tears, but her mother's eyes were relentless. "I know. And I will. It's just—" She struggled to maintain steadiness in her voice. "Right now I just can't seem to calm down enough to . . ." She swallowed. "Enough to see things clearly."

She took her mother's hand in hers and pulled it to her lap, bowing her head.

"I will work to make things right. Just . . . I can't. . . ." She looked up. "Not tonight."

Mrs. Davenport patted the clasped hands in her daughter's lap and said nothing. Then she looked back at the sleeping corporal.

Emma wondered what her mother truly thought of her marriage. Did she see past the effort of it, past the estrangement, to the basic absurdity? Was her mother able to see how stupid her daughter had been? Or did she have such faith in Emma that she believed there was something other than a desperate, momentary expedience to the marriage?

"Please go get some rest, Mother," Emma said in a more controlled voice. "I'd like to keep an eye on Corporal Simon. If I don't I'll just lie awake worrying about him anyway."

Her mother nodded. "All right, then. I'll get up about three and relieve you. But think about what I've said."

"I will. Where's Judith?"

"She's gone to bed. She was taking care of those two little

girls down the street who were scared to pieces after all the gun-fire and didn't want to be alone. When she came back she was exhausted.''

Emma stroked the back of her mother's hand absently. "Poor things. Imagine growing up in times like these."

Her mother's eyes grew dark. "I know it. I think about that often."

Guilt assailed her for adding yet another negative thought to her mother's burdens, and she searched for something positive to say. But her mind flagged with the effort and she could think of nothing to do other than to give her mother a quick squeeze.

"It will all be all right," she said. "You'll see. As soon as the war is over everything will be right as rain." She smiled at her mother's dubious look. "Well, at least don't worry about me. My problems are small and very fixable with some time and some quiet. As soon as things calm down Lawrence and I will talk and everything will be fine."

Her mother's lips curled in a tolerant smile. "Don't wait until things calm down; they may never. Do it soon."

Emma nodded. "I know. I will. Promise."

"All right, then."

Emma helped her mother to her feet. Now that she'd been convinced to get some rest, her mother looked more in need of it than ever. Gone was the tight stoicism around her mouth, the calm, competent look in her eyes. Her youthful face seemed to sag with the prospect of sleep, and her searching gaze turned inward to her own worries.

Emma gave her another quick hug. "Thank you, Mother. And really, everything will be fine."

Fine, fine, everything will be fine. The words echoed in her head long after her mother had left the room. Maybe if she thought it often enough it would become true. A yawn overtook her. As she sat amid the long slow breathing and occasional snores of the men around her, Emma felt a calm steal over her.

Strange that it was just a simple ceremony that allowed her to be here, alone, among these men, when really that ceremony had produced no knowledge that she hadn't possessed before. She was a married woman now, and supposedly well versed in the ways of men simply because she'd spoken the simple words of fidelity. But, ironically, if it hadn't been for Will, she would know nothing of marriage, or love, or sex.

Unexpectedly she felt a warm blush of yearning sweep her at the thought of Will, and making love. He'd been so sweet, so passionate, so compelling, she thought with a tightness in her chest. For the first time since the war began she allowed her memory to present an image she had long since banished to the back of her mind—the sight of Will, white dress shirt unbuttoned to the waist, hair mussed, and eyes fluid with desire as he deftly pulled down the sleeves and the low sweeping décolletage of her ball gown. Her breasts, high and firm over the strict confinement of the corset, stood peaked with excitement, reaching for his touch.

It was again 1860, and they were engaged. The house reverberated with the sounds of the Davenports' annual Christmas ball, as Emma and Will sat alone on a low settee in the pitch darkness of a small sitting room.

Emma's arms encircled Will's shoulders as his burnished head dipped and his lips closed over one taut nipple. She arched back with pleasure, waves of sensuality tingling along her skin, up her neck, down the insides of her thighs. She felt a delicious abandonment of thought as her body gave in to the craving, the scintillation of his tongue on her bare breast, his hands along her naked back.

She reveled in his passion even as the noise of the party swirled two rooms away. Her fingers threaded through the clean softness of his hair. She felt the flush of an uncontrollable hunger when he laid her back against the pillowed arm of the settee. Silk sleeked up her bare thigh as his hands pulled up her skirt and cool air touched exposed flesh. A pulsing desire, a blinding urgency, ruled her and she fumbled at the buttons on his pants.

Her fingers sought and relished the impossibly soft skin of his manhood, the hard, throbbing thickness of it. His callused hand pulled at her thigh and it rose obediently to circle his hips. The other followed. He slid easily inside her, the movement practiced yet ever new, their need mirrored body to body. Sensations rippled through her and she moaned, her head thrown back. His lips found the sensitive skin of her neck below her ear and tickled, teased, devoured, as he dove inside her and back, over and over.

They scaled the pinnacle together, both stiffening, then shuddering the consummation as their love was sealed, yet again.

"God, you taste good," Will murmured against her throat, as they lay spent on the sofa.

"Hmmm," was all she could say.

"Do you think they miss us?" His words were tantalizing breaths against her ear.

"I don't care."

His slow, sensual laugh caused her heart to race. "Can we do this at all of our parties?" Lightly, his hands pushed her sleeves back up, fingers lingering over still-taut nipples as he straightened the bodice. She shivered with delight.

She licked her lips. "Let's tell them all to go home," she said, eyeing him through half-closed, sated eyes.

His smile was soft, his eyes still hungry. "Ah, but then I would have to leave, too, my love."

She sighed languidly. "No. Let's never leave this room. We'll live here forever, together."

She had danced like a sylphid that night, a magical, enchanted maiden bewitched and enthralled by her seducer. But she'd had power of her own, too, for she knew as deeply as knowledge went, that her lover was enthralled by her as well. And it was that knowledge that made life worth living . . . those moments, that feeling, that gave her strength, belief, and even self. What did she have now?

A sudden, loud pounding at the front door brought her instantly to her feet. She must have dozed, she thought sluggishly, straining to determine whether she'd dreamed the unexpected noise. All around her the sedated patients slept.

A moment of silence reigned before the pounding erupted

again. Emma swiftly moved toward the parlor door.

More pounding echoed through outer rooms. One of the men stirred. Emma stepped over the last sleeping man and swung open the parlor door. She pulled it closed just as another barrage threatened the hinges of the front door.

Her heart rivaling the insistent hammering at the door, she fumbled with the lock, then yanked the door open.

"Buck!" she gasped. Her older brother towered in the doorway, in his arms a bloodied, unconscious man.

"I had to get him out," her brother rasped breathlessly, sliding through the entrance and away from the lighted portal. "They'd have killed him. Someone knew who he was."

Emma stepped back and directed her stunned gaze to the man in her brother's arms. She felt her stomach lurch up to her throat as she took in the blood-soaked but recognizably bronze curls. His face was turned into Buck's arm, his features soot-blackened and covered with dried blood, but the curve of his jaw and the fine sweep of his brow gave him away.

"My God." She exhaled.

One arm dangled from his side, and the sight of the limp hand hanging so strangely powerless caused panic to bloom within her.

Buck's firm tone brought her back. "Yes, it's him. But don't fall apart on me now, Em. There's no time. Where can I put him?"

Thoughts blustered through her mind as she struggled to think quickly. "The back parlor." She pointed needlessly. "There's no one conscious there."

As she spoke the words, footsteps sounded on the marble stairs behind them. Buck strode off without heed as Emma whirled.

Judith, thank God. And Emma's mother was just behind her.

"What is it?" Mrs. Davenport demanded, her tone urgent but muted. "Was that Buck?"

Emma opened and closed her mouth, swallowed, then said, "Y-yes. He's got Will." Then, as if awakening to the reality of the situation, she took off after her brother.

Buck set Will gently in the far corner of the room. Emma drew close, moving the candle she'd had next to Cpl. Simon to the floor beside Will's unconscious form.

Blood spilled from a muddy pool at his shoulder, and one leg was twisted at an awkward angle. When Buck moved to push the leg into place, Will groaned and shook his head, then sank back into oblivion.

Emma reached tentative fingers to a vicious knot on his forehead from which brown rivulets of dried blood created a macabre mask down the side of his face. She longed for him to open his eyes, to show her that life still existed despite the carnage his body had endured.

"Where did you find him?" she whispered, pulling a lock of hair free from the wound and smoothing it back with the rest. But before he could answer, Judith and Mrs. Davenport rustled in behind them.

With her candle, Mrs. Davenport knelt beside the body as Judith hovered in the darkness behind her. Her experienced fingers probed the soggy shoulder area, ignoring Will's pained lapses into and out of consciousness.

Emma's heart contracted with every agonized groan.

"The bullet's still there," her mother said lowly. "Judith, get me some clean instruments."

Judith rushed off. Emma fixed intense eyes on her mother. "Mother, you can't." Panic gripped her. He needed a doctor, someone experienced in surgery—and why was his leg perched at such an odd angle?

Her mother began ripping the already torn material of Will's homespun. "I have to."

It crossed Emma's mind that now everyone would know the horrible secret of Will's spying. But at the moment it seemed to matter to no one present.

"I'll run get the doctor," Emma said desperately. "I know that he's staying with the Jacobsons tonight. Surely he wouldn't mind—"

"Don't be a fool, Emma," her mother snapped. Emma flushed at the tone and the direct, hard look her mother gave her. "This man's an enemy soldier," she whispered harshly. "Dr. Wilcox would sooner die than touch him now."

Flabbergasted, Emma protested, "But it's Will! Dr. Wilcox knows him." But her mother was right. A hysterical, inexplicable fear of abandonment threatened to overtake her. "We can't let him die! The doctor knows Will's not *our* enemy."

Buck laid a hand on her shoulder as Judith arrived with the knives and needles. He urged her to her feet and moved her back so Judith could assist their mother.

"Not everyone sees it that way, Emma. Surely you know that by now," Buck said. "In fact, the man who spotted him was Bennett Cole. I believe Bennett even had Will to dinner once or twice before the war. Tonight he called for a lynching."

The occurrence of such bloodthirstiness in someone she knew horrified her. For God's sake, a few years ago those two would have exchanged pleasantries over the punch bowl. And now Bennett wanted to kill him.

A wild, desperate despair hovered at the fringe of her consciousness. "But we can't let him die," she repeated. "Surely the doctor wouldn't just let him die."

"Perhaps not. He might do what he could," Buck agreed. Emma turned optimistic, pleading eyes to him, but her hopes were dashed with his next words. "Then he'd patch him off to Libby where he'd suffer a worse fate. And even if he lived through that, he'd probably *wish* he were dead, which might be worse than the real thing."

Emma clutched her hands before her and twisted them to keep them from shaking. "Can you help him, Mother? Can you save him?"

"I'll do what I can," her mother said vaguely, but her voice was gentle. "He's no worse off than any of the other boys here. Just on the wrong side of the fence."

White-hot rage blinded Emma for a second. "So just because he's a Yankee the good *doctor* would let him die. Oh, damn this blasted war!" she burst.

"Yankees are the enemy, and war is a nasty business," Buck said practically.

Emma sighed in frustration, tears threatening. "But it's Will; doesn't that matter?"

"Not in this case, not to a lot of people," Buck said with a penetrating look. Emma felt confusion rack her—something wrong, something she didn't want to think about—but she pushed the half-formed thought away. Buck's gaze shifted back to the man on the floor. "Most would say he's as much our enemy as any Yankee."

"But you don't feel that way, do you, Buck?" Emma asked, calming herself. "You couldn't, not after what you've done."

He expelled a deep breath. "No. I don't."

A strange awkwardness hung in the air. "You were so brave to take the risk," Emma reflected then. "How did you get him away?"

Buck ran a tired hand through his hair and Emma noticed for the first time her brother's own soot-blackened face and hands. "It wasn't easy. Of course, the explosion helped."

"The explosion?" Emma echoed.

"Though come to think of it, he'd been shot but he wasn't down until the shed blew." Buck's thoughts were on the scene he'd just escaped, she could tell, distracted by the reconstruction of events. "We had to run to avoid getting burned by the flying cinders. I just dragged him along with me. I don't think he even knew who I was."

"Were you hurt?" Emma asked gently, scanning his body for some sign of blood that was not Will's.

He shook his head dismissively. "No, no."

They watched as their mother probed Will's shoulder with a pair of tongs. Will was out cold now.

Emma felt her stomach churn at the amount of blood that Judith swiftly mopped up so Mrs. Davenport could see what she was doing. Emma's head swam dizzily and she felt Buck's hand reach out to steady her.

In an effort to keep her wits about her she asked, "What exploded?'' She had no desire to be sent from the room.

''A shed, near the fort, filled with munitions.'' Buck shook his head ruefully. ''Damn fool. It was on our side of the line.''

''*Our* side?'' Judith's voice rose from beneath them. Emma had not been sure she was listening. ''What was Will doing on our side?''

Emma's mother looked up sharply at that and met Emma's gaze with an inscrutable look. But she made no comment.

Buck just laughed, a hard, disgusted sound. ''He's the one who blew up the goddamned shed.'' He was angry, perhaps humiliated, Emma thought, and yet there was a trace of admiration in his tone. ''He could easily have been killed. We had three men gunning for him before the thing blew.''

''And at least one of them hit him,'' Mrs. Davenport remarked. The *ping* of a lead bullet hitting a metal pan resounded through the small room. ''Stitch this up, Judith, while I take a look at his leg.''

Emma looked away from the sight, quelling her fear. ''But you saved him,'' she said softly, laying a hand on her brother's arm. ''Why did you do it?''

He looked down at her incredulously. ''Honestly, Em, how can you ask me that?''

''But he could have killed you,'' she persisted.

Buck shook his head, his eyes kind but uncomprehending. ''He wouldn't have, Emma. You of all people should know that.''

She looked away, down at the unconscious face of her former lover. An emotion she could not restrain filled her chest and made it ache.

''If the situation had been reversed,'' Buck said steadily, his eyes on the motionless form before them on the floor, ''he'd have done the same for me.''

It was the very position Will himself had maintained in the face of all Emma's arguments those many years ago, when she could not escape the image of him firing into the oncoming line of his enemy—her people, her family. And she knew he fought for principle, not anger, not revenge. But did it make a difference?

An unbidden vision of Lawrence's white, livid face filled her mind. The intrusion repulsed her. She shunted the image away but bile rose to the back of her throat anyway. She'd nearly forgotten about him. Had he heard the pounding at the door? Did he know Will was here? What would he do if he knew?

The chill that doused her body was complete. Whatever he did it would not be kind, either to her or to Will. She found herself searching for a way they could hide Will. He could not be discovered. As it was he was imperiled by not only the Confederate threat outside the house, but by that which was within it—her husband.

Her husband, she thought blankly, almost absurdly. Upstairs, he waited. While here lay her love.

Chapter Fourteen

"He's dead," a woman's voice said gently.

Then a soft, frustrated sigh. A muffled sniff. "Are you sure? Remember the other night?"

"No, this time he's really dead. I'm sorry, Em. You did all you could. There was nothing else we could have done for him."

Thick, swirling blackness clutched at him. He resisted. He tried to lift a limb, or even one useless eyelid, but the weight was unbearable, insurmountable. Then, like a storm cloud racing across the sky, a thunder of noise approached and resounded around him, dizzying, deafening. Footsteps clattered hollowly along wood floors, horses' hooves pounded sun-baked earth, then shattering, earsplitting explosions, splintering glass, the shriek of crushed metal.

Then suddenly it was all barely discernible. All but his own helpless whimpers.

His brain flooded with blood that rushed like rapids; then he heard, once again, the voices. "No! Help me here. Now, damn it!" That voice, hard-edged but distinctly female, cultured, throaty. It was hers. The guns receded as rapidly as they'd approached and a calm stole over him.

"Corporal Simon is already dead. He can wait a moment more. Help me get this man back on his pallet."

Rough hands grabbed his ankles, his arms. A screeching pain shot through his body. The screaming returned, short, sharp, painful, then gone.

Coolness on his forehead, soft fingers stroking. The feeling washed through his body and left him limp. He took a breath and forced out a sound on the exhale. "Emma."

Satisfied that the impenetrable barrier of silence was broken, he slept.

He reached out again, his spirit straining upward toward the thin slit of light he could see through one partially opened eyelid. He could feel his lashes flutter—could *make* them flutter, by God—so he forced them apart. As if moving on rusted hinges, his eyes opened once, allowing just a glimpse of white beyond the heavy veil of darkness, before closing again.

A slight gasp—not his own—then the honeyed voice. "Mercy."

He licked his lips, amazed to find that the idea produced actual movement.

"Water," the voice said. "Do you want some water?" She was very close. He could feel her breath on his cheek.

He tried to nod but could effect no motion this time. A small panic welled up in him at the fear that he'd lost the ability, had forgotten how to make his muscles obey him. He did the simplest thing he knew he could do: he breathed in deeply.

But the air caught somewhere in his chest. His body convulsed with the effort to breathe normally and he gasped, straining for air. He felt not a hand upon him, but his chest was seized by a grip that squeezed all the air from his lungs. A high wheezing sound filled the room. It scared him, for he knew it issued from his own lungs. Fingers clawed at his throat and his chest. Helplessly he continued to inhale, inward, inward, inward—wanting to exhale but powerless to do it.

"No, no, no, no!" Her voice. The words were meaningless, but audible.

Her hands? No, his own. His own hands clawed at his chest in an effort to open it to air. He tried to relax them but they wouldn't obey. He was drowning. He was struggling for his very life.

On the last inhale, his eyes popped open. He saw her. It *was* her. Emma. Then the black tide swallowed him again.

Quiet, evening sounds. Plates and silverware, muted talking. A solitary bird outside.

Will opened his eyes.

It took a moment to focus, to believe what he saw was not just in his own head but actual sight. White crown molding. A cobweb in the corner. He swallowed, a painful, deliberate motion. There was textured wallpaper—strangely, hauntingly familiar. It was beautiful, like artwork. He studied it, its intricate detail of indigo blue flowers and cream background in a close, leafy design. The sight of it made him feel good, comforted; he imagined for a moment a long cherry sideboard with candles set in hurricane lamps. Supper. Supper's ready.

He closed his eyes, realizing he hadn't blinked since he'd opened them. They were scratchy and dry. A split second of fear clutched him before he discovered he could open them again with relative ease. The weight of unconsciousness ebbed.

Turning his head was excruciating. He half expected it to creak with the movement, but he was able to turn it fractionally to the side. Someone's—a man's—dusty, wrinkled feet bottoms greeted his newborn eyes. They were inordinately close, perhaps two feet away, and from this vantage point they looked enormous.

He sighed, careful not to breathe too deeply. There was some reason, some good reason he should not do that, though he could not recall at this moment exactly what it was.

Soft, slippered footsteps sounded on the floor.

"I'm just going to check him," she called.

Another voice, distant: "You just checked him a minute ago!"

"It was half an hour," she replied, but there was lightness in her voice.

The footsteps neared. They were coming to him. He tried to look toward them but the stiffness in his neck prohibited the bend that was required. Then she came into view.

The look of wonder on her face when she looked into his eyes was a sight to behold. He smiled, or he thought he did.

"Will," was the airy sound she made. She knelt fluidly beside him. So close, so close.

He tested his voice. "You . . ." It was reasonably understandable. Raspy, a bit painful. "You haven't looked"—he swallowed—"so happy to see me . . ." He cleared his throat and winced at the pain in his chest. ". . . long time," he finished lamely. The feeble sentence exhausted him. His eyes met hers again.

Tears dripped from her face. He could feel them on his arm. She was crying. And there was the most tender, most disarming little smile on those perfect lips. His whole being relaxed with the sight of it.

"Oh, Will," she said so quietly he barely heard her. "Will, you can't imagine how happy I am." She swiped at the tears on her face. "We weren't sure about your head, the concussion, and of course the doctor—" She waved a slim hand dismissively. "We couldn't let him see you. It's all been so very tense. Once we thought we'd lost you. But you're back now. Thank the Lord, you're back now. How do you feel?"

He felt wonderful, fantastic, lighter than air and sitting on a cloud—she was smiling at him again. This time sincerely. "Too fast," he managed. Confusion marred her perfect features. "Talking too fast."

The smile returned, lovely, reaching her eyes, dark, bottomless eyes of kindness and warmth. "Sorry." Spontaneously, easily, she reached out and caressed his face.

"Ahhhh." That felt good. Even the word.

"Are you in pain?" This time the words were slow, as if she spoke to a foreigner.

Eyes closed, his lips tilted and he concentrated on the feel of her fingers on his face, along his hairline. "Perhaps." He heard her quiet laugh. "But—better now."

"Don't lie to me, now. I need you to be completely honest about this."

He shook his head, the barest of movements. "Not lying."

Footsteps sounded outside the door again, this time heeled, more purposeful. Emma turned, taking her blessed hand away.

"Mother," she said urgently. "He's awake. He's talking."

He walks, he talks, he feeds peanuts to the elephant. . . . Will opened his eyes to see Emma's mother usurp her daughter's place and lay her hand on his forehead.

She harrumphed delicately. "A bit clammy," she said. She peered into his eyes.

"Mrs. Dav—" was all he could muster on the short breath he'd taken. "You—looking lovely," he murmured on the next one.

"Land sakes," she said wryly, looking at him with amusement. "No amount of gunfire's going to change you, is it?"

That was when he made the mistake—he laughed. Immediately the great invisible hands grabbed his rib cage again and squeezed with all their might, robbing him of breath and relentlessly pushing all air away. He gasped and the terrifying wheezing began anew. Worse, he saw Emma's panicked face behind her mother, her mouth screaming something he could not hear.

Again the inward pull of air, again and again and again, stupidly, fruitlessly pulling at a void for air he could not hold. Blackness crept to the edges of his vision but he held it at bay. He would not let go now, not when the dream was this good. Emma, his Emma, everything felt normal again.

He closed his eyes and clenched his stomach muscles, actually lifting his shoulders from the ground with the fight for breath. Then it hit him, the swift, daggerlike pain to the shoulder. He dropped back onto the pallet, suffered another second of blinding pain, then dipped helplessly into darkness.

"Will? Can you hear me? The doctor's going to have to amputate your leg."

A spasm of panic shot through him. Will forced his lips to part. "Ungh," was all he could manage. He swiveled his head, searing pain be damned. "Unn-no, no," rasped from his throat.

"We have to, Will; you've got some shrapnel stuck in there and you've dislocated your knee."

His eyes cracked open and he could see her face, so calm. "No," he articulated more clearly. "No amp—"

"What? I'm sorry, I didn't understand that." She bent close.

His entire body shook with agitation. "Amput—n-no, no."

Her head shook. "No, not amputate, *operate*. We have to *operate,* Will. If we don't get the metal out it'll fester . . . gangrene. Do you understand me?"

Relief washed over him. He tried to nod, but the blast of terror had not yet left his nerves. She took one of his shaking hands in hers. He hated his weakness, his fear. He wished he could take that hand and grab her, hold her, bury his fingers in her thick mass of burnished hair.

"No amp—" he repeated, just to be sure.

"That's right. They won't take your leg. You'll be fine if we just get the metal out and straighten the knee." She laid her hand on his cheek, turning his face fractionally to hers. He couldn't stop the groan that rose to his lips with the movement. "But, Will, listen, this is important. We have to bandage your head before the doctor sees you, not for long, just so he can't tell who you are. Do you understand why, Will?"

Her eyes radiated intensity and concern. He understood thickly that her point was important. The doctor, his face . . .

"If he sees you, he'll send you to prison. You'll be a prisoner of war."

He cleared his throat. "Got it." That was pretty clear. He was beginning to wake up. The throbbing ache in his shoulder and the numbness of his limbs were a dead giveaway.

She smiled tentatively. "Good. You'll be Corporal Simon, Fifth Georgia Cavalry. All right?"

"Can't—" he began when an awakening sliver of pain sliced quickly across his shoulders. He waited a moment, then resumed. "Can't talk like"—he took a shallow breath—"hayseed."

Her laughter was music to him. He felt his lips move into an actual smile, though something pulled and stung over his right eyebrow.

Her hand squeezed his. "Don't talk at all, Will, all right? Shall we bandage your mouth so you don't forget?"

He knew she joked but panic danced over him anyway. "Non-ono, breathing . . . bad 'nuf now."

She stroked the side of his face. "I know, I know. I was teasing." Her voice was suddenly somber. "It should get better with time. You can't breathe because you've damaged your lung. The doctor said you might have punctured it."

He took a deliberately shallow breath. "Don't tell me . . . *I* didn't do it. Talk to—your boys."

She straightened beside him. Something indefinable changed. He turned his head, forced his eyes to her. "Kidding," he said earnestly, almost desperately. It would be too cruel to lose her again now, so soon. "Just, just—not funny."

Her expression was kind. "Don't worry," she whispered. "Please, no more talking now. You need to rest."

He clenched his teeth against an onslaught of pain, from where he could not tell—everywhere, it seemed. Sweat popped out on his forehead and ran down his temple. "When? Emma?" Was she still there? "The doctor, when?"

He heard the rustle of her skirts as she shifted. "Soon. Today." Her next words were close to his ear. "Will, if he asks, what's your name?"

Words scattered through his mind. "Corp—corp'rl . . . damn."

She clutched his forearm. Something to focus on, a part of his body that could feel good for a moment. "Simon. *Simon,*" she said urgently.

"Simon," he breathed. "Corp'rl—Sime. Fifth Johnny George cracker cav'ry." The words cost him, but he wanted to make her laugh again.

Her voice was dry. "You're from Atlanta."

Good enough. He could hear the smile in her voice. He wished he felt less sluggish, less broken. "Beg . . . beg pardon," he said. He let his lips curve with contentment.

She left then, and came back a while later with the other woman—Judith. He remembered Judith from before, tall, pretty, serious, not at all impressed with Will's jokes. But she'd liked him, he'd felt. She didn't banter with him or flirt, but she'd liked him. He vaguely remembered something about fixing her up with Brendan, but it hadn't worked out. Judith had proven too smart for that. Will was glad. Because he liked her, too, and because he wouldn't wish his buffoon of a brother on anyone.

The thought raised an unpleasant feeling in his breast, something he'd tried to forget but remembered now with enough clarity to be disturbed. . . . Emma turning her subtle flirtations on Brendan, Emma's hand on Brendan's sleeve, Emma giving Brendan that look, that sly inviting look that had always made his own insides quiver. The look sailing clear over Brendan's head.

He blocked the images as Emma knelt again beside him, Judith on the other side. He felt her hand slip beneath his head and bit back the nearly overwhelming moan that rose to his lips. Pain sliced downward from his shoulder, straight along his side to his toes. Involuntary tears sprang to his eyes; he felt them dribble down the sides of his face and into his hair.

"Not so high, Emma," Judith's voice whispered.

Immediately his head was lowered, the pain lessened, and he took a breath. "I'm sorry, Will," Emma said quietly.

But he was too tired to answer. Suddenly his brain felt as if it were swamped by a deep, cloying fog. He wanted to tell her not to worry, that he was fine. He wanted to tell her to keep talking, that just the sound of her voice soothed his pain, but he couldn't get the words out. And he'd just begun to notice that he couldn't feel his right foot; he'd have mentioned that for sure, if he could have. But the blackness was descending again and this time it felt so comforting. . . .

Just before he let himself go, into the fog, he heard Judith say, "Oh, God, Emma, he's bleeding again."

A gasp. "Oh, my God, it's so much. It's my fault. I lifted his head too high."

No, no, no, Will thought dreamily. Not your fault, Emma. Never your fault, my beauty, my love . . .

"No, look at this pool of it. He's been bleeding for some time. . . ."

The voices became fainter; his heart fluttered delicately, like a bird taking flight.

"Oh, Lord, oh, God, why didn't I notice that?" Her agony tugged at him, weighted the ascending lightness in his chest.

"None of us did. You couldn't have. . . ."

"Oh, where *is* the doctor?"

It wasn't important anymore.

"Quick. You finish this; I'm going to find the doctor." Emma jumped to her feet and sailed through the door. Terror propelled her; the abyss of abandonment dogged her heels. Two orderlies momentarily blocked her way as they passed with a stretcher between them, but she shouldered around the second man as they moved through the doorway.

She passed through the living room and scanned the rows of cots there, eyes grazing nurses, servants, and volunteers bending over the wounded or sitting by their beds to read to them. But the doctor was nowhere to be seen.

Sweat sprang instantly to her hands and forehead as anxiety outweighed effectiveness. In her panic she found herself searching the same row two or three times before believing the doctor was not there. All she could see was Will, his face whiter than some of the corpses they'd loaded on the cart this morning, his hands shaking, his breathing weak and wheezing.

He was going to die. She knew it with a certainty she'd never felt before. And the knowledge was terrifying—as if the cavity where her heart should be was rendered an empty, echoing canyon. The feeling was like those dreams of falling she'd had as a child, but so much more horrible because she was grown up now—and awake.

She spun through the archway, crossed the foyer, and pounded up the steps. Only two rooms upstairs were used for the wounded, and one was used for surgery. The rest housed family and the volunteers who came up from the country or who, like Judith, had lost their own homes and stayed to help in the hospital.

Controlling her panic, she opened the first door quietly and glanced about the tiny room. No doctor. But Mona, a young newlywed from down the street, stood upon seeing her.

"Emma?" Her pale face was taut, her eyes naive but not quite as young as they'd been a just few months ago.

"Have you seen Dr. Wilcox?" Emma asked.

"Not for a while. But Emma, I'm a little concerned," she started hesitantly. She was new to the hospital and obviously nervous about her responsibility for a roomful of men. "The sergeant here has been calling out—"

Emma shook her head. "Not now, Mona. I can't—not now." She closed the door on the girl's frightened face. Vaguely she thought that she should have said something comforting, that they all call out, especially in the beginning. But that thought was lost in the next one.

The other sick ward was the one that used to be her mother's chamber. It was the largest room upstairs and held perhaps fifteen men. She swung open the door.

The room was bathed in soft evening light, and for a moment Emma's eyes were dazzled by the unexpected brightness. For just a second she thought she saw the room as it used to be—with the high tester bed, the deep oriental carpet, the plush drapes. Her mouth slackened with the unexpected beauty of it and she closed her eyes.

When she opened them, the rows of wounded men had returned. A pile of brown and crimson bandages in the corner waited to be picked up for the laundry; pails and dippers for water, chamber pots, and an occasional stool were scattered between the beds.

But there was no doctor.

She brought her hand up to the side of her face, feeling the stickiness of perspiration, the heat of anxiety. Mrs. Jenkins sat on the far side of the room near the windows, nodding off in the afternoon warmth.

Emma entered the room with a swish and deftly stepped between and over men on pallets and cots.

"Mrs. Jenkins." She shook the woman awake with less gentleness than she'd intended. "Mrs. Jenkins."

The older woman snorted loudly and started awake. Her wrinkled hands fluttered to her hair in confusion before her eyes focused on Emma.

"Oh! Dear Emma, you frightened me," she said feebly.

"Where is Dr. Wilcox?" she demanded.

Daunted by the intensity emanating from Emma, the old woman shook her head. "I don't know. I'm sure I don't know." Then, remembering her status as head matron in the household, her expression firmed. "What is it, girl? What's gotten you into such a state?"

But Emma was no longer listening. Clutching her head in her hands, she turned to the door. But she made no move toward it. Panic engulfed her. Where could he be? He could have gone anywhere. If he wasn't in the house as she'd thought, he could have gone on to any one of a dozen other homes full of wounded in need of medical care.

Tears of dread fogged her vision. Stiffly, she skirted back through the prone figures on the floor to the door.

Would he have gone home? How could he have thought he was finished? They'd spoken about Cpl. Simon. He was to operate before the leg became infected. But now . . . now it was even more critical. . . .

She braced her hands against the doorjamb and looked down the empty hallway. The Fishburnes had a hospital just five doors down. The Wallaces had one two blocks over. The Pennerys over on Cary Street had just found one of their sons on yesterday's five-twenty with a bullet hole in his hand and his feet burned by an explosion. How long would it take her to search all of those houses? How much time did Will have?

"Emma," the sharp voice croaked closely behind her, causing her to jump. She turned to face Mrs. Jenkins. "I believe the doctor might have mentioned something about grabbing a bite."

"He's gone home to supper?" she asked in sudden breathless hope.

"Well, now, I remember saying something to him about Cass's shepherd pie—how we all thought we'd never taste the likes of it again—and what a good job she'd done with what—"

Emma clutched the woman's frail forearm. "You mean he's still *here?*"

Mrs. Jenkins frowned at her and pulled her arm out of Emma's grasp with deliberate asperity. "I don't pretend to know at all *where* he is. I only mean to say there's a chance he is still here. Check Cass's kitchen."

"Thank you, Mrs. Jenkins!" Emma pushed off the doorjamb and ran down the hall. She rounded the top of the stairs at full speed and grabbed the railing to guide her down the stairs. Skirts lifted high in one hand, she hit the front foyer running. She spun around the corner where the hat rack used to stand and entered the hallway leading to the back of the house. Skirts flying behind her, she burst through door into the kitchen and skidded to a halt.

Three heads jerked around to glare at her sudden intrusion. Cass's dark, glistening face, eyes wide in surprise; Dr. Wilcox's red, florid countenance with an expression not unlike Cass's; and Lawrence's pencil-thin, paper-white mask of displeasure marked her arrival.

Stunned silence reigned for a moment before Lawrence got slowly to his feet. Emma felt her nerves melt into confusion.

"Emma? What's the matter?" he asked in a voice he might use for an embarrassing child.

"I—ah—it's Dr. Wilcox I need." She flicked her eyes to the doctor.

"Yes, Mrs. Price?" he asked solicitously. But he made no move to rise and she had the abrupt, irrational thought that they believed her to be crazy.

"It's one of the patients, Doctor. He's worsened considerably." Her hands twisted before her as she glanced from one face to another.

Cass gave her a strange look with one raised eyebrow and turned back to her baking. Lawrence eyed her icily, with much more interest than she would have liked. And Dr. Wilcox, blessedly, wiped his hands on a napkin and got to his feet.

"Oh, thank you for coming right away," Emma could not help gushing. She cast an uncomfortable glance at Lawrence. He still watched her. "He's just worsened so suddenly. It caught us all by surprise. It's Corporal Simon, from Georgia," she added more to Lawrence than to the doctor.

Emma backed toward the door as the doctor approached and pushed it open behind her. "It's his shoulder. We suddenly found a great pool of blood under it when we had thought the shoulder wound was healing properly. And you were to operate on his leg, do you remember?"

The doctor's great bulk followed her through the door. She felt relief war with trepidation as they started toward the hall. If he would just walk a bit faster, if they were just a little farther away from Lawrence . . .

Then that which she had dreaded, but had not articulated even to herself, came to pass. Lawrence's voice followed them down the hall. "I believe I'll come with you, Amos. Perhaps I can be of some assistance."

Chapter Fifteen

Emma led the way down the hall with damp palms clenched nervously in her swinging skirts. She kept her head bowed in a desperate bid to regain her composure and studied the worn, lusterless floorboards beneath her. Once, not so long ago, these floors would have been buffed and polished once a week. Emma could remember sliding along this very hall in her stockinged feet as a child, seeing how far she could go on the sleek, shiny surface. Now raw wood showed through the finish like a dirt path through grass.

The two men clomped heavily behind her. Part of Emma screamed at her to run, to drag the doctor by the hand to Will's side. But the cautious part, the part always aware of Lawrence and the direction of his attention, was unreasonably frightened by his presence. It was not as if Lawrence would recognize Will any faster than the doctor would. She'd prepared for the fact that they both would know his face. But with that covered was there a chance one of them might know him anyway?

The doctor, at least, was not likely to notice anything about the person beneath the bandages, not after analyzing literally hundreds of bodies a day. Dr. Wilcox's careful eye probably did not extend past the wound at this point. But Lawrence, what would he see? Emma had the irrational fear that he could somehow read her mind and, hence, *she* would be the one to give Will away. It was silly, almost superstitious, but why had Lawrence chosen this particular time to visit the hospital?

They arrived in the dining room, now known as the critically wounded ward, and Emma stepped across the threshold, sliding immediately aside to let the men pass. She pointed them in the direction of the corner where Judith knelt, mopping up Will's blood with a tablecloth. She should go to Will's side, should explain the situation to the doctor, but with Lawrence here she did not trust herself to appear objective.

Halfway across the room Lawrence turned to look back at Emma with a frown. "What's the matter?"

"Nothing," she replied quickly. "I have other patients to check."

Lawrence eyed her coldly for a moment. "Don't you think, now that you've robbed the poor doctor of his supper, that you should tell him what the trouble is?"

Argument was useless, she knew. She gritted her teeth and moved to the corner.

"He got here late, a couple of nights ago," Judith was saying. "So Mrs. Davenport removed the bullet. I thought I'd stitched everything but then we found this enormous pool of blood under him. It seems to be abating somewhat now, but he's very weak. He lost such a lot of blood."

Emma stood by, kneading her fingers together, as the doctor knelt beside the body.

Lawrence shot her a look so she added, "She's right."

The three of them peered down on the body and the doctor's probing hands. It was so obvious to Emma who it was she could hardly restrain her panic from making her do something stupid. Every muscle, every scar, even just the shape of his limbs beneath the sheet looked familiar to her.

As the doctor investigated the shoulder wound and repositioned the compress Judith had applied, Emma watched Lawrence out of the corner of her eye. He studied the patient with care, which might or might not portend something, as he eyed everything intensely. The bandages around Will's head were completely concealing, but they did not seem sufficient disguise to Emma. Now that she stood here with two men who could be the death of Will if they knew him, she was sure that her meager attempt at subterfuge had failed.

Dr. Wilcox angled his head to her. "This is the man whose leg I was to be settin'?"

Emma nodded and swallowed hard. "Yes. It's not broken, merely dislocated, but there's some shrapnel as well, so we didn't do it ourselves."

The doctor knelt and raised the sheet to view Will's knee. He held the covering awkwardly to protect the unmarried Judith's modesty, but Emma could see all. The heat that flushed her cheeks dried her mouth and made her look away to still the sudden rushing of blood in her ears.

"And the face?" the doctor questioned, placing practiced fingers gently around the lower part of Will's well-muscled thigh, an area studded with cuts and gashes. "What happened there?"

Emma and Judith exchanged panicked glances. Why hadn't they thought? Of course the doctor would want to look at all the wounds, particularly one that warranted as large a bandaging as was required to cover an entire face. Dr. Wilcox paused at the silence, then looked up at Judith.

"Not—nothing serious. Scratches and whatnot. A bump on the forehead." Judith's hands moved to Will's bandaged face and needlessly tucked in a loose end.

"Yes, you know how cuts to the face bleed so," Emma added, drawing the unwanted attention of the doctor to herself.

"Well, I'll take a look," he said kindly. "I want to get a look at his complexion anyway."

Emma sent Judith a desperate plea with her eyes. If Judith were to say something to stop the doctor, Lawrence would not be as suspicious as if Emma tried to.

But Judith's mind had obviously gone blank, and the doctor's hands were reaching for the knot of the bandage on Will's head.

"Uh, Doctor," Emma said, laying a hand on his shoulder. "I'd really appreciate it if you could take him right up to surgery. He's unconscious now, but when he's awake he's—he's quite loud. I think it might be due to the knee."

She glanced at Judith, whose face lit with the excuse. "Yes and we do so hate to have the other patients roused. They're all so quiet and need their rest. And this one's just so *loud*, not stoic about it at all."

The doctor frowned. "Hard to be stoic when you've been sprung like a keg of brandy by a bunch of blood-hungry Yankees, missy," he said gruffly.

Judith flushed to the roots of her pale hair. Emma closed her eyes in mortification. It was bad enough that Judith had to look inept because of her own oversight in discovering Will's bleeding, but to look unsympathetic, too, was just unfair.

"Dr. Wilcox, no, it's my fault," she blurted.

He turned to her, irritation showing on his face. "What's your fault? Did you shoot him?"

Emma stepped back, aghast. "No!"

He rolled his eyes and gestured to Lawrence. "Come on, give me a hand here. We'll take him to surgery. I've heard enough of this women's prattle. I get it all night from the missus; I don't need it all day, too."

Emma and Judith shared a look of frustration. Lawrence, in as genuine a show of good faith as Emma had ever seen from him, moved immediately to help lift the unconscious man from his pallet. But where Emma would have preferred him to take Will's feet, Lawrence moved immediately to his head. So close, too close . . .

"Emma!" Dr. Wilcox's voice made her jump, jolting her from her thoughts. "Wake up. What's gotten into you today? Acting dreamy as a schoolgirl."

"I'm sorry—"

"Get us a stretcher. Did you think we'd just heft him over our shoulders?"

"Of course not." Good Lord, what had gotten into her? "Right away. I'm sorry." She made the mistake of glancing at Lawrence before turning to leave the room, and his surprising look of virulence caused her to stumble over the feet of the man behind her. She caught herself before tumbling face-first onto the patient, but not without doing some fancy stepping to avoid treading on unconscious fingers and toes.

She grabbed up her skirts, and without another glance backward she stepped purposefully out the door. She located a stretcher in the front foyer and took an extra minute to look in the adjoining front room for Dee. Surely there was someone else who could help carry Will to surgery besides Lawrence. But the front room was empty and silence reigned in the hall. She stood motionless a second, hoping to hear a voice, a scuffle of feet, anything; but nothing stirred. Time weighed on her with the force of her own urgency. She gave up and hurried back.

They moved Will easily from the pallet to the stretcher. His head lolled sideways with the movement and Lawrence reached out a hand to stay it, causing Emma's stomach to butterfly. They heaved the burden up and started for the door, Dr. Wilcox backing up stiffly and Lawrence trying not to look as if he struggled under the weight.

"Do you think he'll be all right, Doctor?" Emma asked anxiously as they negotiated the turn from the top of the stairs into the upstairs hallway.

Dr. Wilcox smacked his lips after obviously dislodging something from between his teeth and thought for a moment. "Hard to say, though I've a pretty good feeling about this one," he said. "The wounds don't look so bad. It's the loss of blood we've got to worry about. Wish I didn't have to cut into his leg, but what with the threat of gangrene . . . can't really be helped."

Emma felt a moment of hope—the wounds didn't look bad!— mixed with the dread of the unknown. How much blood had he lost? Could he sustain one more operation?

They slid the stretcher onto the raised operating table—once a dressmaker's table gotten from a downtown millinery shop that closed at the beginning of the war. Mrs. Jenkins swore the shop had been run by Yankees who were chased out of town the second it was known who their relations were, but Emma could find no evidence to support this story.

"Where's Porter?" the doctor asked, referring to his aide.

Judith, who had followed from below, said, "I think he's gone to the Polivers. I can assist you."

The doctor shook his head. "Nope. Need somebody strong. We've got to set this leg, pull it back into the socket there. That takes more brawn than you've got, I'm afraid."

Emma held her breath. *Dear God, no. Not Lawrence.*

"I would be happy to help in any way that I could," Lawrence offered with a short inclination of his head. "If you would but tell me what to do."

"I'll get Dee," Emma interjected. "I think he's just downstairs."

Dr. Wilcox's shrewd eyes looked from one to the other of them. "Well, now, Mr. Price. That's right nice of you to offer, but I think Dee might just be the better choice."

Lawrence drew himself up straight. "It would be no trouble. And I'm already here."

The doctor shook his head, as if rejecting a fish at the market. "It's a messy piece of work, surgery is, Mr. Price, and—no offense now—pullin' a man's leg back into place takes quite a bit of muscle. Ain't nothing for the book-learned type man to be tryin'. Can get quite gruesome, what with the patient screamin' and all. Got to hold 'em down tight."

Lawrence knew something, Emma was sure of it. Why else would he suddenly be so solicitous? She brought her hand to her forehead.

"Will it be so bad, then, Dr. Wilcox?" She closed her eyes a dramatic second.

"No worse than usual," he answered gruffly.

Emma sighed and moved her hand to her heart. "Good," she said faintly. Then, "I don't know why . . . but I'm suddenly not feeling . . ." She staggered back a step, after which the doctor looked at her closely and Lawrence grasped her forearm in a cool, weak hand. "I'm so sorry, I think I need some water. Please, could you help me, Lawrence?"

She would pay for it, of that she was certain. But she was compelled to take advantage of the fact that he would not refuse to help her in front of the doctor.

"Certainly, dear," he said, his tone neutral. "Dr. Wilcox, I apologize for my inability to assist you."

The doctor had begun to roll up his sleeves. "Well now, you can help by sending Dee up. I'll be ready for him in just a minute."

Lawrence nodded and led Emma from the room. They spoke not a word as they moved down the hall, Lawrence's hand still on her elbow. Judith followed and told them that she would locate Dee, and they separated at the base of the stairs. Lawrence and Emma headed for the kitchen.

They were greeted in that room by the comforting smell of baking. Though flour was astronomically priced, Lawrence had secured some from someplace and had asked Cass to make him up a loaf of bread. Whether or not he intended to share this with the household was unknown, and Emma did not question him.

Cass was not in her kitchen, so Lawrence sat Emma at the table and brought her a glass of water himself.

"Thank you," she murmured when he'd set it before her.

He did not reply, but sat across from her at the table, glaring at her over his folded elbows. Emma sipped, then dipped her fingers into the glass to press some cool water against her temples. It felt good, reviving, regardless of the fact that she had not for a moment felt faint. And then, too, it was an excuse to close her eyes against the pale hostility emanating from the man across from her.

But after several minutes of this Emma got tired of hiding and opened her eyes to glare back at him. "What?" she asked finally. "Why do you look at me so?"

Lawrence did not answer, but neither did he shift his eyes from her. Instead he sat back in his chair, arms folded across his chest.

"I don't know why you're acting so peculiar," Emma said. She took another sip of the water, her mouth inexplicably dry. It must be the same technique he uses when he interrogates prisoners at Libby, she thought, determined that the practice should not work with her. "So what do you think of our little hospital, now that you've laid eyes on an actual patient?" she asked caustically. She would much prefer an argument to an interrogation right now.

"How long has he been here, Emma?" the icy voice asked calmly.

An unsuppressible chill racked her. His eyes pinned her motionless where she sat. "Who?" she asked, unsuccessfully attempting nonchalance. She raised the glass to her lips again with a suddenly stiff arm.

His eyes were relentless. "You know who I'm talking about."

Emma took several short breaths before answering. "The man you just saw? Corporal Simon? He came in about two days ago."

"Corporal Simon is dead, Emma."

Air burst from her lungs as she looked at him in disbelief. The man was unholy. He saw all. He knew all. Or did he just have the ability to read Emma's mind?

"What are you talking about?" she asked weakly. "Corporal Simon is in surgery."

Lawrence leaned forward and placed his arms on the table in front of him. Emma drew back fractionally.

"You and I both know," he said deliberately, "that the man upstairs in surgery is not Corporal Simon."

She felt herself engulfed by his glare, found herself shaking her head. "He's not?" she asked uncertainly.

Lawrence almost smiled; she saw his lips twitch, but the near-expression did nothing to lighten her dread. "No," he said, drawing the word out lengthily. "You and I both know that the man

218

upstairs in surgery is William Darcy.''

Emma shook her head jerkily but could not bring the denial to her lips.

His hand slammed on the table with a loud crack. Emma jumped and upset the water glass with her hand. ''Tell me!'' he demanded.

They sat still as hunter and deer in the woods as the water puddled and eased toward the edge of the table. It dripped slowly onto the floor, loud in the silence.

''I'll tell you nothing,'' she said in a quaking voice. Every nerve in her body shook so that she felt her head move like an old person's.

''Then I'll tell Dr. Wilcox to examine beneath that head bandage.'' He let the threat sink in. Then he added, ''Emma, he has a scar on his left forearm, crescent-shaped, very deep. Very unusual.''

She couldn't help it; her gaze dropped from his.

''I can see you know the one I mean,'' he said, slight disgust in his tone. ''I know it is him. This secrecy of yours is laughable.''

She stared at the rough-hewn wood of the table between them. Every muscle tensed stiff as iron, every nerve taut, as the silence stretched long. Finally, conceding defeat with the words, she asked quietly, ''What will you do with him?''

Lawrence leaned back, eyelids drooping fractionally with satisfaction. The cat who'd crippled the mouse and now could play with it. ''Of course, as loyal Confederates we should turn him over at once. He's a spy, as you and I well know.''

Emma's eyes flicked quickly to his. ''How do we know that?''

''As loyal Confederates we should not even treat him,'' he continued, ignoring her question. ''We should leave that to the doctors at Libby. He's an officer; he may be treated well.''

She stared at him hard, her hands fisted and on the table in front of her. ''He won't be and you know it. He was your friend—long before this war started. Could you really turn him over, just like that?''

Lawrence scoffed. "He was more than your friend, was he not? Yet you threw him over, tossed him back to his own kind as if he were nothing more to you than a dress you'd outgrown." He paused, then continued smoothly, "As a loyal Confederate, it was the right thing to do, no doubt. Yet now you ask me to risk all, everything I've worked for, to harbor this man in our house?" One of his brows raised. He looked as superior as a judge in an ugly court battle. He held all the cards and knew it.

She could not deny him. How was it he was always able to corner her with her own behavior? Was she so wrong? So confused? Yes. She was confused, and she had been wrong. Now, in the midst of this life-or-death situation, when it was up to her to preserve Will's safety as he lay possibly dying in her house, now it was obvious that politics—even war—were no barrier to love.

"Lawrence," she started slowly, "surely you see the treachery in ignoring personal loyalties. You and I feel one way about the war, about freedom and family, what is right and just, and Will disagrees. He and I fought about it; perhaps you and he fought also. But is that any reason to stand aside and watch as death takes one more? One we loved so well for so long?"

"That is the nature of war," he said mildly. "Particularly the nature of this war. A Confederate should not plead for the life of a Yankee, not when her countrymen have done all they could to end that life."

"My God, is it always so clear to you?" she burst out, frustration and confusion infusing strength into the words. "Yes, I am pleading for the life of a Yankee, of a spy even. But I'm also pleading for the life of Will Darcy. Your friend, your neighbor, a man you've known since childhood. Does all of that mean nothing now that he wears blue, and now that he's helplessly within your grasp?"

He snorted. "Prettily put, Mrs. Price," he said, obviously unmoved. "But do you plead for the life of *my friend,* as you so effectively phrased it, or do you plead for the life of *your lover?*"

Emma flushed—in anger, not in shame. "What difference does it make? He was something to both of us. It's inhuman to send him to prison in his current state of ill health. You know as well as I do that he'll die there as surely as if you put a gun to his head this minute."

Lawrence brushed a piece of dust from his sleeve. "So dramatic, my dear," he countered with infuriating calm. "Do you flatter yourself that you'd argue this persuasively for any Yankee, that your altruistic nature would prevent you from turning your back on any wounded man? Or do you see in your heart of hearts that you argue out of lust and desire for this man who's had you, this man whose hands have feasted on your sinful flesh?"

She could suddenly see the rage that simmered just below the surface of his control. Emma knew from experience that he was at his most dangerous when he began this talk of sin, but she had never been able to turn him from it once the idea had seized him.

"The past is over," she said desperately. "I plead only for his life, not our history, nor any future." She stopped and took a deep breath. "Lawrence, it's time to stop tormenting me and yourself with images from the past. Yes, I made a mistake. I-I sinned." For some reason she had a hard time getting those words past her lips. "But I will not do so again. I made a vow to you and I intend to hold it sacred—"

"As if someone with your morals could hold anything sacred," he spat. But she got the feeling that he was baiting her, pushing her to make her break—again.

Anger propelled her and she stood so quickly the chair toppled behind her. "I will not stand by and watch you turn him in!" she declared.

He looked at her, mock confusion on his face. "But my dear, you have no other choice. Do you?"

She stood breathing heavily with her desperate ire. She hated him. God help her, she hated her husband. "I'll leave you," she growled. "I'll tell everyone what a low, despicable character you really are. I'll tell General Carruthers that you're not to be trusted—he'll listen to me, you know he will."

"And I will have turned Will in." His expression was stony, his eyes dead as quartz. "You would gain nothing and lose all, for when you sabotage my character you assassinate your own, as well.''

But she knew the one thing he needed her for, wanted her for, was respectability. It was a small thing, but it was something.

"I don't care." Her fingernails dug into the soft wood of the table. She wished it were his face.

"They would only think you crazy, that the pressures of war had warped you."

She stood stock-still, glaring down at him contemptuously. "It would still be a scandal. I can *make* it a scandal."

The only sign that her words affected him was the muscle that tensed repeatedly in his jaw. "And I could lock you in your room from this day forward."

She laughed in disbelief. "Here? In my own house? With my family all around?"

"I am your husband. A fact I'd advise you to remember." He rose, considerably slower than she had, and stepped purposefully around the table toward her. She felt a trembling deep inside herself. "No court in the world would deny me the right to subdue my own wife."

She felt the wood pull against her nails as she dug deeper. "It would never reach a court," she uttered lowly. But he frightened her, and the words lacked force. The thought flitted across her mind that he could kill her right here and now and no one would be the wiser. But that was ridiculous. He wouldn't even fight in the war; of course he wouldn't kill anybody.

He stood very close, seething with rage at her perfidy. "I believe," he said slowly, obviously controlling his wrath, "that the sentries are performing nightly searches for those who would defect from our glorious cause. It would be nothing to call them into the house this very evening. What a coup it would be for one of them to capture a Yankee spy—possibly even resulting in advancement."

She gritted her teeth. Her defiance had done nothing to change his mind. And she realized now that persistence would only make him more determined. The only thing she had not tried, the only thing that might possibly sway him now, was the hardest to endure—complete submission. "I'm begging you," she said, the words coming from deep in her throat. She turned blurred, angry eyes to him. "I'm *begging* you, Lawrence. Don't do it. Don't send him to his death."

Lawrence's eyes narrowed. "You beg," he sneered, "but your haughty jaw betrays you. Lower your chin, my dear; you look positively defiant. In fact," he added snidely, "should you not be kneeling as you plead for the life of your lover?"

She bowed her head stiffly, rage and fear causing her breath to tremble.

"Kneel to me," he snarled ominously. "Kneel to me or I'll not hear another word from you."

Slowly, as if every inch were another decision, she gripped her skirts and knelt before him.

"Lower," he taunted. "You do not yet appear abject."

Willing her mind to go blank, she placed her hands on the gritty floor. Anger shook her voice. "I'll do anything, anything you say, if you will spare him this once."

He reached out a booted toe and placed it over the fingers of her hand, pressing gently. "Anything," he repeated thoughtfully. "But you have already vowed to obey me. I recall it from our wedding day." His foot pressed harder. Tears of mortification stung her eyes.

"I'll do anything," she repeated. She had nothing else to give.

He slid his foot away from her hand, grazing the knuckles, breaking the skin. Pinpricks of blood emerged bright against her white flesh. "You'll do anything I say," he said then in a harder voice, "the moment I say it. Supplication is what I demand of you. You'll not question, nor defy. You'll kneel just as you are now whenever I ask it. You'll *worship* me for all our time together. For this I'll give you one week before I turn him in."

Her head snapped up. "Two weeks."

His lips curled. "This is a weak show of obedience."

223

"We have not yet agreed." Her voice was hard.

He sighed. "Ten days. Then I take him."

She glared hatefully at him, employing every ounce of loathing she possessed in the look. "Agreed."

Chapter Sixteen

Five days later, Judith spooned a mouthful of broth into Will's mouth where he lay, partially propped up by a pillow, on the floor. "I'm so glad you're better. You can't imagine the turmoil this place was in while you were unconscious," she said.

Will swallowed and watched her beneath hooded eyes. Her light blond hair was pulled severely away from her face in a tight, practical bun, at odds with the soft color. Her movements with the spoon were deft and precise; she was practiced at feeding helpless men. "I'm sure I was not the only one unconscious. Why should I produce a turmoil?"

Judith smiled mildly, softening the tired lines of her young face. "Mr. Darcy, you surprise me. Are you fishing for compliments?"

One side of his mouth lifted wryly. "Are there any to be had?"

Just then the boy, Dee, popped his dark head in the door and hissed at Judith—his way of being careful not to wake the patients.

"What is it, Dee?" she asked patiently.

"You seen Miz Price's shawl, the one carryin' a hole in it?"

She thought a moment, empty spoon poised in the air in front of her. "In the front parlor, I believe. Underneath the sewing box."

"Thank you, ma'am." He nodded his close-cropped head and disappeared.

Judith turned back, her eyes averted, and continued their conversation. "You produced a turmoil, Will, because you were practically one of the family at one time. There are many people here who still care about you."

His eyes sought hers but she kept them shielded. "Who, in particular?"

Judith knew what he asked, he could tell, but she evaded the obvious prompt. "Well, I do, for one; can't you tell?"

Will closed his eyes and turned his head as another spoonful of broth approached him. "I've had enough."

"No, you haven't. You've lost a lot of blood. The doctor said fluids were the best treatment we could give you. Open up."

Will turned back to her, amused. "Have you any children? Have you married since I last saw you?"

She looked surprised, but slipped the spoonful into his mouth anyway. "No, why?"

He shook his head. "Because you've got that mother's imperative to your tone. Perhaps it comes naturally to some."

She dipped the spoon again and brought it toward him. Her expression sobered. "No. I've not married." Her expression was odd and the words sounded somehow pointed, he thought. He first wondered if she'd lost someone she cared about; then something inside him jumped nervously as another idea took root.

A question sprang to his mind but he found he was too afraid of the answer to ask it. He swallowed more soup and asked instead, "Where's Emma?"

Judith readied the next spoonful, her long, slim fingers delicate on the implement. "She's out tonight."

He raised his brows. "Out?"

Her eyes remained placidly downcast, concentrating on running the bottom of the spoon against the edge of the bowl before lifting it. She nodded.

A tiny particle of alarm gnawed at his stomach but he

"Yas'm," he replied and disappeared again.

A long moment prevailed during which the only sound was the *chink* of metal spoon against bowl.

He steeled himself against the almost overwhelming dread licking at his heart. "Who is Mrs. Price?" he asked quietly.

Not even a flinch did he detect as Judith tipped the bowl for the last of the broth. She brought it up to him, but kept her eyes on his lips as he opened his mouth.

"I think you already know," she said finally. She sat back with the empty bowl in her lap and raised her eyes full of pity and sadness to his.

Will felt the roar of an ocean invade his head as he stared back, suspended in sluggish comprehension. "You're not married," he said, repeating her earlier words. A pain swelled in his chest and threatened to block all air. "*She* is," he forced out flatly. "Emma is married."

Judith nodded slowly. He expelled the breath he'd been holding and let his head drop back against the pillow. He stared at the ceiling, feeling his heart drain in his chest. "Who is he?" he asked.

Her skirts rustled as she stood, and he bent his head forward to look at her.

"I think that's something you should discuss with her," she said firmly. "I've said more than I probably should have anyway."

"Do I know him?" he persisted. "How long has it been?" *Does she love him?* was the question he could not voice.

But Judith shook her head at him. She would say no more, no matter how difficult his questions became for her or himself.

"She'll come to see me," he asserted, as Judith turned to leave. "You said she would, is that right?"

She looked back at him, her sympathetic sorrow infuriating. "She will. Yes, I'm sure."

He nodded, trying to control the swift and unjust anger that billowed within him. "All right, then," he said. "All right." As if that proved anything at all.

* * *

When he awoke again his head was splitting and his mouth was dry. It was dark, and a ghostly moonlight washed through the window. The strange ambience allowed him, for a moment, to forget why he was here, to forget that this was a sick ward and not the formal dining room he'd known so well. He imagined the room as he'd seen it a hundred times before, lit by candles, with sumptuous arrays of food laid out on the long, cherrywood table.

He could almost hear the clinking of glasses and the swishing of crinolines, the undulating waves of a crowd's conversation waxing and waning. If he reached for it, he could imagine the orchestra tuning up out back on the flagstone patio, where torches lined the open space and ladies and gentlemen danced, champagne in their hands. The low, haunting cry of the mourning doves would sound at dusk. The bobwhite would whistle its redundant tune from the pear tree.

How many parties like that had he been to at this house? Mellow, gracious gatherings of charming men and women. He and Emma would move as one through the crowd, his hand on her elbow, sometimes drifting to the small of her back. How proud he was of her, even back then, before he knew what agony it would be to lose her. And the look she would give him, that trusting, amused, adoring look that would make him feel ten times the man he was—what he would give to have that back again.

A noise from the hall interrupted his reverie. It sounded like the click of a door closing, but so quietly as to be almost inaudible. A second later he heard soft footfalls on the patio outside. Ten, fifteen steps faded into the near distance, then stopped at the edge of the stones.

The feeling that invaded him was intense. Need, like an alien will, possessed him. The presence outside was a tangible thing, a conviction, a compulsion. He had to know who it was, outside alone in the moonlight.

He pushed himself onto his elbows and craned his head to look out the window. But he was too low; all he could see was the deep indigo of the sky and the tops of the tallest trees. Slowly, sheets bunching and rustling beneath him, he slid himself to a sitting position. It was the first time he'd been completely upright since he'd gotten here, and his head swam with the effort it took to stay that way. He gazed above him, wishing he could stand, just a moment, to look out the window. Such a small thing, a tiny desire that would not have qualified for a thought a week ago, but now burned inside him like a craving.

He bent his good leg, and thanked God that it produced no pain, unlike virtually every other limb he possessed. The chair rail was reachable, but too narrow to serve as much of a hold. If he could move himself up against the wall, then push with the good leg, he could possibly get himself high enough to grasp the sill. He started to make preparations for this move when the footsteps turned back. He listened to see if they reentered the house, but they turned away again. Then back. The cadence was unusual, not the *clop-clop-clop* of walking, but a step and a shift, with an occasional shuffle. He cocked his head like a dog, straining to hear.

Dancing, he thought illogically. Then, no, that was absurd. He listened hard. Yes. Someone was dancing. After a moment he thought he could detect the rhythm of a waltz. One-two-three, one-two-three—no, there was a stop and the rustle of fabric.

He pushed himself against the wall, then down along it, toward the window. It was only a matter of four or five feet, but it seemed to take forever. Sweat beaded on his forehead, but the pain was negligible against this strange, intense desire to see out the window. His good foot somewhat beneath him, the splinted leg out straight in front, he pushed himself upward. He bit back a curse as pain shot through his thigh, and his hip joint popped with the unfamiliar movement. He flattened the palm of his right hand against the wall and used it to push with the one leg.

With an enormous effort he was able to grab on to the sill. Between that, the wall, and the leg that was even then sliding slowly out from the wall on the corner of sheet he'd snagged, he managed to rise. Contorted with pain, he propped his weight briefly on the splinted leg before jerking his good foot under him.

There. He was standing. He was sweating, and panting, and

gritting his teeth against pain that traveled along every nerve in his body—but he was standing. He rested his head against the trim by the window and gazed out, trying to keep his breath from fogging the glass.

The scene that met his eyes was one he would never forget. Emma, her hair loose and hanging in long waves almost to her waist, clutched her arms to her middle and spun in a slow circle on the flagstone patio. A strong breeze molded her skirts to her legs and flung locks of her hair out to the side. The moonlight was eerie and unreal, bright enough to cast shadows like a weak or dying sun. Her eyes were closed, her cheeks wet. She swayed, reedlike, for a moment, back and forth, then spun out gracefully and resumed the one-two-three, one-two-three of the soundless waltz. Her fingers tensed and released the flesh of her upper arms.

Will felt raw tears gather and sting his eyes. Grief expanded in his chest. She did not unclasp her arms, nor did she open her eyes. The wind swirled around her, bending the distant trees in a graceful parody of her own willowy steps. She was not dancing in freedom, or happiness. She was bound by herself, isolated, and yet in the grip of something much larger, much more sorrowful than mere thoughts or reckless mood.

Upstairs someone opened a window. Emma froze. Her eyes flashed open and up, fear of discovery in her every line, though she'd barely moved. She was a startled, fragile bird in the moment before deciding the direction for flight. A second later she moved, swiftly, on silent feet, back into the shadows of the house. He heard the quiet whoosh and click of the door opening and closing. Then her footsteps disappeared into the depths of the sleeping house.

Late the following afternoon Judith bustled in with a crutch in one hand and a wad of clean bandages in the other.

"Good afternoon, Corporal Simon," she said, using the alias they'd decided was best in case of eavesdroppers. "You slept late this morning. Did you rest well last night?"

"Passably," he answered vaguely.

In truth, he had not slept late. He had barely slept at all. The memory of Emma's melancholy dance had clung to him all night and into the morn, torturing him with visions of her tragic face, her arms clutching each other, her hair blowing wildly in the wind that presaged this morning's storm. It was a reluctance to engage in conversation that had him feign sleep when Judith had come to check him earlier.

"Well, rainy days are best for sleeping." She set to work unbuttoning his shirt, a castoff someone had donated, to examine the wound at his shoulder. He tried to look down as she uncovered the afflicted area to see if he'd done any damage to it the previous night, but it was hard to see so close. "Hmmm," she murmured.

"What is it, Doc? Bad news?" He was not in the mood to muster a smile, but he tried anyway.

It didn't matter; Judith had eyes only for her task. Perhaps she knew that after her revelation the previous day he'd be in no mood for jesting.

"No, it looks all right. In fact, it looks pretty good." She poked gently at the skin surrounding the stitches. "No redness. Normal swelling." She helped him lean forward so she could inspect the exit wound behind.

After Mrs. Davenport had found the bullet in his shoulder, Will had been told, they had assumed that the wound in his back was just a graze. It had been late, dark, and they'd been operating in extreme secrecy and agitation, according to Judith. It hadn't occurred to any of them that he might have been hit twice in the same area. But that was the reason for the surprise bleeding Emma had found later that necessitated his emergency surgery. The doctor, who had fortunately been too busy to inspect under the facial bandages, had rapidly stitched up the shoulder, straightened his leg, and removed the shrapnel from his knee and thigh, and now all appeared to be on the mend.

"I hope you've been counting your lucky stars, Corporal," she continued, efficiently folding and applying the clean linens. "It's just a miracle neither one of those bullets struck bone. At the very least you'd have lost the ability to use this arm, if not the whole arm. As it is, the doctor said it'll only be stiff."

Will made a cynical face. "It's a charmed life I'm leading, that's for sure." He eyed the crutch leaning against the wall. "Is that for me?"

Judith followed his gaze. "Yes. A gift from Peter."

Will's brows shot up in surprise. "Peter Davenport? How is he doing?"

She sighed. "Not too badly, considering. You know that he lost his leg, don't you?"

Will nodded, mentally uttering a silent, unpracticed prayer of thanks that such had not been his fate. "Yes. They were able to save the knee, though, were they not?"

Judith nodded. "And Mr. P—someone was able to procure a wooden leg for him. He's getting around quite well on it. Really, you wouldn't even know it was false, his limp is so slight." She lifted his arm and pulled the ends of the bandaging around. "Of course, if he gets moving too quickly he loses his balance, but I'm sure even that will improve with time."

"That's wonderful," he said sincerely, as she knotted the ends of the fabric. He slid his arm back into the sling. "And so I've inherited the crutch?"

"That's right. And now, Corporal Simon," she announced, securing the last of the buttons on his shirt, "today you shall rise. We've got to get you moving around some or the blood's all going to settle."

"God forbid." Will pushed himself delicately into a fully upright sitting position.

A moment later he heard a ponderous step in the hall and Peter appeared in the doorway. His youthful face gazed in their direction with dark eyes so like Emma's. Then he smiled faintly and ambled in. Judith was right; the limp was remarkably slight. With normal pants and boots on, if Will didn't know better, he might have thought the leg merely injured, not missing.

Will watched him approach, feeling a small but tight knot of apprehension in his gut. When Emma had broken their engagement, Buck had been the one to champion Will's cause with his sister while Peter and the rest of the Davenports had remained conspicuously silent on the matter. That silence had hurt Will almost as much as Emma's anger.

Of course, it was ludicrous to be hurt, as if a war were not a big enough reason to justify their rejection of him. His mistake had been that while he offered his opinions freely enough if asked, he never made it clear to them or to Emma that if it came down to it he would fight for his beliefs—just as they would for theirs. It was the shock of that fact that had thrown Emma. She had known his views all along, but she'd never believed, first of all, that it would come to war. None of them had, really. And secondly, she had never thought if it did come to war that he would fight against them. He should have prepared her for the worst, he knew now, rather than turning a blind eye to the possibility and hoping it never came to pass.

Peter stood over him now, thinner but looking hale in spite of it, regarding him thoughtfully. "Well, I won't say it's good to see you," he began, confirming Will's fears, "considering the circumstances. But I can say it's good to see you alive." It was then Will noticed the smile in his eyes. "The last thing I wanted to do was haul *your* dead carcass out the front door." He extended his hand.

Will raised his and they clasped solidly. "Nor would I wish to be hauled. Thank you for your consideration."

The small smile Peter wore blossomed into a grin. "You look close to death, my friend," he added. "Get up; let's get that blood moving. You need it more in your face than your arse."

"I seem to be suffering a general dearth of the stuff in all areas, thank you." Will grimaced as he shifted his leg off the pallet.

"Wait; Dee is coming," Judith interjected quickly. "You can lean on him while I pull you up."

"No, no," Will said as he pushed himself to the wall as he'd done the night before. "I can do it."

"Don't be silly. You'll hurt yourself." Judith grabbed his arm. "With Dee here it will be simple."

"Let him do it," Peter commanded, taking her elbow in his hand and pulling her gently away.

"But it's too much," she protested.

235

"No. If he thinks he can take it, let him try," Peter insisted. "We'll pick him up when he falls."

Will raised an ironic brow. "Thanks." With his back against the wall he bent his good leg under him and pushed. He slid up about a foot. "The crutch," he said tightly, waving his hand in that direction. Judith rushed to hand it to him.

With the help of the crutch Will was able to gain a standing position with greater ease than the night before but no less sweat. He stood for a moment panting shallowly, afraid to take too deep a breath but feeling dizzy with exertion.

"Hear, hear!" Peter cheered, clapping quietly. "Well done. You're a natural cripple. Come on, then, I've got a surprise for you."

Judith turned stern eyes on him. "Peter," she warned. "What have you got up your sleeve this time?"

He grinned and moved to Will's side. "Nothing illegal, don't worry," he answered. "Here, put your arm around my shoulders. We'll take a quick spin around the patio."

"The patio!" Judith said. "But it's raining."

"Pah," he scoffed. "A little rain. I don't mind it. Do you, Will?"

Will shrugged his one good shoulder, wondering if he was up to one of Peter's "surprises." "Ought to reduce the crowd out there somewhat."

Peter laughed and winked at Judith. "We won't be long."

Judith planted herself firmly in front of them. "Peter," she repeated sternly, "he's very weak and much more susceptible to pneumonia right now than normal. You can't possibly take him outside."

"Outside!" The shocked voice from the doorway commanded all of their gazes.

"Emma," Judith and Peter said simultaneously. The word echoed silently in Will's head. She looked pale and tired, but no more so than she had before last night. He wondered just how often she visited her ghostly orchestra on the terrace at midnight.

"You will under no circumstance take this man outside,"

Emma stated, stalking gracefully into the room. The line of her pretty mouth was pinched and the sight of it made Will sad. Another small violation on the war's long list of heinous acts. "Honestly, Peter, do you want to be the death of him?"

An awkward silence fell after the words. Emma glared at her brother until she realized the odd truth behind her careless sentence. At one time Peter had wanted to be the death of at least a few Yankees.

Will broke the silence. "I think it was subtle of him, really," he said, hopping slightly on his good leg to get it more directly under him. "I've needed a bath for days now. A good soak in the rain might have ensured me a few more visitors." He let his eyes linger significantly on Emma.

"A good point," she said dryly. "If you had more visitors you might monopolize fewer of the staff."

Underscoring her words, Dee entered the room. He stopped dead in his tracks at the sight of Will, hanging like a dropped bird off Peter's shoulder. "Saints preserve us!" he announced gleefully. "The dead's arisen!"

The small group broke into relieved laughter, and Judith whisked Dee away with her to attend to other tasks.

"I was just going to take him on a tour of the house," Peter said. "He needs to move around a bit and he hasn't seen our most recent changes. For example"—he turned to Will—"the sitting room has been changed to a lying room. The keeping room is now the sleeping room; the parlor, the pestilence ward. Doesn't it sound better? After all, everyone has *sitting* rooms." Will smiled and Emma rolled her eyes. "The bedrooms," Peter continued, "however well named, fell far short of what was necessary to earn the title, though—so we added a few more beds. Dozens, to be exact. It's something you really must see."

Will could not contain a reluctant chuckle, though he worried it would send him into another convulsion, and he was already feeling the effects of being upright for so long. "Sounds charming," he managed.

"Charming?" Peter echoed, an exaggerated look on his face.

"Now that's intriguing. What do you say, Em? Do you suppose we could get a witch doctor? I've got it—the washroom to—"

"Enough," Emma pleaded, a smile tugging at her lips. Will was glad to see it. He felt better just looking at her as the lines of strain and fatigue fell away with her smile. "Look at him," she directed Peter, her hand suddenly indicating Will where he swayed on his crutch. "I think perhaps standing up was enough for today. He can barely even do that."

Will tried to straighten his shoulders, as he was suddenly the center of attention, but the pain it caused did nothing to ease the dizziness in his head. "I'm all right. I'm fine. I've done this a lot, really. It's just been a while."

With that, he started to slump inexorably forward, but Emma caught him. Her surprisingly strong hands pressed against his ribs, and her body supported her hands to keep him from toppling. The touch sent shards of both pleasure and pain through him, and it was the pleasure that hurt the most. But he realized that Peter was not yet skilled enough in his balance to keep the two of them from sure disaster, so he let her help him.

"All right, you've convinced me," he said, ashamedly grateful to sit down. "I've stood today; maybe I'll walk tomorrow."

Emma helped him lower himself to the ground while Peter divested him of the crutch. "Here," she said, propping him against the wall. "Sit up for a while first; then you can try walking."

She arranged a pillow behind his back, and her nearness increased the reeling in his head tenfold. She was so close, just beside him, and it would be no effort—even for him—just to reach out and touch her. Just a touch, a finger on her arm, a small taste of the skin he'd longed to feel for so long.

He couldn't help it; he gave in to the temptation. But he could not limit the move. His hand touched her forearm; his fingers curled softly around it, then slid down her arm to grasp her fingers as she backed rapidly away. She froze and looked at their hands, color rising to her cheeks. He squeezed the delicate fingers, gently, so gently, and imagined he felt an answering squeeze, as he would have—before.

Then she snatched her hand away and slipped back to straighten his splinted leg. "Now, I've got to get some water to the men in the other room," she said, all business. "Will you be all right here for a while?" She didn't look at him as she asked, just continued to straighten the bedding around him.

Peter cleared his throat. "I'll do that, Emma," he said, already moving to the door. "You stay here and visit a minute more."

Will smiled at the maneuver to himself, he thought, until Emma said sharply, "And what are you grinning at?"

"You," he said. "You can't avoid me forever, you know. Just when you least suspect it, I'll show up in your house."

Emma sat back on he heels. "I'm not avoiding you."

Will laughed shortly, hating himself for pushing her, especially now that he knew why she avoided him, but unwilling to give it up. "Oh, come on. I see more of Judith than I do of you. A lot more."

"I have a few more obligations than Judith happens to at this time," she said defensively.

"So I've been given to understand," he said vaguely. He raised a hand to his sweating brow and pushed away several locks of long, roughly cut hair. He wished he didn't feel so woozy. He would have liked to get things straightened out between them, or at least to hear the dreadful reality from her own mouth. As it was he found himself fantasizing that Judith was somehow wrong, or even lying, as doubtful as that was.

He decided to throw caution to the wind. "Were you ever going to tell me, Emma? Or did you hope I would leave without having to find out?"

He was almost sorry he asked, so completely affirming was her reaction. Her face closed up and her hands balled into fists in her lap. "Find out what?"

He chuckled without humor, closing his eyes in fatigue. "Ever the cautious one, eh? Well, it's no good this time." He opened his eyes and searched her face sorrowfully. "I know all about you, Mrs. Price."

Chapter Seventeen

"Who is he?" Will asked.

Emma blanched and looked at him stonily, gauging him, he thought. Her hands bunched in her lap. "No one you know," she said. "He—he's for the South."

He nodded. "Ah."

It was clear neither of them knew what to say. For Will just the sight of her held him arrested. Her dark eyes and fine skin seemed impossibly pure compared to the lifeless memories he'd survived on for so long. And her stillness, her untouchable repose, was as daunting as a wall to all the questions piled up inside of him, a talisman against the harsh, precarious truths he wished to unearth.

"It—" she began, then stopped as if surprised by the word in the quiet room. He looked at her questioningly. She continued more quietly, as if coerced, "It's not as if it should matter."

His brow furrowed. "Matter?"

"To you," she said, shaking her head. She appeared to be forcing the words from her lips, then suffering some embarrassment from them. "I mean, after our last—parting. And I know how you felt about me, about my actions. I know that you wished me—gone." She tossed her hands just slightly in her lap in exasperation, or frustration.

Will felt the cloudiness between them and spoke as if feeling his way through a fog, afraid of scaring away the revelations that lurked there. "Yes, I wished you gone. Of course." Her eyes snapped up to his, aghast. The look took him aback. Why should that shock her? "Emma, I never wanted you in prison."

She closed her eyes at that and issued a short laugh that had nothing to do with amusement, her hand to her heart. He thought he caught a trace of dampness between her lashes before she bent her head, fingers clenching into a fist on her chest.

"You must have known," he began softly, then thought again. How could she have? He'd turned out to be such an accomplished actor, he thought in disgust. "That is, I hope you know now, that it was an act, a ruse. I had to do it. I wasn't as angry as I appeared. Well, perhaps I was, but"—he sighed at the inadequacy of words—"I had to—"

"Will, don't." She raised her eyes to him with an embarrassed kind of pain. "There's no need to explain. You had every right to be angry. I—well, I guess I betrayed you, though I sought only to help...." She cast a slim hand out, indicating the unconscious soldiers, the hopeless, doomed men, all around them. "But I never"—and at this she pinned him with an abruptly hard look—"*never* slept with that man, that person you all accused me of—" She broke off, red with humiliation, hard put to control rough, embittered breathing.

"I know that," he whispered. God help him, he knew that now. But he was mortified to the core that she had to doubt it. She would never have doubted him that way, he was sure. The extent of his shame was immeasurable. There was nothing adequate to say, nothing adequate to do, to make up for his monumental loss of faith in her, or to make her forget the cruelty he'd perpetrated in his anger. "I'm sorry," he muttered meagerly. "I'm so, so sorry."

She smiled wanly, then muttered, "Don't be. It's nothing compared to what I've done to myself."

Her bitter words aroused a dreadful feeling within him. "What do you mean?"

She shook her head dismissively.

"Emma, what happened to you . . . that night?" he asked.

Her eyes jerked to his. "What night?"

He almost couldn't ask, so afraid was he of the perils that could have befallen her alone in Washington, struggling to get back to her home while the land all around her bloodied itself in conflict. "How did you get back, after the escape? Were you alone?" His eyes searched her face, watched her eyelids descend to veil the fathomless depths he so longed to plumb. What was she hiding? What did she do that night? Why hadn't she come to him?

"No, I had—help." She looked surreptitiously to the door, then began to rise. Will laid a hand on her arm to stay her, his own heart twisting at the contact. "I have to go," she protested weakly.

"Just tell me one thing—please. Are you happy? This man, your husband"—the word almost caught in his throat—"does he make you happy?" There was so much more he wished to know but simply could not ask. *Does he love you? Does he keep you safe? Does he know that you are the lifeblood, the world, the soul of another man?* "Does he?" he prompted at her silence. Though he was not even sure he wanted to hear the answer.

"No one is happy now, Will," she said sadly. With that she rose swiftly. "I'll come back later," she promised. Then as if on impulse, she grazed a swift, cool hand over his forehead, pushing aside the now lengthy hair that fell into his eyes; then she pivoted and was gone.

Will sat immobile for a long time, her touch lingering on his skin, her words echoing in his head. *No one is happy. No one is happy now.* His right hand squeezed and released, squeezed and released, driving his nails into his palm, kneading a pain he could not handle. *No one is happy now.*

But that could change, he thought with a certainty that hurt. I could be happy, Emma. I would be happy if I had you back.

Peter came again several times in the following days. Will, shamed by his inability to move without awkwardness and self-pity even while possessed of two entire legs, forced himself to rise and ignore the dizziness in his head and distress in his limbs each time Peter came. Sooner than he would have thought, he was able to stand for long periods with no dizziness whatsoever and found he could maneuver with the crutch, if clumsily, even with one arm in a sling.

Peter encouraged him by alternately cajoling, then insulting him, and then cheered with great sincerity the first time he crossed an entire room alone without so much as a stumble.

Will felt a measure of success at the feat himself, but these days nothing, absolutely nothing he did or thought was divorced from the insidious knowledge that Emma was gone from him in a way so intangible and elusive that he could not fight it. She was there in his sight; he could even talk to her, but their conversations were little more than that of two strangers. After their last conversation she'd withdrawn from him, treating him as if he were any other patient in the ward—indeed, as if he actually *were* Cpl. Simon, Fifth Georgia Cavalry. He almost began to prefer talking to Judith, for their conversations were real, and with her he felt a connection to the past Emma that talking to the real thing did not accomplish.

He'd never felt so frightened or sure of her loss before, even when they'd been separated by distance, by argument, by passions that alternately drew them, then forced them apart. Because during that separation when they looked into each other's eyes they knew what they saw, *who* they saw. Now . . . now their remoteness was so complete they might never have met, Will found himself thinking illogically.

It was a warm, still evening and Will was just spooning the last of his soup to his mouth when Peter's distinctive step sounded in the hall. Will watched the empty doorway until the mischievous face he was beginning to know so well appeared in the space.

"Well, you're up late," Will drawled. "It must be after seven o'clock. Why hasn't anyone put you to bed yet?"

Peter's eyes narrowed. "Very funny. But you'll be glad I'm here. I'm on a mission," he said mysteriously, entering the room and limping toward him. When he reached his side he took the crutch from its place against the wall and handed it to him. "I've been given a special dispensation to help the especially needy."

Will blinked blandly. "And that would be me, I take it."

Peter smirked. "You betcha." He glanced stealthily behind himself. "Come on, up with you. Remember that surprise I had for you a few days ago?"

"Ah, the surprise." Will hefted himself onto his good leg and rose, clinging to the crutch. The procedure had become a bit simpler in the last week, particularly since the wooden splint on his leg had been replaced with a stiff bandaging. He almost thought he could have done without the crutch had it not been for having to get up and down off the floor whenever he wanted to move. He made a mental vow to himself never to be without furniture again if he could help it.

Peter's smile was born of the devil himself. "Ready?" he asked.

Will shrugged, amused. "Lead on."

When they reached the doorway Peter stopped him with an outstretched hand and peered around the opening like a small child hoping to see St. Nicholas. "All right." He waved to Will to follow. "But be quiet."

They moved as furtively as two full-grown men with serious leg impairments could down the bare wood hall and around the corner to the back door. As Peter opened it Will could not help thinking of the night that Emma had crept so secretly out this very door; the same click and whoosh met his memory with reality.

Negotiating the stairs was a trick Will had only done once since he'd arrived, and this time, in dim light and with Peter's hurry, he gave up trying to do it gracefully and hopped down the three steps on his good leg. The jarring awoke an aching sensation in his shoulder but he was to the point now that he could ignore the pain. It was the breathlessness that would not leave him.

At the bottom of the short flight he paused to rest. Thankfully, he was no longer sent into convulsions every time he tried to inhale deeply, but moving around still required more lung space than he apparently had available.

"Come on," Peter hissed, waving a hand at him.

Will shook his head and crutched across the patio. Peter remembered to help him down the step leading to the lawn, then brought him around a large rhododendron to the flower garden. Here were wrought-iron benches, as Will remembered well, where couples would come during parties to be alone. The line of bushes along the edge of the patio effectively blocked anyone sitting here from view. He and Emma had been here many times.

Peter motioned him to one of the benches. "Have a seat."

"Why, Peter," Will said in a mocking tone, "you haven't got any unscrupulous intentions toward me, have you?" But he sat slowly, gratefully lowering himself with a sigh. He turned his head to see Peter kneel, plunge his head into a bush, then apparently dig through the leaves and dirt at its base, rustling branches and causing dried leaves to fall down along his back. He watched bemused as the younger man rooted through first one, then another bush in the line beside the patio. "I don't know why you can't just sit in a chair like everyone else," Will complained blandly.

"Ouch!" Peter exclaimed and suddenly backed out of the bush. A feline squeal erupted and a gray cat darted out of the foliage a few feet away.

Will started to laugh. "What the—"

But Peter had dived back into the task. A moment later he backed out more slowly. "Feast your eyes, my boy," he announced, and turned dramatically, holding aloft a clear bottle two-thirds full of an amber liquid. "A whole bottle of unscrupulous intentions!"

Peter's wide smile beamed out of the darkness of rapidly approaching nightfall, and Will felt an answering one split his own face, his first genuine grin in days. "My dear and clever friend," he said, "what have you there?"

Peter pulled the bottle in to his chest protectively. "What would you have it be, in your wildest dreams?"

Will's mouth salivated at the thought. It had been months since he'd had a drink of any quality, of any kind even. "My wildest dreams? Brandy. But I'd settle for whiskey, and happily."

The grin on Peter's face became increasingly delighted. "William, you lucky dog, close your eyes. Your wildest dream is about to begin."

The first sip went down with the power of a fireball, burning a path through his chest to explode in his stomach. But the sensation was delicious, and almost immediately, long tendrils of searing heat stretched over Will's nerves and muscles, imbuing them with a cloudless relaxation he thought he'd never again feel. Pain, his constant companion the last week, skulked behind a wall of bliss, no longer ruling his helpless body.

"My boy," Will drawled after his third—or was it his fourth?—mouthful of the blessed liquid, "you've secured yourself a place in heaven."

Peter snickered and held out his hand for the bottle. "Yep, and with any luck at all, before the night is through I'll see God."

The two of them chuckled companionably. "Where on earth did you get it?" Will asked. "I didn't think there was brandy like that left anywhere in the country."

Peter hiccuped after taking too large a gulp. "Ah—excuse me," he murmured. "Emma's husband." He made a disgusted face, then widened his eyes at Will. "Oh—sorry." His face was all concern but Will only shook his head, ignoring the abrupt tightening in his chest. "Anyway, the old skinflint had it hidden away, but I found it. I knew he wouldn't make a stink when he found it missing because nobody was supposed to know he had it!" He crowed with laughter. "And he claims he doesn't even touch spirits!"

Something niggled at the back of Will's mind with the words, but he was already feeling enough of the effects of the brandy to know he'd never figure it out now.

"So," Will said, deliberately casual, "he's an ass, then?"

"Ha!" Peter burst disgustedly. "Like none I've ever seen. The man must have held a gun to her head when they married. I swear, I just can't believe she doesn't see it." He lifted the bottle again, then thrust it at Will.

Will downed two, three, four large gulps before lowering the bottle and sighing. He wiped his mouth on his sleeve and closed his eyes.

"But enough about her," Peter said charitably. "Do you remember the last time we were out here? You and me and a bottle?"

Will narrowed his eyes. The drink was really hitting him; his tolerance must be way down, he thought. "No, I don't."

"Actually, your brother was here, too, and Scaley Johnston."

"Scaley Johnston . . ." Will murmured. "How could I forget someone named Scaley?"

Peter held a wavering finger out toward the area just beside them. "Over there, remember? Scaley was asking us how to get into Barbara Samuelson's dress and you were dem—*hic*, 'scuse me—demonstrating on Brendan the proper way to—to *navigate a corset,* I think was what you said." High laughter issued from him and threatened to overtake his ability to talk. Will couldn't help laughing with him, the scene becoming clearer in his head. "And—and remember, Scaley started supplying the dialogue . . . 'Oh Barbara, oh Barbie . . . ' " Peter was convulsed with laughter.

Will's laughter mingled with his, the scene returning to him. "When who should appear, but—"

They said the name in unison: "Barbara Samuelson!"

The memory assailed him, the warm night, the drunken camaraderie, the easy conversation. "And I believe she was with Paulie Morgan, if I recall," Will added, chuckling deeply.

"Yes, yes!" Peter squeaked through tearful giggles. "Paulie the prude!" His hilarity caused Will to succumb completely and the two of them rocked with laughter.

Will glanced down at the bottle in his hand and saw that they'd already downed close to half of what had been in it. He handed it to Peter, who slurped at the stuff gleefully.

"And then there was the time"—he handed the bottle back to Will—"when my father caught Buck and Hilda in the buff down at the pond. Do you remember that?"

Will swallowed hard the mouthful of brandy he'd just taken and barked out a noise between a cough and a laugh. "Remember it? I was very nearly part of it. If Buck and Hilda hadn't been in the water, Emma and I would definitely have been caught back in those trees. Remember how your father chased them back up the lawn—"

"And Hilda didn't even have time to—"

They both lost control, wiping tears from their eyes as the mental image of a naked Hilda danced between them.

Peter slapped his hands to his chest. "She had the nicest ti—"

The distinct sound of a feminine cough caused him to bolt upright in panic. Will moved his gaze slowly over his shoulder.

"Yes, thank you for not finishing that sentence," Emma's cool voice said, glaring at them both. "And *you.*" Will's brows raised in innocence as her irate look scorched him. "I just finished searching high and low for you. If your crutch hadn't been missing I would have sworn they'd come and carted you off to Libby."

While her attention was diverted Peter tried unsuccessfully to slide the bottle behind his back, but Emma's head whipped around and caught him.

"What is that?" she demanded.

Peter held it up limply, looking at it as if it had just appeared in his hand. "This?"

"Good heavens, aren't you two sick enough?"

Will smiled languidly despite the sudden racing of his heart. "Have a nip, Em. You don't look very relaxed."

This sent Peter into another volley of giggles, during which he popped off the cork and took another sip. Then he held the bottle out to her. "Come on, sis. You can't imagine how good it feels."

Emma tried to maintain a firm look, but Will could tell it was an effort. He slid several inches over on the bench and patted the empty space with his hand. "Just for a minute. *Five* minutes," he amended. "Five minutes of respite from the grind won't do anybody any harm."

She started to smile but pinched her lips to hide it. "You always did think it was too easy to corrupt me, Will Darcy," she said. But she did not turn to leave.

His lips curved. "That's not true. I never thought it was easy. That was the sport in it."

"Sit, sit," Peter encouraged, sensing victory. "You can tell me what you were doing in the trees during Hilda's mad dash from the pond."

Emma's widened eyes turned in exasperation to Will. "You—"

"I didn't say anything!" He held his hands up in innocence. After a second he fought his way to his feet, musing how fortunate it was that he was already so practiced on the crutch while dizzy. He lurched to her side, took her forearm in his, and led her back to the bench. She let him take her.

"I'd forgotten how bad you two were together." She sulked, but it was unconvincing.

Will took the bottle from Peter and handed it to her. "One sip. It's my turn to play doctor to you, Miss Em," he said firmly. She took it but did not lift it to her mouth. "Wouldn't it feel good," he said quietly, close to her ear, "to not think about things—just for a little while?"

It was too dark to see, but he could tell by the demure lowering of her chin that she blushed. A few years ago he would have added a kiss on her smooth cheek to that intimate whisper.

"Hey," Peter objected, "no secrets."

Will laughed and leaned back. "I told her to wipe the lip of the bottle before she drinks. You've been saying some foul things."

Will snickered and Emma chuckled reluctantly at the look of

249

exaggerated offense on her brother's face. In the moment of joined laughter she raised the bottle to her mouth and sipped.

The cool liquid burned hot as it blossomed inside her, descending to her stomach. And she hoped from there it went straight to her head. Will's soft persuasion had caught her in a weak moment—after fifteen minutes of terror as she searched for him and worried that Lawrence would arrive home before she found him—and the idea of not thinking, just for a few minutes, appealed to her in a way she could not resist.

The bottle was nearly empty, she noted, as she handed it back to Will, and she wondered how full it had been when they'd started. They were tipsy, to be sure, but they did not seem completely drunk.

Will tilted his head back and drank. Emma could not keep her eyes from the side of his face, his throat, his broad chest, as he drank. She wanted to trace the muscular cords in his neck with her fingers from that square jaw to the strong collarbone beneath his shirt.

When he handed the bottle to Peter it contained barely a sip. Peter downed it and scowled. "That's a bad piece of luck for you, isn't it, Emma? After all, you can't fly very well on one wing."

She shrugged nonchalantly, not about to admit to wanting more, to wanting oblivion above all else.

"We were pretty selfish, I guess," Will said. She saw his hand lift and thought for a second he would place it on the back of the bench around her, an old habit, but he dropped it back onto his lap.

"*You* were," Peter agreed and stood uncertainly. "But I'm about the most selfless guy there is." He held a finger up and winked at them, swaying as he stood. "Wait there." He shuffled off into the darkness. After a moment the sound of his progress through the grass and leaves disappeared.

For Emma, the air was suddenly charged as her brother left them alone in the dark. Will was very close—they practically touched—and every nerve in her body stood at attention to his nearness.

"I'll be amazed if he's got more," Will murmured.

She turned to answer and found herself swept up in his sleepy gaze. "I won't be," she said, trying to maintain a sense of distance. "He's always got something up his sleeve."

Will sighed and his warm breath caressed her cheek. "You're beautiful, Lady Em," he said softly.

She felt her breath catch in her throat at the old endearment. She told herself it was the brandy that caused her head to swim suddenly and her cheeks to burn, but he was so close, his face, his eyes, his heartbreakingly soft lashes.

She could think of not a thing to say, and yet she could not tear her eyes from his face. Her lips parted.

Will looked intense, coiled, undecided. Finally, as every fiber of her being reached for it, he raised his hand to her cheek. His thumb caressed the skin as he gazed searchingly into her eyes. "I still love you, Emma," he said so quietly she barely heard, but hear she did. The words melted her, sliced through any resistance she might have offered, and she leaned into his hand.

Slowly his head came down and his lips met hers gently. Her heart tripped in her chest. She felt the urge to lean into his arms but the thought scared her. If she gave in even halfway . . . Instead she held perfectly still.

He withdrew slightly, their lips separating. His hand stayed on her cheek and his eyes penetrated hers.

Her chest rose and fell rapidly as she struggled for control. But when he dropped his hand from her face she grabbed it, folding it between both of hers. She brought it to her chest and held it dear. Then, as he looked at her with the question clear in his eyes, she took her left hand and brought it softly to his jaw, then slid it to the back of his neck, lacing her fingers through his hair.

He pulled his hand from hers and with a fierce look took her by the waist. "Damn it, Emma, kiss me before I go crazy," he commanded.

She dissolved into him.

Their lips met in frantic need. He crushed her to his chest and she slid her arm around his neck, pulling him as close as close could come. Her other hand rested on his leg to avoid the sling and kneaded the hard muscle of his thigh. Lips slid over lips, and tongues reached and twined. Will's subtle growth of beard scratched her face but she didn't care. Emma's heart was sailing somewhere over her head as the rich sensations of Will, brandy, and love united to send her spiraling away from reason.

A familiar fire burned in her loins, and a desire that mocked all others gripped her. She felt her hips pushing forward, and sensed his answering obsession in the rhythm of his tongue. This was it, the thing she'd dreamed of when she'd awakened all those nights with her flesh burning and her husband lying like ice beside her. But this was real, this was Will, and she could feel his hot hand on her waist, his hot breath in her own lungs.

The sound of breaking twigs in the near distance broke them apart. They split, scanning each other breathlessly, with similar expressions of stunned intensity. The irregular footsteps neared. Anger flared within Emma, for she did not want it to end. She leaned forward just as the steps got close, and planted a hard, wet kiss on his lips as if to seal the passion. Then she backed slowly away, her eyes still on his, as Peter returned to the garden.

"Look what I've got," he sang, swinging a full bottle of the same dark liquid in one hand above his head.

Emma and Will tore their eyes apart and looked at Peter.

Will recovered first. "Well, well." He cleared his throat of the rasp it had developed. "Our master magician conjures another one. Hand it over." His tone was compelling, and Peter handed the bottle to him at once.

Will popped off the cork and downed several slugs. Then he passed it to Emma. She followed suit.

Peter watched them blearily, the ghost of a notion lighting his eyes. "My, so thirsty in my absence," he said with a sly grin.

Will settled back into the seat, and Emma sat still as the fire burned again from her stomach through her limbs. "Peter," she said slowly, "do you think you could find something to do"—

she shot a wary glance at Will, who watched her carefully—
"over there somewhere for a while?" She pointed away from the
benches to a separate area of the garden, out of the way.

Peter shook his head mournfully. "Just like the old days," he
lamented, words slurring. "But I'm taking the bottle with me. It's
mine, after all."

"Take it," she said, smiling at his pitiful act. "Just give us a
few minutes alone."

Peter sauntered off singing *The Southern Soldier Boy* in an
indeterminate key.

Emma waited until his voice was reedy with distance, then
turned her head to Will. He'd moved his arm to the back of the
bench, as she thought he'd do earlier, and leaned back, watching
her. One eyebrow raised, his lips curved slightly.

"Will," she said, the somber note in her voice causing his
smile to fade. "You're in great danger here."

The smile returned. "That's not news, Em."

"No"—she shook her head—"I'm serious. It's worse than
you know." She glanced away quickly and lowered her voice.
"There's someone here, someone who knows you and does not
wish you well." Will sat up straighter. "He's sworn to take you
to the authorities in three days. You must make plans to leave."

"Who is it?" he asked.

She clasped her hands together and avoided his eyes. "I can't
tell you, but you have to trust me. You can't stay. Are you able
to walk at all? I don't think I can get you a horse; there just aren't
any anymore." The panic she felt at the thought of him daring
to escape while he was still so weak was extreme. It might have
been exacerbated by the drink, but she felt suddenly as if the
whole situation were hopeless.

Obviously sensing her mood, Will leaned forward and took her
hands in his. "I'll be all right; I can get away. But, Emma, sweetheart, you have to tell me who it is so I'll know how to avoid
them. Is it someone in the house?"

Tears blocked her throat. She nodded.

A horrible suspicion twisted his features. "Not Judith—"

253

"No, no," Emma burst out on an angry sob. "It's no one who's helped you. It—it's my husband." She could not disguise the disgust she felt with the words. "He's discovered who you are and I guess he's jealous or something and he said he'd only keep the secret for ten days and that ends—"

"Shhh, shhh," Will soothed, pulling her to him with his good arm. She buried her face in his shoulder. "It's all right. I might do the same thing if I were him. . . ."

She wished he *could* do the same thing. There was nothing she'd like better than to see her husband behind bars.

"I'm sorry." She wept, feeling absurdly emotional but unable to control herself. "Will, I'm sorry for everything. God—it's all such a m-mess." She forced herself to sit up. Rubbing her cheeks free of the humiliating wetness, she straightened her shoulders. "I'll help you," she said with great determination.

"No." He shook his head. "I'll do it myself. I don't want you involved."

"But you can't do it alone!"

They both heard the rustle of leaves. Will turned on the seat, still holding Emma's hand. Peter emerged none too gently from the bushes.

"I think someone's coming," he blurted. "I heard the door—"

All heads whipped around as sharp steps sounded on the patio. Whoever it was was moving fast, and Emma felt herself frozen where she sat.

Like a specter emerging from a fog, the pale form of Lawrence Price appeared in the clearing.

Emma made a choking sound and stood swiftly, unable to look at Will. He rose slowly beside her, his hand on the small of her back, supporting her.

"Lawrence?" his voice was soft, incredulous.

Lawrence surveyed them coldly. "Will," he murmured. Then, "I'll thank you to take your hand off of my wife."

254

Chapter Eighteen

Will saw first the look of terror on Emma's face; then his suddenly sober brain took in the utterly shocking, stunningly white face of Lawrence Price.

The enormity of it hit him in the gut like a fist. *Mrs. Price.* Mrs. Lawrence Price. Emma had married Lawrence Price. The idea was staggering, blinding. He could make no sense of it.

How well could they know each other? They'd only spoken once or twice during the time they'd met at his house. Had they known each other before and not let on—did they meet each other again afterward? The lack of logic in the facts made his head spin.

Emma moved rapidly to Lawrence's side. "I was just coming in," she said quickly.

Will watched in horrified fascination as Lawrence's long, thin hands took hold of her arms. "I came home early, darling," he said, smoothly bending to place a kiss on her cheek. "Why don't you go on up?"

"No, I'll wait." She was stiff in his grasp. She turned to face

Will and Peter, who both stood mutely gaping at them. She had the look of a child who'd been caught stealing, Will thought.

Lawrence's eyes raked Peter, flicked over the bottle with a raised brow, and came to rest on Will. The look was superior, knowing, and Will felt rage ignite within himself.

He was the spy, Will suddenly knew. *He* was the one who'd gotten the information Emma had been caught with. Only Lawrence was high enough in the hierarchy to have access to that kind of knowledge. And the coward had employed Emma as his messenger.

The realization must have paraded across his face because Lawrence said then, ''We have a lot to talk about, Will.''

His fist contracted by his side. ''Funny. I was just thinking there was nothing more to be said,'' he answered, deceptively calm. *Someone knows about you, someone who does not wish you well. . . . My husband.*

''But that's where you're wrong. How are you feeling, by the way?'' His tone was genial and made Will want to strike him.

''At this particular moment or in general?'' Will questioned wryly. No point in pretending he wasn't shocked. Lawrence would have seen through that in an instant.

But Price . . . of all people. He *hated* the Confederates, railed against them with the fervor of a priest amid sinners, and he punished all who fell into his hands with a ruthlessness that had shocked Will on several occasions. It had all been a masquerade, then, a show to distract everyone from his real work—spying for the Confederacy. The notion was mind-boggling.

Lawrence smiled. ''I always enjoyed your wit, Darcy. What I meant was, how are your wounds?''

Will couldn't help it; he stared in abject wonder at the man. A Confederate. And married to Emma. *His* Emma. He tore his gaze from the cadaverous face and reached for his crutch. ''I'll just go in now,'' he said flatly.

Lawrence did not budge. ''We have a lot to talk about, Will,'' he repeated.

Fury possessed him. Will shook his head. ''I don't think so,'' he bit out. He limped toward them to pass.

Emma tried to step back, but Will could see Lawrence's hand tighten on her arm. She tried to wrestle free discreetly, but Will saw it, saw her caught by the devil's white pincers.

"Let go of your wife's arm," he said, ominously low, as he neared. "You're hurting her."

A breath of air escaped Emma's lips, and for a second Will thought Lawrence had only tightened his grip. Then he let her go. She stepped quickly back and away, allowing a space through which Will could pass to get to the patio. She did not look up from the ground.

He thought of the kiss they'd shared, the passion that still burned between them. He thought of Lawrence's clawlike hand on her flesh. He remembered that last fierce kiss she'd placed hard on his lips. None of it meant anything. And at the same time it all meant everything.

He walked away.

Carrying the crutch and limping badly, Will walked away from her. Emma wanted to cry, wanted to race after him, wanted to soothe away the horrid, stunned look on his face.

Peter cleared his throat. She'd completely forgotten about his presence. "Well, guess I'll be going, too," he muttered. "Good night."

Neither Emma nor Lawrence said a word as he turned and moved in the opposite direction. She stood abjectly beside her husband. Had Lawrence heard her warning Will? No, certainly not. If he had, he would have taken Will off immediately rather than risk his escape. But still, she could not stop the trembling in her limbs.

"Come, darling," he said, taking her firmly by the arm again. "Let's go to bed."

She walked obediently into the house, her mind in a turmoil. Surely Will saw now why he must leave so quickly. At least she'd been able to warn him before they were caught. Perhaps even now he made his plans. She turned her mind from the memory of his face, the shock, the utter stupefaction upon learning who her husband was. Did he feel doubly betrayed? By her and by his friend, his supposed compatriot? She didn't know. She could not bear to think about it.

It was sobering, she mused sullenly, to be confronted by the sight of a livid Lawrence Price. Though he was only a few years older than Will, his looks and bearing gave him the air of someone from her parents' generation.

She ascended the stairs, remarkably steady for the brandy she'd consumed, and contemplated how she hated going up to bed with him. He would berate her, she knew, for her behavior. With a fluttering of apprehension, she wondered if he would strike her as he had before, but she knew the reason that time was because she'd argued with him. Tonight, she would let him rant. Then they would lie awkwardly beside each other until sleep could no longer be denied. She felt tired just thinking about the scene to come.

He opened the door for her, ever courteous in public places, and she entered numbly. She did not have the energy to fight him, so she turned ready to allow him whatever raving he might wish to exercise on her.

She was unprepared for the fist that caught her in the chest, just above her right breast. She twisted with the blow and clutched her arms to her chest.

"You whore. You drunken, adulterous whore," he seethed through gritted teeth. "What did you think you were doing out there in the dark?"

"I—I—" She had no answer. This was no slap, no irrationally justified punishment. This was pure wrath.

Slowly she straightened to stand again before him, her left hand pressed against the throbbing spot where he'd struck. She knew, deep inside, that if she turned away from his anger it would double; yet she was not sure how to respond to counteract it.

"Out there indulging in your filthy, physical pleasures," he fumed, pacing three short steps to the right, then three steps back again. "You wanted him, didn't you? Admit it. You drank with him, evil, sinful spirits, and you wanted Will Darcy again with your wicked body.''

Emma watched him, overwhelmed by his anger again, confused by the display of possessiveness when he wanted nothing of her anyway. She began to nod slowly, incredulously. ''Yes,'' she said clearly, her heart demanding that she speak it. ''I did want him. I wanted him more than I've ever wanted anything.'' Blood pounded in her ears with the admission.

Lawrence glared at her, eyes radiating more heat than she'd ever seen in him. ''You disgust me,'' he hissed.

Hatred reared up inside her. ''As you do me,'' she enunciated in a similar tone. She stood before him, feeling rage strengthen her as it never had before in his presence. ''Who are you to judge me? Who are you to demand loyalty—fidelity even—when you show nothing to me but cruelty?''

His hand whipped out, palm flat, but she saw it coming and averted her head. The strike was hard, catching her on the back of the head, tearing through her hair. It jumbled her vision so that she could not immediately focus.

''I am your husband,'' he snarled.

Perhaps it was the alcohol, but she felt her own ire rise up to meet his. Before she could think twice she raised her hand and slapped him back, full across the face. Her fingers prickled and stung with the impact. In the ensuing moment of astonishment she stared at his reddening face. Then, without bothering to conceal her satisfaction, she said, ''I can't stand you.''

Like the strike of a copperhead, his hand shot out and grabbed her by the throat, fingers punishing, as if to dig clear through her skin. She gasped and involuntarily clutched his arm. Her feet stumbled to stay under her as he pushed her backward, across the bare wood floor, until her shoulders hit the wall and drove the last breath from her lungs.

Her eyes burned as Lawrence pressed harder. She dug her nails into his arm, felt his flesh give beneath them, but his face was rabid, unhinged. He did not even feel it.

''I'm going to turn him in,'' he growled. ''I'm going to get rid of him. You're lucky I don't kill him.''

Abruptly he let her go. Her weak knees barely held her and she sagged against the wall, clutching her neck and gasping for air. Her head swam and terror shot through her veins. He was capable of anything.

Eyes on the door, she tried to calculate how many steps it would take to reach it. He was turned away from her now, pacing short steps away, his hand in his hair; but he was still between her and escape.

''Obedience!'' he barked, and her eyes snapped back to him. He approached her slowly. ''You promised obedience. You *begged* me, remember? You begged me for time and I gave it to you, because you promised to honor me. And what do I get instead? *This*—this sinful, lustful, *disobedient* wife!'' He shouted the words directly into her face. She twisted her head away.

He was insane. She had to get out of there. But with his madness came an uncanny quickness, she knew, and an ability to know her thoughts almost before she had them.

''Did you let him touch you? Did you kiss him?'' he demanded.

She felt herself blush, yet met his eyes steadily. ''What does it matter to you?'' she said lowly.

He raised his brows, looked at her consideringly for a moment, then turned to pace away again. ''What does it matter to me? She asks what does it matter to me?'' He was about ten feet from her when he turned abruptly with an icy, narrowed glare. ''I'll tell you what it matters. You are mine, Emma. Mine to do with as I please. You were unwise to forget that.'' He started back toward her.

''You cannot escape me. You will never escape me, not until death takes you.'' Her racing heart threatened to burst from her chest the closer he came. ''You see, I can see right through you. You're an open book. You have no secrets from me.''

If he reached her, he would kill her; she was sure of it. She watched, paralyzed, as he came inexorably forward.

Her entire body shook. It was true, he knew everything she

knew. She feared even now he read her mind. But when he got within three feet of her she pushed herself off the wall straight into his chest. In shock, he staggered back, hand grasping for her. His fingers grazed her arms and she pushed again, this time off of him and toward the door.

She dove for the knob, hearing him pound after her. She twisted the handle and pulled, saw four inches of escape, when his palm hit the wood above her head and slammed it shut in front of her. She whirled and raised her leg to kick him, but he was so close her knee caught him in the groin.

He grunted and pitched forward, his head hitting her shoulder. She pushed him off with all her might. He stumbled backward, bent over, mouth open, saliva dripping onto the floor.

Emma wrenched her eyes away. She spun, yanked open the door, and slammed it behind her as she fled.

Instinct propelled her down the hall. Her mother's door was closed but not locked. She barged through it, panting and gasping and sobbing so hard she could not speak.

Her mother's face registered shock first; then she slid quickly from the bed as Emma slammed the door behind her and collapsed against it.

"Emma, what is it? What's happened?"

Emma could force no words from her lips. Hysteria clutched her. She could barely keep air long enough to breathe, so great were her sobs. Her mother's hands made long, soothing sweeps down her quaking back as Emma buried her face in her mother's shoulder. She was racked by grief and horror. All the emotions she'd held in check for so long exploded within her like so many fireworks.

"L-Lawrence," she choked out.

Her mother stroked her hair. "What's wrong? Have you had a fight?"

Emma made a sound, a vicious growl that came from a place deep inside. "He's evil," she snarled. She could feel her own face contort with hatred. For the first time in her life she thought she could kill someone.

"Emma!" her mother gasped.

But she dissolved into tears again. "He—he wants to kill me. He's going to kill me, I know it."

"Emma." Her mother's voice was sharp. "Get hold of yourself. You're exhausted and overwrought. Now tell me exactly what's happened."

Emma became suddenly aware of herself, of her hands clutching her mother's arms, of her face and hands drenched with tears, her hair stuck to her skin and neck. She straightened slowly, pushing away the wet locks with desperately shaking hands, but she succeeded only in making a bigger mess. She clawed at her fingers, trying to disentangle the hair from them, at the same time trying to master her own breathing. But her stomach wobbled like jelly in a bowl and her nerves were seized by staccato bursts of trembling.

She had to pull herself together. She had to regain her anger, because this disintegration of her spirit was more frightening than anything Lawrence had done to her.

"What happened? Tell me from the beginning." Her mother's voice, so matter-of-fact, so commanding.

She sniffed and took a deep breath. "Out—outside, I was— with Will and Peter. It was all so harmless." Her hands fluttered before her and she pawed at them again, as though the long tendrils of hair still clung to them. "I-I only wanted a minute—just a minute to sit. It felt so good. . . ." Tears coursed down her cheeks again as she thought of Will's kiss, his arms, his love. She brought her hands to her face. "I can't stand this," she breathed.

Her mother nodded. "I think I understand. Lawrence was jealous. He was angry."

Emma laughed harshly through her fingers, dragging her hands down her face until her fingertips were at her mouth. "Jealous," she repeated bitterly. "He has nothing but hatred inside of him." She stared blankly across the room, seeing Lawrence's hideous face.

"Honey," her mother said, "it's understandable. Of course he would be jealous. Perhaps it may seem as though he hates you, or hates Will, but don't you see? He's threatened by Will.''

Emma stared at her mother in wonder. How could she be so wrong? How could she possibly believe that Lawrence was normal in any way? That his actions were anything but deranged?

A knock sounded at the door. Emma started violently, terror propelling her to her feet. ''No!'' she heard herself cry as she tripped over her skirts toward the bed. ''Don't let him in. For the love of God, don't let him in!'' She watched in horror as her mother moved decisively to the door.

She clutched the pillow to her breast as her frantic eyes roved the room—the window, the closet—was there no other escape?

Unstoppable, the door widened. Standing in the hall, in the light of a single candle, was Will.

Disbelief made her eyes swing shut and relief made her head spin. When she blinked her eyes open he was still there. She threw herself from the bed, grabbed up her skirts, and plunged across the space into his arms. Will dropped the crutch and encircled her with his right arm. The left in its sling tentatively clutched the candle away from her.

''Will,'' she sobbed. ''Take me, please, take me away with you.'' She could feel his arm tighten around her—warm, strong, protective. She wanted to melt into its comfort.

''What's happened?'' he asked gently.

Emma's mother drew herself up and levelled a steely gaze at him. ''If I thought you would perpetrate such harm, William, I would not have allowed you to stay.''

''No!'' Emma protested.

''What happened?'' he ground out.

''You've succeeded in arousing the worst kind of suspicion in Emma's husband,'' her mother said.

Emma tried to swallow the panic in her throat but blustered desperately, ''He hates me, Will. He wants to kill me. Please, you've got to help me.'' She stared up into his dear, anguished eyes. The strangeness of her panic, the chaotic madness in her blood, frightened even her. As she looked at him, she began to doubt her own sanity.

She brought a hand back to her face and started to turn away. "Dear God, what's become of me? He—he tried to kill me." For a second, she did not believe herself.

Will's hand grabbed her as she slipped from his embrace. The feel of it, kind and firm, on her arm brought her back to a semblance of reality.

"Emma," he said urgently. He pushed the candle at Mrs. Davenport, giving the woman no choice but to take it. Then gently, so gently, he brushed away the hair that matted against the wet skin of her neck. She winced as his fingers passed over the area that Lawrence had grabbed. "My God," he breathed. He turned his head angrily to Mrs. Davenport. "Did you see this?" he barked. "Is *this* what you consider a normal expression of suspicion?"

Emma's mother leaned in, a look of astonishment blanketing her face. "Oh, Emma," she said mournfully and reached out a hand.

Emma felt the tears well into her throat again at the pity and sadness in her mother's voice.

"I'm going to kill him," Will uttered lowly.

Both women started. "Will, no," Emma said. "You can't. And there's so much he can do to hurt you." She turned her face to his, bringing her hand up to his chest. "You have to leave. Now, tonight. He's going to turn you in."

"I'm not going to leave you with him," he said incredulously.

Mrs. Davenport raised her chin. "You must remember that *he* is her husband," she stated. "And nothing short of God can alter that."

Emma flinched with the words but said nothing to deny them.

"Then let me be the instrument of God," Will retorted. "How can you propose to leave your own daughter in the clutches of someone who could do *this?*" he demanded, holding Emma's hair in one hand to expose her neck.

"I've known of other men like that who've had to learn to change their ways," Mrs. Davenport said in a hard voice. "I shall speak to him about it."

Humiliation stung Emma's cheeks and she backed slowly out of Will's grasp. He turned bewildered eyes on her. "You have to get out of here," she said, her voice a harsh whisper.

His face betrayed confusion as his eyes searched hers. He turned to her mother. "Mrs. Davenport, I beg you. Let me speak to Emma alone, please."

"I think not." The older woman wrapped her robe more closely about herself. "There is already impropriety enough in your very presence here. I suggest you take Emma's advice and leave immediately."

"Impropriety!" he repeated, the absurdity of the idea in every line of his face as he glared at her. "The man has beaten your daughter and you won't allow me a private word with her?"

"The man is her husband," she maintained stonily. "And think what he might do if he knew you'd been alone with her."

Will expelled a gust of air.

"She's right," Emma said, finding strength from somewhere to put into her voice. "I can handle him. But you are at his mercy and I can tell you there's precious little of that to depend on."

Will stared at her, pain stark in his eyes. He turned again to her mother, defeat in his shoulders. "*Please.* Just a word. Then I'll leave."

Emma watched her mother's face register an inkling of pity. "Five minutes," she pronounced. "I will talk with Mr. Price."

Emma shuddered at the thought, but already the wild events of the evening had taken on the surreal aspect of a nightmare. It was over. Could it possibly have been as bad as she'd felt at the moment? Even now the thought of Lawrence killing her seemed little short of dramatic.

The door closed quietly behind Mrs. Davenport and Will's expression changed to one of ardent intensity. "Emma, you mustn't stay with him. I've seen what he can do when he's angry. He's— he's—" Words failed him and Emma saw that he knew the real Lawrence Price, as she did.

"I know," she said quietly. "But the only real harm he can do me is to hurt you. So you must leave. Do you understand?"

Will came toward her and grasped her hands in his. "Come with me. I can keep you safe," he said, his voice low and compelling.

The surge of desire she felt at those words nearly weakened her resolve. "Where, Will? Where would we go?" she asked hopelessly.

His hands gripped hers. "Out of the city. I know a hundred ways—"

"He would find me no matter what. And how far do you think you would get with me? Alone you can disappear. I saw you—that day in the market—no one else would know you." She felt tears drip down her cheeks again, but this point she could not lose. "You must disappear, just like that. You must use one of those hundred ways and save yourself. For me."

"And leave you here with him? You must be mad. I'd sooner cut off my own arm."

"Once you're gone I'll be fine. It's your presence that angers him. I'll be fine," she repeated doggedly, to convince herself as much as him. "Really, he's never done this before."

Rough, agonized breathing issued from Will's lungs. "Why, Emma, why did you marry him?" he rasped.

She opened her mouth to speak, to say—something. But she was saved from the lie by her mother.

"You must go," Mrs. Davenport said sternly. "Now. He's no longer here. Now is the perfect time."

Will looked from Emma to her mother and back again. "Go, Will," Emma said softly. "Please do it, for me."

He sighed in frustration. "I'll come back," he promised, eyes boring into her. "I'll come back for you. Lawrence Price be damned."

Will moved into Emma and slid his arm resolutely around her waist. Emma gazed up into his eyes, eyes so full of pain and confusion it made her want to weep, and worse, to hold on to him so tightly that she followed him right out the door. But the thought of what would happen if he were caught checked her.

The only way Lawrence would not pursue him was if he left alone.

His breath caressed her cheek as he spoke. "I love you, Emma Davenport," he avowed. "And I'll come back for you."

Her lips parted to reply, but they were captured in his. Right there, in front of her mother, he kissed her savagely, passionately, with all the power of fear and desire.

Emma slid her arms around his neck and pulled herself into him. *Just once, this one last time, and then he'll be gone. . . .*

He pulled away abruptly and turned for the door. Emma's breath came in short rapid bursts. "Godspeed," she whispered as he yanked opened the door.

He did not reply or even look back, but moved down the hall with his awkward, limping gait. She saw him pull the sling over his head and toss it to the ground as he rounded the finial to descend the stairs.

Emma stood staring at the empty space down the hall for a long moment after he disappeared from view.

Then she felt her mother's roughened hand on her arm. "You did the right thing," she said quietly.

Emma nodded jerkily. Desire and frustration skated along her nerves. Fear washed though her veins. But at that moment nothing felt more wrong than standing there alone, without Will.

The stillness in Emma's heart was jolted to a start a minute later when the unmistakable sound of horses pounding up the street was heard. The once ordinary sound now rang ominously unfamiliar, as there were no horses to be had by anyone but the military, and even then the lower ranks went without.

The hoofbeats stopped abruptly in front of the Davenport house and Emma ran to the window. Her mother followed and the two of them peered out the wavery glass at three Confederate officers on large, winded horses. They dismounted simultaneously, tossing the reins around the wrought-iron fence, and strode in their heavy boots up the front stoop to the door.

Emma turned but her mother had already started for the stairs. "Don't let them in," she said impulsively. But she knew they had no other choice, and her mother did not even deign to reply.

When they reached the hall the knock at the door sounded loud in the cavernous void of the foyer.

Mrs. Davenport started down the stairs, and Emma followed on quaking, uncertain knees. They were halfway down the long curving staircase when Lawrence stepped out of the front parlor, his boot heels echoing on the marble floor of the foyer. In his hand was a long gray pistol, cocked.

"I believe that's for me," he said coolly. "Please go ahead and let them in."

Emma and her mother stood frozen on the stairs. The knock sounded again. Her mother started down.

"What are you doing with that gun?" Emma asked.

Mrs. Davenport reached the door and unbolted it. It creaked open and a cool night wind blew in, billowing her robe.

Lawrence's reply was quiet, but it sounded in Emma's head like a bell tolling. "Apprehending a spy."

Emma's eyes scanned the empty foyer as she crept down three more stairs, hands gripping the railing as if she might fall, white knuckled, damp palmed. Surely he'd gotten away; he must have made it at least out of the house. Out the back door? Somewhere through the garden? Could they hold off the soldiers long enough for him to at least get a decent head start?

But her vain hopes were quickly dashed.

"Captain Merton," Lawrence said to the head officer. "Thank you for coming so quickly."

The officers doffed their hats upon entering the house. The youngest of them looked sheepishly up at Emma with a tight smile.

"Message was you'd caught a spy, sir," he said. "Beg pardon for disturbing your evening, ladies." He inclined his head politely.

Emma stared at them in blank disorientation. Suddenly they were her enemies. These brave, worn men who fought so hard for her cause, her family, her state and country, they now stood to destroy that which she held more dear than anything.

"No," she heard herself say.

But they did not hear, or did not pay attention. For at that same moment Lawrence turned back to the parlor door and spoke clearly. "Right this way, Captain Darcy. Your escort has arrived."

"No," Emma said again, and this time the officers' heads rotated to her.

Her mother, panic in her eyes, moved swiftly up the stairs to take her hand and put an arm about her waist. "Emma, be quiet," she whispered harshly. "Do you want to be arrested as well? A traitor to your own country?"

But Emma's eyes were riveted on the parlor doorway. A traitor? For wanting the man she loved to live through the war? Right and wrong congealed in her mind into a muddy mess. North and South were braided together too intimately to separate, she thought with ludicrous clarity. Why couldn't they all see it now, as clearly as she could? These soldiers were not her enemy, and neither was Will. How was it that things had come to such a pass?

Everything moved in slow motion before her. Will stepped into the hallway, his hands tied securely in front of him with a burgundy-colored cord from the parlor draperies. She could feel her mother's grip on her wrist tighten enough to bruise.

"No!" burst from her again, an agonized protest wrenched from her throat.

Her mother's hand constricted and shook her harshly. "Be still!" she commanded.

But Will's eyes had found hers and they connected across the distance. His expression was fierce and imploring at the same time. She swallowed and bit her tongue.

"Have you anyone who can vouch for you, sir?" the captain inquired perfunctorily. "To attest that you are not, as this man asserts, a Yankee spy?"

"No, I do not," Will answered immediately, his voice clear and strong in the barren room. His eyes shifted to the captain, who shuffled uncomfortably under the vehemence of the glare.

Emma understood then as clearly as if he'd somehow whispered to her across the room. She was not to fight for him. She would keep quiet. Fighting now would do no good, for he needed someone on the outside—someone who could set him free.

Chapter Nineteen

Will stopped his laborious pacing around the tiny room and lowered himself to the bare plank floor. It was the cleanest spot he could find but it was still sticky to the touch. Gingerly, to avoid awakening the old pain in his shoulder and the new pain in his ribs, stomach, and face, he leaned against the wall. He'd been there for four days. Four days of imprisonment with no light and only water to drink. The tactic was something called solitary confinement. He'd been interrogated when he first arrived—beaten, cajoled, and threatened—then left completely alone to change his mind about revealing the Union Army's plans, as well as whatever he'd gleaned in his spying about the Confederates.

But he was not a spy, he'd maintained, somewhat doggedly and frequently by rote, throughout the interrogation. He'd been wounded in the battle at Fort Harrison and brought to the hospital by someone who'd mistakenly thought he was a Confederate wounded.

"Why didn't you tell anyone?" the beefy, red-faced corporal had asked, again and again, angrier each time he got no answer.

But it was an idiotic question, one that no self-respecting officer of any intelligence would have asked, so Will refused to answer.

Finally, tiring of the repetition, he'd countered mildly, "Would you?" An answer that got him considerably more attention, if unwanted, and fewer stupid questions than his silence had done.

But for the last four days he'd been alone. Alone to contemplate his own stupidity and the hopeless state in which he'd left Emma. Now that he was incarcerated the desperation of her situation was unbearable. There would be no rescue for her if he were to die in here, only a lifetime of subjugation and abuse. It was a thought that filled him with pain, and had him thinking, with a morbidity that frightened him, that she might be better off dead. For he'd seen what Lawrence was capable of. . . .

He did not think about his own situation, his own future. That would be an exercise in self-pity. God only knew what would become of him. Even the most lenient sentence would be no better than exactly where he was right now. Caged, away from Emma, and as good as dead himself.

He laid his head on his arms and closed his tired, scratchy eyes. It was amazing. As exhausted as he was he could not sleep. As limp and beaten as his body felt, it would not succumb to unconsciousness. That was the real torture—the wakefulness to think, to lament, and to wish. He suffered his own worst nightmares consciously, with the difference that now he knew them to be true.

The metal scrape of a key in the lock made him raise his heavy head and look to the door. The dense wood-and-iron portal swung back on unoiled hinges that protested every inch of the motion. He pushed himself up straighter and blinked dry eyes hard against the light from a lamp the visitor bore. He rose stiffly, sliding up the dirty plaster of the wall to stand limply on his left leg.

The intruder stood motionless just inside the closed door, saying nothing, until Will's eyes adjusted to the light and he squinted into the pale face.

"I'm sorry I couldn't get here sooner," Lawrence said, his voice odd in the small, silent room. "I had to make it look good for them, Will. I hope you understand.''

Will tried to put the man's words together into some kind of sense but, whether from lack of food or lack of rest, he could not. "I don't," he rasped. "I don't understand any of this." It hurt to speak and he wondered briefly if they'd cracked his jaw when they'd hit him. He raised his good hand to the spot, his other arm held tightly against the side of his body. Impossible to tell.

Lawrence's features were eerie and distorted behind the lamp. "That's partly why I'm here. You deserve an explanation."

Will scoffed weakly. "When did I earn that?"

"You must understand," Lawrence repeated, his voice tinged with urgency. "I had to make it real. They mustn't suspect me. But trust me, I'll have you out within the week. Two at the most. They're prepared to ignore you now. They think you've nothing more to give."

"Trust you," Will muttered. "Trust *you*." He laughed, a dry, worn sound.

Lawrence listened to him a moment, then stepped forward and handed him something wrapped in a cloth. "Here," he said. "I'll bring more later."

Will hesitated, then took it. Inside was a biscuit. He stared at it. A real, tender, fresh biscuit. He brought the morsel to his instantly salivating mouth. He choked as the dry crumbs hit the back of his throat, but he devoured it anyway. The bread awoke a powerful growling in his stomach. Eyeing Lawrence warily, he wiped his hand on his pant leg.

"So. You'll have me out in a week or two. To what sort of warped loyalty do I owe this? Or is it just more convenient to have me out of the way?" Will felt slightly more awake after the minuscule meal, enough to feel anger return and to control his words.

"Don't be a fool," Lawrence said harshly but low. "We're on the same side. You don't honestly believe I'd turn coat for these infantile barbarians, do you?"

Will's understanding was slow. The same side, he repeated to himself, a spy for the Union after all, not Confederate but fooling them all. He felt confusion trip him. "But you, you're—does Emma know?"

Lawrence snorted derisively. "You're pitiful, do you know? Besotted. No, she doesn't know. Who would entrust information like that to a woman? No, she thinks I'm as obsessively Confederate as anyone in her household. More so, even. That's one reason she married me."

"Trust you," Will repeated ironically.

Lawrence cleared his throat and looked, for a split second, disconcerted. Then, with a lift of his chin, he regained his imperious air. "I want you to know that I have never touched her in a sexual way. She was just a means to an end. The same end, Will, that you work toward."

Shock caused Will's jaw to drop. Then he laughed in disbelief. The notion, as agreeable as it would be to believe, was absurd. Though what possible reason Lawrence could have to lie about such a thing was beyond Will. He squelched the involuntary surge of relief that threatened at Lawrence's words and scowled at him. "You can't seriously expect me to believe that," he said.

The man was up to something, it was obvious, and with Lawrence that was always dangerous. The fact was he *had* touched Emma, in a brutal, disgusting way. "*You're* the barbarian, Lawrence," he continued, awash in visions of the bruises on Emma's neck. "I've seen your tactics and you're nothing more than primitive yourself. There's no virtue in what you've done to her. Not for any cause. Not for any end."

He wished he could think more quickly. He wished he could stand on his own two feet and beat the last breath from Lawrence Price's body. Instead he stayed, leaning heavily against the wall.

"But there is," Lawrence replied intently. "You would be astonished at the amount of information we've been able to gain here. And it's prisoners like you that I am able to liberate who convey it to our troops. Which brings me to my point. I will have several imperative messages to send with you, and you must be sure to get them to the proper people immediately upon your release. I'm not sure yet of the exact timing, but you shouldn't have to be here long. This information could mean the difference between invading Richmond now or waiting out the siege.''

Will's mind worked slowly over all he said. Information, freed prisoners, timing. ''I'm here now on purpose, then. You planned this.''

Lawrence smiled deprecatingly. ''Well, not all of it. I hadn't anticipated your presence, specifically, fortuitous though it may be. And I would have waited until you were feeling a little better—if you had been able to keep your hands off of Emma. But, yes, I must confess this time I was aided a bit by luck.''

''This time.''

Lawrence shrugged, a light smile on his thin lips. ''I had to—engineer a few things in Emma's case.''

Emma's case. Emma's case had been planned. Col. Harding's words, as he revealed the cipher Emma was carrying with the smuggled medicines, came clearly back to him. *We have a very reliable source implicating Miss Davenport in the scheme. Very reliable* . . . His tone had been thick with meaning.

''You set her up,'' Will said incredulously. Connections exploded in his mind like sequential mines. ''*You* intercepted her in Washington. It was you who brought her here.''

Lawrence laughed triumphantly. ''Not bad for no food and very little sleep,'' he congratulated. ''Yes, I'm sorry but I had to. You're lucky no one else found out about your little escape scheme though, or you could have been in a lot of trouble. But your secret's safe with me.'' He eyed him significantly.

''So—your advice—your help—everything—you used me too,'' he said, dumbfounded and disgusted with himself for being so easy to manipulate. ''The guard worked for you, then.''

''Pah,'' Lawrence spat, waving a hand in disgust. ''That guard—a good-for-nothing, self-aggrandizing panderer. He was handy, for a time. I took care of him.''

Will stared at Lawrence. ''You took care of him,'' he repeated.

''Then there was you, too, Will. You forget how well I know you. It didn't take a genius to figure out you'd do something for her.'' He let those words penetrate for a moment, chilling him with his pale, penetrating eyes, then continued offhandedly, "Anyway, I always keep a close eye on my own interests. I had plans for my prisoner, long-standing plans. No one was going to interfere with those—not even you, my dear boy. So I decided to take advantage of a situation that would have occurred naturally anyway." He laughed and leaned back against the wall. "But don't feel bad, Darcy; it'll be years before you reach my level of competence in the spy trade, though you're off to a good start. I can put in a good word for you—if you continue your fine work."

Will shook his head, hoping to clear it of the fog that muddled everything he heard. There was so much to think about, so many things he'd done wrong.

"I've been living with subterfuge most of my life," Lawrence went on. "I have eyes and ears everywhere. I knew before Emma left Richmond what her plans were. It was almost too good to be true."

"You mean you knew it would be her? Did you target her specifically? Was she coerced into going?"

"Not exactly. She was one of a group we hoped to convince. But I had a very able young lady in Richmond who made sure Miss Emma Davenport knew just how simple an operation it would be—especially with her valuable connection to the Darcys in Washington." He flicked an eyebrow up casually. "It's really quite simple if you know what you're doing. And," he added ominously, "if you know how to keep your people loyal. I know how to keep my people loyal."

Loyal—like the guard. Despite Will's handsome sum of money, together with what had been ample threats and inducements to secrecy, the guard had turned on him for Lawrence. Had they ever found the guard? Will wondered. Or had he turned up dead like Bondurant?

"Very impressive," Will murmured, his mind racing furiously over the subsequent details of Emma's fall. "And I imagine you were responsible for Bondurant's confession as well."

"Ah, yes, the old brain's awake now, is it?" Lawrence raised the lamp and looked at him sharply. "Bondurant was key, of course. Ferguson had to believe she was capable of further and extensive damage or he would never have kept her so long. It took me a while to get all my ducks in a row, as they say, and I needed some time. And the ruse had the added benefit of turning you into an ally. I guess you were not always so blindly besotted, eh? Amazing how easy it is to believe the worst of people, isn't it?''

Will felt humiliation and self-loathing burn him to the core. How easy it had proven to rock his faith in Emma. Child's play to manipulate even himself. He was nothing but a pawn in someone else's game, all the while believing himself master of his own fate.

But Emma was the real pawn now. She was the one in the most danger. For what possible use would Lawrence have for her once his plans had been carried out? Once she was no longer necessary, she would be as disposable as—as Bondurant. The realization sent a shot of panic through him.

"What will you do with Emma? What will become of her when your assignment is over?" he asked.

Lawrence shrugged. "She and I will go our separate ways— once the war is over and the North has emerged victorious. I shall return to Washington, of course, most likely to be assistant secretary of the War Department. My deeds are well respected in certain important quarters, I understand."

"Your deeds," Will repeated, adding impulsively, "Such as killing Bondurant?"

Lawrence's eyes narrowed dangerously. "That is one that shall remain between us, I should hope. Bondurant was a danger. A drunk. Whether he passed information when I said he did or not, he would have eventually. No one even batted an eye when news of his treason was made public. It was that believable."

Will felt cold through to his bones. "So you killed him. . . ." His mind struggled to keep up with all the implications. "Very smart," he added mildly.

Lawrence remained silent, considering. Will felt danger clasp him in its clammy grip. So far everyone who had outlasted their usefulness in Lawrence's plans had died or disappeared. It could well be that once this phase of his operation was finished Lawrence would do away with Emma, and Will if he proved uncooperative.

"I have to say," Will forced out as casually as he could, "as much as it galls me, using Emma was brilliant. No one could have greased your way into Richmond society the way she could. The respectability of the Davenports is unparalleled."

Lawrence's smile was pleased, but not as gullible as Will would have liked. "Yes, those are the obvious benefits."

Will could not think what the unobvious benefits might be, but he hoped whatever they were that they did not expire anytime soon. But no matter what, it was certain Lawrence would not need Emma once the war was over.

"And she's so true to her cause—no one would dare question her husband," Will continued.

"Right again," Lawrence said smugly. "But I can see you don't approve. Not really. Such a shame," he mused, "because without her you and I could be such a team. You're smart, Darcy, and you're cunning. I could teach you a lot."

Will could not stop the disgust that came out with his words. "Cunning," he scoffed. "So cunning you manipulated me with the ease of a puppet master."

"But you forget," Lawrence said, "I'm very, very good at what I do. I know how to get what I want from people."

"By beating them?" Will asked quietly. It was no use. Lawrence must surely see the hatred in him now.

But he merely shrugged again. "You speak of Emma, I'm sure. She's headstrong, you know that. You'd have done the same yourself, eventually, if you'd married her. It was for her own good."

Will closed his eyes. *For her own good.* Out of his tired delirium came an old vision, a memory. Lawrence, perhaps ten years old, with a black, swollen eye, in his hands a starling with its neck freshly broken. "It was for its own good," his boyish voice had said, his tone bland, dead. "My father would have killed it anyway, if I hadn't."

The bird had been a pet of Lawrence's, something he'd trained for months to take bread from his hand. Later that day Will had seen Lawrence crying in back of the carriage house. The sight had been so strange, his sobs so broken and uncontrolled, that it had frightened Will away. Lawrence never knew he'd been seen, and he always maintained he was glad the bird was dead.

Will opened his eyes to see the mature face before him, so similar to the pale little boy's it had been. "You say you know me," he said quietly. "But I know you, too, Lawrence. I know you well. That starling wasn't any better off dead and neither will Emma be."

Genuine confusion clouded Lawrence's eyes for a moment before comprehension dawned. The transformation in his face was immediate and shocking. The mobility of his features seemed to freeze into a rock-hard mask. His jaw clenched, his eyes hooded, and he straightened with an ominous stealth. "What are you talking about?"

"The bird," Will said, dizzy with his vision from the past and its implications for the future. "That bird you trained as a child. You weren't glad it was dead, Lawrence. I saw you. You cried." He looked at him, sympathy, anger, and determination in his eyes. "You didn't enjoy the killing," he enunciated, understanding for the first time the strange, lethal impulses his friend possessed and did not fight. It was like a disease that had been latent in him as a child and had now grown into a horrifying obsession, validated and hidden behind the laudable guise of warfare.

"I'll get you some more food," Lawrence said woodenly. "You appear to be hallucinating."

Will took a deep breath, suddenly unsure that Lawrence wasn't right. His head swam, but it was with fear for Emma's safety more than hunger.

He rubbed his hand across his face. "I could use some food," he agreed. He needed to keep his mouth shut. The more he said,

Elaine Fox

the more he saw, the less Lawrence would be inclined to keep him alive.

Lawrence turned to the door and pounded for the guard with a ferocity that gave away his buried emotions. When it opened he turned back briefly, his eyes glittering in the lamplight. "Don't do anything stupid," he said harshly. Then he disappeared with the light, leaving Will to be swallowed by darkness.

Will was not sure how many days passed before the arrival of his next visitor. But he did know that things had improved for him since Lawrence's visit, if only in the most basic of ways. He was being fed now, and once a week he was given a cloth and some tepid water with which to wash. They'd even given him a candle once or twice and portions of a novel that was being passed around the prison. He was still not allowed outside the tiny cell, however, and so had to make a concerted effort to move to limber his stiffened muscles and strengthen the limbs already weak from injury.

In any case it was days later when the great portal again heaved open to reveal the large, armed guard and a woman in wide sweeping crinolines. Though she was hooded and covered to the gloved fingertips by her cloak, the moment she moved to enter the cell Will's heart leaped with the knowledge of who it was.

"Fifteen minutes," the guard growled.

She nodded her cloaked head once.

He waited for the door to close before rising to his feet. She carried a candle and a basket, which she set on the floor by her feet.

"You shouldn't have come," Will said, though he could not stop the rushing of his blood and the gladness in his heart to see her.

Slowly she raised a gloved hand and pushed back the hood. The light from the candle struck sharp, gyrating shadows across her face, accentuating the lean cheekbones and making dark pools of her eyes.

"You shouldn't have either," she said, the wry tone in her

voice perhaps an attempt at humor. But Will was too stunned, too grateful to see her, to react. She bent to her basket then, placing the candle on the floor, and busied herself unwrapping a parcel. "They searched this—spilling everything," she muttered, her voice muted as her head was turned away and down.

"Emma," he said, and took a step toward her. But he was acutely conscious of his filth and stopped before he could reach her. "Emma, what are you doing here?"

She rose and handed him a bowl, stepping back away from him after he took it. In it was something that looked like pudding. "I'm not sure where Dee got the eggs. I think he stole them." She issued a short, breathless laugh and her hand fluttered in dismay. "But we decided to use them for you. It's Indian pudding. I hope it's all right—we only had a tiny bit of molasses and no sugar."

Will stared down at the mixture, the sweet smell of it wafting up to him. He lifted the spoon and tasted it, then proceeded to scrape the bowl clean. Finished, he looked up at her in embarrassment. "I'm sorry. I've become something of a beast lately."

"Oh, Will"—she sighed anxiously—"how are you feeling?"

"Fine. I'm fine," he answered quickly, and saw the doubt flicker across her face even in the dimness of the single candle. "I will be fine, anyway. How did you—did Lawrence let you come here?"

Even though it seemed Lawrence was to take care of him, he found it hard to believe the man would be generous enough to give his wife, even for fifteen minutes.

"No. He doesn't know I'm here." She folded her hands at her waist and clenched them together.

"Doesn't he—"

"Oh, he'll find out about it, I'm sure." She laughed harshly. "I had to use my *influence*"—she said the word scornfully—"as his wife to gain an audience with you. But right now he's somewhere else, I'm not sure where. He doesn't tell me such details."

"You must not stay," he said with considerably more force than he felt. He longed for her to stay, longed to take her soft, clean form into his arms and bury his face in that shining mass of hair. She was thin, worried, and fragile; but she was beautiful. He wanted to smooth his palms gently over her face and wipe away the strain of anxiety, kiss away the stiffness of her stoicism, and love her until her eyes shone with happiness and light.

Her glance flicked to the solid wood door. There was a small barred window high in the middle, but the wooden gate to that was closed, too. "We only have a short time. I've spoken with a woman named Elizabeth Van Lew. Have you seen her? She comes here quite often."

Will scowled and turned away. If he continued to look at her he would take her in his arms and never let her leave. "I know who she is, Emma. *Damn it.*" The curse was a harsh whisper. Was there no way to keep her safe? He turned back. "I don't want you to get involved—"

Emma stepped forward decisively. "But she can help you! They all think she's crazy but she's not. She helps people to escape, Will." She stopped before she touched him. Will was unsure if her reluctance was due to his appearance or his anger, but either way she hesitated. And he took advantage of it; he backed away until his shoulders met the wall. If the guard were to come back and find them—it was too risky even to think about.

"I've got a way out, Emma," he said quietly. He glanced involuntarily at the door, sure that at any moment five guards would come storming through the door with leg irons and manacles. "Please tell me you won't see her again."

Her brows drew together. "What way? How will you get out?"

He shook his head. "I can't tell you. But—"

"You're only telling me that to make me stop trying. But it's too late. I've made an agreement."

"Break it," he snapped. Fear made his words hard. If she were to get caught here, by her own people, with Lawrence's deeds as heavy on her unknowing head as any of her own small patriotic infractions where he was concerned, they would kill her faster than Lawrence could. But he could not tell her that. He could not even warn her of Lawrence's lies because nothing would make er more vulnerable, more of a target for Lawrence's wrath. No, she had to remain ignorant of it all, and useful to the loathsome man. "Damn it all, break the agreement and get out of here."

Confusion marred her features. "I'm going to help you—"

"Well, you're not," he said sarcastically. "Do you have any idea how they'll make me suffer for this visit? Do you know what your whim is costing *me?*" The pain and guilt on her face made his heart twist in his chest.

"It will cost you nothing if you would just listen to me," she said, a slight quake in her voice belying the determination of her words.

"No, Emma, I won't listen," he said, forcing the anger into his words, converting frustration to rage. "Think about it. Just *think* for a second. This is not a game. Whatever little scheme you've hatched is not going to outsmart a whole building full of soldiers. These men are smart and they're not going to forget Mrs. Price's little visit to the man in solitary. This is *war,* damn it. People are serious. People are devious."

He saw the trembling of her chin even as she straightened her spine. "Don't you think that I know that by now?" she asked owly.

They glared at each other a moment, Emma's face a study in self-control, Will's pain consuming him. "Sweetheart," he let slip so quietly he might have thought she didn't hear him, but for the slight relaxing of her shoulders. "I know you feel you need to help me. Maybe you think you need to somehow pay me back for getting you free from the Old Cap, but I'm telling you, I've got a way out. You can help me most by being safe. And coming here to help a captive Yank is not going to do much for your safety."

She stood stock-still before him and he wondered what he'd said that had gotten through to her. Her lips were parted and her chest rose and fell rapidly with her breathing. He thought for a second she might cry.

"Will you be all right with Lawrence until I can get back?" he asked.

"You?" she asked quietly. "It was *you?*"

"What was me?" He scanned his own words for the source of her question.

"*You* freed me from the Old Cap." It was not a question. And with it Will realized the enormity of his gaffe. Not only had Lawrence intercepted her after her escape, but he'd altered his own instructions to the guard. She would have known, in Will's scenario, who she was to meet. "I thought it was you," she said, "but then . . ." She expelled a sudden breath. "My God." She closed her eyes.

He could not let her see Lawrence's plot. If she caught on to that there would be no saving her. "Emma, it didn't work out, not the way I planned. But"—and here he had to drive the words from his mouth—"thank heaven Lawrence could come through with help."

Her eyes flashed open and pinned him where he stood. "You wanted him to help me? Did you plan it?"

"God, no." The words were harsh. "But he got you here safe, and for that I am thankful."

She eyed him skeptically. "You're being quite cavalier about it. I would think you'd be bitter, considering he's turned out to be such a traitor."

Will sighed heavily and closed his eyes. "Nothing surprises me anymore."

"How are you getting out, Will?" she asked stonily. "Tell me, I need to know."

The key scraped in the lock, and the door started to open. Emma stepped forward and shoved it closed. "Tell me," she hissed.

Will shook his head, his eyes steady on hers. She would figure it out. God help her, he thought, she would figure it out and Lawrence would kill her.

"What're you doing in there?" the guard shouted. Emma stepped away and the door crashed back against the wall.

She stood composedly before the huge man. "Please, Sergeant. Might I request five minutes more? I'll mention your kindness to

half-folded sheets and flat, worn pillows as they looked apprehensively at each other.

"Maybe it was thunder," Judith ventured. No one replied. No one for a second thought it was anything other than a renewal of battle. But this time it sounded closer than it had in the past.

With trembling hands, Emma continued to fold the sheet, taking inordinate care to smooth all the creases from each fold.

"They won't be able to hold out long now," Mrs. Davenport said in a low voice. "I think we should move the rest of the patients in the morning. Take them down to the depot. There's nothing more we can do for them here."

Emma's heart pounded a question, but before she could bring it to her lips her mother answered it.

"We shall leave, too." Mrs. Davenport studied the sheet in her swift, efficient hands, then pulled another one from the lessening pile of laundry. "We'll go to the Randalls'. We'll take the train as soon as the wounded are gone."

Emma felt the breath leave her body. "The Randalls'? In the Shenandoahs?" It was the house they had visited with Will just after she'd become engaged to him. She recalled with a nearly overwhelming twist of her heart the lake where she and Will had first known love. It would be too much to return there. Her carefully constructed defense of withdrawal would be destroyed in such a setting.

She stared nervously at her mother's delicate profile. "Why would they have us? They're Yankees," she attempted.

Her mother turned and fixed her with an inscrutable stare. "They were friends first. Mr. Randall and your father went to school together. They'll have us."

Emma closed her mouth, her teeth coming together with a soft click. She couldn't bear it, she thought wildly. She and Will were to have honeymooned there. . . .

A deep trembling started low in her abdomen. She wouldn't be able to stand going back to that spot, to see Will in every room, every chair, by every tree and shrub, wherever she might wander.

"Besides," her mother added in the ensuing silence, her voice muted by an emotion Emma could not identify, "we've nowhere else to go."

Emma's fingers went nerveless as she felt her insides begin to crumble. For some reason now, at the thought of that house, she felt the truth, the reality of Will's death. Looking forward into the future, realizing perhaps for the first time that the war was really ending, she saw that she would now have to spend a lifetime without him. The world itself would be without him. The depth of her loneliness shocked her.

"Emma?" Judith's voice penetrated her anxiety. "Are you all right?"

She looked wide-eyed at her friend, panic bubbling just beneath her skin. "I'm all right," she managed, her throat tight.

Judith dropped her sheet and moved around the basket to take Emma's hands.

Mrs. Davenport stopped folding and looked at her daughter. Her expression was flat, controlled, but her eyes were imbued with an arresting energy. "Emma," she said firmly. "You absolutely cannot fall apart now."

Emma's eyes shifted to her mother. It was all too unreal. How could they expect her not to? How had she lasted this long, all these months since his death, not realizing it was permanent? Will was never coming back. How did they think she could survive knowing that he was nowhere in the world?

"Emma," her mother repeated. And this time Emma grasped the dread in her mother's tone. This time she heard the minuscule tremble in her voice, saw the appeal in her eyes. "Emma, go upstairs and dress the wounded up there in the warmest clothes you can find." She took a deep breath and glared at her daughter. "They'll have to go out on the first train in the morning, and with the weather we've been having we can't risk their getting pneumonia."

"Pneumonia," Emma repeated, nodding her head. She couldn't allow her feelings to reign now, she told herself. She had to hang on for a few more days, a few more hours. "Yes. I'll dress them." But she did not move. She stood staring at the sheet in her hands, picturing the sun dimpling off the ripples of a mountain lake.

"I'll send Dee to get some men to take them down to the station. Judith will tell Peter we're leaving; he'll have to leave something for Buck so he'll know where to find us. If he comes back here."

Emma bit her bottom lip. "Oh, Buck." She felt tears threaten to choke her. They still hadn't heard from Buck.

"Get on with you now," her mother directed. "And when you're finished with that, put a few things in a bag for yourself. There won't be much time in the morning."

Emma clenched her hands into fists and concentrated on the pain her nails produced as they bit into her palms. "No, there won't be. I'll go do that now."

"Emma?" Judith asked, touching her forearm lightly. Emma looked up at her friend. "Do you know where Peter is?"

Emma thought for a moment. "He's in the cellar, gathering the root stores we have left." Her brow furrowed. "But you know that, Jude," she added. "You asked him to do it."

Judith smiled, relief evident in her face. "That's right. I'd just forgotten." She patted Emma's arm. "You go on, then. I'll get him."

The following morning brought unexpected sunshine and the enormous task of removing all the wounded soldiers but two from the Davenport household. The two men left were in conditions so tenuous any movement would surely be the death of them, and those they intended to leave for the Federals to care for. It was the only option short of taking them on a trip that would surely be their last.

Emma found herself with a frenzied kind of energy to tackle all they had to do. She supervised the removal of the wounded and the painstakingly slow loading of the rickety old wagon, which had somehow escaped the looters, even as the sounds of battle neared and people ran frantic in the streets.

Guns blasted steadily across the short miles to the front, with an occasional explosion close enough to rattle the windows. When that happened, everyone seemed to still for a second, suspended in uncertainty, before chaos regained its hold. The day dragged on, and the prospect of leaving right away seemed slim.

Rumor had it that during church that morning, Jefferson Davis had been given a note that caused him to leave the service before the pastor had finished. When the hush of foreboding had lifted from the crowd, people had surged out of the church to rush home and continue their packing with renewed frenzy. Amid the tumult on the streets, more than a few people could be seen staring about themselves in a kind of dazed wonder as wagon after wagon bustled past and old men, women, and children plodded out of the city with their belongings on their backs.

They were leaving their homes. They were leaving their things, those who had any left. They were separating from friends and leaving the place where loved ones fighting in the ranks would know to find them. And for most it was uncertain, at best, that they would ever be able to return.

Emma did not think about leaving the house that had been the only one she'd known since childhood. She did not think about all the things she'd lost, the things she would leave, or the things she might hope to find again. She thought only of the moment, the next task.

As day became evening, quartermaster wagons careened by at a gallop outside the house, carrying what was left of the Confederate government, its gold reserves and archives. A few blocks away smoke billowed blackly into the deepening blue of the sky as government papers were burned in the street. People continued to stream past the house in wagons and buggies, trunks and boxes strapped to the backs. Others walked, carrying satchels and carpetbags. But all were leaving.

Emma had pushed the last of her garments into her own bag and secured the straps when she heard the shattering of glass and a voice yelling from below. Amidst the encroaching clamor of battle, the sound shredded what was left of her nerves. She ran into the hall, leaning breathlessly against the banister to see Peter teetering on his good leg in the doorway.

"Get out of there, you damned drunkard!" he yelled out the door, shooing at someone with an irate hand. "Go on, move along, or I'll get the bloody pistol, you half-assed imbecile."

Harsh words pelted back at him but he merely shook his head in disgust, watching whoever it was proceed down the street.

"Peter, what is it?" Emma asked, descending the staircase.

He turned and entered the foyer, slamming the door behind him. "Damned idiots don't know when it's in their best interest to get the bloody hell out of town." He flung a hand back at the door as he approached. Then he glanced sheepishly at his sister. "Sorry, Emma. Someone had the bright idea to get rid of the liquor supplies by dumping them in the streets. I'll be damned if there weren't half a hundred men down there on their hands and knees sucking whiskey out of the dirt."

Emma moved to the long window by the door. "Oh, my," she murmured, watching the rabble stream down the street. "It's really happening, isn't it?"

Peter took her arm and pulled her from the glass. "I wouldn't stand there, Em. They've been taking potshots at the houses along here all day. That idiot already got the parlor window. Standing right in the middle of Mother's rose garden."

Emma took his arm and patted it. "I know," she said consolingly. "It's so infuriating to watch. The whole city falling and all they can think to do is get drunk."

They moved down the hall toward the kitchen, Emma slowing her stride to match Peter's uneven one. "I don't know." He sighed. "Maybe that's the best thing to do."

Emma gazed thoughtfully at the floor. "Did you find out anything about Buck?"

Peter shook his head, his lips clamped together in frustration. "No. But I saw Emil Hawken, and he said he was sure Buck was with Longstreet. But who really knows anymore?"

Emma sighed as they made their way into the kitchen. "We'll find him," she said. "Or he'll find us. I'm sure of it."

Emma's mother was packing what was left of the crystal and

china into crates, wrapping them in the clean but stained linens they'd used for bandages.

She looked up hopefully as Peter and Emma entered the room. "Anything?" she asked.

Peter shook his head. "But the banks were open and I got the deed to the house and the stock certificates."

Mrs. Davenport nodded. "That's good. We should come out of this with something, at least."

"You should have seen it, though," Peter continued. "The streets were papered with Confederate currency. I kept thinking if Lee could possibly manage some kind of miraculous comeback, we could be rich as Croesus. People were literally blowing their noses with it."

Mrs. Davenport made a grimace of distaste and Peter apologized perfunctorily. "And the shops—nearly all of them had been broken into. If we had a bigger wagon, we could have set ourselves up for years in knickknacks and books. Of course all the food stores were wiped clean."

An explosion that rattled the windows made them all jump and head for the windows. In the distance a huge black cloud of smoke billowed up toward the sky, blocking the sun.

"They're firing the arsenals," Peter said in an awed tone.

"Who are? The Yankees?" Emma asked in shock. Could they possibly be that close?

He shook his head. "No, our boys."

Another explosion sounded, and Emma heard more shattering of glass from somewhere in the house. She whirled toward the hall. "They *are* here! They're firing on us," she said in a high voice.

Peter grabbed her arm. "It's probably just the force of the explosion," he said. "Let me check."

Emma turned back to her mother. "Where's Judith?"

"She went to the Wilsons for a while."

The Wilsons lived two doors down and planned to stay throughout the invasion. They had tried to maintain a neutrality during the conflict, as one of their sons had fought for the North and one for the South. Unfortunately the Confederate one had been killed in his first battle at Bull Run. Now they simply waited for their other son to come to them with the invading victorious troops.

"Should I get her?" Emma asked.

"No, leave her be. She's just as safe there as she would be here. It'll be dark soon enough and then she'll be back."

Emma began helping her mother wrap the china, but she could not keep her mind on the task, and every time another explosion sounded she jumped, nearly dropping whatever she held.

"I wish we could just leave now," Emma declared, her nerves as worn as the threadbare linens they wrapped the plates in.

Mrs. Davenport continued steadily on. "We wouldn't get far now. Best to wait for morning."

Several hours later, as Judith, Emma, Peter, and Mrs. Davenport sat nervously in the front parlor, trying to mimic sociable conversation, a loud wave of voices from the street drew their attention to the window. It grew louder as they sat, mesmerized by the sound, until Emma rose and moved to the window. At the same time someone pounded at the door.

She'd just altered her course toward the front foyer when the door swung open and Mr. Wilson from down the street burst in. Emma gaped at the unlikely spectacle of the elderly man in his nightshirt with his gray hair mussed and his eyes wild.

"Fire!" he yelled, moving swiftly toward Emma. "The whole city's on fire!"

The rest of the small group pushed out of the parlor.

"What're you talking about, old man?" Peter questioned rudely in his agitation.

But Mr. Wilson did not seem to notice. "The sparks!" he quavered, wagging a gnarled finger in the air. "They're alighting on the rooftops! Our whole upstairs is in flames!"

Mrs. Davenport bolted for the stairs. Emma pounded after her. Even as they ran, Emma thought she could feel the acrid sting of smoke in her lungs. It was just her imagination, of course, she thought, until they reached the landing and the heat nearly bowled them over.

"The attic," her mother said. "The roof must have caught. Hurry, Emma, get your bag." She dashed toward her room.

Emma stopped, paralyzed with shock as she realized that smoke was indeed filtering down through cracks in the ceiling. She stared, fascinated, as smoke trickled out of a nail hole in the wall where a Landau watercolor had once hung.

Behind her Judith dashed up the stairs. "Grab your things," she said, pushing Emma hard from behind.

Emma stumbled, catching herself on the wall. It was warm to the touch.

She jerked her hands away and spun in the direction Judith had taken. She sprinted down the hall and slid to a stop at Judith's doorway.

"The men!" she gasped. "There are two in the sitting room, remember?"

Judith turned frantic eyes on her. "What?"

"Remember? The two who were gut shot? We have to get them out." Already her eyes were burning. She brought her fingers up to rub at one of them.

"Oh, Lord," Judith squeaked. "We can't move them. They're too heavy."

The two stood locked in indecision, every nerve screaming at them to run for their lives. Then, as if words had been spoken, they both raced for the sitting room.

They opened the door and smoke ballooned out, over and past them.

"Oh, God, oh, Emma," Judith wailed. "The ceiling'll come down on our heads!"

But they simultaneously ducked and pushed into the blinding smoke. They located the men easily. Emma knelt and felt the first man's neck.

"No," she said, curtly shaking her head. "The smoke . . ." She shook away tears.

They both moved on to the next man. "I've got a pulse,"

Judith stated. "You grab his feet."

The two women lifted but could not get the man completely off the ground. They dragged him to the door. Coughing and spluttering, they emerged from the densely fogged room to the relative clarity of the hall. Emma's mother emerged from the other end carrying two large carpetbags. She threw them over the balcony and moved to help with the wounded man.

As the three of them dragged the poor wounded man, bumping down the stairs, Peter waited at the bottom to help.

"He's never going to make it," Judith cried. The man neither moaned nor moved the whole way down.

They got him out of the house and somehow lifted him, with Peter's help, onto the wagon. Judith jumped up beside Mrs. Davenport while Peter and Emma moved as swiftly as possible around to the buckboard.

As the horse pulled at the weight, and the wagon creaked slowly to life, Emma watched the flames licking upward at the air from the roof of their house. They were coming from the back side of the roof and had yet to reach the lower floors. Emma was glad they would not see the complete destruction of the house. As it was, seeing the flames stroke the sky from far side, she could almost believe it was not their home that burned, could almost pretend that there might still be a way to save it.

When they'd gone barely twenty feet she remembered that her own bag and Judith's had been left in the house when they'd gone to get the wounded.

She jumped off the wagon. "I'll catch up!" she yelled. "I forgot my bag."

"Are you crazy?" Peter yelled.

"It's all right. You can see the fire's only on the roof!" She waved her hand. "I'll get yours, too, Jude."

"We'll stay on Franklin till you find us!" Peter yelled, as she took the front stoop two stairs at a time.

She entered the house and closed the door behind her, realizing with a strange feeling how misplaced the old habit was. She

309

started swiftly across the floor, but at the base of the stairs she hesitated.

It was quiet in the house, the outside noise effectively muted by the closed front door, the rushing of adrenaline through her veins, and the rushing of blood in her ears. She looked about herself in eerie wonder. So this was it—the last time she would see this house. She gazed around, at the marbled foyer, the rich dark wood of the doors, the chain where once had hung a crystal chandelier. That chandelier had fed them for three months, she thought briefly, with a sudden insight into how bizarre this would all seem years from now. For some reason, she was able to feel as detached as if the whole moment were already a memory.

She was tempted to go back to the dining room, to look at the spot where Will had lain, where she'd agonized over whether he would live or die, where she'd seen—in a moment possessing the power of a religious epiphany—Will open his eyes and speak her name, after they'd all thought he surely would die.

An explosion, unexpectedly close, rocked her from her reverie and propelled her up the stairs. The upper floor was thick with smoke now and she could see where pieces of plaster had separated from the lattice and fallen to the floor. She ran first to Judith's room and grabbed her bag, lugging it behind her to her room. But when she entered the bedroom she'd shared with Lawrence, her suitcase was gone.

She knew she'd left it on the bed. She remembered clearly leaving it there when Peter had called out the front door at the drunks. Dropping Judith's things in the hall, she moved into the room, thinking perhaps the bag had fallen to the far side. But when she made it to the other side of the bed it was not there. She was on the verge of kneeling to look under the bed when the bedroom door slammed shut.

She jerked around to see a tall, thin form standing in front of the closed door. Her carpetbag dropped with a thump on the floor from his hand.

''Looking for that?'' Lawrence's voice asked, chilling her to the bone.

Light from a healthy flame on the roof across the street flickered in the window, layering the room in gyrating orange light. Her breath caught in her throat.

"I don't know why you're so shocked," he said smoothly. "It is I who should be surprised. *You* should be dead."

Emma found her voice, the peculiar surreal feeling she'd had in the hall returning to her. "You used pennyroyal. It's always made me sick," she said in an oddly conversational voice.

"Ah," Lawrence said. "My mistake."

He advanced on her a couple of steps and she noticed with a jolt that he carried a revolver. "You're going to kill me? Now?" She felt laughter bubble to her lips. But it was a weird sort of laughter that had nothing to do with amusement.

"Mrs. Price," Lawrence purred, an expression of true perplexity on his face. "How would it look to have the new assistant secretary of the U.S. War Department saddled with a Confederate wife? I can assure you, the position of the grieving widower is much more appropriate."

She noted distractedly that smoke oozed into the room from the crack under the door. "Many's the day the title of widow would have suited me, as well," she said. She felt, more than looked, for her avenues of escape. She had basically two options: either try to push past him to the door, or jump out the window. Neither of which felt very realistic.

Lawrence smiled and she noted abstractly that she had rarely seen the sight before. "Clever," he murmured.

Emma heard something outside the door, and evidently Lawrence heard it, too. He paused, head cocked, listening, the pistol unwavering at her chest. A moment later a chunk of plaster fell from the corner ceiling of the bedroom and they realized simultaneously what they'd heard was more of the same in the hall.

Before Lawrence could react, Emma charged across the room and threw herself into his chest. His gun discharged as he was knocked straight into the door, his head smacking the wood with an audible crack. Emma didn't pause to discern what he'd shot as she whirled and headed for the window.

Pressing her hands on the glass she tried to push it up, but it wouldn't budge. It came into her head that the wood must have swelled with the heat. Behind her the gun exploded again and a shower of plaster rained down the wall just next to her head.

She spun to face him. Lawrence pushed himself to his feet and took careful aim.

Emma thought she could feel the floor shake beneath her, and wondered if the house might collapse, swallowing them both up and answering the whole question of who would win this war of wills.

She prepared herself to dive. When she saw Lawrence cock the pistol, she threw herself to the floor.

The gun erupted. Lawrence's body was suddenly thrown forward toward her. The gun skittered across the bare floorboards to smack against the wall.

It took Emma a second to realize that the door had swung open behind him, clipping him in the back and sending him flying. She rolled away from the flailing body, pushing with arms, legs, body, to slide across the floor. Wood scraped her palms and bruised her knees as she clamored for distance, and reached for the gun.

"Emma? Emma!"

The voice froze her. She peered through the smoke that billowed in from the doorway and barely made out the shapes of two men. Her hands gripped the warm gunmetal and she pulled it into her skirts.

"Price!" A deep, unfamiliar voice sounded loud in the murky room, demanding and hostile. As the two men clamored through the smoke, she squinted through the frustrating fog, anxious to see who had called her name. Booted heels beat solidly on the floorboards as a large man in Yankee blue hauled Lawrence to his feet. Dear God, had they come to help him?

She scrutinized the Yankee's face, not recognizing it, and cocked the pistol on her drawn-up knees. She could make out only shapes in the burgeoning smoke, but she was prepared to fire at any that came close to her.

She had the dim thought that what she must have felt through the floor were these two Yankees pounding up the stairs. The first of the invaders . . .

"I know she's in here," that startling voice said. She started again and strained her ears in shock, longing for the sound once more. Her eyes streamed tears from the smoke, further impairing her sight.

"Will?" she whispered. But her voice was a silent croak. She pressed herself back against the wall, wondering if she really was going crazy.

"Where is she, Lawrence, damn you," the voice growled.

Emma pushed herself up in the fog, one hand pressed firmly against the wall, the other clutching the revolver.

"Will?" Louder this time, but the words caused her breath to catch on the smoke, and she coughed.

Through the smoke a man strode across the room, in his hands something large and unwieldy. She raised the pistol uncertainly in violently trembling hands.

The man reached her side of the room and, with a sweeping motion, hurled the large object out the window.

Glass shattered and smoke was sucked out into the cool night air. In the sudden clarity, the man who'd broken the glass turned to face her. She gasped. Coughing besieged her. She brought her fist to her mouth and bit hard on her knuckles, willing herself not to blink, not to turn away from this smoky, ghostly specter.

She felt suddenly dizzy. "It is really you?" She pushed herself back into the corner. "Have I died?"

Will Darcy strode through the scudding smoke to take her roughly in his arms. "It's me," his deep, familiar voice, thick with emotion, said against her hair. "And I thank the grace of God you're not dead."

She dropped the pistol from hands yearning for the feel of his solid, live body. She pulled herself hard against him, the reality of it causing her to sway, light-headed.

"Emma," he rasped. He held her steady, one arm around her waist, one hand cradling the back of her head and pressing it to

313

his shoulder. "Emma, thank God, we reached you in time."

Her hands clutched at his shirt, moved across his back, his arms, his ribs, everywhere they could touch. "I thought you were dead," she said faintly. She pulled her head back to look up into his dear, relieved, intense face. "Will, they told me you'd died."

He covered her face with kisses, his own hands clutching her with a force that might have hurt in any other circumstance. "I nearly did, sweetheart. And if I lose you again I will."

The sudden blast of a gunshot shook the tiny room. Emma jumped and Will turned swiftly, pushing her behind him.

"He's got the gun!" the other soldier shouted, from a place on the floor where he clutched at his reddening belly.

Another shot rang out and more plaster clattered to the floor beside them. The room was again filling with smoke, and the warmth of the fire could now be felt. The draw of the open window was probably pulling it right toward them, Emma thought. She heard the other soldier cough, a dangerous gurgle in the sound.

"Where is she?" Lawrence's unmistakable voice growled from the opposite side of the room.

"Over here," Will said, his voice cutting clearly through the smoke. Emma clutched his shirt in her hands.

Through the fog, the eerie, ominous figure of Lawrence Price emerged. Emma watched in morbid fascination as his long, thin fingers cocked the heavy Union pistol.

"Don't do it," Will warned. And Emma noticed for the first time that his own pistol was cocked and aimed straight at Lawrence's chest.

"Don't you do it," Lawrence said. "You may have forgotten, *Captain* Darcy, that I outrank you. And I'll have you court-martialed for this."

Will's mouth tilted up on one side. "This is no time for jokes, Lawrence. You've just shot a Union officer. I'm not sure I'd be able to avoid mentioning that at my trial."

Lawrence coughed, then spat on the floor. "Then I guess I'll have to kill you, too. Three more charred bodies in the remains